CORNFIELD SOLDIERS

Utah Beach to the Elbe River

The story of
the 238th Engineer Combat Battalion
During World War II

Paul Michael Frazeé

Cover design by Lorraine Bollinger

Printed and bound in the United States of America

Another fine historical book by
GRAPHIC PUBLISHERS
Santa Ana, California 92705 USA

PREFACE

Cornfield Soldiers—Utah Beach to the Elbe River is a work of fiction. While great attention has been given to its accurateness, it should be noted that this book is a novel. Any resemblance to actual events or locales or persons, living or dead, is entirely coincidental.

It should be noted that the author tried to be as accurate as possible with the events in which the men of the 238th Combat Engineer Battalion took part, but all of the conversations in this book are fictional.

Books by Paul Michael Frazeé

Waiting for a Rainbow—Coming of Age in Vietnam

Summer Storm—Prelude to Pearl Harbor

Cornfield Soldiers—Utah Beach to the Elbe River

DEDICATION

The 238th Combat Engineer Battalion probably built more bridges than any other unit in the United States Army did during World War II.

The first Allied bridge in Europe was theirs, and they were the first to cross the Seine, Marne, Meuse, and Roer rivers. With other engineers, they built the second bridge across the Rhine at Koningswinter about the time the Remagen Bridge fell.

These fine young soldiers fought their way from the sands of Utah Beach all the way to the Elbe River. It is to all of them, living and dead, that this book is respectfully dedicated.

THEY ARE ALL BRAVE, BOTH OLD AND YOUNG.
ALL ARE HEROES, SOME UNSUNG.
THEY GAVE THEIR LIVES WITHOUT REGRET.
THESE MEN, THESE MEN, WE'LL NEVER FORGET.

—Written in a foxhole by William Gentry,
Company A, 85th Engineers

238th Combat Engineers Honor Roll

PVT Anderson, James M.	Jacksonville, Florida
CPL Camano, Freddie L.	Boca Grande, Florida
CPL Cameras, Lewis	McComas, West Virginia
SGT Cash, Henry V.	Montebello, Tennessee
PVT Cias, Ezequiel	Juarez Chi, Mexico
PFC Downs, Harvey F.	Larkinville, Alabama
PFC Dunham, Victor H.	Leaf, Mississippi
CPL Gravette, Donnell C.	Rutherford, Tennessee
PFC Hardy, James C.	Ruffin, North Carolina
CPL Harling, Robert M.	Detroit, Michigan
CPL Hood, Lonnie A.	Sanderson, Florida
PVT Joyner Dan P.	Madison, North Carolina
CPL Long, Dwight L.	Crescent, Oklahoma
SGT McDowell, Jesse A.	Woodward, Oklahoma
2LT McClure, Eugene L.	Shreveport, Louisiana
CPL Miller, Richard R.	Beltsville, Maryland
PFC Mills, Harold W.	Blanchard, Oklahoma
PFC Rael, Alberto L.	Arroyo Hondo, New Mexico
PFC Scenna, Tony A.	Vitondale, Pennsylvania
SGT Smith, Daniel J.	Philadelphia, Pennsylvania
PVT Spencer, Homer V.	Pilot, Kentucky
PVT Webb, Julius E.	Kerrville, Tennessee
SGT Weeks, Columbus P.	Murfreesboro, Tennessee
PFC Weiss, Sam	Chicago, Illinois
CPL Willis, Luther C.	Crystal River, Florida
2LT Wise, Stuart S.	Youngstown, Ohio

ACKNOWLEDGMENTS

Years ago, while gathering up material for my first book, *Waiting for a Rainbow—Coming of Age in Vietnam*, I was carousing one of the many Sacramento area used book stores in Fair Oaks. There I bumped into a World War II veteran named Ernie James. As we talked, I knew that some day I would write about Ernie's unit, the 238th Engineer Combat Batallion, during the Great Crusade.

Ernie was a tremendous help. We spent countless hours on the phone discussing many facets of the operation. He always made time for me. Please note that, as you read this book, you will come across letters Ernie wrote to his future wife, Faith. I want to thank Ernie for letting us share his most private thoughts.

In all honesty, *Cornfield Soldiers—from Utah Beach to the Elbe* could not have been written without Ernie James' guidance and assistance.

Another fine man who assisted in this book is Albert E. Davis, a retired U.S. Army master sergeant. We met at the Camp Roberts Military Museum during an annual training period while I was serving with the California Army National Guard. After telling him about this book, Sergeant Davis spent countless hours with me, walking me around the Army Guard training facility. His knowledge of Camp Roberts was staggering. He even knew the names of the commanding officers of the training cadre during World War II. We kept in contact for many years. However, regretfully Sergeant Davis has since passed away. The "Sharon" portion of *Cornfield Soldiers–From Utah Beach to the Elbe* is dedicated to him. He was a true professional.

I am also indebted to the Arizona Wing of the Commemorative Air Force, of Mesa, Arizona. Their technical expertise on the workings of the Boeing B-17 heavy bomber was very helpful.

Credit must also be given to Colonel Ross Davidson (USAF, Retired). Colonel Davidson flew B-17s during World War II with the 8th Air Force. Awarded the Distinguished Flying Cross for a particularly harrowing mission over Berlin, he was a great deal of help with the chapters that pertain to mission 115, the raid on Schweinfurt of October 14, 1943. Thank you, colonel!

In 2003, I retired from the California Army National Guard, closing a military career that spanned four decades. I will always cherish fond memories of our citizen-soldiers who gave—and continue to give—so much of their time, and their lives, to our country.

A big "thank you" is order for my wife, Deanna, who allowed me to spend far too many hours away from chores. Finally, to my two daughters: Maybe now Daddy can take you to all those wonderful places we have talked about visiting.

However, before closing these notes, I would like to share an experience I had while serving with the 115th Area Support Group during the 1980s. The 115th ASG was a top-notch Guard unit, and as such was always requested by the German High Command (OKW) during the Cold War for the annual Return Forces to Germany (REFORGER) exercise.

During one such exercise, I managed to get time away from Kaiserslautern to visit General George Patton's grave in Luxembourg. As I walked around the military cemetery I could not help but notice how many of those young Americans who gave their lives during World War II had come from Midwestern America.

On my way back to "K-Town," I kept thinking about those brave young men. That evening at the NCO Club I commented to another NCO about my sojourn, mentioning that "They were from the cornfields of America."

With the memory of all those fine men in mind, I respectfully dedicate *Cornfield Soldiers—from Utah Beach to the Elbe.*

CORNFIELD SOLDIERS

BOOK ONE: CALIFORNIA

PROLOGUE

ON THE PORCH OF THE RESIDENCE OF
MR. & MRS. SEAN KENNEDY, SR.
VOLCANO ROAD, SUTTER CREEK,
AMADOR COUNTY, CALIFORNIA
THANKSGIVING DAY, 1991, 2:00 P.M. LOCAL

As the eldest son of a retired Army chaplain, Sean Kennedy Ohara knew from the minute he got up from the Thanksgiving dinner table that he had committed one of the Seven Deadly Sins—Gluttony. He also knew that unless he wanted to be the recipient of an ungodly harangue from his junior varsity basketball coach next Monday afternoon, he had better get off his butt and go for a walk.

"Going somewhere, Sean?" his mother asked, taking another sip from her coffee cup.

"I was thinking 'bout moseying on up to Volcano," the teenager replied.

From the opposite side of the dining room an older man jumped into the conversation. "Mind if I tag along?"

"Mr. Dannenberg, from what I remember when we were back in Iowa two months ago, I'll be the one who's tagging along."

The old man smiled. "Chalk it up to good breeding and good feeding."

Almost as if it had been planned, another guest now spoke up. "If you're going to let that old geezer walk with you, how about letting me come along, too? At least my war stories are believable."

"Great! Just friggin' great!" the teenager answered. "Now I'm gonna have to keep up with two guys who haven't got the message they're in their seventies."

"Quit your bellyaching," quipped the second septuagenarian. "And go open the door before Dannenberg fires up another one of his nasty cigars."

"Oh, yeah—which cigar are your referring to? The one you smoked this morning, or the two you smoked last night?"

"Well, now, if you are offering me a cigar, that last Cohiba wasn't too bad...."

"Christ, Sergeant Major, why can't you smoke a two-buck cigar?" said Dannenberg, as he reached in his shirt pocket, pulled out a fresh stogie, and handed it to his old friend.

As they headed outside, Sean Ohara thought about the two men he was about to begin walking with. He'd met Dexter Dannenberg the previous Labor Day, on a family vacation in Iowa. But he was introduced to the second man only a couple of days ago, when he and his wife showed up at the Kennedy compound late in the afternoon.

The truth of the matter was that young Ohara felt he'd known the man much longer than just two days. Because the old soldier was one of the main characters in a yarn Dannenberg had told while they were visiting one of his father's Vietnam War buddies, Ronald Banks, Republican congressman from southwestern Iowa.

How things can change! After hearing the story Dannenberg related two months ago, Sean Kennedy Ohara's initial impression of Charles Wilkes was that he was the biggest horse's ass to have ever lived in Montgomery County, Iowa. But after spending two days with him wandering around the haunts of Amador County, he knew he had misjudged the older man. Sean had found new meaning in the biblical verse, "Judge not that ye may not be judged."

Now Sean's father got up from the dinner table and walked outside to the Kennedy's front porch. A retired colonel in the Army chaplaincy, he had been subordinate to Dannenberg during his second tour in Vietnam. To say the two men had a "history" together would be a gross understatement.

"Dexter, if you'll continue telling that same story you told us in Iowa, I'd like to come along, too. But you'll have to promise to take it easy on me. I'm getting up in years now."

Dannenberg chortled. "Ohara, quit whining. I promise to be as easy on you as Michigan will be on Washington in the Rose Bowl on New Year's Day."

Having earned a degree in political science (with a minor in Vietnamese language) at the University of Washington after his first tour in Vietnam, Ohara glanced over at his former boss. "Despite the fact that I'm not much of a drinking man anymore, and that you've never been a gambling man, I would like to propose a small wager."

Smiling, Dannenberg responded, "Go ahead, you lying Mick."

"I'd be willing to bet you a cold beer that the Dogs rip Michigan a new one, come one January."

"You're on," said Dannenberg, with a twinkle in his eye.

Colonel Ohara sensed he was about to be had, as Dannenberg continued. "Of course, Colonel, you understand it means I'm going to have to come to your house after Christmas—or vice versa—as it's the only way to guarantee that I'll collect that bet."

Before Dexter could respond, a distinctly feminine, English accent was heard coming from the next room. "Dexter, there's always room for you at our house. Why don't you plan on coming a bit earlier this year, though? Say… sometime around December fifteenth? That way, you can escort me to the various Christmas events that Michael is too busy for, what with his church, and all."

Dannenberg glowed with delight. Being Jewish, gay, and as a result single all his life, the Christian holidays were essentially foreign to him. But Dexter had been around long enough to realize that Christmas was a time that his Christian friends celebrated with their families. And since Labor Day, he had pretty much been "Uncle Dexter" to the Oharas' son, Sean. As for the boy's father—well, more than likely that relationship was going to need more time.

Maybe this holiday season would be that time.

Dannenberg looked over at Colonel Michael Ohara, to his son, and to CSM Wilkes. "Why don't we head on up toward Volcano? It's a beautiful afternoon."

Mrs. Ohara chimed in. "Yes, please do go on your walk, so we girls can clean up. And get to know Brigitte better."

The woman Mrs. Ohara spoke of was in her late seventies. She was the mother of Mr. Kennedy's son, Jean Pierre LaFoche. Their wartime romance had been the by-product of a special mission that Brigitte coordinated after the elder Kennedy's B-17 was shot down on October 14, 1943, near Frankenstein, Germany, following a bombing run on Schweinfurt.

Jean Pierre LaFoche also figured in the final line of Dexter Dannenberg's three-day tale of the exploits of a few of the people from Villisca, Iowa during World War Two. In a distinctly British accent, Jean Pierre inquired if the men would like some additional company.

"As long as you don't complain about my cigars," Dexter said, offering LaFoche another of his prized Cohibas.

"The only way I would complain, *Monsieur* Dannenberg, is if you had not offered me one of your fabulous smokes."

Mrs. Ohara walked onto the front porch of the house just as the five men were putting on windbreakers. "How about I drive over and pick you all up, around dusk, if you're not back by then?"

"Sounds like a wonderful idea to me," her husband replied.

None of the men disagreed with her suggestion, as the group headed out into the afternoon chill.

Charlie Wilkes had known Dexter Dannenberg since his high school days back in Iowa during the Thirties. So he felt completely comfortable shortening the former CIA bureau chief's name.

"Where'd you leave 'em, Dex? Pearl?"

"More or less...."

"Then what do you say we do a team-tag approach? I'll continue from Pearl and work my way up to North Africa."

Dannenberg's reply was typical. "Okay, Charlie, but knowing how bad your memory is, I'll reserve the right to add tidbits here and there."

The older Ohara almost choked on Dannenberg's words. "Hell, Dex, when did you ever offer just a 'tidbit'?"

Dexter's response was classic Dannenberg: He reached into his Pendleton shirt, extracted another Cohiba and gave it to Ohara. "Then I guess, Colonel, you'll just have to smoke this fine cigar, and listen up."

Ohara played along. "Okay. Personally, though, I'm interested in hearing how Sergeant Major Wilkes won World War Two single-handedly. Of course, we'll reserve plenty of time for you, Dexter, to correct any of his lies."

Despite loving the attention he was getting, Wilkes feigned a poor imitation of Sesame Street's Miss Piggy: "*Moi*? Lies? I protest!"

"As long as you don't get too carried away," Ohara added, "I could probably work in some time for a confession when we get back to the house."

Everyone in the group laughed, as Command Sergeant Major Charles Wilkes, (U.S.A., Ret.) began relating his tale.

"Within a very short time after joining the Iowa National Guard I was activated and sent to Camp Roberts. The camp was down on the Central Coast of California, near San Luis Obispo...."

CHAPTER ONE

Yesterday, December 7, 1941—a date which will live in infamy—the United States of America was suddenly and deliberately attacked by naval and air forces of the Empire of Japan....

 —U.S. President Franklin D. Roosevelt, address before Congress on December 8th, 1941

SMALL ARMS RANGE #1, CAMP ROBERTS, CALIFORNIA
SATURDAY, 20 JUNE 1942, 1:00 P.M.

As Corporal Charles Wilkes, U.S. Army, sat beneath a spindly scrub oak tree he thought of his predicament: He was two thousand miles from home in some god-forsaken hell hole, close to heat exhaustion and, at the moment, in deep shit with his company commander.

Looking off to his left, he spotted a deuce-and-a-half truck driving up to the rifle range, signaling the return of basic trainees from the mess hall. He knew he could not put off his commanding officer, Captain McDonald, any longer.

"I'll bet you that, by the time the Old Man gets through chewing on my butt, I won't be able to sit down for a week." Wilkes muttered to nobody in particular.

Wiping the sweat from his brow, Charlie went over the events that conspired to bring his twenty-two year old fanny from Villisca, Iowa to what had to be the end of the world—Camp Roberts, California. First, he thought of his deceased mother. Then, of his childhood sweetheart who had died after a back-alley abortion went south on her while he was in basic training at Camp Claiborne.

You loved them both, Charlie.

Next, he thought of his insurance business. It had belonged to the man he believed was his father. After the local sheriff confronted Charlie's "father" with enough evidence about the murder of Charlie's mother to send him to the electric chair, the would-be death row inmate killed himself. Charlie, being his sole-surviving heir, inherited the business.

Charlie now thought of the man who arrested his "father." That would be Leroy Wilkes, the town sheriff. A smile came over Charlie's face. He recalled the day when he learned that Sheriff Wilkes actually was his father. Soon afterward, Leroy convinced Charlie that he would be better off "getting out of Dodge" while the dust settled. To Sheriff Wilkes, "out of Dodge" meant Camp Claiborne, Louisiana, as a proud member of the Iowa Army National Guard.

Getting the young man into the guard hadn't proved difficult, as Sheriff Wilkes and the company commander of the local unit were notoriously good friends. It seems that many of Villisca's "finest" had decided to enlist into the Army Guard after spending some quality time with the wiry, not-so-subtle Sheriff Wilkes. First, though, his "volunteers" usually experienced some good old-fashioned "wall-to-wall counseling," meaning that the youthful offender's body was thrown against the wall a few times to assist him in making his decision.

What this meant to young Charlie Wilkes was that he'd received an all-expense paid vacation to the garden spot of Western civilization—Camp Claiborne, Louisiana—where he learned to peel potatoes, scrub latrines, burn human waste, operate a radio and be a combat infantryman!

After what seemed like an eternity, now Charlie's mind came back to his original question: Why was he here at Camp Roberts?

That's easy, bonehead—the fucking Japs bombed Pearl Harbor!

After the Japanese sneak attack the bureaucrats in Washington began sending anyone they could find, to defend the West Coast of America from invasion. Last month the War Department had finally got around to federalizing his Army Guard unit, Company F, 168th Infantry, and ordered it to California. After his unit reported in at the Presidio, in San Francisco, he was attached to Baker Company, 90th Infantry, as part of the cadre in an infantry training unit.

But that was all history now. Iowa, the Japs, and the searing California heat were all secondary concerns. The things really worrying Charlie now were the thoughts of how irked his commanding officer was at his involvement in some off-post activities he'd gotten involved in after leaving Theater #4 last night.

How Charlie wished that, after watching Jane Frazee in "Almost Married," he'd remained on base. Instead, he and some friends wandered into "downtown" San Miguel. Until just recently San Miguel had been a one-horse town, known primarily for its early Spanish mission and railroad station. However, since the U.S. government had announced its plans for turning 37,000 acres of the Nacimiento Ranch into an army base a year-and-a-half ago, San Miguel had become both a boomtown and a soldier's shortcut to perdition.

So, instead being ready to soldier when he got up this morning, Charlie woke up on the floor of San Miguel's hoosegow with a monumental hang-over, smelling like urine. To make matters worse, he was stone-broke. And that was the good news!

You still have to deal with Captain McDonald. Who, by the way, didn't seem too impressed with your story when he bailed you out of jail at 0500 hours this morning. I should have known to go back to the base after those two smart-assed MPs jerked us around last night at the prophylactic station.

Charlie Wilkes looked down at his wristwatch. It was five minutes past one o'clock, time for him to report in at the ammunition shed. As Charlie stood up, his head pounded with a vengeance and he wanted to upchuck. He tinkered with attempting to strike a deal with God: If he wasn't busted, he would swear on his mother's grave never again to drink more than three shots of whiskey at a single sitting.

Charlie, you are without doubt the biggest idiot on the Central Coast. What type of God would go along with that sort of deal? Certainly not the God his Methodist momma had worshiped.

He looked off to the east, where the ammo shack stood. Beyond it ran the rail line that served this part of the Central California. In the far distance, a small river flowed in a basin created by the waters of the Nacimiento River. There was hardly enough water in it for the few flea-infested deer that inhabited the area to take a drink. However, that had not always been the case. Just last year that same trickle of water had been a raging torrent, swollen by the heaviest rainfall this part of California had seen in decades.

Slowly Charlie began walking toward the ammo shed. As he ap-proached, he heard McDonald speaking. "From what that commo guy told me, we kicked the snot out of the Japs. Some shave-tail said the battle took place near Midway about two weeks ago. Says we sank four of the bastards' carriers, two heavy cruisers and three destroyers. Along with that, G-2 says we shot down more than 250 of the sonofabitches' Zeroes."

McDonald stopped talking when Charlie entered the hooch. For both soldiers it was an awkward moment. Charlie had hoped to come in unnoticed, but now that goal was impossible. Fortunately for him, as he entered, the staff sergeant running the rifle range asked McDonald if he wanted him to start up the range again. McDonald put down his coffee cup.

"Let's try to have 'em qualified by sixteen-hundred hours, Sergeant. I gotta get off base early tonight so I can run into 'Paso to pick up a gift for the battalion XO's wife. He's throwing her a surprise birthday party, and I can't go empty-handed."

Charlie took the hint, and started out the door for his communications post. But he didn't get far.

"Hold on, Wilkes. I need to talk to you."

After the other troops had left, McDonald walked over to where Charlie was standing.

"Wilkes, I hope you realize that this morning was the very last time I bail your sorry ass out of jail."

Quickly, Charlie agreed. "Sir—yes, sir. It will never happen again, sir."

"Well, young man, you make sure that it was the last damned time, because if you screw up once more I'll bust your ass so low that you'll be looking up at a snake's belly. Do I make myself clear?"

Now realizing that his commanding officer wasn't going to bust him, Charlie replied, "Yes. Perfectly clear, sir."

"Be advised that I'm restricting you to Camp Roberts for seven days. I've also had the first sergeant assign you some extra duties."

As it turned out, those "extra duties" would play an important role in Charlie's life.

McDonald continued. "And, as far as your bail goes, you'll pay me back next payday."

"Sir—yes, sir. And thank you, sir, for being so understanding."

"Is that what you call it, Wilkes? Understanding?"

"Like you said, sir, you could have busted me," Charlie replied.

"Call it what you like, soldier. But if I busted every one of my cadre who screwed up once in a while, they'd all be privates. What saved your sorry tail, is that I believe that you are smart enough to learn from your mistakes."

Breathing a sigh of relief, Charlie acknowledged his commander's admonition.

"Besides, I can't have the best radio operator in Baker Company—and my new company driver—a buck-ass private, can I?"

A smile came over Wilkes' face. Just yesterday, the first sergeant had told Charlie that he was being considered for the captain's driver. When he'd seen his commander's eyes glaring through the bars of the jail this morning, however, he'd pretty much kissed off any such notion. Apparently Captain McDonald was not so willing to give him the boot.

McDonald continued with both his staring and his lecture. "Starting this afternoon you are to assume the position of my driver. My last one has been kissing some colonel's hind end across the base, and has managed to finagle a transfer over to said colonel's unit. I've been screwed for the past two days."

Charlie thought that this was the first time in a long time that the gods had smiled on him. If things had gone their usual way, he would still be in the brig.

Now McDonald changed the subject. "After we get these recruits qualified, report to the motor sergeant. He'll issue you a driver's license. Since you'll be driving me over to Major Houston's house this evening, take a shower and put on your short-sleeved khakis before picking me up at the orderly room. In the meantime, get your butt up to the firing line and help us whip these sorry excuses for human beings into shape."

Charlie saluted his CO and ran back to the firing range.

You lucked out, Charlie. You lucked out.

BUILDING 5005, BAKER COMPANY,
90TH INFANTRY MESS HALL
CAMP ROBERTS, CALIFORNIA
SUNDAY, 21 JUNE 1942, 6:45 A.M.

As Charlie Wilkes sipped his morning coffee he took notice of the soldier sitting next to him. If he weren't wearing a United States Army uniform, Charlie thought, Private Clayton Forrest, from Barrettville, Tennessee, could pass for a soldier in the old Confederacy. Charlie attributed such thoughts to Forrest's speech patterns—they were straight out of the Tennessee backwoods.

Forrest often referred to non-cooperative pieces of equipment as being "as fucked up as Hogan's goat." To any GI who refused to loan him money, he claimed the soldier in question was "tighter than a tick." The list of his off-the-wall similes was endless. But on the rifle range Forrest's marksman-ship rivaled another Tennessean's: Sgt. Alvin C. York. Forrest could also put away the hooch. Scuttlebutt around Baker Company was that Forrest single-handedly downed an entire fifth of firewater at the Elkhorn one night and still made reveille the next morning at 0530 hours.

Charlie also suspected that the soldier from the small town northeast of Memphis had never had a pair of boots to call his own before being draft-ed, let alone three square meals a day and a warm place to sleep at night. The twenty-one bucks a month he was receiving from Uncle Sam probably made him feel as rich as Andrew Carnegie.

Taking notice of Corporal Wilkes' stare, Clayton Forrest nodded his head and smiled. Then he turned his attention back to the plate of grits sit-ting in front of him that was dripping with butter and swimming in pepper. His eyes glowed. He picked up his cup of hot coffee and took a sip. This being Sunday morning, Private Forrest planned to take his time eating.

Charlie began to daydream. Suddenly he was back in Iowa. It was Fri-day night and he was about to score with two girls from Clarinda. Unfortu-nately, Charlie's erotic thoughts were interrupted when he noticed Forrest staring at the plate of food that he hadn't touched since sitting down.

"If you ain't gonna finish them vittles, give 'em to me. 'Cause, as sure as Sherman burnt Atlanta, I know I could eat the ass off a hog this morn-ing."

"Clayton, I swear you ought to go on sick call and have the medics check you for a tapeworm. Damn, I ain't never seen anyone who eats as much as you do," Charlie replied.

"Jist the same, if you ain't gonna eat all of that-there food, slide yer plate over my direction."

Charlie did just that. His stomach had been acting up for the past three days, and the thought of another plate of chipped beef on toast nearly caused him to upchuck. Forrest dug right in, all the time grinning like the cat who had just eaten a canary.

Angry at Forrest for interrupting his daydream, Charlie decided to jerk his subordinate around a bit. Charlie knew that Clayton had met what he considered to be a floozy at the Elkhorn two weeks ago, and had been screwing her every since. So he began chastising him about his newly-ac-quired girlfriend.

"You know, Clayton, all that whoring you've been doing is gonna catch up with you, don't you?"

The dumb bastard is probably in love with her by now.

"Charlie, you know I don't cotton to no one callin' my girl a 'whore,' so why do you do it? Ya' know danged well it pisses me off." Forrest angrily swallowed some more coffee.

"For just that reason—to piss you off," Charlie answered.

"If I didn't know better, Charlie, I'd swear you done got a burr up your ass over women."

"Calm down, Clayton. You know I'm just jerking you off. And the funny thing is—you fall for it every stinking time."

"Well, as long as you was jist jokin' I guess it's all right. But I do wish you'd quit callin' Betty Mae a 'whore,' because she ain't one. She's a nice girl, and after we get through kicking the Huns' asses, I think I'm gonna come back to Californy and marry her."

Shit, I was right. He is in love with her.

Charlie looked at his watch. It was seven in the morning. On any other day he already would have been at work for two hours, but, since today was a Sunday, training was curtailed so the soldiers could attend worship services.

The number of recruits who suddenly discovered they loved Baby Jesus after joining Uncle Sam's Army was no surprise to Charlie. Even those recruits who professed heathenism at the induction center now claimed a miraculous conversion, since being assigned to Baker Company, 90th Infantry. These latter-day Road to Emmaus events could directly be attributed to First Sergeant Jeffery Calhoun Lee, of Holly Springs, Mississippi.

The routine went like this: All newly arriving recruits would be yelled at until they got into some sort of military formation in front of the company orderly room. They were left there until more than two soldiers passed out from locking their knees. Then the senior NCO would suck in his gut and start acting as pompous as if he had just ridden in on Astor's horse. He would introduce himself by asking if there was anyone one in the formation who thought he could kick his ass. If there were any soldiers dumb enough to respond affirmatively to his question, the first sergeant would respond by saying "then you're my assistant."

After the ensuing laughter died down, he would launch into a twenty-minute diatribe that began with the admonition, "My name is First Sergeant Jeffery Calhoun Lee. And, gentlemen, it ain't no mistake that my initials are 'J.C.'! You will address me as 'First Sergeant.' Behind my back I am called 'His Holiness.' I have only two rules: Don't ever piss on my boot and tell me it's raining… and never lie to me."

J.C. Lee went on into great detail as to what he expected—*demanded*—from his men. After ranting and raving for a quarter of an hour, Lee would suggest that it "behooved all newly-assigned recruits to go to their favorite Sunday morning meetings."

Then he would do a dramatic pause, usually lasting a full minute. Standing on his porch at parade rest, the first sergeant would look every soldier in the eye. Rumor had it that more than one soldier had pissed himself while being glowered at.

Next, the senior non-commissioned officer would put on a look of utter disgust, followed by the spitting routine. After nearly all his hell-raising was completed, Lee would conclude his welcoming speech by saying that he despised "…atheists, communists, malcontents and smart-asses." The implication being that, if you were not among the church-going type, you automatically fell into of the four aforementioned classes of utterly depraved individuals.

"So," the senior NCO would say, grabbing himself, "If I catch any of you green pees hanging about in the barracks during 'church-going time,' I'll personally arrange for ya'll an alternate activity, like peeling a hundred-pound sack of potatoes that'll be finished by ten-hundred hours, or else! Then, I might just bust your balls!"

Most recruits came away from his "welcome to hell speech" convinced that their senior enlisted man was one tough sonofabitch. Nor was it very surprising that by the second week of basic training, nary a non-believer in the Baby Jesus could be found in all of Baker Company.

Charlie's dog tags claimed he was a Methodist, but the truth of the matter was that he'd had it stamped on them only to avoid having to listen to all the bullshit sure to be directed his way by the first sergeant if he'd had "No Preference" on them.

It wasn't that Charlie Wilkes didn't believe in Jesus, or anything like that, but since losing his momma he hadn't held too many discussions with God. That is, other than to call out His name when getting laid. But, to Charlie's way of thinking, God understood.

Most of the other men in his unit were not as jaded about religion as Charlie was. In fact, one of the soldiers newly assigned to his unit, a PFC named Ian Henry, not only went to Catholic mass every Sunday, but he even went to church on Wednesday nights! So far as Charlie was concerned, that was overdoing it—all the kneeling and carrying on. But the way Charlie looked at it was this was America, and if the mackerel snappers wanted to spend their lives on their knees, lighting candles, going to confession, genuflecting and saying weird stuff in Latin, that was their business.

He took a long sip of Java from his cup, and thought about how he'd come to know PFC Henry. Six weeks ago Charlie had been sitting in the company orderly room, minding his own business and watching the phones for 1SG Lee, who had stepped out to perform his morning necessary business (a trip to the latrine —or at least that's what he told the CO). The truth of the matter was that he had gone out for a wee shot of Old Fitzgerald Kentucky straight bourbon whiskey.

Charlie hadn't been alone for more than ten minutes when Chaplain John R. Wright of the 12th Field Artillery strode in, unannounced.

"Is First Sergeant Lee in?" Wright inquired.

After advising the 0-3 of the lead noncommissioned officer's absence, Charlie asked the man of the cloth if there was anything else he could do for him.

Not at all used to someone of Charlie's low rank showing any initiative, instead of shining on the two-striper the captain proceeded to tell him how he had lost his chaplain's assistant. "The young man got into a fracas down at the Elkhorn Bar a few weeks ago and stabbed another soldier in the back!"

Charlie replied with one of his Iowaisms. "Well, I'll be go-to-hell."

The minister had already come to the same conclusion. But, right now, he was more concerned with getting a new assistant than saving another soul from the flames of hell.

Maybe this trooper could help me find a new chaplain's assistant.

"Even though he probably was the biggest scoundrel in the Church since Judas, my now locked-up assistant was very good at handling many of my day-to-day things."

Charlie asked how he might be of help.

"Well, if you could get me a replacement, I'd sure appreciate it. But, then, I don't suppose that's your line of business."

"What qualifications does your assistant need, sir?"

"To start off with, I want someone who can stay away from those houses of ill-repute downtown, who doesn't gamble, swear up a storm, and drink whiskey as if it were water, or cheat at cards."

Damn, doesn't this Papist know the Twelve Apostles are dead?

The chaplain looked at Charlie. "Don't suppose you know anyone like that, do you, Corporal?"

"Nobody I know around here fits the bill, but as soon as the first sergeant comes back from the company library I'll tell him you were in and what you need, sir."

The chaplain thanked Charlie, and left the orderly room.

As things turned out, First Sergeant Lee ended up indulging in more than one shot of Old Fitzgerald and didn't wish to risk showing up at the office until after the noon meal. When Lee finally did grace the orderly room with his presence, Charlie was off doing an errand and consequently forgot to tell him of the chaplain's visit. It wasn't until late evening when Charlie was having a particularly delightful nocturnal emission that he woke up remembering the priest's request. He vowed to take care of his oversight the first thing the next morning. Yet, as is often the case with such vows, one forgets. The same thing happened to Charlie.

It wasn't until he walked by the chapel on an errand for his platoon sergeant later the next afternoon that Charlie remembered. Not wanting to screw up again, he did a one-eighty and literally ran back to Baker Company. Out of breath (and smelling like a he-goat), Charlie filled the first sergeant in on the chaplain's request.

Having just returned from his afternoon appointment with Old Fitzgerald, and again not feeling any pain, 1SG Jeffery Calhoun Lee wasn't in the mood for small talk. Curtly, he asked if Wright was "that ring-kissing 0-3 from Base Chapel 4?"

"One and the same, First Sergeant," Charlie hurriedly replied.

The first sergeant leaned back in his chair, passed wind, and looked up at Charlie.

"Well, hell, boy! Don't just stand there with your finger up your butt, gimme the damned company roster."

To Charlie, Lee's request seemed idiotic, as he could plainly see the unit's manning roster sitting in plain view of the senior NCO. All the man needed to do was swivel his fat butt around and pick it up. However, Charlie knew from the first sergeant's demeanor that he'd better keep his mouth shut. So, instead, he quietly walked behind his superior's desk and handed him the document. As Lee began thumbing through the document, Charlie asked him how he planned to make a selection.

The 1SG just grunted, and replied, "If I thought it was any of your friggin' business, I'd tell you."

From the way the senior non-com was leafing through the sheaf of papers, Charlie figured his boss didn't have an inkling as to how he was going to pick a soldier for the chaplain.

"You know, First Sergeant, if it were me I'd call base personnel and let them fool with it."

The sergeant put the papers down on his desk, then again passed wind. This time Charlie nearly upchucked. He'd been raised around hogs all his life and knew that being downwind from them on a hot, windy Iowa summer afternoon was a close to hell he would ever want to get. Nevertheless, by God, the first sergeant's flatulencies made the fecal matter from a thousand pigs seem like Old Spice, in comparison.

Charlie turned away to avoid the putrefied air. His eyes were burning. After a few seconds had passed the air had cleared up somewhat, but not enough for Charlie to turn around and face his boss. From behind Charlie heard, "Well, hell, do I gotta do every thing around here, boy? Call them sonsabitches over in base personnel and git 'em on it."

Now, as far as Charlie was concerned, all the men working over in base personnel where a bunch of sonofabitches, so he was at a loss as to how to fulfill his superior's request. When he turned to ask the senior noncommissioned officer for clarification, he discovered the man had gone outside for a 'walk-around'—that is, another drink. Although he was still a green pee, Charlie knew better than to interrupt his superior's pursuit of liquid refreshment.

Corporal Wilkes picked up the phone and asked the switchboard operator to connect him with base personnel. To say that the senior noncom in charge was thrilled at the prospect of talking to some 'numb-nuts from a training unit' would be an egregious error, and he took his sweet time answering the phone.

Charlie introduced himself and began explaining the reason for his call. He had just started with the requested qualifications when the personnel clerk stopped him cold. "So, just what the hell makes you think I have time to go through the names of the forty thousand-plus soldiers at this base to find some Latin-speaking, pope-worshiping bastard an altar boy?"

Instantly Charlie was incensed. He didn't really care if the chaplain ever got an assistant, but for damned sure he wasn't about to listen to some nitwit at base personnel chew on his hindquarters. So he fired back. "Personally, Mack, I don't give a damn what you do. You can go pound salt, for all I care. I promised my first sergeant that I'd call you bastards to see if there was anybody over there, who knew what the hell he was doing. Obviously there isn't! That being said, I'll give you a suggestion: Why don't you go down whatever master list it is that you primadonnas have, and find someone with an Irish-sounding name? Chances are, some Mick would jump at the chance to serve God. Or is that just too damned simple of a solution for you?"

Finishing his outburst, Charlie slammed the phone down and stormed out of the office.

If that doesn't get me tossed in the brig, nothing will!

But the amateur bureaucrat in personnel was used to being talked to like a halfwit, and didn't take offense. After thinking about it briefly he concluded that the rude asshole on the other end of the phone might have had a good idea, after all, so he began thumbing his way through a list of newly arrived soldiers. The first Irish-sounding name to surface belonged to a soldier from Hooksett, New Hampshire. His name was PFC Ian Henry.

Ian Henry wasn't only a good Catholic, he was also good-looking and intelligent, having passed all of his freshman courses at Dartmouth with honors the previous year.

In Chaplain Wright's opinion, having such a smart soldier being assigned to him as assistant seemed like Divine Intervention. And to show his gratitude, Wright decided to personally thank the soldier who had found him PFC Henry. Two days after Henry was assigned to the chaplain, he dropped in at base personnel to look up whoever was responsible for finding such an upright soldier.

Unfortunately, the sight of a priest walking into personnel nearly caused the NCO responsible for Henry's transfer to go into cardiac arrest. When told the priest was there to see him, he even felt a sharp pain in his chest.

Struggling to stand, the admin spec's head was filled with horrible thoughts: Had the Army found out about his uncle—the one who'd served with Franco? Or maybe they'd learned about the fourteen-year-old boy from Boston that he'd spent the summer with out on Cape Cod, in 1939?

The sound of dozens of metal trays crashing to the floor knocked Charlie Wilkes out of his daydream. He looked up and saw none other than soldier he'd just been thinking about, Ian Henry.

"Grab a cup of Joe and some of that slop they call food, and sit next to me. I gotta tell ya about last night!" Charlie insisted.

Coming from a town in southern New Hampshire of less than three hundred souls, Ian had never before been exposed to anyone as worldly as

Charlie Wilkes. Nevertheless, Ian liked hearing about Charlie's bedroom conquests, so it was with great interest that he worked his way through the chow line, pulled a chair up next to Charlie, and asked, "What happened at the XO's potty last night?"

Because Charlie had never been farther east than Indiana, he didn't have a clue about what the soldier from New England had just said.

"What the hell are you talking about… what 'potty'?"

"That potty you went to last night at the XO's house, Charlie," Ian repeated.

From the confused look on Charlie's face the other soldier sitting at their table, a twenty-year-old from Shelbyville, Tennessee, named Chester P. Jackson, could tell that Charlie was completely screwed up.

"Charlie, I know you might find this difficult to reckon, but if I'm right, Ian done asked you about the hoedown the XO threw fer his old lady last night. He ain't talking about no damned outhouse." Looking over at Ian Henry, Jackson commented, "Am I right, Bluebell?"

"Yeah, Charlie—the potty, not the toilet," Henry piped up.

After getting over his feeling stupid, Charlie began with his tale.

"Well, to start off… it was hotter than hell inside the Old Man's house, so the doings moved outside. There were only a few women there. And the ones who were there were so damned tanked up I bet you they still ain't got out of bed."

"Any of 'em make a pass at ya?" Ian asked, having heard through the grapevine that Charlie's good looks had got him into trouble often in the past.

However, ever since the summer of 1939 whenever Charlie Wilkes needed to get laid, he paid for it. It wasn't that he couldn't get any girl he wanted, because he could. In fact, that was his problem. Not only had Charlie been physically blessed (a handsome six-footer, with black hair and dark blue eyes), but he was exceptionally talented in talking his way into the girls' hearts. Charlie was so adept at ending up in Montgomery County's feminine underdrawers, in fact, that the old Jewish owner of one of Villisca's grocery stores used to claim that Charlie "could sell pork chops at a Bar Mitzvah."

Among Charlie's many conquests had been one of his high school classmates, Dotty Andrews. But Charlie never viewed Dotty as another notch in his pistol. In fact, of all the women he'd boinked, Dotty was the only one he'd ever loved. Yet, much to the chagrin of the local populace, Charlie and Dotty had been openly tee-heeing ever since their sophomore year. Were it not for the fact that both kids were considered "white trash," the local citizenry might have raised hell about their openness.

Many Villiscans figured that Charlie and Dotty would elope someday and, therefore, what they did before marriage (even though it was not proper) should be overlooked. All of that changed one torridly hot afternoon late that summer of 1939, however, after Charlie had experienced a particularly bad bout with Demon Rum.

His drinking binge was the result of a venomous argument he'd had with his employer, the man Charlie believed was his father. While Charlie's relationship with his dad had not been the most ideal in history, it certainly wasn't the worst in history, either. There had been other arguments, but that day's fight was so vile that it pushed Charlie to the breaking point. To deal with the situation, Charlie got stinking drunk. Had that been where it ended, nobody in town would have even been inclined to recall the incident.

But that was not where it ended. Instead of drinking himself into a drunken stupor, Charlie got such a load on that he strolled over to Dotty's house completely blasted out of his mind. Dotty was enraged on seeing him that way, as she'd been led to believe by some of the town wags that Charlie planned to propose to her that evening. Obviously, that wasn't going to happen now, and she threatened to end their relationship.

Again, had that been where matters ended, the pair probably would have still got married, as no doubt Charlie would have been able to calm her down after a few days. At least that was the way things had always gone in the past.

But when Dotty told him to go somewhere else and sleep it off, he became physically abusive and demanded that Dotty have sex with him. Dotty proceeded to tell Charlie that if she wanted to do it with some drunken sonofabitch who would beat the shit out of her after he was finished, she'd go fuck her stepfather. She then told Charlie to perform a certain sexual impossibility on himself. Charlie yanked her down by the arm, covered her mouth, dragged her off behind a rosebush and repeatedly raped her.

After sobering up the next morning, Charlie begged Dotty to meet him at the Marsh Café, the town's only restaurant. At first Dotty refused, but finally relented and agreed to meet him for lunch. She planned then and there to permanently break off their relationship. However, no sooner did she enter the eatery than Charlie became sloppily apologetic. Having been subjected to the same treatment by her stepfather so many times, and for the same offense, Dotty knew the drill.

"I'm so sorry, Angel. It won't happen again. Please forgive me."

Although Dotty had intended to end their relationship, she forgave Charlie one more time. Forgiveness was one thing. In reality, things never did get back to the way they were before the night of the rape. Even the most casual observer around town could tell their feelings toward each other had chilled considerably.

Then disaster struck. Dotty missed her menstrual cycle. The memory of Charlie forcing himself on her became overpowering, causing her to go three days without sleep. On the fourth day, exhausted and nearly suicidal, she made a fateful decision. She would rid herself of both the unwanted child and the man who made her pregnant. She began the cleansing process by breaking up with Charlie for good that afternoon.

The next day she confided her secret to a local boy she'd known since first grade, Randy Roberts. Dotty trusted Randy implicitly, because he had never tried to get into her or her girlfriend's pants. What she didn't know, was why he hadn't tried to score with either of them.

Charlie suspected that Randy Roberts was homosexual, and had confronted him with his suspicion on a couple of occasions. At first Randy tried to ignore Charlie's line of questioning. When that proved impractical, Randy told Charlie it was out of devotion to fianceé, Miss Sharon Lorraine Eddy. Charlie thought Randy was an idiot for not trying to get as much tail as he could, but did respect his friend's integrity. He also remembered that he was a guest in Randy's house!

In September Charlie felt like a complete ass for even having suggested that his friend was gay, when Randy married Sharon Lorraine Eddy. If the marriage wasn't enough to make Charlie feel like a heel, he certainly did when Randy asked him to stand in for his older brother as best man at the wedding.

Charlie had pretty much forgotten about the entire episode, until the newlyweds named their firstborn son Dexter Charles Roberts. The name "Charles" was bestowed on the lad in honor of Charlie Wilkes.

Another high school classmate, Dexter Dannenberg, had just returned from a harrowing European trip—one in which he'd barely been able to stay one step ahead of Hitler's *Gestapo*. Dexter was Randy Roberts' secret lover.

Suddenly, Ian Henry interrupted Charlie Wilkes' flashback. "So, tell me, Charlie, did any of the ladies make a pass at ya?"

Charlie apologized for having drifted away from their conversation about the last evening's events. "Sorry, I got lost in some old memories of a friend of mine."

"From Iowa?"

"Yeah, we played football together in high school. After graduation, he got married and moved to California. His uncle's an FBI agent in 'Frisco, and he fixed Randy and Sharon up with an apartment in Berkeley. Randy joined the ROTC while attending college at Cal, and they had a baby. Then, during his sophomore year something happened to Cal's regular place kicker... and from nowhere, Randy got the position." Charlie picked up his coffee cup and took a couple sips from it, gazing away reflectively.

Ian frankly wondered where Charlie's story was going. But he couldn't realize that Charlie's coffee drinking was a ploy to buy some time, so he could relive bittersweet memories of his dead friend. After taking a long swallow, Charlie continued his story.

"To make a long story short, Ian, Randy was killed at Pearl Harbor. The ironic thing about it, is that the only reason he was there in the first place was because he pulled a groin muscle and was off the team for the rest of the season. As 'luck' would have it, Randy's uncle got transferred to Honolulu. He felt like he was deserting Randy and his wife, so he invited them over to spend a few days in the Hawaiian territories before Christmas. Well, bigger-than-crap December seventh comes along, and of all the lousy luck, Randy and his uncle are on none other than the fucking Arizona when those bastards attacked. Amazingly, his uncle survived."

Ian said nothing, but made a mental note to light a candle for Wilkes' friend's soul the next time he was in the chapel.

A few awkward seconds passed without Charlie saying anything. Ian rightfully suspected that his friend's silence was due to the story he'd just related. Ian offered to leave the table, but Charlie asked him not to.

"The story doesn't end there, Ian. See, before I shipped out to Camp Claiborne, I got this girl knocked up."

Ian Henry was dumbfounded. He'd always suspected that Charlie was pretty much a gigolo, but this nearly knocked him off his chair.

"I didn't find out about it until I was shoveling shit in Louisiana."

"What did you do?" Ian asked.

"Well... the way I found out about it was when the base chaplain told me about her death," Charlie said, his voice now nearly inaudible.

"Shit, Charlie. She died?"

"Yeah. You see, with me being gone, and the way I treated Dotty—that was her name—she decided to go to one of those doctors and get rid of the baby."

"Shit the bed!" Ian exclaimed. "She killed her baby?"

His use of the verb *kill* hit Charlie hard.

I guess that's what an abortion is, isn't it? You kill the baby? Shit, you'd think he could come up some other word, wouldn't you? Hell, Charlie, you and this Mick are two peas in a pod!

Instead of getting his trousers in a twist at his friend's poor choice of words, Charlie figured God was speaking through his Irish Catholic friend and that he deserved the abuse.

Charlie continued. "This is where Randy comes back into the story. You see… Dotty asked him to drive her over to Omaha for the operation. Randy refused."

Ian gripped his coffee cup, his mouth agape.

This is certainly the juiciest story I've heard since I left New Hampshire.

"So what happened next, Charlie?"

"Randy was an Episcopalian—a damned fine one at that—and so he refused to take Dotty to Omaha. Moreover, you know what? When I got back from Claiborne, Randy and Sharon met me at the train station. That night, after I went to Dot's grave, Randy and I had a long talk. He told me that the reason he didn't take her to Omaha was because he thought having a child out of wedlock was a small-time sin, but that if he helped Dotty to get rid of her baby God would never forgive him."

"We Catholics call that a mortal sin," Ian added.

"Yeah, but like I said, this guy wasn't Catholic."

Ian laughed nervously, then said, "Truth is, the only difference between Catholics and Episcopalians is that the Episcopalians have money."

Charlie was not churched enough to catch the subtleties of Ian Henry's attempt at humor, so he ignored it.

"In the end, it didn't matter what Randy thought, or wouldn't do, because Dotty took a bus to Omaha by herself. And… damn!" Charlie said, his eyes glistening. "That's where she died—in a back alley, all alone."

"Shit the bed," Ian repeated, as his mind attempted to understand what his buddy had just told him. Even though he was a tried-and-true Roman Catholic, and firmly believed that abortion was a mortal sin, Ian felt sadness for the girl who died such a horrible death, the baby who was innocent, and for his friend—who obviously was in great pain.

For Charlie, telling his story was a catharsis. This was only the second time he'd been able to talk about his loss to anyone. Feeling drained, he changed the subject.

"Back to your question about broads at the XO's wing-ding. There was one old babe there I'd say was pushing forty. Back in Iowa, we'd say she'd been 'rode hard and put away wet.' A redhead, and hope to crap, she had the biggest set of jugs I've ever seen. Hell, her boobs would give Mae West a run for her money. And did she ever have a load on."

Ian interrupted Charlie. "You know, I heard about her from that beaner lieutenant from El Paso who runs the rifle range. He calls her 'Malina.' I couldn't pronounce his last name if my life depended on it, but according to the lieutenant Malina was an Aztec goddess who could eat your heart while looking at you."

"I dunno about that, but I can tell you this broad has danger written all over her," Charlie said, taking another sip from his cup of coffee.

"Ian, I can assure you that it ain't gonna be a problem. The last friggin' thing I need in my life is to be screwing some officer's wife. But that didn't stop that broad. She kept asking me to take her home. Hell, she asked me twice. The first time I acted like I didn't hear her, but that only pissed her off. Then she demanded that I drive her home. Honestly, I didn't know whether to shit or go blind. But one thing's for sure—there was no way in Hades I was going to leave that party without McDonald's permission."

"Well, yeah…." Ian said, feeling dumb, as it was obvious that his friend would no-way-in-hell do something that stupid.

"The trouble is that McDonald wasn't readily available."

"What do you mean, Charlie—"he wasn't available?"

"You know Mac. If there's a card game within a hundred yards he can sniff it out. That's exactly where I found him—in the back room with the XO, playing seven card stud. I told him there was this woman that needed a ride home."

"What did Mac say to that?"

"What do you think? He had a full house. He just told me he didn't give a damn what I did, just so I was back within two hours."

"So… did ya take the old cow home?"

"No."

"Well, I'll be a suck-egg mule," said the soldier who up to this point had been happy just to listen to Ian and Charlie's conversation. "Y'all mean to sit there, bigger 'n' shit, and tell me you turned some down last night,

Wilkes?"

Charlie looked at the soldier disgustedly.

"Listen, 'Johnny Reb,' the reason I never took her home was because by the time I got through dicking around with MacDonald, she'd flown the coop."

"Ya' know, Charlie, it might not seem like it, but I think God was looking out for you," Ian said, laughing.

"Somehow, I think she'll be back," Charlie thought aloud.

For the next few minutes, the three soldiers ate their breakfast and shot the bull. Just about the time they were getting ready to leave the mess hall, another PFC from their unit sat down at the table. Charlie thought that seaweed had more brains than this halfwit. Just looking at the soldier made Charlie ill. His military bearing was an abomination. His boots looked like he had shined them with grits and a Hershey bar. His uniforms always looked like he had spent the night in them, and his breath always smelled like he had just brushed with Clorox.

Added to those less than complimentary observations, Charlie firmly believed that nothing had occurred north of the man's neck since birth.

In an Oklahoma accent that would give Tom Joad an inferiority complex, the Okie soldier blurted out, "Wilkes I done heard tell that you 'n' Henry got coast-watchin' duty tomorra' over at Camp SLO."

"Now, ain't that the cat's behind?" Charlie groaned.

"I think the saying goes 'cat's whiskers,'" corrected Ian.

"Well, one things for sure," Charlie said as he reached for a cigarette. "I doubt if we'll actually see a Jap sub this time."

Now the Tennessee soldier's curiosity had been piqued. "What the hell do you mean, 'this time'?"

While Charlie fiddled around with his Camel, Ian Henry began relating the story of the first time Charlie Wilkes had pulled coast watching.

"If my memory serves me right, after Charlie's unit was federalized he got orders to report to the Presidio up in 'Frisco. The Army was using the Presidio as a marshaling area. Well, after three days of wondering what the heck he was going to do during this war, his name came up on a roster to pull guard duty down at Half Moon Bay. I think the only reason they called him was that he was a corporal and had been in the Army for two years. That's right, isn't it, Charlie? I got it right, don't I?"

Charlie took a puff from his smoke. "Yeah, me and five other numbnuts were selected. The NCO of that goat-rope was from the 159th Infantry.

His name was James something… *Ernest James*, as I recall. Anyway, James had pretty much been pulling coastal duty since the Zips bombed Pearl. Just so you'd know, Oklahoma, Half Moon Bay is about a forty-five minute drive south of 'Frisco."

The Norman, Oklahoma soldier nodded, and Charlie continued with his story. "But you know, I knew from the time they called my name that this duty was going to be a problem," Charlie said, taking another drag off his smoke.

"How so?" the Tennesseean asked.

"Sounds dumb, but I swear to God that I got a bad feeling in my gut from the time I climbed on board that truck going down to Half Moon Bay. And, sure as hell, if we didn't end up spotting a Jap sub that evening! It was no more than three football fields off shore!"

The soldier from Tennessee suspected Charlie was jerking him off.

"Wilkes, you lyin' sack of crap… you ain't never seen no Jap sub."

"We sure as hell did," Wilkes said, laughing. "And the damned thing about it was that if some local yokel hadn't been poking his girlfriend on the beach that night, we probably wouldn't ever have seen it."

"That's crap, Wilkes… ain't it?" the Okie soldier said in disbelief.

"Listen, you dumb-ass Okie, that's the way it was. You see, in between rounds the guy gets to looking around for his smokes and that's when he saw the Japs. He and his girlfriend got the heck out of there real fast, and called the cops. The police went down to the beach, verified the sub's presence and called the Army. We arrived just as the cops were getting off the phone to the Presidio, whereupon Sgt. James called Hamilton Field to apprise them of the situation. When he got hold of them, do you know what they told us?"

"I ain't got the slightest idea," the soldier from Tennessee admitted.

"Well, hold on to your hat, because those nitwits in the Army Air Corps told us to 'Keep an eye on them.'"

"That's bullroar! Ain't it, Wilkes?" the Okie added in disbelief.

"No, as a matter of fact, that is exactly what they told James to do—to keep an eye on them."

"It gets worse," I an added. "We didn't even have so much as Enfield to take a pot-shot at the Japs! And, it turned out, Hamilton Field didn't even have any combat planes to send out to bomb the bastards, either!"

"What ended up happening?" the would-be Joad family member asked.

"Other than James putting in for officer candidate school (OCS) the next morning? Absolutely nothing.

"Well… that's not quite true. We did honk our horn at the Japs."

"Oh, I'll bet that put the fear of MacArthur into them," the soldier from Barrettville, Tennessee replied.

"Which leads me to believe it's going to be a long war," Charlie said, as he stood up and began walking toward the door.

CHAPTER TWO

*We must hate with every fiber of our being. We must
lust for battle; our object in life must be to kill. There
need be no pangs of conscience, for our enemies have
lighted the way to faster, surer, crueler killing. They
were past masters. We must hurry to catch up with
them if we are to survive.*
> —Lt Gen. Lesley McNair, US Ground Forces command-
> er, Solomon Islands

THE BEACH AT MORRO BAY, CALIFORNIA
SUNDAY, JUNE 28, 1942, 2:00 A.M.

Charlie had gotten the message: When Captain McDonald told him he
was going to be assigned extra details because of his lack of good judgment
and subsequent incarceration—he had meant it.

*But Jesus, Mary and Joseph, seven days of this miserable coastwatch-
ing is a bit much, don't you think, captain?*

As he looked at his watch for the fifth time in the last six minutes, Charlie could feel his temper rising.

Where are those sonofabitches who are supposed to relieve us?

Until tonight, Corporal Wilkes hadn't been part of the usual bitching
and complaining soldiers did, as before now in his army career he'd actually
felt as though he was accomplishing something....

But after seven nights in a row of freezing his butt off in someplace that
had to be twelve miles from East Jesus....

God, to think that my enlistment says "duration, plus six months!"

Charlie pulled his field jacket tighter, and yanked on the zipper again. It
was no use. Until he got inside there was no way he was going to get warm.
He took a draw from his Camel and rubbed his hands together—again, a
wasted effort. He thought about scanning the ocean's horizon to pass the

time, but gave up on that idea rapidly.

What the hell good would that do in this fog? I can't even see Morro Rock from here, so what makes me think I could see a Nip sub? Besides... remember the last time I actually did see a Jap sub? There wasn't even so much as an Army Air Corps plane available! What a helluva way to run a war! It's kind of like the ordeal with that civilian up in Avila Beach on December 7th crap—all they had for him was a friggin' 24-inch iron bolt as a weapon.[1]

How in the hell did the strongest country in the world end up in this mess?

Despite Charlie's youth, this monkey business was beginning to wear thin. For a few minutes Charlie was amused by feeling sorry for himself. Then he did some jumping jacks, but because it was so damned cold each time his feet hit the macadam he felt the ground shock in his brain. He then thought of the thousands of soldiers he'd seen milling around Camp San Luis Obispo every day for the last week, and wondered why one of them could not be here, freezing his young ass off instead of Charlie.

"Hey, Charlie," PFC Henry hollered from the distance, "Pack up your stuff, our relief is here."

"What the hell kept them?"

"They told the watch commander they ran out of gas," Ian replied.

"I'd bet next month's pay that those sonofabitches stopped off at the Elkhorn for a few toss-downs or a roll in the hay with one of the whores upstairs," Charlie mumbled as he walked toward the guard shack.

Wilkes' suspicions proved correct, as the instant he walked into the guard shack he caught a whiff of hooch. Then it became overwhelming. Every soldier on the detail smelled of rotgut booze. Ten minutes ago he'd been pissed—now he was ready to kill! But the truth of the matter was that there wasn't a damned thing Charlie could do about flirtations with perdition that night. He was a two-striper and therefore powerless.

"Heard you fellers ran out of gas," Ian Henry said as he came in the shack.

"Bigger 'n' Göring's ass!" one of the soldiers replied.

Charlie recognized one of the soldiers and walked over to him.

---

1. For more information about California's Central Coast during World War II, readers should refer to *War Comes to the Middle Kingdom—California's Central Coast Enters World War II*, EZ Nature Books, San Luis Obispo, CA. ISBN 0-945092-24-5

"You're Crosby from Chicago, aren't you?"

"Yes, Corporal," the midwestern private answered.

Standing close enough to mar the Kiwi on the other man's boots, Charlie leaned over and said, "If you ever pull a stunt like this again, so help me God, I'll break your balls."

Even as intoxicated as he was, the young man Charlie had just threatened got the point—Corporal Wilkes was not one to screw with.

"It won't happen again."

"If it does, you'll answer to me personally," Charlie whispered.

His business finished, Charlie followed Henry's lead and signed off-duty. As they headed for their vehicle, Charlie heard his name being called out. Turning, he spotted a butter-bar lieutenant coming in his direction.

"Go ahead and get her warmed up," Charlie directed Henry, as he began walking toward the junior grade officer.

After Wilkes saluted the OIC, the second lieutenant began talking. "I just wanted to thank you and PFC Henry for doing such a good job for the past seven nights."

"Thank you, sir. I appreciate that."

The lieutenant continued, "And I want you to know that I told Captain Mc Donald the same thing this morning after mass."

"Thanks, sir. Maybe now he'll pull us off of this shit detail."

The lieutenant only smiled. "This is an important job, corporal."

Charlie knew he had screwed up again.

My damned big mouth gets me into more trouble. Maybe someday I'll learn to keep it shut.

The lieutenant looked as though he'd just read Charlie's mind. He grinned and added, "If it makes any difference to you, tonight was your last night on this 'shit detail.'"

Wilkes thanked the officer, saluted him, and headed for the jeep. As he was climbing in, he noticed in his side-view mirror that the lieutenant was behind him.

"Sir?"

"I forgot something. Wilkes, I know you think you were chosen for this job because of your recent run-in with the law in San Miguel. But that's simply not true."

Charlie didn't believe a word he was hearing. "Then, how in the hell did I end up here, sir?"

"Remember Sergeant James?"

"Certainly, sir. He's the NCO who I was working with the night we spotted that Jap sub. Yeah… he's at OCS now."

"Well corporal, he's the one who requested you—not Captain McDonald. Staff Sergeant James told me he thought you had a lot of potential, the way you remained so cool the night of the sighting of the Nip sub. Therefore, when I drew this shit detail, the first thing I decided was not to be on it with soldiers who didn't know their asses from an Enfield. So I called my old high school buddy, Captain McDonald, and asked him to send you."

Charlie began to laugh, while the lieutenant continued speaking. "Don't tell Captain Mac I'm telling you this, but he didn't want to release you. He told me he thought you were the brightest junior enlisted man he's seen in years. But he did say you were somewhat of a hothead."

"It's the Irish in me," Charlie joked.

"That's why your Mick captain overlooks half of the crap you do, because he's done the same stuff himself. Sometime I'll have to tell you some of the stunts we pulled back in high school."

"I'll be go-to-hell," Charlie said, as he saluted the officer again.

Just before he closed the jeep's door, the lieutenant joked, "That's exactly what the base chaplain told me about you yesterday morning after mass."

2ND PLATOON, BAKER CO, 90TH INF,
19TH TRAINING BATTALION (GAY 90TH)
TOP FLOOR OF THE BARRACKS,
MONDAY, 6 JULY 1942, 12:55 P.M.

After finishing his morning's duties Charlie went upstairs to his room to catch up on some sleep. His snoring was proof-positive that he'd accomplished his mission. For all he cared, he could have spent the rest of the war sleeping.

At five minutes to one he was awakened by PFC Henry's rendition of a limerick that was currently popular with the troops at Camp Roberts:

A cheerful old mammy named Hannah
Who'd lived eighty years in Savannah
Said "Sho' 'nuff I'll buy Defense Bonds
'cause I'm in love with the star-spangled bannah.

Had it not been time to get go downstairs for the 13:00 formation, Charlie probably would have kicked Henry's butt twice: the first time for waking him, and the second time for singing that little ditty he'd already heard at least fifty times this week!

When Charlie stood up to put on his trousers, someone knocked on the door. Because Charlie wasn't dressed, Ian did the honors and opened it. Outside stood a buck private. From the way the young soldier was shaking in his boots, Charlie figured he hadn't been in the Army more than two weeks.

"You have something to say?" Ian Henry inquired.

"Ah... yes, private," the soldier offered in a hesitating voice. "I have a message for Corporal Wilkes."

Henry opened the door wide open and pointed to Charlie. "There he is. Give it to him."

The nervous soldier slowly walked into the room that had been set aside for permanent cadre. As soon as he reached Charlie, he handed him the note. Written in massive block print, the note from the first sergeant read, "See me IMMEDIATELY after formation! First Sergeant J.C. Lee." The word *immediately* had been underlined three times.

Having finished his mission, the private requested permission to leave.

"Yeah, go ahead. And don't be late for formation," Wilkes responded.

After Henry closed the door, Wilkes showed him the first sergeant's message.

"Have you ever seen one like it?"

"I haven't, but that may not mean anything," Ian replied. "It could be that he wants you to do something right away."

Charlie wasn't buying it. "He would've said that in the note, Ian. Nope, from the way this thing is written I think ol' Lee wants to break my balls for something."

"Why do you say that? You ain't done anything stupid again, have you Charlie?"

"What do you mean by that, dick-head?"

Ian Henry hesitated a bit, then blurted out, "Well, you know yourself Charlie, you're always fucking up somehow."

"Fuck me," Charlie replied. "Haven't you noticed that I ain't done a damned thing out of line in the last week? Why, hell, I ain't even yanked off this week."

Charlie was about to say something else when he noticed Ian's face was beet red.

"What's the matter with you?"

"What do you mean, wrong with me?"

"Your face is beet red."

"To be honest, Charlie, I'm embarrassed that I just said the word 'fuck.' I haven't ever said that word in my entire life before."

Charlie was dumbfounded. To him, *fuck* was a noun, a verb, an adjective, and could be used at least ten times in one sentence. He was about to say just that when his eardrums were nearly shattered by the first sergeant's whistle.

Having heard what the senior NCO was about to say at least a hundred times since coming into the Gay 90th, Charlie began mimicking him.

"All right, you sick, lame and lazy, malcontented malingerers, get your sweet asses down here, now. I ain't got all fucking day!"

Wilkes' mimicking of their superior was impeccable, and Ian began to laugh. It wasn't a half-second later when they heard the first sergeant yelling, "All right you sick, lame and lazy…."

IN FRONT OF BUILDING 5005, FACING J STREET
MONDAY, 6 JULY 1942, 1:15 P.M.

The first sergeant was in unusually rare form. For the past fifteen minutes, he'd accused his trainees of every vile deed since Adam and Eve. His list of misdeeds had started with bestiality. At present he was accusing them of being Sodomites.

PFC Henry was about to burst out laughing at the spectacle the top kick was making of himself, but knew if he did so he risked emasculation. Wilkes rightfully suspected the first sergeant was tanked, which meant that Charlie was likely to get reamed-out royally for whatever transgression he might be accused of doing this time.

This B.S. is getting tiresome. Bring on the Japs!

The first sergeant continued to rant and rave for ten more minutes, and then from nowhere he just stopped screaming and dismissed the lot of them. That is, with the exception of Corporal Charles Wilkes—whom he directed to be in his office in post-haste fashion.

Is this what John Wilkes Booth felt like before going to the gallows?

As soon as Charlie walked into the first sergeant's office, he knew his suspicions about the senior non-com being stinko were correct.

My God, I can smell hooch on his breath from here.

His mind flashed back to that bunch of drunks the other night on coast watching duty.

Christ! Does everyone in the army get rip-roaring shit-faced? No wonder we ain't winning this war.

The unit's top-ranking NCO didn't even give him an opportunity to report in before he started raising hell.

"Wilkes! How many more times are you gonna screw up before you and me go out to the motor pool and discuss your behavior without my stripes on?"

"Would the first sergeant please tell me what I'm being accused of, so I'll know how to answer him?" Charlie came back.

"How 'bout *rape?*"

"'Rape,' for Chrissake? Who's accusing me of that this time?" Charlie said, and then regretted it."

"So, you've been accused of it before?"

"Three years ago, first sergeant, and I've lived with it every day of my life since then," Charlie admitted.

Suddenly the top sergeant lowered his voice. "When are you young bucks gonna learn to either pay for it, or marry some broad and screw her brains out? I mean… shit the bed… you're one of my best soldiers. So why am I am having to talk like a Dutch uncle to the provost marshal to keep him from hauling your ass off to the stockade?"

"But, first sergeant, you haven't told me who this woman is who's accusing me of poking her. And, besides, I swear to God that ever since that incident back in Iowa, every time I've knocked off a shot of tail it's been in a whorehouse."

"Well, fuck me," the first sergeant said, as he sat down in his chair and reached into the top drawer of his desk. Out came a pint of Old Fitzgerald Kentucky straight bourbon. The first sergeant looked across to Charlie. "Now don't get the wrong idea here, corporal. I'm drinking this strictly for medicinal purposes."

"Whatever the first sergeant says," Charlie wisely responded.

After swilling down half the bottle of sour mash the first sergeant put it back in his desk, then returned to the subject at hand.

"Corporal Wilkes, there's some young babe out at the train station at the front gate, with her belly half-way to SLO. Name's Sharon. She's been asking for you. Do you know anyone named Sharon?"

Charlie knew the woman. He also knew that there was no way in hell he'd ever slept with her. A feeling of relief came over him. He started to tell his superior that the woman in question was the wife of a friend who had been killed at Pearl Harbor. But he decided to wait a bit, instead, to teach him a lesson.

"First sergeant, what does this young lady look like?"

"Hell, from what the MPs done told me, she's a looker. Definitely ain't no bimbo. And you know what, Wilkes? Because she ain't no bimbo, I done told them military police pricks that there's no way in God's green acres that you would know her."

He must've taken etiquette classes from Ian Henry.

Charlie decided he would go along with the first sergeant's questioning. If for no more reason than to make him look stupid, when Charlie admitted he did know the woman in question—and that their relationship was respectable.

"Could you be more specific in his description of this woman, First Sergeant? You know, is she a redhead, brunette or a blonde?"

The senior enlisted man stood up from his desk and walked out into the hallway, where he passed wind.

"Phew, I must've ate rat for lunch," he said, coming back into the office.

"Well, she's blonde, about five-foot-seven. She ain't got much in the way of boobs on her, but the MP says she's one swell broad."

She has to be Sharon Roberts. Charlie decided to end his prank.

"First Sergeant, she sounds like a girl from my hometown. Her name is Mrs. Sharon Roberts. I was her husband's best man. He was killed on the *Arizona*."

"So you ain't the father of her baby?"

"No, First Sergeant. The closest thing I am to being a father is her son's godfather."

"Well, I'll be a suck-egg mule," said the man with a diamond in his rank insignia. "And do I feel like a damned fool, too."

Charlie felt relieved to know he was off the hook. But he also felt sorry for his superior, as he'd plainly made an ass of himself. That was something the rarely did.

Suddenly the first sergeant stood up, walked over to the window and looked out. Outside the orderly room stood a military police vehicle, and in its front seat was a woman who was definitely in the latter stages of pregnancy. In the back of the vehicle sat a very young boy who was being tended to by another MP. The first sergeant turned to Wilkes.

"Is that your lady?"

"Yes, First Sergeant, that's Mrs. Roberts and her son, DC."

"Then, what in tarnation are you doing in here? Get your young butt out there and greet that girl. What's that matter with you anyway? Ain't you learned anything about bein' nice to women?" The NCO had a broad smile on his face.

Charlie thanked his superior and began walking outside. As he closed the door, the first sergeant hollered, "After you give her a nice howdy-dowdy, you bring her in here. I want to meet her. Any woman that young made a widow 'cause of them damn Japs, needs to be taken care of."

The walk outside only took a few seconds. But for Charlie Wilkes it was long enough for him to relive virtually every incident that had ever occurred between him, Sharon Lorraine Roberts, *née* Eddy, and her now-deceased husband, Randy.

The instant he saw her, Charlie's eyes welled up with tears.

Dressed in a flowing maternity outfit made of pink material and wearing a wide-brimmed straw bonnet, Sharon greeted Charlie with a soft kiss on his right cheek.

"Hello, soldier," she said, touching his face.

Images of her wedding came to his mind. He recalled the slow dance they did, after Randy's first stroll around the dance floor was finished.

As Charlie stood there, he realized for the first time that he'd loved Randy Roberts. Charlie was consumed with guilt, remembering the hateful things he used to say about Randy behind his late friend's back. Now the only thing that mattered was that Randy was dead, and that his wife was a widow with a two-year-old child and another one due in less than three months.

"DC," Sharon said to the little boy standing beside her, "I want you to meet your Uncle Charlie. He's Daddy's brother."

Whether or not the two-year-old understood what his mother had just said was debatable—but he did understand what his eyes told him: that the man in front of him had a smile on his face and open arms. DC tried to walk to Charlie, but tripped. Charlie reached down and picked up the youngster.

"Hello, little guy." DC responded with a hug.

As Sharon joined them, Charlie noticed that she'd been crying.

"Randy's gone, Charlie."

Instead of saying anything, Charlie pulled Sharon closer to him and whispered, "He's with God."

Watching the scene from inside his office, the first sergeant reached into the desk for his bottle, but decided against it.

You've already drunk too much of that firewater today, Lee....

Instead, he raised the office window and yelled, "Wilkes, I thought I told you to bring that little girl in here... and that handsome lad, too."

Charlie broke away from Sharon's embrace, whispering, "He's my first sergeant, and he's got a real Garfield on."

Sharon Roberts immediately understood what Charlie meant, as there had been many times when Charlie Garfield (Charlie's last name before he changed it) had been so drunk he could hardly function.

Sharon looked at Charlie. "Lead the way, soldier boy."

When the trio walked into the office, the senior NCO introduced himself. He appeared as sober as a judge.

How the hell does he do it? That's probably how he's managed to stay in the army so long.

"Pleased to meet you, First Sergeant," Sharon said, as she put her son on the floor.

"And who is this?" the top-kick asked, looking at the little boy standing in front of his desk.

"His name is Dexter Charles Roberts," Sharon replied.

"Good-looking little rascal," the first sergeant answered.

"Well, his father was a looker," Sharon said, holding back her tears.

"Corporal Wilkes told me about your husband, Mrs. Roberts. I want to tell you that I am terribly sorry for your loss."

He looks like he really means it.

"How long are you staying, Mrs. Roberts?"

"Until the six p.m. train to Paso Robles, if it would be all right with you, First Sergeant."

"Do you have a room in 'Paso?" the senior NCO asked.

"Yes, sir, at the Robles Grande Hotel, for tonight. At ten tomorrow morning little DC and I are headed down to Anaheim to meet my parents. They're out from Iowa, staying on a piece of property I inherited from my grandfather after he passed away."

"Sorry to hear about that, Mrs. Roberts," the first sergeant replied.

"It's okay, sir, he was ninety."

A few uneasy seconds passed before Charlie asked Sharon if she was planning to move to Southern California, or was she going to sell the inherited property.

"Charlie, I can't do anything for five years."

"Why?"

Sharon was about to say something when she felt the baby inside her womb kick. She stopped speaking and rubbed both sides of her belly.

"Can I get you something?" the first sergeant asked.

"Thanks, no. But I'll have to say this baby feels like he's going to be a place kicker like his daddy."

It was yet another reference to Randy, which Charlie tried to ignore. Instead, he asked her to clarify why she would have to live in Southern California for five years.

Sharon's mood changed dramatically. Looking at Charlie, she said with a Scarlett O'Hara accent, "Didn't I tell you that I was going to become a strawberry farmer?"

That's a good sign. She used to do those Scarlett O'Hara imitations when Randy was alive.

"Sharon Roberts, stop fooling around. You know the closest you've ever been to a farm was driving by one in a car," he joked.

"Apparently it was good enough for my grandpa, because he left me sixty acres of strawberries down there in Southern California."

"Are you going to keep them?" Charlie inquired.

"That's why I have to be in Southern California, Charlie—because Grandpa's will specified that in order for me to gain ownership of the property I have to live on it for five years. And that the whole time I have to keep at least a third of it in berries. After that, I'm free to do with it whatever I feel like."

"Why do you think he included that in his will, Mrs. Roberts?" the NCO asked.

"From what my mother tells me, grandpa believed that if I live there that long and raise strawberries, that when the five years is up I won't want to sell it. Quite honestly, though, I believe he thought we'd be living there raising his great-grandchildren—and that Randy would be the strawberry farmer...."

It was another awkward moment. Charlie attempted to say something to comfort Sharon, but the right words would not come.

Then the first sergeant started to walk over to where she was standing, but stopped when he felt a slight pain in his chest. He looked uncomfortable to both Charlie and Sharon.

"You all right, First Sergeant?"

"Aw, hell," he replied, "I ate too much again, and it's giving me gas."

Charlie had been on the other end of the first sergeant's gas attacks, so he didn't think too much about it except to snicker a bit. Sharon gave Charlie a quick look to make him toe the line, but then she too saw the humor in the situation and giggled.

The first sergeant saw an opportunity now to change his tack.

"Corporal Wilkes, I want you to take the old man's jeep down to Paso Robles and help this young lady get checked in."

Charlie was nearly bowled over by the senior NCO's magnanimous offer. He tried to thank him, but the first sergeant would hear nothing of it.

"And you are to remain there until after you have taken her and her son to dinner."

Charlie nearly fell to the floor.

The sonofabitch is a softy, after all!

"And, Wilkes," the sergeant continued, "If you can find a place to stay tonight down there in PR, you may do so until you see her off on the morning's train to Los Angeles."

"First sergeant, that's very kind of you to let Charlie stay with me and DC," Sharon said. Turning to Charlie, she added, "And if he doesn't mind sleeping on the couch, I'd like to spend some time with him."

"Aw, hell, Mrs. Roberts, it's the least a man can do for a pretty young lady like you," the first sergeant replied.

"Nevertheless, I just want you to know how much I appreciate your letting Charlie have the rest of the day off. And I'll make sure he comes right back in the morning."

"Do you want me to sign out, sergeant?" Charlie asked.

"No, I'll tell the captain myself," the NCO replied. "You just skedaddle on outta here, and make sure you're back no later than noon, tomorrow."

Sharon Roberts walked over to the first sergeant and gave him a hug.

"Thank you, sir, for letting Charlie have dinner with us tonight. I hardly know how to show my appreciation."

"Honey, you just raise up those kids to be good, God-fearing Americans, and that'll be pay enough."

THE ROBLES GRANDE HOTEL—
AN HOUR LATER

Although she had a room reservation for the night, Sharon thought she might part the Red Sea with greater ease. When they arrived with little DC in tow, the guests sitting in the hotel's small lobby cleared a path for her to get to the check-in counter.

The show of civility ended, however, the second she reached the counter. Behind the cigarette-burned barrier stood what had to be the surliest woman on the West Coast, who looked like a crossbreed of Ma Kettle and James Finlayson. In addition, she was obviously blotto. And it was painfully obvious that she was not having a good day.

Exhaling the smoke from her cigarette into Sharon's face, the woman said, "I suppose you'd like a room, huh, Toots?"

Ignoring the clerk's reference to her as "Toots," Sharon replied, "Yes, and I have a...."

Without giving her an opportunity to finish the sentence, the clerk blurted out, "Well, Toots, unless you got a reservation I'd suggest ya hit the road, as we ain't got any extra rooms. You know, the 'no room at the inn,' sorta thing."

Unaccustomed to being treated like a common streetwalker, Sharon reverted to her Midwestern upbringing. To do otherwise would have been inappropriate. Calmly she explained to the female Attila the Hun that indeed she did have a reservation, and politely suggested that she re-read her reservations list. She ended her comments by saying that she understood how the woman might be mistaken, considering how busy the hotel was.

Totally ignoring her, the desk clerk replied, "Honey, the last time I made a mistake I thought I was wrong. And from what my records here say [which she didn't bother to read] you are shit out of luck. So... hit the road."

Having secured the jeep, Charlie grabbed Sharon's suitcases and made his way to the hotel's check-in counter. Charlie could see that Sharon was upset.

"Is there a problem, Sharon?"

"Are you the husband?" inquired the old clerk.

"No, just a friend"

"That's good, 'cause even if Sugar here had a reservation I couldn't let you stay. I mean, this is a respectable establishment. We just can't let any floozy in...."

Sharon had heard enough insults from the old broad, and was about to say something unpleasant when Charlie unloaded on the woman instead.

"Listen, you old bitch—I don't know why you've got a hair up your ass, nor do I personally give a damn. But if you don't give this lady her room, you and I are going to discuss it outside. You got that?"

"Charlie! Just because this woman is being rude is no excuse for you dropping down to her level. Besides, I don't appreciate that sort of language in my presence."

Sharon was angry. Charlie turned back to the clerk and apologized for his crude comments.

"Is there a problem?" The question came from a room behind the lobby.

Turning around, Charlie and Sharon saw a gargantuan man approaching. He looked as though he hadn't shaved in a week, and smelled like he'd just finished cleaning out a pigsty. For a top, he wore a mustard-stained T-shirt that barely reached his hairy belly-button. In his tobacco-stained teeth was clenched a cigar that looked like a dog had left it at a fire hydrant, and smelled even worse.

"Yes, there is, sir," Charlie replied pointing to the woman. "You see, this Wicked Witch of the West is saying that my friend here, Mrs. Roberts, doesn't have a room reservation. I know that is incorrect because I have a copy of her reservation in my pocket."

The man came closer, which caused both Charlie and Sharon nearly to upchuck.

"You say this broad has a reservation?" The man passed wind.

"What is it with you folks, anyway?" Charlie asked.

"What do ya mean by that crack, soldier boy?" responded the human pile of debris.

"Well, to be honest with you, mister, under most circumstances I'd think that a woman who'd lost her husband on the *Arizona* would be treated with just a bit more respect than you two are showing—or is that asking too much?"

"Look, sonny boy," the smelly man continued, "you don't have no idea how many times a day someone comes in here swearing on a stack of bibles that they have a room. And if Mrs. Hudson says she ain't got room, that means you're SOL—baby about to pop, or not."

"Come on, Charlie," Sharon said, grabbing DC's hand. "Let's go find another place. I refuse to suffer these fools any longer."

Charlie was inclined to knock both creatures on their asses, but knew that if he did he'd probably end up in the hoosegow again. And this time—regardless of how justified he might be—he doubted if Captain McDonald would bail him out.

Fortunately for the two clerks and for Charlie, at that very instant an MP walked in the door, having been flagged down by one of the hotel's guests.

"What seems to be the problem?" he inquired in a drawl that fairly screamed "Alabama."

"Nothing, sonny boy," the old woman replied, "save for the fact that this twat thinks she can strut her ass in here and demand I give her a room without her having a reservation."

The MP had heard enough from the hotel clerk. After all, he'd been raised to think of women as saints, not sluts!

"Ma'am, I don't know what your problem is. But I'll suggest that you shut your filthy mouth right now, or so help me God I'll have the provost marshal close this place down before you can finish that cigarette."

"But she ain't gotta room!" the male clerk protested at the top of his lungs.

"She does, too," Charlie replied, producing Sharon's reservation from his shirt pocket.

After briefly scanning the document, the MP collared the obese man and walked him outside. The two weren't gone for more than five minutes. When the clerk returned, his voice was filled with contrition.

"Mrs. Hudson, there appears to be a mistake. Mrs. Roberts does have a reservation. And for all her trouble, she is to be our guest."

Looking at Charlie, he continued, "And that goes for you too, corporal."

"Well, fuck me!" the old woman said, in a voice half the hotel could hear. "I guess that's the second time in my life I ever made a mistake." She picked up the reservation book and scanned it again.

"Oh, yeah. Here it is…. Mrs. Randy Roberts, from Anaheim."

TEN MINUTES LATER, IN ROOM 14
THE ROBLES GRANDE HOTEL

As Charlie walked into the small room he noticed it was cleaner than he thought it would be, and that it had two beds. A ceiling fan kept the room at a tolerable heat level.

"What did the MP tell you?" Sharon asked, putting DC down on one of the beds.

"He told me he was going to report those two to the provost marshal, anyway. Said they've been under investigation for quite some time. Apparently they've been running off anyone who wants a room for anything longer than two hours until late afternoon. Once they've run through as many hookers and GIs as they can get away with, they go ahead and rent the rooms for the night. It's a pretty good scam—they keep all the money they've made during the day and the owner doesn't have a clue what they're up to, because the hotel is booked up every day."

Sharon sat down next to DC. The boy was fast on his way to deep slumber. Sharon looked over at Charlie and smiled.

"What's that look for?"

"I just noticed how handsome you look in your uniform. It reminds me of the day you came back from Camp Claiborne after boot camp. Remember? Randy and I met you at the train station."

"It seems like an eternity ago." Charlie thought back. Sadly, in returning to that time Charlie's mind replayed the whole series of events that lead up to him being on the train. Suddenly he was overwhelmed with memories of the man who had raised him—the man Charlie thought was his father—and how that man killed himself after Sheriff Wilkes' confrontation with enough evidence to send him to the electric chair.

Charlie tried to shake the terrible memory from his head. But instead his mind shifted from his father's death to the death of the one girl he'd truly loved—Dotty Andrews. Deep in his psyche he knew he was the reason for her death after a back-alley abortion in Omaha. He had raped her in a drunken stupor, and had refused to take any responsibility for it.

After he'd relived those painful memories, Charlie recalled the afternoon he returned to Villisca after boot camp. It was an Iowa afternoon—off in the distance he could see a summer storm coming in from Nebraska. The humidity was stifling, just like when he left. The only difference when he stepped off the train was, instead of his father being there, Randy and Sharon were there. He remembered Sharon's smile.

But something was up. As the trio exchanged hugs, Randy asked Charlie if he would be his best man. Charlie was taken aback. Why would Randy ask him? He assumed Randy's older brother would do the honors.

In his typical fashion, Randy had been straightforward with Charlie. He told him that, while his older brother had been his first choice, Princeton's football team was getting ready for their first game of the year against Williams College and missing a week's worth of training probably would have put his brother's scholarship in danger. After Randy said that his older brother had suggested him for the job, Charlie acquiesced.

Last of all, Charlie remembered Randy and Sharon's wedding. Performed at the Episcopal Church in Red Oak, it turned out to be the social event of the season and both the service and the music came off without a hitch. Sharon certainly had been the most beautiful bride in Montgomery County that year. Charlie would never forget it.

Now Charlie walked over and sat down on the bed next to Sharon. The he leaned over and kissed her on the forehead.

"How do you do it, Sharon?"

"Do what? '

"How do you stay so strong?"

Sharon looked at Charlie. Softly she put her hand against his cheek.

"Because I have to."

"All the same, I admire your courage."

Sharon's eyes began getting misty as she began talking about Randy's death.

"It wasn't until three days after the Japs hit us, that the Navy found his body. Since I was in Hawaii, I had to arrange the funeral."

Charlie handed Sharon his handkerchief. After wiping her eyes, she said something he already knew.

"Randy's Uncle Dickson was on the *Arizona*, too. He got badly shot up, and had second-degree burns over nearly a quarter of his body. He took a long time to recover."

"How's he doing now?"

"Well, last Monday he reported back to work at the FBI. And… from the looks of it, his friend from California is going to move out to Hawaii. They… they're going to get back together…."

That's a nice way of saying Randy's uncle is homosexual. I wonder if she ever found out her husband was, too.

Charlie instantly regretted his thought, changing the subject.

"So, I guess this means you're gonna be a berry farmer?"

"Can you imagine that? Me—the strawberry farmer!"

"Are you up to it, Sharon?"

"By myself—no. But Dad and mom sold their house in Iowa, and they're going to help me. Dad loves little DC so much, he couldn't bear to have him this far away. I think dad was sort of looking forward to getting out of Iowa after he retired, anyway. The winters were getting to him."

"What did he do with the auction yard?"

"He sold it, along with most of their belongings, too. Both he and mama are down in Anaheim now, setting up the new place."

Suddenly something moved within her, causing Sharon to reach for her belly.

"Oh, I do hope this baby comes soon."

"Let's hope not too soon!" Charlie grinned.

"I'll say. We—I mean I—haven't even given him... or her... a name yet."

"Well, I just want to say, Mrs. Roberts, that you are one strong woman. And I really admire you for it."

Sharon leaned against Charlie's shoulder. She began to cry.

"God, I miss him, Charlie."

Charlie gently dried her eyes.

"So do I, Sharon. So do I."

CHAPTER THREE

*The wind blows where it will, and you hear the sound
of it, but you do not know whence it comes or whither
it goes....*
—John 3:8

ROBLES GRANDE HOTEL DINING ROOM, MONDAY,
TUESDAY, JULY 7, 1942, 9:00 A.M.

"These eggs don't look any better than the ones back at Camp Roberts," Charlie said as he looked down at his plateful of greasy food.

Sharon picked up her cup of coffee and flashed Charlie a smile.

"At least the company's better."

"Why, Sharon Lorraine! Are you fishing for a compliment?"

Charlie's response caught Sharon off-guard. But the truth of the matter was that she was fishing for a compliment, and Charlie had caught her redhanded, causing her to blush.

Charlie decided to change the subject. "Well, one thing's for sure, that chesterfield made a better bed than that miserable thing I have back at my quarters."

"You know what the funny thing is?" Sharon asked.

"What?"

"That you and I spent a night in a room together, and you didn't try to put the make on me. I must be losing my touch."

"Well," Charlie replied, a huge grin on his face, "it ain't like you're in any condition for fooling around."

"God," Sharon said, pointing to her belly, "look what happened the last time I did."

Charlie laughed. Then a serious look came over his face. "Do you really think the last time you and Randy made love was when you got pregnant?"

"No, I was already almost two months along when we arrived in Pearl.

I never told Randy, because I was waiting for the right moment."

The last thing in the world Charlie wanted to talk about was sex, as during the middle of the night he had awakened with a monumental erection. He felt ashamed of himself for being such a cad.

There I was, sharing a room with the pregnant widow of one of the only real friends I've ever had in my life, and what did I do? Got a hard-on. You're truly a jerk, Charlie.

Charlie remembered how he'd tried to go back to sleep, but instead he'd ended up fantasizing about having torrid sex with Sharon. After an hour of tormenting himself he made a trip to the bathroom and took care of his "problem."

Charlie looked over to where little DC was sitting. The boy was struggling with a glass of water, so he reached across the table to help him with his drink. The child practically purred at Charlie's attention.

"He really likes you, Charlie."

"He'll be okay, Sharon, just as soon as you get down to Los Angeles with his grandparents."

"I hope so, because until we met you yesterday afternoon he's been just about all I could handle."

"How so?"

"Since we left Uncle Dickson at Pearl he's thrown a tantrum every five to six hours, just like clockwork. He stopped raising the dickens yesterday afternoon, after you showed up."

"Must the uniform," Charlie joked.

"Could be. But personally I think it's because my little guy misses having a man in his life."

That got Charlie to thinking of his early-morning trip to the bathroom and his newly discovered feelings for Sharon Roberts. He feared that if this conversation kept going where it was headed, he might end up saying something he would later regret. Charlie tried to defuse the situation.

"Well, I still think that once you get him down to Los Angeles, he'll settle down."

"Papa says he behaves wonderfully for him," Sharon replied, "but Mom tells a different story. Says he won't mind her for a hoot."

Charlie took a sip of coffee then changed the subject, asking Sharon if she was going to work her farm or get a job at a defense plant and leave the farming to her father.

"Dad says that Grandpa left me enough money to stay home and raise the children, so that's what I plan on doing. How 'bout you, soldier? Do you have any plans—other than chasing skirts?"

Charlie laughed. Sharon noticed the twinkle in his eyes.

"You won't believe this, Mrs. Roberts, but since I've been in California I haven't exactly had thousands of opportunities to meet women."

Sharon feigned a shocked look.

"Why, Corporal Wilkes, are you going to sit there and tell this poor woman that you don't have a girl on every street corner?"

"Seriously, Sharon, since coming to California the only women I've been with have been on a professional basis."

Sharon looked surprised at Charlie's revelation, but the truth of the matter was that she'd already assumed as much. After a bit more teasing, she became serious.

"Is that because you don't want a girlfriend—which I can't believe for a minute—or is it because you still blame yourself for Dot's death?"

When Charlie didn't immediately reply, Sharon felt she had overstepped her bounds for asking such a question. She was about to apologize when Charlie admitted he still loved Dotty, and that he did indeed blame himself for her death.

"After all, I was the one who...."

Sharon cut him off. "Then I guess we have something in common."

Charlie didn't understand her meaning, and asked her to repeat what she'd just said.

"I said, 'We have something in common.'"

"What do ya mean by that?"

"Do you have any idea how many times I've asked myself if Randy would still be alive if I'd refused to go to Hawaii? I mean, it wasn't like we could afford to go, or anything. And I'd just started a new job at the department store in Oakland...."

"It never occurred to me," Charlie admitted.

"Well, it has to me, and more than once."

Except for the sounds made by DC while he ate his breakfast, the table became very quiet. Both adults spent the time soul-searching. After DC was finished, Charlie paid the bill and asked Sharon if she was ready to leave.

"Oh, I guess so. My train comes in an hour." There was reluctance in her voice.

Charlie went back upstairs to retrieve their luggage. When he returned, he saw that Sharon had paid the hotel bill and was waiting for him outside in the parking lot. As the trio walked toward the jeep, Sharon attempted small talk, but it was obvious to Charlie that her mind was elsewhere. As they approached the vehicle, Charlie began feeling nauseous. He knew what was causing his sudden pain, yet lacked the courage to tell Sharon about the way he felt toward her and DC.

Sharon suddenly turned and faced Charlie. "I won't let it end this way, Charlie."

"What?"

"I said, 'I won't let it end this way.' I mean that, outside of DC, this child I have in my womb and Mom and Dad, you are all I've got now! And I'll be darned if I'm gonna let our friendship end this way."

"What are you talking about, kiddo? Who said anything about anything ending?"

Sharon hugged Charlie. "Don't you get it?"

"Get what?"

"In less than an hour DC and I'll be on a train heading to my farm in Anaheim… and soon you'll be heading off to fight this war."

"Yeah." Charlie still didn't know where she was going with her thoughts. Sharon began to cry.

"Charlie, regardless of what I told you last night, the truth is I'm not strong enough to go it alone. I need someone to love. And I need someone to love me."

Had Charlie thought about it, he probably wouldn't have done what he did now: He kissed Sharon with all the passion his twenty-two-year-old lips could muster. To his surprise, Sharon didn't resist his advances.

When he broke off their embrace, Charlie was overcome with remorse. He began to apologize for his behavior, but Sharon cut him off.

"You didn't do anything I wasn't hoping you would do."

"Do you mean that?"

"Yes."

In the distance a train whistle blew. Sharon dried her eyes.

"We need you, Charlie."

Charlie tried to speak, but ended up mumbling.

Sharon wasn't at a loss for words. "Most men would run, Charlie. I hope you won't."

At that instant the sun's rays shone through one of the majestic valley oaks standing nearby. Charlie's mind flashed back to the first night he'd spent in the Roberts house, after being kicked out of his own. He thought he could hear Randy Roberts talking.

Someday you'll amount to something.

Was this that someday?

MAIN GATE, CAMP ROBERTS, CALIFORNIA
ONE HOUR LATER

As Corporal Wilkes pulled the jeep up to Camp Roberts' main gate, he recognized the military policeman manning the gate. It was the same MP who'd helped him at the Robles Grande Hotel yesterday.

"Good morning, Sergeant," Charlie said, pulling out his identification card.

The MP did a fast double-take. "Dammit, Wilkes! If I'd have known you were AWOL yesterday afternoon, I sure as hell wouldn't have busted my butt getting you a hotel room."

"Sergeant, what do you mean, 'AWOL'? I'm not AWOL. My first sergeant gave me permission to go in to PR for the night. Just ask him."

"That'll be a little tough to do, considering he's dead."

"Dead? What the hell do you mean? I just talked to him yesterday afternoon. How can he be dead?"

"Fuck if I know. He was dead when your CO came in from the rifle range last night."

Charlie briefly tuned the MP out. The first sergeant couldn't have been more than fifty. How could he be dead?

"After the medics left, your CO began looking for you to help him with the paperwork. He had the barracks searched for you, but you weren't anywhere around."

"Of course, I wasn't. I was in PR, like I said," Charlie replied. "And, I might add, with the first sergeant's permission."

From the way the military policeman looked at him, Charlie could feel a BOHICA (Bend Over, Here It Comes Again) heading in his direction.

"The problem with that, Corporal Wilkes, is that your top kick never wrote down anything that said you could leave base. Either that, or he died before he was able to tell anyone."

"Fuck me!" Charlie said, lighting up a cigarette.

"Maybe your captain wouldn't have listed your butt as AWOL this morning. But being that every swinging dick on this base knows that your first sergeant kicked the bucket last night, there's no way in hell he could hide it. So, unless you can prove Sergeant Lee gave you permission, your ass'll remain on the AWOL roster."

"Sergeant, look at me. Do I look like the sort of soldier who'd go AWOL?" Charlie feigned a pathetic look on his face.

"Corporal, I don't know diddle about you. But I'm gonna give ya a break. Park your vehicle over yonder and wait 'til I can get McDonald down here."

Charlie Wilkes did as told, all the while wondering how deep was the hole he was about to be tossed into. As it turned out, Shanghai would have been just about right.

IN FRONT OF BUILDING 5126, 2ND PLATOON, BAKER COMPANY 90TH INFANTRY, 19TH TRAINING BATTALION TUESDAY, 14 JULY 1942, 6:00 A.M. MORNING FORMATION

For all hundred and twenty-five men standing in formation outside Baker Company, the ranting of their company commander was clearly audible. McDonald's tirade against Corporal Wilkes would go down in the unit's history as his most memorable.

"And another goddamned thing, Corporal Wilkes! If you so much as fart without my permission, I'll personally break your Irish balls!"

"Sir, yes sir! You will break my balls if I even pass wind without your permission," Charlie replied, at the top of his voice.

To PFC Ian Henry, all this hellraising was outright foolishness. Certainly, the CO knew by now that Corporal Wilkes did have permission from his since-deceased first sergeant to escort the Roberts widow to Paso Robles on the day in question. So why the charade?

McDonald continued his ranting. "And unless you are driving me off base, young man, your name had better be on the company sign-out sheet and you'd better tell the new first sergeant where the hell you're going. Is that clear, Corporal Wilkes?"

Again Wilkes shouted his reply. "Sir, yes sir! I understand that unless I am driving off base with you as a passenger, that I am to sign out and notify the new first sergeant of where I am headed."

"You do that, Corporal, or so help me Sweet Jesus, your ass won't be worth a plugged nickel. In addition, by the time I get through with you the next time, you'll volunteer for firing squad target practice. By God, I'll rip your ass from here to Berlin!"

Among those standing in formation outside Baker Company's orderly room was a newly-arrived soldier from Red Oak, Iowa. Due to Red Oak's proximity to Villisca, Daniel Erickson's and Charlie Wilkes' paths had crossed back home. Like Charlie, Dan had joined the Army National Guard in 1939, straight out of high school, and he too had been sent to the West Coast to beef up the coastal defenses.

The son of Red Oak's only Presbyterian minister, Dan Erickson wasn't familiar with the sort of language being used by Captain McDonald in his chewing-out of Charlie. As McDonald launched into another round of verbally reaming Charlie's posterior, Erickson quietly asked PFC Henry if the CO always carried on this way.

"Only with the soldiers he likes."

In uncommon vernacular, the new soldier replied, "Fuck me."

ON THE ROAD TO SHERWOOD FOREST TRAINING AREA. CAMP ROBERTS, CALIFORNIA. TWO DAYS LATER

As Charlie maneuvered the commanding officer's jeep down the dusty road leading to where Baker Company's trainees were being instructed in quickly setting up a firing position, he thought about his relationship with Captain MacDonald. It was more like that of an older brother watching out for a younger sibling than of one between an officer and a junior enlisted man. He wondered why the captain had taken such a liking to him. Was it, as the lieutenant at Morro Bay had suggested, that Charlie reminded his CO of how he had been as a frat boy in college?

Maybe it's time for something good to happen to you, Charlie. Sure beats the hell out of going to the stockade every friggin' time I pass wind.

As Charlie drove, he couldn't help but notice how quiet MacDonald was this morning. Usually the captain would talk the entire time he drove, but not today.

Wonder what's eating him? He seems lost in thought.

At times like this Charlie knew to keep his mouth shut, and drive. Then suddenly McDonald spoke up.

"That was a real good show you put on this morning, Corporal Wilkes."

"Sir?" Charlie replied, not understanding the point his CO was making.

"Get off it, Wilkes. You know damn well what I'm talking about."

"If the captain is referring to his dressing-down of me, and my replies to the captain, then yes, sir, I do know what you are referring to."

McDonald laughed, and took a sip of coffee from his steel canteen cup. It was the signal for Charlie to speak his mind.

"You know, sir, there were a couple of times I thought you were serious."

"Only a couple?" McDonald swallowed.

"Sir, I knew the minute the MP said I was AWOL, that my tit was in the wringer. But what really pisses me off, is that I knew when Sergeant Lee told me to take Mrs. Roberts to Paso that I should have documented it somehow—either by telling PFC Henry, or somebody."

McDonald lit a cigarette and suggested to Charlie that, although he'd been screwed by the system, he'd also been the beneficiary of a very good lesson.

"If you ain't got it down on paper, so far as the Army is concerned the job ain't done."

Charlie glanced over at the captain. "Sir, I would've liked to have learned that lesson somewhere other than in the stockade."

"Well," McDonald replied, exhaling smoke from his cigarette, "I hope you understand that it wasn't my idea to slam your ass into the brig for a few days."

"I figured the order came from higher up, sir. But that doesn't mean it didn't piss me off. I mean… having to spend a week in the tank was a pain in the ass, especially when Mrs. Roberts called back the next day to thank the first sergeant for giving me the afternoon off."

"Wilkes, it beats the shit out of me how her phone call got routed to headquarters. It also bugs the hell out of me that not one damned soul up there at that puzzle-palace had the brains to let me know Mrs. Roberts called. Anyway, just so long as you know that I didn't have anything to do with your butt being tossed into the brig…."

"I know that now, sir, but I was pretty damned sore about being in jail," Charlie admitted.

"Had it had been left up to me, nothing would have happened 'til I talked to you. But with Sergeant Lee dropping dead, you know, and the paperwork of the incident going all the way to General Lane's office, there really wasn't much I could do to stop your incarceration."

"I know that, sir. But it still pisses me off." Charlie pulled the jeep under an oak tree and turned off its engine.

McDonald was not a man to waste time. So why he remained in the jeep puzzled Corporal Wilkes. His usual pattern was to bolt from the vehicle as soon as Charlie shut off the engine. But today he stayed in his seat. After saying nothing for a few seconds he resumed the conversation that Charlie thought was finished.

"It's none of my business whatsoever, corporal. But have you been sticking your pecker anywhere you shouldn't be?"

What the hell kind of question is that?

"What do you mean, sir?"

"I'm not talking about the working girls down in Paso. What I want to know, is if you've been humping a certain redhead. You know… the one at the XO's party a few weeks back?"

Charlie was dumbfounded. That his commanding officer was even talking about his trysts surprised him, but that he was being grilled about a woman he'd done his level-best to steer clear of caused him even more consternation.

"No sir, I haven't even gotten laid in Paso."

From the look on MacDonald's face, Charlie could see that his 0-3 wasn't happy discussing the subject.

"Well, mind you, corporal, it's really none of my business…."

"I understand that, sir, and quite honestly I'm surprised you would ask. Which makes me wonder why you're doing so."

"To be honest, Wilkes, I don't know. However, somehow I think that redhead is involved in this mess. I couldn't tell you why, it's just a hunch. And it might take me some time to sleuth out an answer. In the meantime, I want you to disappear."

"Might I ask what you mean by that, sir?"

McDonald paused briefly, as if gathering his thoughts. Then he began speaking again. "Wilkes, something has come up that involves you. It's highly classified. But before I go into it, I want you to understand something."

Charlie didn't have a clue about what his commanding officer was alluding to, nor were the captain's next comments of value in deciphering the riddle.

"Wilkes, you and I both know the first sergeant was an alcoholic. I never said anything about it, because Sergeant Lee never let his boozing interfere with his job. But do you know that if this damned war hadn't come up, he would have retired?"

"I knew he hit the sauce pretty hard, sir, but I never thought anything about it because he always did right by me."

"Do you know he thought a lot of you, Corporal Wilkes?"

"No, sir. All I know is that he always treated me fairly."

"Well, he and I had a long talk the night we came back from that last bivouac. It was way past quitting time, but Sergeant Lee just kept hanging around the orderly room. When I asked if he was going to his quarters, he got up, locked the door, and told me he'd been having chest pains. Apparently he knew his days were numbered, and he asked if I would see about getting him discharged. He told me he wanted to look up his ex-wife, find his daughter and meet his grandson, who apparently he'd never met."

"Didn't he have any leave he could take, sir?"

"It wasn't what he wanted, Wilkes. He'd been in thirty years, and knew it was time to put his riding boots away. I said I'd check into it for him, and I did."

"Did you get an answer from personnel, sir?"

"Amazingly enough, I got a packet in today's distribution for him to fill out. I guess the sergeant had friends in high places. I figured there was no way in hell the War Department would let him go with all his experience, but apparently he had a lot of markers out. Too bad he didn't do it sooner...."

"You know, sir—now that you mention it, his entire attitude changed the afternoon Mrs. Roberts showed up. Before the MPs brought her to Baker Company, I thought he was going to ream me a new ass. But, sure as hell, once he saw Sharon and her son his entire disposition changed. Now I know why. Sharon probably reminded him of his daughter, and the grandson he never met."

McDonald laughed. "It's funny, Wilkes. You know what else Sergeant Lee told me?"

"No sir. What?"

"I remember his words as clear as if it was yesterday. He said that once you became a part of Baker Company's cadre, he realized it was time to turn the reins of command over to some younger trooper."

Charlie was stunned. "He really said that, sir?"

"As sure as I'm roasting my ass off, sitting here," said the captain.

"Damn."

"With that in mind, corporal, I'm going to finish what I started telling you a few minutes ago. If you want to look at this as your holding onto the reins for the first time, I don't suppose First Sergeant Lee would mind."

Charlie sat quietly, hanging onto every word his commanding officer spoke.

"Corporal Wilkes, what do you know about the Battle of Midway?"

"Just that we kicked the little Nip bastards' asses, sir."

McDonald laughed before he continued, "Well, I'm going to let you in on something. But before I do, I have to tell you that what I'm about to say is highly classified and that you cannot repeat it to anyone. Do I make myself clear?"

"Yes, sir. Very clear, sir."

"We think the Japs' hitting Dutch Harbor was a ploy to get our navy to draw their carriers away from Midway. The Nip in charge of that attack was an admiral named Kakuta. But during the second air strike on Dutch Harbor, one of their Zeroes was shot down. According to G-2, some nineteen-year-old pilot named Tadayoshi was flying the damned thing. When his oil feed line got shot to pieces, he was forced to land on Akutan Island.

"Again, from what G-2 says, they suspected the Japs had some I-boats stationed near Akutan to rescue any downed pilots. Anyway, this kid flipped the plane over on landing. That little stunt killed Tadayoshi's petty officer.

"Apparently, the Nips flying cover had orders to destroy any plane that crashed. But they failed to do it because they didn't know if there were any survivors. As it turns out, a couple dogfaces found the plane last week. And—hold on to your hat—that plane is damn near in flying condition."

"Shit the bed, sir. You mean to tell me we got us a flyable Zero?"

"You bet your sweet ass, I do. And that's where you come in, Wilkes. While you were at breakfast this morning, I was summoned over to Headquarters by the colonel who heads G-2. He took me into his office and asked if I had an enlisted man who I could trust to keep his mouth shut. I told him the only one I knew well enough was you."

"Thank you for your confidence in me, sir." Charlie replied.

"He sent for your 201 (personnel) file. I'll have to tell you, Wilkes, you were a hard sell. But after I explained to the G-2 colonel that you were wrongly charged of going AWOL, he relented and talked to the general. It was General Lane, himself, who approved you for this mission, based on my recommendation.

"So, don't screw me over on this one! Got it?"

"Yes, sir, I'll go strictly by the book."

"You're scheduled to leave Camp Roberts tomorrow morning, just as soon as two officers arrive here from the Presidio," McDonald said as he stepped out of the jeep.

Charlie started to secure the jeep, but was directed by McDonald to drive over to the motor pool and draw the sedan he was to drive down to Los Angeles the next day.

"Make sure it's fully serviced." McDonald then added, "One of your passengers is a colonel, the other's a captain. Both were airplane designers before Pearl, so you can bet your ass they'll go through that Zero like crap through a goose.

"During your absence, I'm going to task that new soldier from Red Oak, PFC Erickson, to be my driver. So I want you to spend some time with him tonight and explain to him what it is that pisses me off."

"Yes sir, colonel."

Captain McDonald now had walked completely away from the jeep. He added, "I wish I was going with you, corporal—anything to get away from this hell-hole."

Charlie figured the captain's last words were his cue to depart the area. As he started the engine and began driving off, McDonald shouted, "If you get anywhere near the Roberts woman, stop in and see her!"

Charlie waved his acknowledgment, knowing that the commanding officer's final order was one he wouldn't have any problem following.

HIGHWAY 1, NEAR SANTA BARBARA, CALIFORNIA
THURSDAY 16 JULY 1942, 1:00 P.M.

For Charlie Wilkes, getting paid to drive California's Coast Highway of was one hell of a way to fight a war. Never in his life had he seen anything as beautiful as the California coastline. He wondered why more people didn't live on the West Coast.

Had it not been for Captain McDonald, Charlie probably would have missed the entire show. When the two aeronautical wizards from the Presidio showed up around ten the previous evening, raring to get on with their mission, McDonald wouldn't hear of it. He based his objection on the fact that Corporal Wilkes had worked all day and needed to grab some shuteye. Charlie was keenly aware that, had he been down in Paso Robles "wick licking and sticking," his CO would've had no compunction whatsoever about ordering him to hit the road as soon as the two officers grabbed a cup of coffee.

It was well known throughout Baker Company that Captain McDonald believed the word sympathy was found in Webster's book right between shit and syphilis, for any soldier suspected of jerking around. But the word in no way fit Charlie Wilkes.

He'd worked all day at the rifle range, and then spent the better portion of the evening at the unit motor pool instructing PFC Erickson on both the idiosyncrasies of the CO's jeep and of their commanding officer himself. For his efforts, McDonald believed that Wilkes deserved a few hours of sleep before heading out to Los Angeles.

Initially neither officer was pleased with Mac's refusal to supply them with a driver at the exact time they wished to depart, but when the captain whipped out a bottle of Old Fitzgerald Kentucky straight bourbon whiskey and a deck of cards, they quickly got over their wanderlust.

Even though the staff car had a commercial radio in it, Charlie knew better than to turn it on, as he had a suspicion that neither officer would appreciate jitterbug music this early in the afternoon. It wasn't that he had a new-found liking for jive music, but he would rather have had something block out his overhearing what was doubtless a highly classified bull session.

"You know, colonel," the captain was saying, "G-2 says that those Japs are up to something on Guadalcanal. According to the guy I talked to two days ago, those bastards started landing soldiers on the eighth of June."

"There's no doubt about it, captain, the Nips are up to something in the Solomons," replied the colonel, taking a sip of his coffee.

"Hell, sir, it only gets worse. According to my man over in G-2, those sonofabitches started to build an airfield on the twentieth. Then it gets much worse—just within the last ten days they sent in a twelve-ship convoy loaded with construction equipment and at least another twenty-five hundred men."

"That sure as hell isn't going to sit well with Nimitz."

Charlie couldn't believe it. He'd just heard what had to be top-secret information, yet neither officer even bothered asking him if he was cleared to hear anything above scuttlebutt.

What ever happened to "Loose Lips Sink Ships"?

Almost as if the colonel were clairvoyant, he stopped talking and asked Charlie Wilkes if he realized that what he'd just heard was highly classified intel.

"Yes, sir, I do."

The colonel simply replied, "Good."

For the next ten minutes each soldier in the vehicle seemed content to sit back and enjoy the scenery. When the silence was broken, the colonel asked the captain if he'd heard the latest scuttlebutt concerning General Stone, Chief of Army Intelligence, and "Wild Bill" Donovan.

"Are you referring to the botched break-in of the Japs' mission in Lisbon?" the captain asked.

"See... that's the whole point. I have a friend back in D.C., who knows Bill Donovan and the Office of Special Services [precursor to the CIA]. He tells me Wild Bill says Stone is full of shit, and that his operatives didn't break into the Japs' liaison. According to my guy, a couple of Portugues sympathetic to the Allied cause managed to purloin some documents from the trash can."

"So why would that bother Stone?"

Pausing for a second to find his smokes, the senior replied, "It's the same old shit, captain. The regular Army hates Roosevelt and most of his appointees. From what I gather, this Donovan character just rubs General Stone the wrong way. Hell, he's accused Donovan's men of screwing up so badly that now the Japs will change their naval attaché's code—which'll be a disaster."

"That's a pretty serious charge, sir."

Lighting his Camel, the colonel replied, "If it's true, heads will roll— FDR or no FDR!"

Charlie tried his best to ignore the conversation going on behind him. But he was unable to, because the information he was hearing was just too juicy.

"Corporal Wilkes, are you aware that you are to drop us at the army base in San Pedro?" the captain asked.

"Captain McDonald told me about it this morning, sir."

Now the colonel chimed in. "Captain McDonald told us you have a girlfriend down here somewhere. Is that true?"

"Well, sir, she ain't exactly my girl, just a lady I know from Iowa."

"Would you explain that?" asked the captain.

"Yes, sir. Sharon's the widow of my best friend, who got killed at Pearl. She's out here because she inherited a strawberry farm from her grandfather, and in order to keep it his will states she has to live on it for five years."

"Whereabouts does this young lady live?"

"Anaheim, sir."

"Well… that settles it, corporal. Once we get to Pedro, I want you to call this woman and see if she'd like your company."

"Sir?" Charlie asked, not fully understanding what the superior officer was getting at.

"Without going into a lot of details, son," the colonel answered, "the good captain and I have a lot of work to do. And, quite honestly, I think if you were seen around Pedro with nothing to do, some sonofabitch down there might just want to put you to work."

Charlie laughed, as the captain now entered the conversation.

"And the truth of the matter is, corporal, your captain whipped our butts at poker last night. But instead of taking our money, he convinced us to let you have the next ten days off with your lady friend. Who, according to your CO, is about due."

"Sir, you two officers knew all along about Mrs. Roberts?" Charlie asked naively.

"Sure did, corporal. But, tell me, what is it you have on your captain that caused him to give up a twenty-dollar jackpot on your behalf?"

"You won't believe this, sir—but not a damned thing."

FIVE HOURS LATER, ANAHEIM, CALIFORNIA

Finding a telephone proved was harder than Charlie Wilkes had anticipated, so when he spotted the empty phone booth at the Flying A station he drove straight in. After dropping in a few coins he asked the operator for Melrose 1-1898. While Charlie waited for the call to be put through he took off his field cap and reached for a Camel, quietly passing a few moments listening to the line ring before someone answered at the distant end. But when they did it wasn't the voice Charlie hoped to hear. In a heavy German accent, a woman said "Hallo, who's calling, please?"

"Pardon me, ma'am, but is this Mrs. Sharon Roberts' residence?"

"*Ja, ja,* it's the Roberts residence and this is Helga, the next-door neighbor. Who is calling, *bitte?*"

"Corporal Charlie Wilkes. I was wondering if Mrs. Roberts is available?"

"*Mein Gott!* You are Charlie, the soldier boy Sharon keeps talking about? You are this same Charlie?"

Are you the soldier boy that Sharon keeps talking about?

"Well, unless Mrs. Roberts knows more than one Charlie, I guess I am."

"Where are you calling from, young man?" Helga inquired, anxiously.

"I'm here in Anaheim, Mrs...."

"Helga Brüder. My husband Helmut and I have the truck farm next door. But, listen, young man, you are here in Anaheim, *ja?*"

"Yes ma'am. I'm at the Flying A filling station, out on the highway."

"You stay right there, young man. My Helmut will be there in a few minutes and he will show you how to get here. And if everything goes all right, you will be here in time to welcome the new baby."

"Shit! Oh—excuse me—is Sharon in labor?"

"*Ja, ja, das ist richtig.* Her water broke two hours ago. This is why I am here. I have eight children myself, and have delivered more than twenty fine, healthy babies these last three years. This is what I do.

"But now I must go. You joost stay where you are, and Helmut will be there before a quarter of an hour's passing."

Click. The line went dead.

How's that for German efficiency? She didn't even say goodbye.

JULY 17, 1942, 2:00 A.M.

"I haven't been this nervous in twenty-two years!" Thomas Jefferson Eddy lit another cigarette with the one he'd just taken out of his mouth.

"I ain't in much better shape, myself." Charlie replied.

Mr. Eddy walked over to where Charlie was standing, looking like he wanted to say something. Charlie started to make small talk, but Eddy cut him off.

"I don't know how you were able to get the time off, son, but I must say the missus and me sure appreciate you being here."

Due to the classified nature of his trip south, Charlie just said that his being in Anaheim was more of a fluke than anything else.

"Well, fluke or not, you're here, and that's the thing that matters."

Mr. Eddy hesitated. "No, there is something else that counts—and that's what I want to talk to you about."

Charlie sat down on the davenport and looked at Sharon's father.

"You know, young man, since Randy was killed my little girl has had it pretty rough. Oh, she's putting on a good show, but I know she's having a tough time dealing with him being gone."

"I feel the same way, sir. But I think as time passes, she'll feel better."

Mr. Eddy looked at Charlie. Then he blurted out, "Other than us, you know you're all she's got, don't you?"

"Sharon told me that, back in Paso Robles."

"Listen, Sharon's a pretty tough girl on the outside, but the truth of the matter is that it's all window-dressing. She's carrying a lot of guilt about Randy's death. She blames herself for them being at Pearl in the first place, you know?"

"Yes, she told me that, too," Charlie answered.

"Both the missus and I have tried to tell her that's nonsense, but we haven't had much luck."

"I still say that as time passes, so will those feelings," Charlie replied.

"I hope you're right, Charlie," Mr. Eddy said, taking another drag from his smoke. A few awkward moments passed, during which neither man spoke a word. From the sounds emanating from Sharon's room, both guessed her baby would soon arrive.

When Mr. Eddy finished his smoke, he put it out and began talking again.

"Sharon thinks pretty highly of you. And, I might add, so do me and the missus."

Sonofabitch! Did I just hear what I think I heard? Does that mean he's willing to overlook my carousing back in Villisca? And how about what I did to Dotty—is that forgiven, too?

"Damn!" Sharon screamed, "When is this little bugger coming?"

Frau Brüder replied, "One must be patient, *kleine Liebschen*. This baby won't get here one second before God wants him here. In the meanwhile, keep pushing."

Mr. Eddy looked over at Charlie. "Do you think it's gonna be a boy or a girl?"

"I think she'd have an easier time with another boy."

"That may be true, Charlie. But what she really needs is a husband— someone to help her raise these children."

"Don't you think it's a bit soon for that?" Charlie wondered where their conversation was heading.

"Five years ago I would have said 'yes.' But, since Pearl, things have changed. No, I say Sharon ought to be married."

"What does Sharon think of that? Charlie grinned. Have you asked her?"

"I ain't one for telling people what to do," Mr. Eddy replied. "But, Charlie, the day you joined the Iowa National Guard you proved you're capable of making your own decisions. So hear me out. Sharon's talked to me about this, so don't think I'm speaking out of turn."

"Would you mind if we discussed this outside, Mr. Eddy?"

"If that's what suits you, let's go."

For the first minute or two after they went out of doors neither man spoke, choosing instead to take in the star-filled night. Between Sharon's screams the two men could hear the area's many crickets chirping and the frogs bellowing.

"Charlie, I guess I should begin in the beginning. By that, I mean that when Sharon first told me she was sweet on you, I wasn't any too happy about it."

Charlie braced for what he suspected was heading his way: chastisement for his many past dalliances and bouts with Demon Rum. Instead, what he got surprised him.

"Charlie, I suppose it's no secret that me and the missus pretty much thought Randy Roberts walked on water. And when I found out those goddamned Japs had killed him out at Pearl… well… I was sick to my gut. You see, Sharon really loved Randy."

"So did I, Mr. Eddy."

Of course I cared for Randy—so why did I need to say so?

"I know that, Charlie. And I'll tell you why I know that. You know how people talk back in Iowa—or need I remind you?"

Charlie grinned. "No sir, if there's one thing I don't need to be reminded about, it's how much Iowa people like to gossip."

"No, I reckon you don't, with all the things said about you after what happened to Dotty. Or, for that matter, after Charlie Senior killed himself. But that ain't my point, son. My point is that I've heard the whispers around Villisca, how some folks said Randy was a bit light in the loafers."

"Now, Mr. Eddy, you don't really…." But he was cut off by the older man.

"Listen, Charlie, I was told you might even have spread some of those rumors, yourself. But the truth is Randy's gone, no matter what was said, and nothing's gonna bring him back. And that other stuff don't matter a shit to me, 'cause he did right by my Sharon. So there's no time for recrimination."

"I appreciate your understanding, Mr. Eddy. I want you to know that if

I did repeat any of those rumors, I feel like an ass for doing it."

"Charlie, let's just say that it's water under the bridge. Yesterday's over and gone. You and I need to talk about today. And tomorrow."

"What do you mean, sir?"

"What I mean, is that my daughter's in there having a baby whose father ain't gonna be here to raise him up. For me, that's unacceptable."

Again Charlie started to speak, but Mr. Eddy interrupted him. "You still haven't figured out what I'm about to ask, have you, young man?"

"No, sir. Quite honestly, I haven't got the foggiest."

"Well then, I'm just gonna lay it on the line—I'm asking you to marry my daughter."

Holy Christ!

Charlie almost fell off the porch. Instead, he asked Mr. Eddy what he thought Sharon's response would be to a marriage proposal coming so soon after burying Randy Roberts.

"In normal times, Charlie, people would talk. But these ain't normal times. Hell, that sonofabitch Hitler has conquered half of Europe. And with the exception of the battle out there at Midway, it looks like the Japs are kicking our asses, too. No, these ain't normal times, and that's why I'm asking you to marry her."

"Mr. Eddy, I've thought about it. But, to be honest with you, I don't think she'd have me."

"Why do you say that?"

"Well, for one thing, there's my past...."

Sitting upright on the porch railing, Mr. Eddy looked Charlie straight in the eyes. "Young man, what you did then is over with. You need to move on with your life. It's what you'll do in the future that people will remember."

"You know the army doesn't pay me much, don't you, sir?"

"About twenty-one bucks a month, ain't it?"

"Yes sir. And as far as the insurance business goes, back in Iowa, what little money Mr. Roberts makes at it I let him keep. After all, he's the one doing the work."

"Speaking of Eric Roberts, when I talked to him on the phone a few days ago about buying a life insurance policy for this new baby, we talked about Sharon's situation."

"What did he say?" Charlie wondered aloud.

"He told me he thought it would be good idea for you to marry Sharon."

Sonofabitch, those Roberts people sure have class.

"That must have been real tough for him to say."

"Like I said, times are different nowadays. Things that used to be unnatural are now as common as sliced bread."

"But, Mr. Eddy, no matter how you slice that bread, twenty-one bucks a month isn't enough to raise a family on."

"Charlie, look around you. This farm will make more than enough money to support you and Sharon and the children after the war's over. Maybe I shouldn't tell you this, but I'm half-way to coming to an agreement with a family here in Orange County to sell all the strawberries we can grow. You see, they just got a huge contract to supply the Army a half-million cans of jam next year. And you know what? I plan on growing most of the strawberries that go into those cans."

Charlie smiled. "Good thing Mrs. Eddy isn't out here listening to us. She'd accuse you of auctioning off her daughter to the highest bidder."

"Charlie, two years ago we'd have caught hell for this conversation. But the truth of the matter is my wife was the one who came up this whole idea."

Well, call me a suck-egg mule!

"As I said, young man, times aren't normal these days."

Right then, *Frau* Brüder came out onto the porch and announced they'd just welcomed a new addition to the family. He weighed eight pounds, four ounces.

Sharon named her newest son Charles Jefferson Roberts.

And three days later the little boy's name was changed to Charles Jefferson Wilkes, in honor of his new daddy—Charlie Wilkes.

CHAPTER FOUR

He who rides the tiger dares not dismount.
—Chinese Proverb

LA IGLESIA AT MISSION SAN MIGUEL, CALIFORNIA
SUNDAY, 30 AUGUST 1942, 12:05 P.M.

Never in Charlie Wilkes' life had he been as uncomfortable as he was this minute. He hoped the priest would finish his sermon—and fast.

I've been lost since he said something about "dominos and biscuits."

He wondered what he was doing in a Catholic Church, in the first place. Wasn't he Methodist? Or… was he anything?

Then Charlie remembered just how much his mother loved the Lord. How she looked forward to putting on her Sunday-best clothes, fixing her hair and putting on ever-so-little lipstick… then singing "Fairest Lord Jesus."

He remembered how he'd promised both Sharon and Captain Mac-Donald he would start going to church. How the subject had come up with his commanding officer seemed odd to Charlie, as officers usually didn't get personally involved in their men's spiritual lives. However, last week when the two were out scouting for the unit's new bivouac area, MacDonald told Charlie he should start attending church. When Charlie asked why he brought up that particular subject, the CO simply replied, "You can't be a good father or a good husband without going to church. End of story, Wilkes."

To Charlie, that sort of discussion was a *non-sequitur*. But since Mc-Donald seemed sincere, Corporal Wilkes took his commanding officer's suggestion as an order. The fact that his CO had gone way out of his way to help Charlie marry Sharon, also entered into the equation.

Charlie's thoughts now returned to the religious service, back in to the priest's words.

This mackerel-snapper's Irish accent is so thick it would give St. Pat-

rick an inferiority complex.

"Now remember, lads, you mustn't be takin' our Lord's name in vain. And a life of fornicatin'… is a sure pass into the bowels of Hell. Instead of carousin' after wanton women, you should be helpin' others out. Look out for each other. Say your prayers daily, and write your wives, girlfriends and mommas every chance you get. Remember that our Lord Jesus loves every last one of ya! Amen."

I may be guilty of most of those sins, but, by God, since I married Sharon I ain't been to the cathouses. That has to be worth something. After all, this place is hotter than hell itself. It's like being on the A-train to Hades.

Then Charlie remembered what his father-in-law told him, on the night that his son was born: "Times are different, nowadays."

As the organist started to play the recessional, Charlie tried to remember the last time he visited one of San Miguel's six brothels.

These last three weeks have been the longest I've ever gone without getting laid, since the first time I got laid. I wonder if all men get less once they get married?

"Bow, Charlie," whispered Ian Henry as the crucifer recessed past them on his way out of the church.

"Bow?"

"Yeah, you big palooka, *bow!*"

"Bow-wow, yourself! What the hell are you talking about?"

"Sheesh!" Ian said, as he genuflected and begged God not to strike Charlie dead on the spot. "You're supposed to bow when the crucifer recesses from the church."

"You mean that guy who just walked by, carrying the cross? Is he the one you're talking about?"

"What's with you, Wilkes? Ain't you got *any* religious training?"

"Not as some mackerel-snapper, I don't," Charlie replied.

"Jesus, Mary and Joseph, Wilkes! This's the last time I bring you here. I am not risking getting struck dead by a bolt of lightning because of you. Go find some other church," Ian said while waiting for the priest's final blessing.

As the parishioners made their way out of the adobe church building, Ian and Charlie followed. Once outdoors, they sought shelter from the hot sun. Standing in the shade of one of the patio's two fig trees, laden with fruit, they enjoyed the cool spot while taking a minute to allow their eyes to adjust to the bright sunlight. Charlie reached for a smoke while Ian spent his time looking off into the west.

"Damn, it's drier than a popcorn fart out here," Charlie commented, lighting up a smoke.

"There isn't enough water in the Nacimiento River for a kit fox," Ian replied, as he stared at the valley's rolling, golden-brown hills. Intermingled with a slight breeze in the air, Charlie could hear bees buzzing in the background. The air smelled like autumn was on its way.

"This sure is beautiful country, ain't it?" Ian said in his ever-present Yankee accent.

"Beautiful? You call *that* beautiful? Look out there, Ian. The only things growing out there are oak trees and poison oaks. How the hell is that beautiful?"

"It's true, but with some water you could grow a lot of stuff here," Ian said as he sat on the ledge of the patio's main fountain.

"What good is that? I mean, it ain't like there's anybody around here to eat it."

Ian looked at Charlie, and shook his head. "No, but there will be someday."

"Yeah, about the time this war ends," Charlie deadpanned. "That's what I like about you, you worthless Mick. You're such an optimist. Here you're talking about your life after this war is over, but I'm beginning to wonder if we're gonna screw around and lose the whole damned thing."

"You sound like Quisling. What in hell do you mean by a crack like that?"

"Ian—the Japs have taken everything they've wanted since they bombed Pearl Harbor, and the Krauts are knocking at Stalingrad's front door," Charlie wisecracked. "Oh—and don't forget that the U-boats are sinking damn-near everything afloat. Other than that, not much."

"That's okay, Charlie. We ain't in the thick of it yet. When we get ready, trained and over where we need to be, I'll feel sorry for those fascists. We'll kick their butts all the way back to Berlin. And after we're done with them, we'll kick the snot out of the Japs."

"Well, something's got to happen, and pretty damn soon, or the Brits are going to be out on their asses in Libya. Ian, that Kraut Rommel drove the Brits out of the Gazala line and back into Egypt. Hell, he took Tobruk in twenty-four hours!"

Ian Henry refused to be baited, firmly believing that once Uncle Sam was ready to fight, the Axis would be in for one hell of a licking. And that was one ass-kicking he looked forward to participating in.

When Charlie was in one of his defeatist moods, Ian knew better than to argue with him. So instead he began talking about his desire to return to San Miguel after the war and become a farmer. But before he could speak, Charlie asked, "What would you grow in this godforsaken wilderness?"

"I don't know, Charlie. Something—maybe grapes."

"Well…" Charlie said, taking a drag from his cigarette, "The way things are going on the war front, you just might get a chance to do that, sooner than you think."

"Are you still on that?" Ian wished Charlie would get over his foul mood.

"I'll spell it out for you, Ian. Since the Nips blew the shit out of our navy at Pearl and took Wake, they've overrun Corregidor and Singapore. Burma followed so fast it made my head spin. The Philippines now belong to Tojo. And, in case you haven't noticed, the Brits ain't exactly kicking ass in North Africa. Add to that, the damned Huns are raising hell with the Bolsheviks. I'd say this war is about over," Charlie commented sarcastically.

Ian couldn't take any more of Charlie's defeatist attitude.

"I'll tell you one more time—that's only because we ain't ready. Look at what we did to the Krauts, once we got to France in 1917."

"That was twenty-five years ago," Charlie shot back.

"Well, then, look what Nimitz did to the Nips at Midway when he was prepared for them! Nope, I say that when we get over there, Hitler had better call it a day. We're gonna kick his Austrian fanny all the way to hell. I know we are. If there's a God in heaven—I know we are!"

Charlie pulled another Camel from his shirt pocket, lit it, and asked, "Do you really believe that?"

"Of course I do! I mean, crap the bed, Charlie, just because you and me are stuck here at Roberts don't mean diddle. You know as well as I do, that we have to train as many troops as we can to fight. I know there ain't no glory in it, but it's what we've gotta do."

"Okay, so it's our job. But I gotta tell you, I'm going stir-crazy driving around this place all day. I mean, hell—what am I gonna tell my kids when they ask what I did during World War Two?"

"Tell them the truth, Charlie. Tell them you were in the United States Army."

"Yeah, tell them I drove a jeep over the hills and dales of Camp Roberts. They ought'a be real impressed with that, don't you think?"

"What's with the burr up your butt, Charlie?"

"What do you mean by that?"

"It's just that you've been a horse's fanny all day today."

"What the hell are you talking about, Ian? I'm a horse's ass every-day."

"I know what's pissing you off, Charlie. You need to get laid. Maybe you should talk to McDonald about going back down south and seeing Sharon. You know—soon as she's able to do it again."

Charlie Wilkes laughed out loud, then put his arm around his buddy.

"How about us getting some cold, three-point-twos, instead, and tying one on?"

Ian laughed. "Well, there's one thing you don't have to ask a Mick twice about, and that's booze. Let's walk down the street to the Elkhorn and have a few."

"Lead the way, soldier."

BOOK TWO: LONDON

LION'S PARK ON VOLCANO ROAD
SUTTER CREEK, AMADOR COUNTY, CALIFORNIA
THANKSGIVING DAY, 1991, 2:30 P.M.

As the group of walkers turned the corner and saw the Lion's Park, Colonel Michael Ohara looked up and saw Dexter Dannenberg already sitting one of the park's many tables, engaged in conversation with his son.

Ohara thought about the first time he met Dexter Dannenberg, and how their relationship had quickly evolved into one nasty affair.

My God, it's hard to believe so many years have passed....

The retired Army chaplain thought back to a sultry afternoon in 1974—August, in Vietnam. At the time he was a freshly-commissioned second lieutenant in the Army Security Agency, assigned to the C.I.A., working out of the American Embassy. Although new to the officer corps, he wasn't new to the Army, having served a year in the Signal Corps with the 8th Infantry Division in Bad Kreuznach, Germany, before volunteering to go to Vietnam in 1967.

That combat tour was spent at Nha Trang, with the 1st Signal Brigade at the Back Porch tropospheric scatter facility on Long Vanh Air Force Base. During the Tet Offensive he earned a Bronze Star and a Purple Heart—and saw several of his buddies and one's girlfriend killed in action.

Ohara recalled how it was, that on his second day in-country his officer-in-charge told him of a soirée at the American Embassy that night, and how everyone in the detachment was expected to attend. The light colonel then rattled off a litany of high muckty-mucks that would be there. At the time, it sounded pretty damned exciting....

Because of his rank and prior service as an enlisted man, Lt. Ohara knew to keep his mouth shut at the party, to drink no more than two cocktails, to listen to what the other blabbermouths were saying and watch them drink too much. The first hour seemed to fly by, but as the party wore on he began getting bored. Fortunately, his OIC came back over and told him that he was going to introduce Ohara to CIA station chief Dexter Dannenberg. Initially Ohara was awe-struck with the idea of meeting an honest-to-god spook, but within a few minutes of meeting the CIA big-shot Ohara began to dislike him. By the end of the night Ohara had found Dannenberg to be obnoxious, self-righteous, and a downright pain-in-the-ass.

As he left the embassy that evening, Ohara shuddered to think what his upcoming tour would bring.

As it turned out, how Ohara got on with Dexter Dannenberg would become irrelevant, as during the next twelve months he not only saw South Vietnam overrun by the communists, but the woman he loved perish onboard an Air Force C-5A mercy flight filled with orphans trying to escape to the United States. He would also receive the Silver Star.

Now, however, Ohara pulled out the cigar Dannenberg had given him back at the Kennedy home, and lit it. As he nursed the Dominican torpedo into a viable smoke, he recalled how bitter he felt when his helicopter lifted off from the American Embassy on the 30th day of January, 1975.

And today you're an Episcopal priest doing God's work. Oh, the vicissitudes of life!

And remember how you wanted to kill Ron Banks, your old Army buddy from Vietnam, now the congressman from southwestern Iowa, when he told you that Dannenberg was coming to spend last Labor Day at his home in Villisca?

A car coming down the hill from the small Gold Rush burg of Volcano interrupted Ohara's thoughts. He picked up his pace, walking over to where his son and the older man had briefly stopped their conversation.

"What you thinking about, colonel?" Dannenberg asked Ohara.

"Vietnam. What else?"

Dannenberg smiled. "Which tour?"

"Second."

"Back when we were in the spy business?" Dannenberg had a slight grin on his face.

Ohara managed to return the smile. "Well, sir, as I recall it, you were in the spy business…."

Dannenberg looked Ohara in the eye. "I thought we got past that, back in Iowa."

Ohara felt like a damned fool. Here he was in the "forgiveness business," and he was still carrying a grudge that went back sixteen years. He sloughed off his feelings.

"Forgive me Dex, it's the Irish in me."

Dannenberg tapped Ohara on his shoulder and chimed, "Hopefully your temper hasn't tampered with your memory."

"What do you mean by that, Dex?"

"Do you remember the story I told you on Labor Day, about how I got into the spy business?"

"Of course. How could I forget it?"

"As I recall, I didn't mention anything about my days in London and at Bletchley Park, did I?"

"You alluded to it, sir."

"Well then, my boy," Dannenberg said as he lit up a cigar, "How about I start where I left off from, on Labor Day?"

Always one for dramatic effect, what Dexter did next was characteristic Dannenberg: He unzipped his jacket and pulled out a flask, took a sip and handed it to the colonel and SGM Wilkes. Normally a teetotaler, Ohara took a small sip as a means of fending off the afternoon chill. Having conditioned himself to shun alcohol since his seminary days, the chaplain was pleasantly surprised how the wonderfully smooth Kentucky bourbon began warming him from the inside.

"Wow, that's pretty good stuff, Dex. What is it?"

"Remember Professor Greenwich?"

"Sure do. He was that crazy professor from Creighton University, that you and Thomek cavorted around with back in 'thirty-nine, when you were one step ahead of the Gestapo."

"Well, it's his brand—Old Fitzgerald Kentucky straight bourbon whiskey."

Remembering the story that Dannenberg told him over the past Labor Day weekend, Colonel Ohara now asked how Dannenberg managed to get himself assigned to Bletchley Park.

Dannenberg took a long pull from his cigar, savored its taste, and exhaled. Slowly he began to speak.

"After that hair-raising wagon ride from hell and our brush with death, we made it across the border and into Belgium. Amazingly, that old conniver Greenwich had a car stashed in an old barn in Murrigen, where our immediate goal was to get Thomek medical attention. Once that was done, Greenwich and I flew to London and Thomek limped his butt back to Poland. Of course, by then Poland was a complete disaster.

"The Polish government tossed in the towel on September 28th, after the Wehrmacht broke through their border and completely encircled Warsaw. Hell, the Krauts had two thousand tanks and a thousand planes when they rolled in on the first of September."

Colonel Ohara's son, Sean, had been wondering about something since last fall's holiday in Iowa.

"Before you tell us about your spying days, Mr. Dannenberg, please tell us how the heck Thomek ended up in the Polish Air Force? I remember you saying that's what he wanted to do, but wanting something and being qualified to do it seem like two different things to me."

"To be honest, Sean, I think Thomek bull-shitted his way into it. As far as I was aware, the only thing he knew about flying was what happened after he mixed one of his concoctions for you at the Hotel Wilhelmplatz's bar, back in Ypres."

Dannenberg's comment caused all of them to laugh.

"I got back to England on September 9th. London, of course, by then was a Charlie-Foxtrot."

That's a polite way of saying it was a cluster-fuck! thought Sean's dad.

Dexter continued, "I tagged along with Greenwich. His contact was at the American Embassy, a man named Jack Eggert. Eggert reminded me of Jack Webb."

"Jack who?" Sean questioned.

"Jack Webb played Sergeant Joe Friday on the 'Dragnet' TV show, back 'in the day,' as you kids say. Friday was strictly a no-nonsense sort of guy."

"So you're saying Jack Eggert was a man of few words?"

"Yes—and he didn't suffer fools lightly. He put Greenwich and me on the hot-seat for four days straight. By the time he was done with us, I thought we were the bad guys. But Eggert told me later that the reason he put us through the third-degree was so he could learn how the Nazis operated."

"He left nothing to chance," CSM Wilkes added. "I know that because of my experience with him in Korea in 'fifty-two. He was just a no-bullshit kind of a fellow."

"What did you do, after Eggert was through with you?" Sean asked.

"The first thing Eggert did was to put Greenwich on a flight back to the States. Once that was accomplished, he cut me loose for a few days. So I wandered back over to the Claridge and got reacquainted with the concierge. We spent many an evening together, at Dirty Dick's Lime House," Dannenberg said with a slight grin.

Having for so many years been in a business where an ability to think on one's feet often meant the difference between life and death, Dannenberg knew it was time to stop reminiscing about his gay days back in London. He nodded in Colonel Ohara's direction, which Ohara understood to mean the old man wasn't about to go off on some "whore story."

Ohara nodded his approval of Dannenberg's decision, when CSM Wilkes rejoined the conversation.

"What was London like during the first part of the war, Dex?"

"To quote Charles Dickens, 'It was the best of times, it was the worst of times.'"

"Well, I didn't get there 'til January of '44, when my unit, the 238th Engineer Combat Battalion, was shipped in from Oran," added Wilkes.

Colonel Ohara was curious. "I hate to interrupt your story, Dex. But, Sergeant Major, how did you get from Camp Roberts to the 238th Engineer Combat Battalion?"

"Beats the heck out of me. One day I was out driving Captain McDonald around Sherwood Forest, scouting out bivouac sites, and the next day he handed me and Ian Henry orders stating we were being transferred to the 51st Engineer Regiment down at Camp Bowie, Texas. It came as a shock, to be honest with you. I asked McDonald if he had anything to do with it, but he said no… the Army was getting ready to start its build-up for the invasion of Europe, and they were looking for a few good men."

Sean Kennedy laughed and looked to his father. "Sounds familiar—how many times did that happen to you, Dad?"

"Now, if you're referring to that vacation in Montana we planned before Desert Storm came up," Colonel Ohara replied, "you should remember that Saddam Hussein was the reason it never happened."

"No need to get all defensive about it, Dad. I just want to remind you that I'm still planning on that vacation sometime in the future," Sean Ohara replied with an impish grin on his face.

CSM Wilkes looked over to the colonel. "Sir, that's the second time this weekend your son's brought up that dude ranch vacation you planned last year. Sounds to me like you ought to get on the phone and book another one."

Dexter Dannenberg now retuned to the conversation. "If you wouldn't mind me staying back at the ranch, smoking cigars, drinking Kentucky bourbon and telling lies at night around the campfire, I'd like invite myself on that vacation."

Ohara reached over and hugged the older men. "Okay, you guys. Next summer, it's Wyoming."

Dexter looked Ohara in the eyes. "Perhaps, Michael, that just might be the time for us sit around the campfire and discuss your second tour in

Vietnam… and, just maybe, put that behind us. What do you think? I'm game."

Ohara looked into each face, and asked, "How does next July sound?"

"If you're asking me, I'm game for it, too," Charlie Wilkes replied. "Of course, Chaplain, you'll have to explain my absence to Sharon."

Wilkes' comment brought another round of laughter, and all agreed that come next July, they were going on a seven-day horseback ride in Wyoming.

After a few minutes of joking around, Dexter restarted telling his tale.

"Sergeant Major, you asked me how London was during the Blitz. This is what I witnessed: The first few days were sheer chaos. Hell, Chamberlain's ultimatum to the 'Austrian corporal' had barely expired, and the air raid sirens began going off throughout London. False alarms, of course, but that gives you an idea just how screwed-up things were. Except when it came to civil defense. Somehow, the Brits managed to bus three hundred thousand children out of the world's largest city during the first seven days of World War Two. We all know they had their heads up their asses militarily, but I had to hand it to the Chamberlain government—they were more than prepared in the area of civil defense."

"How so?" Colonel Ohara wondered aloud.

"Without going into all the lurid details, one night my friend from the Claridge and I met up with a friend of his—one of London's finest, a bobby named Brian Clancy. The Irish lad was a gossipy sort, and with an absolute hollow leg when it came to Guinness! I guess it was the second or third night we got together, that he told us the British government had over one hundred thousand body bags ready to go. He said he'd read some official report that gave the formula the Brits used when they ordered all those body bags. To wit: they figured they'd lose four civilians each time a house got bombed. Rather ghoulish, if you ask me, but at least they were prepared for something."

Dexter took another sip from his flask.

"So how did you get hooked-up with the O.S.S?" asked Sean Ohara.

"Well, the O.S.S. came on-line on June 13, 1942. But I'd already been in England for a while before they set up shop, working over at Bletchley Park doing all sorts of nefarious deeds. But, then—you asked me about the O.S.S."

Looking at his former employee, Dannenberg continued, "You'll find this unbelievable, Ohara, but the other intelligence organizations such as the

State Department and the FBI had a bloody cow when the O.S.S. became more than just another of FDR's hair-brained ideas."

Colonel Ohara played along with Dannenberg's joke. "Well, I'm shocked to hear that! I mean, we all worked together so beautifully in Vietnam."

Dannenberg chuckled. "The armed services were so outraged about the O.S.S. that they had FDR sign a decree practically banning it from access to the Nazi communications. Donovan raised holy hell, but in the end nobody gave a damn."

"It sounds like nothing's changed. Remind me to tell about that Charlie-Foxtrot in Grenada, some time," CSM Wilkes interjected.

"Pipe down, Sergeant Major. I have a war to win here!" Dannenberg said, as he got up from the picnic bench. He looked over to Colonel Ohara, and then back to CSM Wilkes. "Do you fellows really feel like walking all the way to Volcano? It sounded like a great idea when Sean suggested it, but now that we're three or four miles into it, I'm having second thoughts."

Colonel Ohara glanced over at his son. Even he looked like his second helping of Mrs. Kennedy's dressing was getting the better of him.

"What do you think, Sean? Could we talk you into walking back with us to the Kennedys'?"

"I was about to suggest it myself," the colonel's son admitted.

"Sounds like we have ourselves a new mission," the retired senior NCO replied, as he got up off the picnic table and started walking.

As Sean Ohara headed back toward the Gold Rush town of Sutter Creek, he resigned himself to a thorough ass-chewing by his basketball coach at Granite Bay High School next Monday afternoon.

Dexter Dannenberg continued with his tale.

"By December the concierge and I were old news, and the bobby was too busy running around London chasing whores, hooligans and homos. I figured that enough time had passed since my tour in Germany, and I should probably head back to the States if for no other reason than to see my folks. But the question arose, how would I do that? Could I simply get on an airplane and go home? Did I need to check in with anyone? Remember, Professor Greenwich had long since gone. Thomek, for all I knew, was still in Poland. As I later found out, he was flying with the R.A.F., and doing a great job of it. I decided to tell someone.

"That 'someone' was Jack Eggert. It wasn't like he was my boss, or anything, just more-or-less that he was the only American official I knew in London. So late one afternoon I waltzed into his bunker at the American Embassy and informed him I was headed back to the States.

Quite honestly, I think he was surprised that I was still in London. Hell—the damned Nazis were threatening to invade! We shot the bull for a few minutes, then he offered to help me get a seat on an Army Air Corps plane heading back to the States the next day. I accepted, of course, and before I knew it I was in Washington D.C., all fat, dumb and happy to be back. It was December 19th, and D.C. was damned cold. The bars were jammed, and the war news was dreadful."

"What do you mean, Mr. Dannenberg?" Sean Ohara inquired.

"Take Finland, for example. In 1939 there couldn't have been more than three-and-a-half million Finns, certainly nothing for Mr. Stalin to lose any sleep over. But with Finland being located right above Leningrad, Stalin feared that Hitler might make a move on it. The Finns tried their damnedest to work something out with Uncle Joe, but because Stalin was the paranoid sonofabitch that he was, nothing came of their talks. The 'fit hit the shan' on November 30, 1939, when Stalin's Red Army opened up with a monstrous artillery barrage. The Finns held out for six months, but in the end they were overwhelmed by the Russian horde.

"But, back to Washington. The first thing I wanted to do was get some sleep. But, finding a room proved to be an adventure in itself. If it hadn't been for the fact that Eggert gave me the name of the reservations manager at the Willard Hotel, I probably would've slept at the YMCA.

"After checking in, I stumbled up to my room and collapsed. God, I must have slept for two days. When I finally did get out of bed, I made my way over to the State Department and met with some low-level bureaucrat friend of Eggert's. He said that, so far as he knew, my services were no longer needed.

"As I sat at his desk, initially I was relieved. I thought I could go back to Omaha, help my father in his business, and just 'fade away.' However, when I went to get up and leave, the man suggested that I come back after the presidential election. Why, hell, the presidential election was eleven months away. By that time, who knew what I would be doing?

"Then he said, 'You know FDR is going to run for a third term, don't you?'

"I remember my response, 'No I don't. He doesn't clear his plans through me.'

"As soon as I said it, I regretted it, because it was so unnecessary. But the bureaucrat just sloughed it off and replied, 'He'll win, you know!'

"It was then I realized he was serious about Roosevelt running for an unheard-of third term, so I asked him why he thought that.

"'I'm basing my judgment on how hard Roosevelt fought to repeal the 1937 Neutrality Act. I mean, if he wasn't planning to be president, why would he give a damn about whether the United States is neutral, or not?' the bureaucrat said.

"What he said intrigued me, because it made too much sense. Then he added, 'I think FDR is worried the Republicans are going to recapture the White House in 1940, and that he is the only man alive who can prevent that from happening.' We talked for a few more minutes. Eventually our conversation came around to Ambassador Joe Kennedy.

In retrospect, I was impressed because this State Department official shared his inside dope with me—a nobody from Omaha. Either that, or he enjoyed mentally jerking-off dumb-assed civilians. Either way, I was intrigued.

"But, back to old man Kennedy. This same low-level guy had a hard-on for Joe Kennedy. Why? I don't know. But, trust me, he hated him through and through. After seeing that he had a sympathetic ear to rant about 'that bootlegging bastard from Boston,' he really opened up. 'You know,' he said, 'the Boss (FDR) has had it with Kennedy and his sympathies toward the Nazis, and I think Kennedy's going to get the boot.'

"The guy was a real gadfly. But, as it turned out, his information was right on the mark. After venting for a quarter-hour about what a bastard Joe Kennedy was, our conversation returned to whether there would be job waiting for me that coming November. At the time, I didn't know if he was for real, or just shining me on. But I have to tell you, after Berlin, the thought of going back to Omaha and working in my father's haberdashery sounded like excitement enough."

"So, what did you do, Mr. Dannenberg?" Sean Ohara asked.

"I dutifully went back to Omaha and helped my father in his clothing business. But all too soon I grew tired of it. After a few months of waiting on my father and all the schmucks that came in the door, suicide felt like it just might be a viable option. The thought of spending the rest of my life being a typical Jewish rag merchant was beginning to overwhelm me. I must have been a real pain-in-the-ass to all concerned," Dexter said as he took a draw from his cigar.

"Spring came and went. Summer was another non-event. And then, from nowhere, who walks in the door, but Professor Greenwich? I hate to admit it, but I was damn glad to see him. He asked me how things were going at the store, which I correctly understood to mean 'Are you fed up enough with this yet?'

"We went out to dinner that night, and Greenwich said he thought he could get me a position at Bletchley Park. He didn't go into too many details, except to say I 'wouldn't be bored there.' That's about all there was to it. Less than a week later I was on a train to Washington, D.C., to meet with that fellow from State again. My passport was rushed through, and I was on an Army Air Corps plane bound for London the next day.

"I remember it like it was yesterday… the date was September 15th, 1940. The war was a little more than a year old, and London had survived—even thrived—in spite of it. Everyone was doing what it took. I remember reading a magazine story during the flight over, about an English woman who practiced shooting her rifle every day in preparation for when German parachutists might land in her rose garden. The article quoted the old gal as saying, 'They'll be easier than grouse.'

"And so it went. Churchill had been in office nearly a year-and-a-half, and Mary Martin's 'My Heart Belongs to Daddy' was on the wireless all the time. It was just like the old days back in Berlin, except that I was twenty-four years old, without a pot to piss in, and full of myself."

"You mean to tell me you were even more stuck on yourself then, than today, Dex?" Colonel Ohara said, grinning.

"Ohara, this is total humility, compared to how full of it I was back then," Dannenberg admitted. "But I'll tell you, it didn't take long for Herr Göering to take the wind out of my sails. My God, you won't imagine what happened the day after I returned to London."

Sean Kennedy was intently listening. From the look on his face, it was obvious to everyone that he was completely caught up in the old man's wartime tale. He urged Dannenberg to continue.

"Well, as I recall, it was a Sunday night. After a day of napping and fiddling around the Claridge, I was just about to step out and meet a friend over at Dirty Dick's Lime House for a few rounds of drinks. That was a night I'll never forget.

"Around seven-forty p.m., the R.A.F. picked up bogies coming in from the direction of Cherbourg and Le Havre. These were the lead planes in the raid; the rest came in from the Dieppe area. They concentrated on London, and by that I don't mean military targets like airfields and naval bases. Hell, the Huns were out to kill all nine million people in London, if you ask me. "The bombing was relentless. Around three-thirty the next morning, another group of planes came in from Dieppe. They bombed us until dawn. I don't know how much ordnance those bastards dropped that night, but it's a bloody miracle anyone survived. Churchill admitted to over four hundred civilians being killed. Personally, I think that number was way too low.

"I say that, because for a fact I know one of those *Luftwaffe* boys managed to drop a bomb down a ventilator shaft where a thousand people had gone to take shelter. The government said only fourteen people died. That's a bunch of 'bovine fecal matter.'

"The truth is that from September 7, 1940 until New Year's Day 1941 there were around thirteen-thousand, three-hundred-plus Brits killed by the Huns. Another eighteen thousand were severely wounded. But you have to hand it to the Brits, the more those bastards bombed them, the more resolve they had. As far as I'm concerned, Churchill was dead on—that was Britain's 'finest hour.'"

Dannenberg looked over to CSM Wilkes. "Charlie, the damnest thing about it was that, if Göering had keep hitting the R.A.F. instead of going after the civilian population, he might have forced the Brits to come to the table. Hell, I later learned that on the morning of September 16, 1940, the Brits only had six hundred and thirty-nine flyable aircraft!

"We now know the Germans had switched tactics... and so did the Brits, I might add. You can count that one up to the Enigma device. Winnie got a message from the 'Fat Sausage' requesting a change in tactics; now Göering wanted to bomb the British people back into the Stone Age. Quite honestly, everyone at British intelligence believed that as long as the R.A.F. was flying, Hitler wouldn't invade England. Even Fat Boy knew he had to have total control of the air in order to protect the German invasion force, if there was going to be one.

"Of course, we know the German invasion plan of England was called 'Sea Lion.' From what I recollect, that term was first used by the Germans after France went 'Tango-Uniform.'"

"Excuse me, Mr. Dannenberg," interrupted Sean Ohara, "but what does 'Tango-Uniform' mean?"

Dannenberg started to say something, but hesitated. He looked over to the teen's father, who added, "Dex, we don't use acronyms at the Ohara household. But since you said it, go ahead and tell him or he'll drive me nuts."

Dannenberg apologized half-heartedly, then said, "Sean, 'Tango-Uniform' is a polite way of saying, 'Tits Up.' Like I said, the Brits were reading all the mail between Göering and Hitler. Hell, they even knew from which direction the *Luftwaffe* was coming!

"Which brings me to my next point: The bombing subsided enough that by ten a.m. I was back at my room in the Claridge, highly annoyed at the Jerries. I hailed a taxi over to the American Embassy on Grosvenor Square. The trip over was an experience in itself, but that's another story.

"Once I got there, I met with Eggert, who after a cup of coffee came right out and asked me if I was ready to go back to work. There was a twinkle in his eye when he asked, which led me to believe he was up to something. After I told him I was up for being gainfully employed again, he got up from his desk and we walked down the hall to none other than U.S. Ambassador Joseph Kennedy's office.

"I'll say, I was scared piss-less. For the life of me, I didn't know what I was supposed to say to old man Kennedy. But the ambassador quickly put me at ease."

"How did he do that?" Sean Kennedy inquired.

"Being a good Irishman, he offered me a drink, invited us to sit down on the sofa, and asked me how my father was doing. Well, I was dumbfounded! I hadn't any idea that my father knew the Kennedys. Our conversation went something like this:

"'How's your father, Dexter?'

"'He's doing just fine, Mr. Ambassador. Business is starting to pick up, and dad thinks the worst of the Depression is finally over.'

"'Has he told FDR that?'

"'I don't think they run in the same circles, Mr. Ambassador,' I replied.

"Kennedy laughed, and said, 'You're probably right. But FDR certainly keeps a lot of Jews around, doesn't he?'

"From there the Ambassador named every Jew I'd ever heard of in the Roosevelt Administration, finishing up with Morgenthau and Bernard Baruch. From the way Kennedy talked, I was beginning to think he was anti-Semitic, but just as soon as he'd finished with FDR and 'his Jews' he shut up and changed the subject. After a few minutes of small talk, Kennedy looked me straight in the eye, and said, 'Professor Greenwich told me quite a story about your adventures last summer in Mr. Hitler's Reich.'

"I nearly dropped my cocktail. 'He did?'

"Yes, he did. And that's why I am going to ask you the following question."

"Go ahead, Mr. Ambassador."

"Are you up for round-two with the Nazis?"

"Well, if I wasn't after leaving Germany, I sure as hell am after last night!"

"Then Ambassador Kennedy glanced at Eggert, indicating that it was time for the bureaucrat to leave. Eggert made some flimsy excuse about having some paperwork he needed to get into the afternoon's diplomatic pouch, and excused himself from the office. After Eggert had left, Kennedy said he wanted me to be his liaison officer with the Brits at Bletchley Park. I was to report to no one but him, 'or the next ambassador.'

"The 'next ambassador' thing threw me for a loop. When I asked Ambassador Kennedy what he meant by that, he hemmed and hawed. Eventually he told me he was going to resign in the next few months. He didn't say why, but I got the feeling that he had pretty much worn out his welcome in England.

"Suddenly it all made sense. Everything that low-level bureaucrat back at State had told me made sense. But how the hell he knew Kennedy was going to resign is another matter. Later I heard that Kennedy was 'sympathetic' to the *Nazi*s, and that was the reason he was 'leaving.' But the guy who told me that was a dyed-in-the-wool Republican, so I didn't know if it was true, or just the words of someone who despised F.D.R. Personally, I think it was somewhere in between those extremes.

"But, back to Bletchley Park. To be honest, I didn't have the foggiest idea what was going on out there. But Mr. Kennedy assured me the job was very important."

Sean Ohara again interrupted Dexter Dannenberg.

"Let me get this right—Ambassador Joseph Kennedy himself asked you to take this job? I'm impressed!"

Dannenberg laughed aloud. "So was I, at the time, young man. But it gets better. When I asked Kennedy exactly what I would be doing at Bletchley, he replied, 'Spying on the Brits.'"

"He really said that?"

"Old man Kennedy said my job was to be a liaison officer for the American Embassy regarding the work that was going on at Bletchley Park, and that I was to report either to him or his replacement, and 'nobody else!' After agreeing to those terms, he sent me to another office, where I was issued the proper identification papers. They told me to come back after one p.m., when someone on the staff would drive me out to Bletchley Park."

"What was it like, working at Bletchley Park, Mr. Dannenberg?" Sean Ohara asked.

"It was like no other assignment in my entire career. And I'll tell you why. Remember last Labor Day, when I told you the Enigma device was put together by the Brits, with the help of a mechanic from Poland?"

"Yes sir, I do," Sean replied.

"Then you'll recall that he worked for the Krauts until he was tossed out after a German security check, but not before figuring out they were making some kind of new signaling device. After being booted, he contacted the British agent in Warsaw, who after checking with the home office told the Pole to stay the hell out of anyone's crosshairs. Then, once they were convinced he was legitimate, the French skirted him out of Poland and into France, where they set up a complete workshop.

"According to the Brit I worked for, named Winterbotham, along with a French carpenter the Pole made a mock-up of the device, which the Brits quickly figured out was an improved mechanical cipher machine called 'Enigma.'

"It wasn't long before the Brits had a working copy of the original German device. It was able to provide them with such precise information that they even knew what air bases the German units were flying from! The ability to read the Kraut's mail gave the Allies a tremendous advantage throughout the rest of the war. But, while it was useful to them they had to be damn careful as to not tip their hand, otherwise the Jerries would have changed their code. God knows how the war would have turned out then."

Sean Ohara returned to the conversation. "Mr. Dannenberg, are you saying that if we hadn't been able to read the German's mail, we would have lost the war?"

"You know, that fellow Winterbotham I worked for was way up there in British Intelligence. In 1975 his book *The Ultra Secret* came out. According to him, the R.A.F. not only knew the Krauts' order of battle, but also where ol' Fat Herman was parking his planes. Hell, I guess it was worse than that—Enigma was so good, the Brits even knew the Germans' maintenance battalions were so ate-up that they couldn't get more than seventy-five percent of their aircraft up at any one time.

But, let me get back to Bletchley Park. You have to understand that when I say 'I worked at Bletchley' I was a mere *peon*. Yes, I was a liaison officer to the American ambassador in London, but that wasn't anywhere on my resumé. My official title was 'Intelligence Coordinator,' which meant I sat in on meetings between Fred Winterbotham and a man named R.V. Jones. Fred referred to their group as the 'Bletchley back-room boys.'"

"It must have been an exciting time, Mr. Dannenberg," Sean added.

The former spy laughed, then said, "When I think about it now, these forty-plus years later, even I become overwhelmed. I mean, think about it. Here I was—a snot-nosed Jewish kid—working in the very heart and soul of the American and British spy headquarters.

"In actuality, I really wasn't any more than a glorified 'gofer,' who set up conferences and drove bigwigs around town. Yet I must have done a reasonably good job, because the next thing I knew it was 1943, and I was working for none other than General 'Wild Bill' Donovan at his Office of Strategic Services.

"You know, my transfer came about all of a sudden. By 1943 the Allies had managed to stop the hemorrhaging, and we were waist-deep in planning for Operation Overlord. I was beginning to think that I was going to spend the entire war at Bletchley— which, by the way, was okay with me.

"Hell, I am not the warrior type. In fact, I considered the O.S.S. assignment a gift from God, and was determined to keep my nose clean and my zipper zipped. But at times I wondered if I was going to go mad."

"How so, Dex?" CSM Wilkes wondered aloud.

"Well, working for the British Intelligence service was a daunting task in itself. But the way they had it set up was enough to make the average man go mad."

Dannenberg's statement intrigued Colonel Ohara. "Was it any worse than that mess between John Paul Vann and Westmoreland?"

Dannenberg stopped walking, and thought about his former subordinate's question. He began his response slowly. "Try this one out: When World War Two started, MI6 was responsible for all intelligence gathering. The problem was that MI6 was scattered from hell to breakfast. They had offices from New York to Istanbul, and everywhere in-between. The old bugger who originally set it up was some nefarious character whose code name was 'Z.' His Christian name was Claude Dansey.

"Now, don't get me wrong. 'Z' was a sharp old geezer. He had a flair for palace intrigue. He used local businesses as fronts, and even had informants in the German Socialist Democratic Party! And when I think about that today, it almost makes me laugh."

"How's that, Mr. Dannenberg?" Sean Ohara asked.

"Young man, can you imagine how hot '*Herr* Schickelgruber' would've gotten if he'd found out the Brits had penetrated his innermost circle? I doubt if they could have found a big enough meat hook at Ravensbrück!"

As the men continued their Thanksgiving Day walk, the conversation ranged from President George H.W. Bush's declining popularity, to Eduard Shevardnadze's reappointment as the Russian Foreign Minister, and what teams were likely going to the Super Bowl. As they approached the Kennedy residence, Dannenberg steered their conversation back to Bletchley Park.

"It was right after Churchill named Stewart Menzies to run Bletchley, when I went to work for 'Wild Bill' Donovan at the Office of Strategic Services."

"How do you remember all this stuff, Mr. Dannenberg? wondered Sean Ohara.

"My mind tells me it was only yesterday. But my body is telling me it was a very long time ago," Dannenberg said slowly. "And, at my age, the body wins. So I think I'm going to take a nap when we get back to the Kennedy home.

"But, young man, I bet if you were to ask nicely, Mr. Kennedy and *Mademoiselle* LaFoche would tell you how the French Resistance got Sergeant Kennedy and his two surviving crewmembers to the English Channel, after being shot down over Frankenstein, Germany on a bombing raid."

"And when they get done with their tale, I'll share with you how I single-handedly won the Second World War," CSM Wilkes said, pointing up the driveway that lead to the Kennedy compound.

"Well, if those stories are half as exciting as the one you told last Labor Day, Mr. Dannenberg, I'm game," Sean Kennedy declared.

"Luckily," his father added, "we've got all weekend!"

CHAPTER FIVE

If your attack is going too well, you're walking into an ambush.
—Infantry Journal

THE DINING ROOM OF MR. & MRS. SEAN KENNEDY, SR.
VOLCANO ROAD, SUTTER CREEK
AMADOR COUNTY, CALIFORNIA
THANKSGIVING DAY, 1991, 7:30 P.M.

Mrs. Kennedy had decided correctly that none of her guests would be up for a large meal after the seven-course feast she'd served earlier that day. But she didn't figure they would literally attack and devour the salad she'd prepared for dinner. Even her husband's French-born son asked for a second helping.

The *pièce d'resistance* came when Brigitte LaFoche asked her for her recipe.

"Oh, it was nothing," Mrs. Kennedy replied. "All I did was throw some fresh baby spinach into a bowl with some toasted pine nuts, add vinaigrette and top it with some dried cranberries."

Mrs. Kennedy's husband now joined the conversation, telling Colonel Ohara's wife, "Chloe, whenever Betty tells you that all she did was throw something into a bowl—she's telling a story. I've known her since 1947, when we were at Cal. Even then, she would try to convince me that whatever she made for dinner was just 'thrown together.'"

Mrs. Kennedy smiled, and winked at her husband. "How else was I supposed to compete with all those debutantes and society girls from Atherton, except to win your heart through my cooking? As my grandmother used to say, 'Kissin' don't last—cookin' does!'"

Brigitte LaFoche just smiled and said, "Betty, I have to compliment you on your cooking—and your choice of men!"

At first everyone chuckled at Brigitte's remark. But as they thought more about it, the room got quiet. Everyone knew that Brigitte's son was the result of her wartime romance with Mr. Kennedy.

Brigitte, however, was nonplused by her comment. Instead, she stood up, excused herself and went into the kitchen. On returning, she was carrying a bottle of Hennessy Paradis Ext cognac. Mrs. Kennedy went to get snifters for all, and Sean Ohara offered to assist her. While the pair was in the kitchen, *Mademoiselle* LaFoche asked Michael Ohara would he mind if she offered a taste of her after-dinner drink to Sean.

"Just so he doesn't expect me to stock it in my bar, it's okay with me," the Episcopal priest joked.

When everyone in the room had their glass, Brigitte LaFoche lifted her snifter and said, "To the United States of America—and to all the brave men and women who have fought for her freedom."

Everyone quietly took a sip from his or her cocktail. Sean Ohara noticed more than one set of moist eyes around the room. He got up from his chair, walked over to Brigitte, and hugged her.

"And if you wouldn't mind, *Mademoiselle* LaFoche, I'd like to propose a toast."

Chaplain and Mrs. Ohara looked at each other briefly. They both knew their son was an exceptional young man, but that didn't diminish their concerns that he might say something that would embarrass the other guests.

Lifting his cognac snifter, Sean said, "May we never forget those who gave their lives for our freedom." He and Brigitte embraced.

As she looked around the room, Brigitte LaFoche cleared her throat. "I would like to tell all of you how the French Resistance assisted in getting Sergeant Sean Kennedy out of Germany, after his plane was shot down during a raid on Schweinfurt in October, 1943."

Colonel Ohara looked around the room, paying particular attention to the look on Betty Kennedy's face. She appeared anxious to hear the story. But before Brigitte could begin her tale, Dexter Dannenberg asked if he could say something.

"Of course, *Monsieur* Dannenberg."

Dexter put down his drink. "When you all were back in Iowa I didn't hit this issue too hard, but you can rest assured that before I introduced *Monsieur* LaFoche to his father I had some friends at a 'certain company' [the CIA] check him out. I've known Brigitte for oh-so-many years. When she contacted me two years ago about her desire to have her son meet his father, we both agreed then that we had to be a hundred-and-ten percent sure before we said anything."

"You always were very thorough, Dexter," commented Colonel Ohara.

"In my business, Michael, it has to be that way."

Jean-Pierre LaFoche looked at Dannenberg. "Mother says that you two met on an airplane."

"We did, and I must say that I was smitten with her beauty. When you consider that I'm gay, that says a helluva lot."

Laughter erupted, as Dannenberg continued his story. "We were on an old Ford Tri-motor flying out of Heathrow to Amsterdam. I can remember it as if it were yesterday. It was a Thursday afternoon in late August. I was lost in thought, believe it or not, thinking about William the Conqueror and how England hadn't been successfully invaded since 1066 A.D."

"You're kidding, right?" Sean Ohara inquired.

Dannenberg chuckled. "I know that might sound bizarre to a young man who is in love, buried waist-high with school reports, and trying to juggle an athletic career, but honest to God, Sean, that's what I was thinking about."

"Amazing," young Ohara replied.

"The next thing I knew, this stunningly gorgeous French girl leaned over and asked me to tighten my seatbelt. I was so taken back by her beauty that I made some catty remark about how I would rather be sipping cognac with her in a nightclub than tightening my seatbelt. The comment was meant to be provocative, but *Mademoiselle* LaFoche refused to be shocked. Instead, she picked up on my line, and offered to take me around to some of Amsterdam's hotter night clubs."

Dexter continued. "When we were in Iowa, I mentioned that Brigitte and I served together on three missions during World War Two. I should clarify that. During the war, I never actually physically worked with Brigitte. Rather, I became her 'controller' after I was transferred to Wild Bill Donovan's cast of rogues and rascals. In fact, the entire Wild Bill Donovan thing in itself is just plain 'out there,'" Dannenberg said matter-of-factly.

"How so, Dex?" Sergeant Wilkes asked.

"The fact that Donovan was there in the first place, should be enough. After all, what were his qualifications, anyway?"

"I'd always heard that he was one of FDR's protégés."

"Well, if you listened to all his detractors in the Regular Army, one might conclude the same thing. But there's more to the story. Without going into a bunch of palace intrigue, suffice it to say that Ol' Wild Bill marched to a different drummer. I mean—just how he and FDR met in the first place is over the top. It goes like this: after Frank Knox became Secretary of the Navy in 1940, he introduced Donovan to FDR. How Knox knew Donovan is even more interesting. It seems they both attended Columbia Law School, albeit I can't say for sure if they had classes together.

"Somehow or another, Donovan gained FDR's confidence, and when an important mission came up the chief sent him to England to see what was really going on with Winnie and the Brits. Franklin wanted to know if our 'kissin' cousins' were in it for the long haul, or would they come to some sort of rapprochement with the Nazis.

"Winnie was desperate for help. He gave Donovan everything he wanted, total access, to all of his country's secrets. When Donovan got back to D.C., he reported everything to FDR. The chief was impressed, and filed Donovan's name away for later use.

"That 'later use' happened when FDR appointed Donovan Coordinator of Information in July 1941. But that ended up being a 'cluster,' so then FDR made Donovan Director of the Office of Strategic Services in July, 1942. Before long, Donovan was in command of agents from Berlin to Burma.

"Can you imagine that—Burma?" Dannenberg said, as he picked up his cognac and took a sip. "And, boy, did he have agents scattered from hell to breakfast. I recall that one of our top guys in Burma was a fellow named Joseph Lazarsky. He worked with our Thai agents.

"I could go on forever, but won't," Dannenberg added, tantalizingly.

"You mean like last Labor Day?" joked Colonel Ohara.

"Yes, as a matter of fact. Moreover, some day I'll have to tell you about the carryings-on within the OSS in France, Yugoslavia and Greece.

"But—back to Bill Donovan. Having won the Congressional Medal of Honor during the Great War, he was chafing at the bit to get back in command of men in combat. His wish might have come to fruition had not fate intervened. By that, I mean he was in a car accident in 1942. Yet, Wild Bill made his way up the food chain, and was promoted to major general in 1944. That didn't exactly endear him to the regular Army, but that's another story. Let's just say that the regular Army hated Donovan, and the feeling was mutual for him."

Dannenberg looked over at Mr. Kennedy. "Well, sir, I believe this is your cue."

Sean Kennedy, Sr. briefly scratched the back of his head with his right hand, and took a sip of cognac.

"I think the best way to tell my story is to begin with some background history of the Schweinfurt raid. Now, as you all know, I was what the Army Air Corps called a 'Flying Sergeant' during World War Two. The program came into being as a means of easing the god-awful shortage the United States had for qualified pilots.

"Congress passed the Army Air Corps Act of 1926 and Public Law 99 in 1941. Simply stated, these laws reduced the amount of formal education one had to have in order to fly the Army's planes. It also meant that the average age of the pilots was now between eighteen and twenty years old. For some soldiers, the payoff came on graduation, as you automatically became a staff sergeant on completing the course. None of this mattered to me, though, because I'd been in the National Guard over in Roseville and was already a buck-sergeant the day the Japanese bombed Pearl."

CSM Wilkes broke into the conversation: "Kennedy, you were a buck-sergeant when we met at Camp Claiborne."

"Small world, isn't it, Charlie?"

"Well, if you'd told me back in August of 'thirty-nine that we would be here, fifty-two years later, I would have told you to lay off the sauce."

Sean Kennedy replied, "It is amazing that our paths crossed again. In fact, I probably wouldn't have even remembered that we'd met, except for the circumstances in which we met."

"How is that, Mr. Kennedy?" Sean Ohara asked.

"I remember it, because when I picked him, I knew the base chaplain was going to tell him that his girlfriend had died as a result of a botched abortion in Omaha."

Charlie Wilkes' wife, Sharon, now came into the conversation. "That sure was a tough time for you, honey. I remember when you got back to Villisca later that summer, and Randy and I met you at the train station. There were two things I recall clearly: one, that you looked sharp in your uniform; two, you were pretty strung out over Dotty's death."

Mr. Kennedy sensed that if he pursued this line of conversation much longer, the evening would turn into a real downer. So he changed the subject.

"Right after those Japanese bastards attacked us, I put in for flight school, and was accepted. Shortly thereafter I found my tail in Arizona in some hellhole. At best, the conditions at the camp could be described as 'Spartan.' Over fifty percent of the men were booted after the flight physical, and out of those who made the cut only twenty-five percent actually graduated. Monday through Saturday you would either be in a classroom, or if you were lucky, in an airplane. Sundays we did PT. Imagine that—it's already hotter than the hinges of hell, and we're out there doing push-ups!

But, being and full of piss and vinegar, I made it through that hellish experience and was transferred to the 8th Air Force down at Hunter Field, in Savannah, Georgia. When General Eaker went to England, I went with him."

"Really? Were you on his staff?" Sean Ohara asked.

"Yeah, sure I was," Kennedy joked. "Remember what I was doing when I met Charlie?"

"Yes, sir—you were driving a truck."

"And that's exactly what I did for the next six months. Then one day, from out of the blue, this butter-bar strolled into my billets and wanted to know why I hadn't told them I was a pilot. I didn't how to react, quite honestly. At first I thought he was jerking me around, but as he kept talking it became clear that he was serious. I had to talk like a Dutch uncle just to get him to believe I wasn't some sort of slacker. It turned out that some admin weenie miscoded me when I got to England, and wrote in my personnel jacket that I was a truck driver!

"I can still remember that scrawny jackass prancing around the billets swearing and carrying on as if I were the enemy!"

Kennedy stood up and started strutting around the room. In a high voice he began mimicking his former supervisor, and his imitation brought forth howls of laughter from all in attendance.

"'Why, hell, sergeant, don't you know the 8th Air Force is destined to become the greatest air armada in history? Don't you want to be a part of that?'"

"I tried to explain to that 'box of rocks' that I wasn't hiding anything, and that the Army Air Corps had screwed-up my personnel records. But it was no use, this latter-day Napoleon just kept carrying on. He called me everything but Benedict Arnold, and implied that I was a coward.

"At that point I was ready to deck the little prick. But I desisted, and advised him that any time the Army Air Corps wanted to give me an airplane, I was ready to fly it. Then I challenged him to be my copilot. That shut him up. He stormed out of my billets like Attila the Hun chasing a virgin. It was a scene straight out of *Catch-22*. The only thing missing was the flight surgeon!"

Mr. Kennedy's parody of the second lieutenant's performance brought everyone in the room nearly to tears. Now Colonel Ohara put his drink down on the coffee table and looked over to Mrs. Kennedy.

"Betty, I think it's time to cut ol' Sean off. He's going to give himself a heart attack."

"Colonel," Mrs. Kennedy replied, "It's the fire-water. Every time that crazy mick gets near it, he gets this way."

Her comments caused the room to nearly erupt into hysterics again. When things finally calmed down, Ohara looked at his wife, Chloe, and smiled. "I guess Sean, Jr. came by it honestly."[2]

Embarrassed, Mr. Kennedy sat down and continued his story. "I can't help it, every time I think of that nitwit chewing on my backside and practically calling me a slacker, my blood boils.

"Anyway, at first I was put on a B-17 as co-pilot, but after ten bombing runs I was given my own plane, the "Nulaid Queen." She did the Mighty Eighth proud."

"The 'Mighty Eighth,' sir?" Sean Ohara asked.

"Absolutely. For your information, Sean, the 8th Air Force sustained fully half of the Army Air Corps' total losses during World War Two. As a matter-of-fact, I think we had more than forty-seven thousand casualties, with more than twenty-six thousand KIAs. Before it was over, 8th Air Force pilots earned seventeen Congressional Medals of Honor, two hundred DSCs, eight hundred-and-fifty Silver Stars, seven thousand Purple Hearts and close to fifty thousand Air Medals."

"That's quite a record, Mr. Kennedy," replied the young man.

Before the former bomber pilot could continue, he looked up and saw his wife. She was holding a framed Army military citation in her hand, which she now gave to the teenager. Mr. Kennedy was obviously embarrassed, but didn't say anything. The young man began reading it aloud.

"The Army Air Corps
This is to certify that the Secretary of War has awarded
The Distinguished Flying Cross To:
SFC Sean Kennedy, United States Army Air Corps
For meritorious service during the period 14 October 1943 through 26

2. Read "*Waiting for a Rainbow-Coming of Age in Vietnam,*" Graphic Publishers, 1995, (ISBN 1-882824-11-3) for the complete story of Michael Brandon Ohara and Sean Kennedy during the Vietnam War and the Tet Offensive of 1968.

October 1943. SFC Sean Kennedy Sr., while serving as a pilot in the United States Army Air Corps during air operations deep inside Germany territory, had his aircraft shot down in enemy action. With great courage and tremendous flying skill, SFC Kennedy managed to fly his plane until his surviving crew was able to bail out. Once on the ground, SFC Kennedy treated his wounded crewmembers and led them to safety and eventual rescue. For his actions, SFC Kennedy is awarded the Distinguished Flying Cross. His actions are a credit to the United States Army Air Corps, and the United States of America.

Permanent Order 093-43
Jimmy Doolittle LTG, AAC, USA
HQ, 8th Air Force
United States Army Air Corps
Commanding Pinetree, England

"That's truly impressive, Kennedy" CSM Wilkes said, sitting up in his chair.

"Well, the truth of the matter is that I couldn't have done any of it without nine other men…," Kennedy replied, his voice about to crack.

Mrs. Kennedy hugged her husband around his shoulders, and apologized. "Sorry if I embarrassed you, honey." She turned to take the wartime document back into their study.

A few seconds passed in thought, before Mr. Kennedy spoke again.

"Let me tell you about my crew. My co-pilot was a kid from 'Dago, named Mark Washington. When I first met him I thought he was a weird duck. I mean, Mark was one of those typical southern California boys: straw-blond hair, muscular build, you know. And indeed he was, having been a lifeguard on the San Diego beaches before the war. The difference was that Mark was always hitting the books, reading some training manual or asking questions about B-17s.

"At first I thought he was trying to impress me, so that I'd recommend him for his own bird. Then I asked him about it one night in a pub. Mark said that wasn't the case at all, claiming that he read to combat boredom. He told me he'd be just as happy reading a girlie magazine.

"My navigator was a good ol' boy from Savannah, Georgia, named Charles 'Sandy' Emerson. Sandy claimed to be a distant relative to Ralph Waldo Emerson, but if he was, he had to be a very distant relative. His grammar was just terrible. But we soon learned that his ability to speak the King's English had damned little to do with his ability to navigate. The thing I remember the most about Sandy was that he had to be the only man in the 305th Bomber Command who actually loved Spam. He would trade anything he could spare for a can of the stuff. Sandy also told some of the raunchiest jokes I've ever heard. When we were out drinking, he was life of the party. But once on board the 'Queen,' he was all business.

"Our bombardier was a lad from New Orleans, named Charles 'Silky' Cantrell. We called him 'Silky' because he was one smooth Romeo when it came to the women. He was close to six feet tall, with blue eyes and a smile that melted the gals' hearts. The joke around the squadron was that he could hit a bulls-eye around London, just like when he dropped his payload on Hitler. Next to me, Silky was the oldest member of our crew—that's to say, he was twenty-five years old.

"He also had to have the worst sense of time that God ever put on earth. He could never be anywhere on time. He used to joke about it, saying that the only thing he ever planned to be on time for was his funeral.

"My next crewmember was an absolute piece of work, my tail gunner. His name was Jack Burns, from Chicago. Burns was probably the only man on my bird that never bitched too loudly about how damned cold it got up there in that un-pressurized aircraft, five miles above the earth at minus sixty degrees.

"Oh, sure, he was freezing his ass off, like the rest of us. But he'd never admit it. It would be so damned cold that if you had to pee you'd have to sit down or you wouldn't be able to find your talliwacker. That was about the time that old Jack would holler up on the intercom for me to "Turn off the heater, Sarge." No matter how many times he said it, we'd all laugh, because that was all you could do. Damn, did it ever get cold up there!

"Jack operated the most important defensive weapons on board, as it was his responsibility to take out the Krauts who were attacking us from the rear. And he was damned good at it, because he knew all too well that the first thing the Krauts wanted to do was kill him and eliminate the threat of his guns.

"It's interesting, how tail guns made their way onto Fortresses. You see, the early 'seventeens didn't have any guns back there, and soon the Germans figured out just how damned vulnerable we were. So tail guns were first installed on the B-17E model. Many changes were made. In fact, on the B-17G, the tail gun area was modified to what became known as the "Cheyenne" turret, which had a better angle of fire and increased visibility.

"I'll never forget the first time I laid eyes on Jack; I thought he had just fallen off a John Deere tractor. Jack looked like the typical hayseed from the Midwest, but I soon learned that he wasn't a man to fool with. He had a rock-solid hatred of everything Adolf Hitler stood for. I still remember how he would rant and rave about the *Nazis*—he accused the 'Austrian Corporal' of being the anti-Christ. Now, don't get me wrong, none of us were Nazi apologists. But that ol' farm boy firmly believed that 'G-D *Nazi*' was one word. Every time he opened up with his weapon, he'd yell out, 'Come get this, you *Nazi* bastards, may you burn in Hell!'

"I asked him about it one day when we were waiting for a P-O-L truck to finish fueling our bird. He told me that the reason he hated the *Nazis* so much was that they were keeping him away from his girlfriend back in Chicago. She must have been quite a girl, for a man to get that worked up over...."

Mr. Kennedy's voice trailed off.

Sean Ohara, Jr. looked around the room, observing the other guests' faces, and correctly assumed that Jack Burns was *not* one of the three men who survived that night when the "Nulaid Queen" was shot down.

"Now, B-17s have two waist gunners," Mr. Kennedy continued. "My guys were Theodore Lake, from Omaha, and a fellow from Reno named Ben Smithson. I never got to know Smithson that well, because he transferred into the unit about a week before we were shot down. On the other hand, Ted Lake was one crazy bastard, who knew all the words to "Praise the Lord, and Pass the Ammunition." By the time the war was over, so did I—because that's what he sang whenever we were out over German territory. You could tell him to shut up, but he wouldn't. He'd just stand there, shooting up all nine yards, singing away. He was a damn good shot, too, downing five Messerschmitt Bf-109s.

"But the most interesting guy in my entire crew had to be our radio operator, Luigi Vigorelli, of the Bronx. He was so Italian—about five-foot-seven, thin, with slicked-back, black hair. He wore a crucifix all the time, and loved to talk about the girls back in New York who considered becoming nuns, because with him out of the picture they knew they would never get laid the way Luigi could do it. Man, was he full of himself! And the damned thing about it—I think he probably was a virgin.

"I remember one night when Luigi was carrying on. Ol' Silky was nursing a god-awful hangover and wanted to rest. Silky told him if he didn't shut up, he was going to take him into the latrine and bust his virgin ass. My god, you could've heard a pin drop! I thought I was going to have to call the MPs. After Luigi cussed him out for fifteen minutes in Italian, he started up in English. Wow! I'd heard some pretty dirty words in my life, but never a string like that before. I was so shocked that my mouth was wide open, and I swear I could have caught flies.

"After Luigi finished his harangue, Silky casually stood up and softly asked him if he 'was going to eat with that mouth.' Luigi was so taken back by Slinky's comment he started to laugh. Before we all knew it, the two of them were off in a corner, laughing and carrying on as if they were long-lost bosom buddies.

"After Luigi, came the brains of the crew: Flight Engineer Sol Weitzman. Sol was so Jewish: Kosher, nerdy, and orthodox. He was a graduate of NYU; in fact, after the war he went back to teach there before going to work for NASA.

"Sol was a skinny kid, as tough as the Bowery Boys, but probably the most religious of all of us. The thing I remember most about him was that he would always tell me before each mission, 'Kennedy, you fly the plane. I'll get us there and back—but no side trips unless we were going to drop our payload on *Herr* Hitler himself!'

"Our ball gunner's name was named Alfred 'Big Al' Norris, from Lincoln, Nebraska. Of course, we called him 'Big Al,' simply because he wasn't big. You see, you can't be big and still fit into a ball turret. I think Al maybe weighed a hundred and twenty-five pounds dripping wet. We all thought Al had the worst job on the 'Nulaid Queen,' the way he was stuck down in that turret, hanging from the plane's belly. It wouldn't have worked for me—I'm too claustrophobic, and lack the testicular fortitude to go on missions without a parachute close–by to save my butt should everything turn to fecal matter. Since the turret would rotate in a complete circle, it provided Al with the incredible ability to see the Krauts before they could do us harm. The guy was a dead-eye shot, too, most likely a distant cousin to Sergeant York. He'd bring pee, death and destruction upon any German S.O.B. who wanted to ruin our day.

"We all thought Al's job was the most dangerous one on board, but the truth was that because he was curled up like a baby with his back against the armor-plated door, he stood a better chance than the rest of us."

"I don't care what you say, Mr. Kennedy—I wouldn't have climbed into one of those ball turrets come hell or high water," Sean Ohara stated, as he stood up and walked into the kitchen.

"I don't blame you. Nor would I," the old man responded. "I was attached to the 305th Bombardment Group (Heavy) in January 1942. They were activated in early March of 'forty-two, then we trained in B-17s before being transferred to England that fall. Once in Great Britain, we were assigned to Eighth Air Force.

"The 305th began flying combat missions in late 'forty-two. They hit the usual targets: submarine pens, docks, harbors, shipyards, motor works, and other places selected by Pinetree. Our first deep mission into the 'Land of the Huns' came in 1943, when we blew up half of Wilhelmshaven. From there we went on to the Germans' war-making facilities in France. As the war progressed, we kept going further and further into the Continent. We bombed the oil plants at Merseburg, the aircraft factories at Anklam and the shipping facilities at Gdynia. But Schweinfurt was the 'ball buster' of all of them."

Kennedy's use of the term "ball buster" in reference to Schweinfurt's ball-bearing factories caused a round of groans to come from all who were listening to his tale. When Colonel Ohara called him on it, Betty Kennedy just smiled and said, "He pulls that one every time he tells his story."

Mr. Kennedy laughed, then began again.

"Nevertheless, here's how it happened…."

CHAPTER SIX

*We sleep safe in our beds because rough men stand
ready in the night to visit violence on those who would
do us harm.*
—George Orwell

HEADQUARTERS 305TH BOMBER GROUP
CHELVESTON, ENGLAND
14 OCTOBER 1943, 0730 HOURS LOCAL

The smoke inside the headquarters briefing hut was so thick that SFC
Sean Kennedy was having a hard time seeing the briefing board, which sat
only about twenty feet directly in front of him.

His copilot, Mark Washington, sat immediately on his right. True to
form, in one hand he held a canteen-cup full of coffee; the other was holding
an Army field manual.

Catnapping next to Washington was Clarence "Sandy" Emerson, their
navigator. Emerson was a true believer in the Army principle that a soldier
should never stand when he could sit down, nor stay awake when he might
sleep.

Kennedy didn't have to look to see who was sitting on Emerson's right,
because he could smell Charles "Silky" Cantrell. Apparently, the *Nulaid
Queen's* bombardier also knew he reeked to high hell with Old Spice. Kennedy tried to ignore Cantrell's odor, but vowed to order his crewmember to
take a shower before they got on board the plane. Otherwise, he feared his
other crew members might toss Cantrell out at ten thousand feet!

From the front of the hut Kennedy heard the briefing NCO call the assembled aircrews to attention. Soon after, Captain Fitzpaugh entered, with
a retinue of junior grade officers.

As Fitzpaugh walked by, Kennedy knew they were headed back to Schweinfurt.

"Be seated, gentlemen," said the O-3 from "Pinetree," as he put down his swagger stick.

"I'm not going to sugarcoat this, men. Your mission today is Schwein-furt."

Kennedy looked over to Cantrell, who was sticking his right index fin-ger into a circle he'd made with the thumb and index finger of his other hand. Cantrell's meaning was obvious: *We're screwed!*

Kennedy smiled, then returned his attention to what was being said by Fitzpaugh.

"Gentlemen, today's mission is number 115. Our mission is once again the ball bearing factories. G-2 reports that more than thirty percent of the Huns' ball bearings are made there, and they believe we can shorten this bloody war by taking them out. We'll be putting up two hundred-nineteen B-17s in a maximum effort to destroy those high-priority targets.

"Fifty P-47s will stay with you as long as possible, but be advised that once they take off, you'll still have about three hours of unescorted flying until you reach the target area. When you get close, the Krauts are going to hit you with everything they have. Photos from previous raids suggest that the Jerries have more than four hundred 88-millimeter guns in the area, which translates to at least five minutes of getting the bloody hell pounded at you before you can drop your payloads and get the hell out of there!

"Now—the last time we went in, many of you recall that some of the *Luftwaffe* pilots braved their own artillery to get a piece of you. So be pre-pared for the bastards.

"Order of battle will be as follows: The 1st Combat Wing will start air operations at 13:30 hours. The 91st Bomber Group will lead with the 332nd, 324th and the 401st, departing Bassingbourne at 13:30 hours local.

The 381st will take off concurrently from Ridgewill. Next will be the 398th, then the 92nd, and then us, the 305th. By order of takeoff, we'll go numerically. That is to say, the 364th, 365th, then the 366th and lastly the 422nd. Once airborne, you'll form up in the following staging areas...."

Kennedy tried to focus on the C.O.'s briefing, but something told him that today's mission was going to be far worse than any he'd flown so far. He tried to shake it off. But it was to no avail—today's mission would be one for the books!

As soon as the C.O.'s briefing was over, Kennedy's crew filed out of the hut and began walking over toward their jeep. Silky was the first to speak. His comments made Kennedy feel even worse.

"I got a bad feeling about tonight, Kennedy."

"I hope the mission isn't as bad as you smell," Washington responded.

"Screw you, man. I just got back to the base and haven't had a chance to shower yet," Cantrell said defensively.

The last thing SFC Kennedy wanted was for his men to get into a beef before they went out on a mission. So he asked Cantrell what he'd based his premonition on.

"Based on how many times we've already been there," Cantrell answered.

"Once was one too many times for me," Washington added.

Kennedy tried some humor. "I think we've made the Schweinfurt run more times than Vigorelli has been thrown out of a whorehouse."

Now Sandy Emerson piped up. "Come on Kennedy, we ain't been there that many times!"

All the men laughed out loud, then proceeded to crowd into a jeep furnished by the squadron. Before Kennedy drove his crew back to their hut, flight preparations were finalized, messages were sent, bombs were loaded, guns were inspected and the planes' gas tanks were topped off. Then Kennedy's crew slept. Or wrote their wills.

THE AIR FIELD AT CHELVESTON, ENGLAND (TRIANGLE G) 14 OCTOBER 1943, 1015 HOURS, LOCAL

As SFC Kennedy and his crew approached the *Nulaid Queen*, the lead mechanic, Jack Marshall, waved them forward.

"She's as ready as she's ever been, Kennedy. I had the boys do better than a usual check-out of her systems, and they're all working fine."

"Thanks, Jack. Your men do a great job, and we appreciate it." Kennedy climbed down from the cab of the three-quarter-ton truck that had transported them out to the flight line.

"Do you know how many birds are going up today, Kennedy?" Jack Marshall asked.

"Well, if you count the fifteen the 305th 'Can-Do' Bombardment Group is putting into the fray, it's well over two hundred and seventy-five B-17s."

Marshall shook his head, saying, "Give those bastards hell, Kennedy, and we'll see you back here!"

"We'll do our best, Chief," Cantrell replied, as he got out of the truck and walked over to the waiting warbird. All the crewmen climbed on board and quickly got to their takeoff checklists.

As SFC Kennedy climbed aboard, he saw his fellow crewmembers were already busy with their duties. Sandy Emerson was busy studying the flight plan and reviewing the route to be flown, all the while trying to figure out the locations of alternate landing fields in case everything turned to fecal matter in the air.

Kennedy walked by Emerson, who looked up and asked in his unmistakable Georgia accent, "Ya'll think the weather might've changed since we was at the briefing, Mister Kennedy?"

"Hopefully, they would have told us, if it had," Kennedy replied, moving forward into the cockpit.

Sitting in Kennedy's seat, Mark Washington was checking out the radio equipment on the pilot's side of the cockpit. Looking up, he noticed Kennedy and quickly moved over into his own seat. Where some other pilot might have got uptight about his co-pilot·sitting there, Kennedy appreciated Washington's thoroughness. He felt confident that if everything turned to crap for them, Mark Washington would get the crew back on the ground in one piece.

In the back of the plane, Luigi Vigorelli was reading over his log and checking out his radio equipment.

While everyone prepared themselves and their equipment for today's mission, Big Al Norris waited for the *Queen* to get airborne so he could lower the ball turret. He busied himself with a wad of chewing tobacco.

While his men prepared for the upcoming flight, Kennedy picked up the microphone and spoke over the intercom. "This is Kennedy. At my beep it is exactly 1030 hours. Synchronize your watches accordingly."

Within a minute of the crew having finished all their pre-flight checks, the tower advised Kennedy that all planes would be taking off at thirty-second intervals.

Kennedy looked at Washington. "Check the time when we start down the runway, and notify me when we've been moving for thirty seconds."

"I'll do that, Kennedy. I'll also make sure that we take off in a medium tail-low attitude...."

Kennedy thought about what he'd just said, and chuckled.

How many times have we done this? Yet, it's the same thing every time. Maybe that's what keeps us from going nuts? [1]

As the *Nulaid Queen* approached five thousand feet altitude, Kennedy

---

1 For a very thorough webpage on the workings of B-17s, check out http://www.303rdbg.com. Known as the "Hell's Angels," this bomber group was one the Army Air Corps' most highly decorated units during WWII.

looked around for the lead squadron.

They should just about be finished with takeoffs, by now.

He looked up and saw that the high squadron was already formed up. The knot in Kennedy's stomach tightened. It was an uncommon feeling. Something was up.

So far, so good.

As the bombers approached Walcheren, Kennedy looked down at the last of the North Sea.

"That estuary down there most likely is the Scheldt," he said to Mark Washington.

"Yeah. And if I recall, it was right about here the Krauts jumped us the last time."

Washington's words hadn't hit the front of the cockpit before Kennedy heard Vigorelli shout, "Hey, Kennedy, lots of chatter up front. The Krauts got at least fifteen Me-109s, and they're mixing it up with the boys in the P-47s. From the way things sound, it's one helluva fight."

Kennedy gritted his teeth.

"Okay men, this is where the fun begins. We're still hundreds of miles from Schweinfurt and the Krauts are on our ass. Stay alert, and God Bless all of you. Now let's keep this old gal up with the rest of the planes, and pray to God one of those Krauts doesn't have our name written on his flight plan."

The dogfights continued. The P-47s shot down five *Luftwaffe* planes and damaged four more. No American planes were lost—not yet.

Over Duren, thirty more Focke-Wulfs attacked the formation. The dogfights still continued, but this time Kennedy's crew saw the first of many B-17s go down.

For the next three hours the Germans sent up everything they had. The list included single-engine Me-109s, twin-engine Me-110s, Junker Ju-88s and FW-190s, along with Me 210s and even a few Dornier bombers.[2]

The noise level inside the *Nulaid Queen* was deafening. The *Luftwaffe* planes seemed to be coming in waves, and each time they made a pass another B-17 was shot down.

Kennedy hollered back on the intercom, "Ted—Ben. For crissake, keep those bastards away from us!"

Ben Smithson replied, "Kennedy, Ted's been hit pretty bad! Get some-

---

2 Sgt. Walter Peters wrote and intense article about the Raid on Schweinfurt for *Yank* magazine. It is available to read on http://www.327th.org.

one back here to patch him up. I can't leave my position or we'll all be dead meat. How much longer, for God's sake?"

From the rear of the plane Jack Burns hollered, "Our fighters are leaving now."

The ack-ack kept exploding. One burst hit the *Nulaid Queen's* right wing, taking out number-three Wright Cyclone R-1820-97 engine in the process.

Washington feathered the engine. But both he and Kennedy could see they had lost a lot of fuel in the process.

"We better get there damn quick, Kennedy, or we're gonna be guests of the German government," Washington said, as more ack-ack exploded right outside their cockpit. "If this shit gets any heavier, we'll be able to walk into Schweinfurt on it."

"Start walking," Kennedy hollered back, as the airspace in front of the *Nulaid Queen* went solid black. Kennedy was about to speak again to Washington when another burst of anti-aircraft fire slammed through the windshield, instantly killing the co-pilot.

Kennedy fought the controls, desperately trying to focus on the mission. All he could think about was keeping their plane in formation, and on the correct target heading.

Before the raid was over, the 305th Bomb Group lost thirteen out of their fifteen bombers. Kennedy debated telling the crew about Washington's death, but decided against it.

Ba-whomb! Ba-whomb! More ack-ack hit the plane.

Now smoke was everywhere. Inside the plane, outside the plane—everywhere.

We have to be close to Schweinfurt. Dear God, get us to Schweinfurt!
Ba-whomb! Ba-whomb! More explosions.

"Holy fuck! That was close!" shouted Sol Weitzman as he tried to regain his balance.

Fire in the airplane! Frantically, Kennedy hollered into the intercom, "What's our status, Cantrell?"

Vigorelli began to say the Rosary. "Hail Mary, full of grace…."

Cantrell shouted over to him, "Say one for me too, Eye-tee boy!"

Ba-whomb! Ba-whomb!

Kennedy turned and shouted to Cantrell, "We're going to be there damned quick, let's do the bomb check."

Cantrell immediately began synchronizing the Norden bombsight.

"What's our air speed?"

"One-twenty, or thereabouts," Kennedy replied, as another piece of shrapnel tore through the plane's fuselage.

"Altitude check."

"Twenty-thousand. Repeat, two-zero-thousand feet," Kennedy replied as another burst of German artillery slammed into the *Queen's* right wing. *One more like that, and the fucking engine's going to drop off!*

Talking to himself, Cantrell said, "The wind is coming from the west. Based on the wind velocity... I'm gonna drop... these five-hundred-pound motherfuckers... right about...."

Ba-whomb!

More shrapnel savaged the airframe, instantly killing the *Nulaid Queen's* navigator, Sandy Emerson. Luigi Vigorelli was hit by flying shrapnel, too, but not as severely. He grabbed the plane's medical kit and began patching up his bloody wounds.

As Kennedy looked out the front of the cockpit, he could see Schweinfurt immediately below the plane. Amazingly, the ack-ack was getting even more intense. Sweat was pouring from Kennedy's brow. His heart was pounding. He wanted to puke.

"Cantrell, drop that shit as soon as you can, and let's get the fuck out of here!"

Silky Cantrell calmly responded, "Maintain present speed and altitude, Kennedy, and I'll do that."

"Roger that!" Kennedy replied, as he gritted his teeth.

Peering into the Norden bombsight, Cantrell thought he saw their primary target: the *Hochgebäude* (high-rise building) of the Kugelfischer-Georg-Schäfer company, the largest bearing manufacturer in Schweinfurt.

"Hold it right there, Kennedy. Hold it... right... fucking... there.... I'm gonna drop all ten of these five-hundred-pounders right down the Kraut bastards' throats!" Cantrell began his countdown.

"Three... two... bombs away!" Cantrell hollered. Then, "Kennedy, get us the hell outta here! Five thousand pounds of bombs are on their way down!"

Kennedy looked at his fuel gauges. Amazingly, they seemed to be working. The old gal had about twelve hundred gallons of gas left.

Again Kennedy shouted into the intercom, "Listen up. Washington is dead. Number three engine is gone. The way I figure it, we've still got enough gas to get back, if we can just get the hell out of here!

"Yeah, and if these fuckers don't kill us all first," Vigorelli said, as he fired one of Ted Lake's fifty-caliber machineguns at some rapidly-approaching Me-109s.

Vigorelli walked his rain of death right into one of the oncoming German fighters, and it exploded into a ball of fire. Flaming pieces pinwheeled down toward the ground.

"Good shooting, Vig!" Cantrell hollered.

"Come on, you bastards!" Vigorelli screamed as another wave of German fighters raced toward them.

Ba-whomb! Ba-whomb! More ack-ack.

Tracers!

As the Me-109s flew past the *Queen*, one of the German pilots squeezed off an unending burst of fire, killing Vigorelli instantaneously.

One hour later....

With number-three engine out, and suffering from numerous ack-ack hits, getting away from Schweinfurt and joining up with the remaining American bombers taxed Kennedy's flying ability to its limits. He looked at his fuel gauge. It seemed to be the only piece of equipment still working.

The Queen has seen better days, but by God she's still flying!

Kennedy had long-since given up on trying to keep up with the other planes that had struck Schweinfurt. It wasn't that he didn't *want* to stay with the formation, but the truth of the matter was that he *couldn't*, with one engine out and losing fuel. He looked at the airspeed indicator. They were flying at somewhere in the neighborhood of one hundred-forty miles per hour, or roughly half the speed the B-17 could normally cruise.

He picked up the interphone and pressed the button. "Cantrell, give me a sit-rep."

"Kennedy, I'm okay. Emerson and Vigorelli are dead; the navigation gear is all shot up, too. Big Al and Ted Lake were both hit pretty bad. I don't think either one of them is gonna make it. Sol and I are okay. Jack Burns is okay, but his gun is out of action. We've transferred his ammo up here."

In his midwestern accent, Jack Burns came on the intercom. "Kennedy, Ted Lake's dead, so is Smithson. That last sweep by the *Luftwaffe* got him."

"Well, there's nothing we can do for them, now," Kennedy admitted. "That is, except get this bird back to England, and flying again. With that in mind, men—listen up. Our fuel situation is okay, at this rate of consumption we should have enough gas to make it to the North Sea. If we have to ditch, we'll send out an SOS and try and get some Allied ship to pick us up."

"Er… any water colder than the Mississippi in December ain't a good thing, Kennedy," commented Silky Cantrell. "The truth is, this ol' boy cain't swim further than a half-dozen yards. I say we fly this sonofabitch toward the French coast and take our chances on the ground. Besides, with the temperature of the North Sea, ain't none of us gonna last five minutes."

Kennedy replayed in his head what Cantrell told them: *We've got five dead—all key personnel. Big Al Norris is wounded. That leaves me, Jack Burns, Sol Weitzman and Silky. I'd say we've got our work cut out for us….*

Kennedy tried some humor. "Well, I wasn't exactly on the swim team at Cal, either. Silky, come forward. Jack, you come forward, too, and man one of the guns, 'cause I'm sure we aren't out of the woods yet. I'd imagine we're about to run into more of 'Herman Göering's favorites' in a few minutes, and we need to be prepared for them."

"Will do, Kennedy." Jack Burns stood up and began making his way through the severely shot up B-17. On reaching the middle of the fuselage, he pulled back the charging handle on the Browning M-2 fifty-caliber machinegun. He did it just in the nick of time, as the first of three *Luftwaffe* fighters jumped the wounded Fortress.

Burns took his time before firing the weapon. At thirteen rounds per second he knew he couldn't waste any ammunition. His aim was excellent. One of his bursts blew away the cockpit of an attacking Me-109, killing its pilot in a heartbeat.

The other two German planes roared past the *Queen* with their guns blazing. Fortunately, none of their rounds did any more damage to her.

"I could use some help back here," Jack Burns shouted as he pulled back again on the charging handle.

Cantrell bolted from the cockpit to the un-manned weapon. He noticed their ammo was getting low.

We don't have more than fifteen seconds worth of rounds… make each shot count!

From his side of the plane, Cantrell watched the two fighters as they did a loop and started back toward the B-17.

"Come on you bastards, hell's waiting for you!" he yelled as he fired a short burst.

"I missed him, Burns. He's coming up... right... *now!*"

The German fighter blew past the B-17 with its guns blazing. Fortunately, all again went astray. Burns waited a second, fixed a bead on the enemy and let loose with a torrent of hot metal. Nearly all of his rounds hit the enemy aircraft and it exploded, spewing parts of the plane in all directions.

"That's two of the bastards!" Burns screamed in relief.

"Maybe his friend's had enough," Cantrell said, more as a prayer than a statement of fact.

Looking out his side of the plane, Burns could see that whoever was flying the third Bf 109 hadn't had enough. He was banking off to the left, to hit them from the rear of their plane.

"The bastard's gonna come up our six!" Burns yelled, dashing back toward the rear of the plane. It was a race against time. Burns steadied himself as the lone "Frederick" model Messerschmitt approached them at a speed topping 370 mph.

"Come on, you bastard... just a few more seconds," Burns yelled and began firing his weapon.

Some of his rounds hit the approaching aircraft, causing the pilot to bank left, and when he did Cantrell picked him up in his sights and began firing again.

This time Silky Cantrell scored a hit, and the German fighter started a long spiral of death toward the ground.

"Hell is waiting for you, you *Nazi* bastard!" Cantrell yelled as he spun around to talk to Burns.

"Jack. I got him." No answer came from the rear of the plane.

Louder, Cantrell repeated himself. "Jack, I got him!"

Cantrell's stomach tightened as he walked back to the back of the B-17. When he got there he knew why his comrade hadn't responded. Jack Burns was dead. A German bullet had blown half of his head away.

Now Cantrell did was what he'd wanted to do ever since takeoff—he vomited.

For a few minutes all he could do was puke. When he finally was able to compose himself he staggered back up to the cockpit.

Kennedy turned around, and shouted at him, "Get back to your weapons, and keep an eye out for bogeys. I'm gonna get us back to England. One way or another."

"What do you mean by that?" Cantrell replied in his Louisiana drawl.

"Look, Cantrell—Sol tells me Big Al just died, too. That's seven of our crewmembers dead; engine number three's out, we're losing fuel, our navigational gear is all fucked-up and we're damn near out of ammo. The way I figure it, we've gotta get the hell out of here," Kennedy said, maneuvering the plane's rudder. "But with one engine out, I think our best bet is to fly an alternate route.

"I think we're about a hundred miles east of Frankfurt. Therefore, Kaiserslautern's about an hour-and-a-half from here, if we fly a southwesterly course. Now... from what I remember from that briefing two weeks ago, when we hit Ludwigshaven, France is only another hundred or so miles from there. I say we fly in that direction and take our chances with the French Underground, rather than drowning in the North Sea."

Cantrell looked at Kennedy. "Well, for damned sure, my French is a helluva lot better than my German! And, the truth be known, we're probably all gonna be killed before we can make it another hundred miles, anyway. So lead the way, Kennedy!"

Now Sol Weitzman came forward. He looked at Kennedy and Cantrell.

"What's the plan, Kennedy?"

"How's your French?" Cantrell asked him.

"I had four years at Hebrew school and one year at Florida A & M."

"That settles it, then. I had two years in high school, plus two at Cal. So, France here we come!"

"That's okay with me," Weitzman said, returning to his weapon.

"Me, too, Kennedy," Cantrell said, as he started back to his fifty-caliber gun.

Before Weitzman and Cantrell could get back to their positions, Kennedy yelled to them. "And check your parachutes. Just in case we end up having to try our luck with speaking German...."

Weitzman yelled back, "Unfortunately, I speak German, too, but I don't think any of those Nazi sonofabitches down there want to engage me in conversation."

"Probably not, Sol. So let's make sure that doesn't happen."

Two Hours Later....

As hard as SFC Kennedy tried to nurse the *Nulaid Queen* to France, he instinctively knew they were going to have to bail out within the next few minutes, as the fuel gauges were either on "empty," or hovering in the neighborhood.

He called Weitzman forward.

"What's up, Kennedy?" Weitzman asked, taking a sip from his canteen.

"We're gonna to have bail out in a few minutes… we've just lost too much fuel. I'm thinking we can either ride this sonofabitch until she begins to drop, or jump out a few minutes earlier."

"Why jump out earlier?" Sol asked.

"We're not in France, and not likely to make it there, either. So, if we jump in a few minutes and the plane keeps flying on a few more miles past where we jump, when it crashes the *Nazis* will spend time in that area looking for us."

Weitzman nodded his head. "To paraphrase General MacArthur, 'I'd rather those bastards try to hit us where we ain't.'"

"Go get Cantrell."

A minute later Cantrell came forward. "You ready to call it day and un-ass this motherfucker, Kennedy?"

"Yes. But before we do, make sure you have a forty-five and ammo for it, plus anything else that can help get our sorry butts to France. You know… extra canteens and medical supplies. When you've got those things, give me a holler."

Cantrell started to leave, but Kennedy continued talking. "I've been looking over the map, and most of the ground underneath us is rolling hills."

Cantrell interrupted him. "So, if we don't get killed jumping out, we can get killed landing in a tree somewhere?"

"That's pretty much the case, soldier."

Sol Weitzman again came forward. "If that's the case, Kennedy, let's get the hell out of here now, before it gets too dark. I'll see you guys on the ground."

"God willing," Cantrell muttered under his breath.

It caused Weitzman to turn, and say, "Talk to Him on the way down, Cantrell. He's been known to help far more worthless bastards than you."

Catching Weitzman's biblical reference, Cantrell replied, "In that case, let's go find the 'Promised Land.'"

BOOK THREE: EUROPE

CHAPTER SEVEN

Whatever happens, the flame of French resistance must not die, and will not die.
—General Charles De Gaulle, 18 June 1940

THE PRIVATE RESIDENCE OF KLAUS KRONSTADT
97 HAUPTSTRASSE, HOCHSPEYER, GERMANY
15 OCTOBER 1943, 14:10 HOURS LOCAL TIME

Klaus Kronstadt and his wife, Hilda, had been the objects of *Nazi* scrutiny for the past four years. At sixty-seven years of age, he knew that if he got caught doing what he was about to do, he and his entire family would be killed—slowly, and painfully!

"Pastor Mueller, are you sure we should try this again? We have done it four times already. Surely the *Nazis* can't be that stupid, can they?"

"I promise you, Klaus, this will be the last time I put your family in danger," the Confessional Church clergyman said as he picked up a glass of *schnapps* and took a sip.

"It isn't that I don't want to help, Father. It's just that I don't think I could stand another beating like the one that bastard *Stürmbannführer* Wilhelm Wolf gave me back in June of 'thirty-nine."

Pastor Mueller smiled. In doing it he made Klaus Kronstadt irritated, and Kronstadt lashed out at him, saying, "What in God's name do you find humorous about a partially-paralyzed veteran of the Great War getting the hell beat out of him by some brutal *Nazi schwein*?"

Mueller put down his drink. "I wasn't going to tell you this right now, Klaus, but I have it on good authority that your 'friend' Wolf was killed last month at Stalingrad, courtesy of the Red Army."

"And, how is it you know this?"

"I was at the *Hotel Drei Konige* two days ago to celebrate a parishioner's thirtieth anniversary, and I overheard a heck of a ruckus coming from the bar. I stuck my head inside and noticed two *Nazi* colonels talking who

113

were rather intoxicated. Somehow, Wolf's name came up, so I made my way into the bar and asked the bartender, Hans Schubert, some innocuous question. While he was answering, I asked him to find out what those two officers were talking about. Well, my request couldn't have made him happier, because Hans believes that one of those officers raped his sister, Ursula.

"Schubert told me later that he heard them say *Stürmbannführer* Wilhelm Wolf was killed three weeks ago, at Stalingrad."

"I know one shouldn't speak badly of the dead," Kronstad said. But, Pastor Mueller, Wilhelm Wolf was of the Devil himself."

"I won't argue your point, nor will I say I am sorry that he's dead. He was a monster who, hopefully, is in hell as we speak."

Kronstadt shook his head in agreement, adding, "You know what is so sad about this situation?"

"What's that?"

"That we, two God-fearing Germans, are happy when our own soldiers are killed."

Mueller briefly considered Kronstadt's remark before speaking. "But Klaus, we mourn the Fatherland's decent soldiers who are killed on the battlefield. I know that I may burn in hell for this, but I'll be damned if I will mourn any of the monsters who got this war started!"

"I feel the same way, pastor. But do you think God will forgive us for being so full of hatred?"

"We'll have to wait until we meet Him, but I can tell you from what the Bible says I don't think God cares too much for these *Nazis*—if for no other reason than the way they treat the Jews."

"Good point," Klaus Kronstadt added, picking up a small glass of *schnapps*.

Mueller continued, "Schubert also heard one of those officers say that Hitler's favorite general, Sixth Army commander General von Paulus', campaign to take Stalingrad is in desperate shape. In fact, they say he is hanging on by his fingernails. It also appears that the Fourth Panzer Army isn't endearing themselves to *Herr* Hitler, either. Apparently, their drive to take the oil fields in the Caucasus isn't going to happen, after all."

Kronstadt shook his head, muttering, "That madman Hitler is responsible for all these deaths, you know."

"Of course, I know that," Mueller replied, in a mildly indignant tone.

Kronstadt could tell he'd pissed-off his pastor friend, and tried to apologize. "Pastor Mueller—again, it isn't that I don't want to help, but I can't keep putting my nephew, Albert, in so much danger."

"I know that, Klaus. But the truth of the matter is that Albert and Judas have a lot in common. I mean, as long as he gets his money, he doesn't care about anybody or anything else. Agreed?"

"Yes, he's certainly the miserable one. But still family, and my sister would never forgive me if she knew I was this deeply involved in the anti-Hitler movement. She idolizes the little bastard."

"You have my word on it, Klaus— no more, after these three Americans are sent to France."

Kronstadt stood up and made his way over where the minister was standing. They shook hands.

"Okay, then…. This one last time."

"That settles it. We'll have the three airmen in Albert's truck by oh-four-thirty hours tomorrow. They should be in France by Saturday."

As Pastor Mueller walked toward the front door he stopped and asked, "You don't want to know the details of how Wolf was killed?"

"Just as long as he's in hell, what difference does it make?"

"Well, from what one of those officers said, he was killed by a sniper's bullet."

"Yes? How do they know that?"

"Apparently, he was raping a young Russian soldier, and the sniper saw him and killed him."

"So, not only was he a miserable Nazi sonofabitch, he was a miserable Nazi *homosexual* sonofabitch."

"Klaus, Wolf gave queers a bad name…."

"Good evening, Pastor. And remember—the last time!"

"Yes, Klaus—the last time!"

IN FRONT OF THE FORMER AMERICAN EXPRESS OFFICE
41 RUE GAMBON, PARIS
MONDAY, 18 OCTOBER 1943. 16:15 HOURS

The afternoon rainstorm that started an hour ago was beginning to fade. Although the precipitation was probably welcomed by most Parisians, for Brigitte LaFoche it likely meant that her 1700-hours meeting with André Tollet would be late. The slender, five-six blonde looked at her watch.

If I stay here much longer, I won't be able to get back home before the eighteen-hundred hours curfew. Damn, how I hate that curfew! For Parisians to have to be off the streets by eighteen-hundred hours—such a travesty!

She lit up her last Gitane, and recalled the events that had occurred in Paris since the Vichy swine surrendered it in June, 1940.

At first, life was almost normal. Everyone made adjustments, but life went on. That all changed after the military commander of Nantes was killed. First, we had military patrols, and then came this fourteen-hour curfew. But we found ways to work around it ... then that Boche General von Stumpage offered a fifteen million francs reward for his killers and promised to murder fifty Frenchmen in two days if we didn't turn over who killed that swine. From then on, everything has turned to shit.

If that wasn't enough, look what they've done to the Jews! They began rounding them up on February first, 1942—the same day the Brits bombed the Renault factories in Boulogne-Billancourt. God, what a tragedy! Five hundred innocent Frenchmen dead!

Taking another drag from her cigarette, LaFoche looked up and down the street. Nobody was coming from either direction. She slipped back into her private thoughts.

Next, the Franc Tireur and French Partisan Movement killed those German officers. It served those Boche pigs right....

As Brigitte leaned against the former American Express Office door, she took one last drag from her smoke, then tossed it into the rain-filled gutter. Brigitte cursed the German occupiers again. Looking to her right, she thought she recognized her contact. Still too far away to be certain, Brigitte wondered aloud if perhaps the older, grey-haired woman carrying a *baguette* and a bottle of red wine was, in fact, *Madame* Roberre.

In her late fifties, *Madame* Roberre worked for Paul Rivet—the clandestine publisher of the anti-*Nazi* paper, *Resistance*, from the basement of the Museè de l'Homme.

Now recognizing Roberre, Brigitte greeted her.

"*Bonjour, madame.* It appears the rain is about to leave us soon."

"May it take the *Boche* with them." *Madame* Roberre suggested, smiling and hugging Brigitte.

"Any news from the Resistance? Brigitte asked.

"Nothing that you would open your last bottle of Napoleon cognac over," replied Marie Roberre. She reached down into her grocery bag.

"Captain André Dewavrin sends his love," she said, handing LaFoche a half-pint of strawberry jam.

"How in God's name did you come up with this?" Brigitte inquired. She quickly shoved the small jar into her purse.

"One has ways…," Roberre replied with a grin.

Brigitte LaFoche started to giggle. "Oh, *Madame* Roberre, if someone had told me four years ago that I would be so happy to get a half-pint of strawberry jam, I would have told him to lay off the champagne. And, now, look at us! The damned Germans have been here since twenty-two June, nineteen-forty, and it doesn't look like we're going to see them thrown the hell out of France for at least another year…."

"That's probably true, darling," the older woman replied. "But savor these days. Remember them well. When the time comes that these bastards have all been chased back to Germany, days like today will have meaning. And, I can assure you—that day is coming."

Brigitte started walking toward her flat. *Madame* Roberre followed her.

"So, what does André want?" Brigitte asked softly.

Looking over her shoulder to make sure that no one was within hearing distance, *Madame* Roberre replied, "The British are requesting help with some downed American bomber crews that were shot down two days ago. They contacted the Great Dane[1], Jean Vinzant, via the wireless yesterday afternoon."

Brigitte and *Madame* Roberre were now approaching LaFoche's flat. Both resistance fighters scanned the area one more time, checking to see if they were being followed.

Once they both had concluded they weren't, Brigitte got out her key and unlocked the door to the three-story building. Neither spoke as they hurried up the staircase.

Once inside LaFoche's apartment, Brigitte turned on her wireless. The French Symphony was playing a piece of Beethoven's work. While LaFoche agreed the piece was beautiful, she nevertheless longed to hear something by a French composer.

"Damned *Boche*," said *Madame* Roberre as she put her coat down over the back of a dining room chair. "You'd think a Frenchman had never written a note of music, the way they flaunt all those damned Kraut composers at us!"

---

1. Due to the treachery of many collaborationists, the French Resistance began to refer to other members by animal names; thus if one of their operatives were captured and tortured, the only names they could give were fictional.

Brigitte ignored Roberre's comment, because ever since Brigitte had been introduced to her at the *Mussée de l'Homme* by Paul Rivet, she'd never heard the middle-aged bookkeeper say anything even remotely positive about the *Nazis*. In fact, Marie Roberre harbored a virulent hated for them.

Brigitte sat down one of the divans in the small flat, and kicked off her wet shoes. Now she got down to business.

"What do you have for me, Marie?"

"The Great Dane says that the Americans had numerous planes shot down over Schweinfurt a couple of days ago. They suspect most of the flyers were killed. But our operatives inside Germany report that one B-17 crashed near Kaiserslautern, and that the *Nazis* only found seven bodies inside the wreckage.

"We have people near there. According to them, the flyers should be in Vichy within the next few days. The Great Dane wants you to get them back to England."

"Are they coming in the same manner?"

"My God, I can't believe the *Boche* are that stupid. Imagine, bringing them out on German trucks!"

Marie Roberre smiled. "There is a certain amount of poetic justice in the situation, if you think about it, yes?"

"I guess that makes as much sense as does anything in this war," Brigitte commented, as she stood up to make some tea.

"Anyway," Marie Roberre said, "Jean Vinzant asked me to see if you'd be willing to make another trip home to see your 'woefully ill aunt?'"

Brigitte laughed. "You know, if the Huns ever find out that my Aunt Pauline lives in St. Lo, my goose will be pâté!"

"But you will do it? Correct?" Roberre inquired.

"I'll leave as soon as I can get the proper paperwork from those dolts in Sécurité," Brigitte said, as she opened *Madame* Roberre's bottle of red wine and poured two glasses full.

Brigitte sat back on the divan and began thinking aloud. "I will do it this last time. But we have to come up with another route. This will be the fourth group of American flyers we've smuggled out on the truck convoy. I'm afraid that somebody is going to get careless and slip up—and all the contacts we have inside Germany will pay a horrible price for helping us."

"The Great Dane said the same thing last night," Roberre said, finishing her glass of wine. She stood up, retrieved her overcoat and made her way to the door.

But before leaving LaFoche's flat, she turned and said, "When you get back, stop by *Museè de l'Homme* and say hello to Jean. He keeps asking about you."

After the other French Resistance agent left, Brigitte sat back down on her divan and poured another glass of the Rhône wine that *Madame* Roberre had left behind. She sniffed its bouquet, smiled, took a sip. The wine tasted so good, that for a brief moment her mind wandered back to her youth. She remembered how her family used to congregate at her Uncle Jacques' small hillside vineyard near Lyon to help him harvest his grapes that made such spectacular Rhône wine.

And now we have the *Boche*!

Brigitte took another sip of wine, then started to think about her mission.

CAFÉ PARISIAN
41 RUE LYON, ROTTLESHEIM, FRANCE
20 OCTOBER 1943. 14:15 HOURS

For late October, today's weather was unseasonably warm. Warm enough for Brigitte and her younger sister, Catherine, to sit with their father and eat lunch *al fresco*. The trio were finishing their bowls of vegetable soup and eating the last of a crusty French *baguette*.

Brigitte longed for a slab of butter. But she knew that such a luxury was not to be, anytime soon. How she longed for liberation!

Although the trio was alone, Brigitte lowered her voice then asked her father when he thought the Allies were going to invade the Continent.

The man laughed. "Brigitte, how could I possibly know the answer to that question? We can only hope it is soon. But, I can say this: last week I delivered some of our potatoes to the German garrison in Kreigsheim. One of the cooks over there heard two high-ranking German officers talking about when they thought the Allies would invade, and according to him, Berlin thinks it will come sometime next summer. But, that could be sheer speculation, too. After all, how would a German colonel in Paris know when the Allies are coming? Personally, I doubt if even General Eisenhower knows the exact date yet!"

"We can only pray to God," Catherine said, as she saw a waiter approaching, "that it happens soon. I am so damned sick of the *Nazis* I could spit!"

Brigitte looked up and recognized the young waiter coming to their table. "Pierre, it's so good to see you. When was the last time we saw each other?"

"The summer before the *Boche* came," he replied, handing her a scrap of paper.

His action seemed odd to everyone at the table, as common etiquette dictated that a meal bill be given to the man of the table.

"How long have you been working here?" *Monsieur* LaFoche inquired.

"My aunt hired me three days ago. Henrí was taken away by the Gestapo...."

As Brigitte's former high school friend started to pick up the dishes, he handed another piece of paper to her father. It was the bill for their meal.

"My aunt wishes to know if you would like to deduct this meal from the potatoes she owes you?

"*Ouí*. That would be fine with me, Pierre," Brigitte's father said, signing his name to the paper.

"I'll tell her, and I hope to see all you back very soon. Who knows, maybe we might even have something other than vegetable soup and baguettes."

The trio got up from the table and began walking toward the LaFoche family's farm.

"Brigitte," her sister asked, "What was in the note? Did Pierre ask you out?"

"I don't know. But I will let you know as soon as we get home."

The trio walked in a leisurely manner the half-kilometer to the LaFoche farm. Once inside the house, Brigitte opened the note and read it:

Brigitte: The postman left three packages for you with Father Frenay today. Please pick them up after Mass. They are a bit roughed up; one may need to be repaired.
Signed,
Marie Duboí

The American aircrew has arrived. But why here, in Rottelsheim?

Not wanting to expose her family to danger from her involvement in the French Resistance, Brigitte looked at her sister and changed the subject.

"Catherine, if you are interested in Pierre, you should pursue him, as his note asks about you."

Brigitte's father suspected his oldest daughter was up to her eyeballs in resisting the *Nazis*, but went along with Brigitte's story nevertheless.

Turning to Catherine, he said, "I guess if you are interesting in marrying Pierre, you'd better have soup with me at the café more often."

Catherine blushed, but did not reply.

TWO HOURS LATER
IN FRONT OF ST. CECELIA'S CHURCH,
ROTTELSHEIM, FRANCE

Brigitte was suffering from a colossal sense of guilt. She hadn't been to confession in over a year. In fact, the last time she even set foot into a church had been last Christmas Eve. She hoped God would understand.

She glanced at her watch. The mass would be ending at any moment. As she began rumbling around in her purse for a cigarette, she heard someone coming from inside the parish church. Turning around, she saw Father Frenay along with a few elderly parishioners coming out of the eighteenth-century wood building.

Father Frenay saw Brigitte sitting on the steps of the church, and began making small talk with her.

"*Bonjour, mademoiselle.* What brings you out this evening?"

"I was out for an evening walk, Father, and stopped to have a cigarette."

"If you have one to spare, I would like one also, *veuillez….*"

Brigitte reached into her purse and handed the priest her package of Gitane cigarettes. But before the Catholic clergyman could light up, an elderly Frenchwoman began to cackle at him.

"Father Frenay, those things are what killed my Pierre. You should not be smoking them."

"*Ouí, Madame* Buissonet, I will take that under advice and ask for forgiveness tonight before I go to bed."

The old lady laughed, "Spoken just like my Pierre, you rascal!"

When the last of the evening's communicants had left the church, Father Frenay changed the subject.

"Your packages are in Claude Montague's barn. I will walk over there with you."

"Are they in good order?"

"Two of them are in exceptionally good condition, considering how far they have come," the small-framed Catholic priest replied. "But the third one is my concern. It's a bit banged up, but Sister Celeste has been working on it all afternoon... and I dare say it should be ready to be moved again in one or two days."

The two resistance fighters walked casually down the old town's main street, *Rue du Rottelsheim*. They turned left at Boulevard Merlot and continued on a dirt path until they came to an old farmhouse. Once on the property, they walked up to an old barn and knocked softly.

"Sister Celeste? It's me, Father Frenay."

The barn door began to open slowly. Brigitte and Father Frenay scurried in, pulling the door closed behind them as soon as they were inside.

"How are they tonight, sister?"

"Considering that they spent a day in the back of a German truck being bounced all over creation without food or water, I would say they are just fine, Father. However, the short one could use a few more days' rest before traveling."

From the shadows of the barn's north wall, two American flyers stood up and made their way into the lantern light, toward the three French Resistance agents. Kennedy and Cantrell got there first. Weitzman was pretty banged up, having spent three hours hanging from his parachute in a tree before Cantrell and Kennedy found his landing place and cut him down.

Looking haggard but smelling worse, Kennedy attempted to brush some of the hay out of his hair to make himself presentable to Brigitte LaFoche. As they inched closer to where she stood, Kennedy said in French,

"My name is Sean Kennedy, and these two men are the only ones besides me that survived a bombing raid a few nights ago over Schweinfurt."

Brigitte smiled at Sergeant Kennedy, then walked over to where Silky Cantrell and Sol Weitzman were standing. She put her arms around them and replied in English.

"My name is Brigitte La Foche. Do you two gentlemen speak French as well as Mr. Kennedy?"

Although he was pretty banged up from bailing out of the *Nulaid Queen*, Sol Weitzman managed a quick response.

"Young lady, I believe a drunken German pig could speak better French than Sergeant Kennedy."

Silky Cantrell joined their conversation.

"Pleased to meet you, Brigitte. I understand you are going to get us back to England. Is this true?"

Brigitte smiled, telling the three American flyers that to the best of her ability she would make every effort to get them back to England. And, that she had already done so several times. She complimented them on their impeccable French and suggested that whenever possible they continue to speak to her in *Francais*. But that when the four of them were alone, she understood English quite well enough.

All three flyers smiled in acknowledgement. Brigitte thanked Sister Celeste and Father Frenay for their assistance, then told them she would take it from here on.

Sister Celeste smiled and said in a very faint voice, "Brigitte, honey, you can have them after I get the Jewish boy healthy, and not one minute before."

Sol Weitzman looked perplexed, then asked the older woman how she could possibly know he was Jewish. Still smiling, the little Catholic nun answered, "Three summers ago I spent two months in Miami visiting my sister. She married a doughboy after the last war and now resides in Florida. While I was visiting her she introduced me to many wonderful people—most of whom I suspect were Jewish—and you sound just like them, although your French is certainly superior to your two friends'."

Sol Weitzman smiled at her. "Guilty, as charged."

Sister Celeste replied, "I am going to change your bandages again tomorrow. You will sleep some more, and then the three of you will be leaving with 'Moses' once the final arrangements are made."

Sol looked over at Cantrell and Kennedy. "I guess that settles it. We're gonna be here for a while—like it, or not."

Silky Cantrell sat down on a small bale of hay and laughed. "That should give me just about enough time to fall in love with one of these lovely French babes."

Father Frenay choked back a laugh. "You know, you Americans took a lot of bad habits with you back to the States after the Great War. Perhaps you should consider behaving yourselves better, this time...."

Brigitte looked at Sean Kennedy. "Well, do you think you can control these two wild men for a week, or so?"

"Moses, I'm gonna issue the first of what may well be many commandments to my men: Thou shalt not screw with anything other than the Germans' minds."

Father Frenay shook his head and walked out of the barn, mumbling something about "blasphemers in Purgatory."

Sister Celeste looked over at the three airmen. "I will bring you some breakfast in the morning. Keep quiet, and stay inside this barn all day tomorrow. Do not go outside for any reason. If you have to use the toilet, use a bucket. And *do not*, for God's sake, smoke in here!"

Now Brigitte smiled, and said she would return as soon as she secured some civilian clothes and the necessary traveling documents so that the trio might "visit their sick uncle in Calais."

"How do you know we have a sick uncle in Calais?" Cantrell asked, half-jokingly.

"All you Americans have the same Uncle—Uncle Sam."

Kennedy laughed then quipped, "I saw that one coming from a mile away."

"Good," Brigitte said. She then added, "Remember, do exactly as I say, and by this time next week you should be back with your squadron in England."

"Can't argue with that," answered Sol Weitzman.

Brigitte looked at him and smiled. "My Heavens—a Jew who doesn't argue."

Sol winked at her. "Moses, I guarantee we'll follow your directions precisely, as I don't have any desire to spend the next forty years wandering around the desert of Vichy France trying to find the Promised Land."

Brigitte winked back at Sol, then strode over to the barn door and peeked out. It was not quite dark outside, so she quietly opened the door while softly calling to Sister Celeste to follow her out into the darkness.

The three American soldiers quickly found a corner in which they could comfortably hide themselves, and get some much-needed sleep.

CHAPTER EIGHT

*Only those who risk going too far can possibly know
how far one can go.*
—Anonymous

THE MONTAGUE FAMILY BARN, ROTTLESHEIM, FRANCE
SATURDAY MORNING, 23 OCTOBER 1943, DAWN

Sergeant First Class Sean Kennedy was finally about to drop off into fitful sleep when a rooster crowed inside the barn. Instinctively, he knew it was time to get up and get moving. He reached over and shook Silky Cantrell's arm.

"You awake?"

"I've been awake for the last two hours."

"Me, too," Weitzman said, as he stood up and brushed the straw off his uniform.

Looking over at Weitzman, Kennedy asked the inevitable question: "You ready to travel?"

"Well… to be honest with you, I've felt better. But we sure as hell can't stay here any longer. As it is, I think we've put these villagers in too much peril."

Kennedy stood up, shook the hay from his uniform, put on his hat and announced he was making a trip to the outhouse.

"Sister Celeste won't approve of that," Weitzman whispered under his breath.

"You're right…," Kennedy started to say, but stopped when he saw the Catholic nun entering the barn. She was carrying a bag that looked like it was for chicken feed. Once she was inside, the airmen could see that the "chicken feed" was in reality their breakfast.

"Good morning, Sister" the three airmen said in unison.

"Same to you, boys. I have some breakfast here. It's not much, but it's all I could manage without drawing too much attention from the other sisters at the convent.

"We understand, Sister." Sol added, "You don't think any of them would tell the Germans, do you?"

"They wouldn't, but I can't say the same for the other workers at the convent."

"Really, Sister?"

"Mr. Weitzman, when it comes to good and evil, absolutely nothing surprises me. Therefore, I suspect there are a few workers at the convent who would turn us in, if they thought it would get them some extra rations or special privileges."

"That's too bad," Kennedy said, peering inside the feedbag.

"Help yourself. There are some hard-boiled eggs you can take with you, and some toasted *baguette*. I wanted to get you some butter, but we don't have any—we haven't had any since the *Boche* took away our last cow, two months ago."

After a short prayer, the men began eating their breakfast. About half way through it, Brigitte entered the barn.

Sister Celeste looked at the three airmen, her eyes glistening. "Take care of yourselves, boys, and get back to England safely. I hope the next time we meet will be after this war is over. Then you can take me out to a real breakfast at some fancy restaurant in Strasbourg."

"You have a deal, Sister," Kennedy said, as he gave the old woman a hug and a kiss on the cheek.

Cantrell also hugged the old woman, as did Weitzman.

As Sol was about to pull away from embracing the nun, she whispered in his ear, "Next year—Jerusalem!"

"Amen to that, Sister."

Brigitte escorted the Catholic nun out of the barn, then sat down on a bale of hay.

"Here's the good news: your papers arrived yesterday and I managed to find you some clothing. The plan remains the same: the four of us are going to visit our 'very sick uncle' in Calais. His name is Henrí Pattique. He's an alderman in the Calais city government, and a "collaborator" of the first order with the Germans. So, if we get stopped by some overly zealous police official, or some *Nazi* swine, and they check with the Calais government, Henrí's family will vouch for us."

"That's brilliant, but what about Henrí?" Weitzman inquired.

"Not to worry, he's in on this, too!"

"Sounds workable to me," Kennedy said, nodding to his comrades.

Cantrell looked at Weitzman and then back to Kennedy. "It beats the shit out of sitting around this damned barn."

"Then it's settled," added Brigitte. We'll get a ride in the back of my father's wagon to the train station down in Krautwiller, a small village about three kilometers to the southwest. Father will be here in half an hour, or so."

"In the meantime, I'm heading to the outhouse," Kennedy said, and started to make his way out the back of the barn.

"I guess as long as Sister Celeste doesn't see you, go ahead." Brigitte smiled.

When Kennedy got back from the toilet, Brigitte spoke again. "I should tell you that, up until last night, my father only suspected that I was working in the Resistance. But I had to tell him this morning in order for him to give us a ride to the train station. His reaction was odd. He said he would have been disappointed, if I was not working in the Resistance."

"My father would agree," Weitzman stated. Silky Cantrell said his father would also expect him to take part in the Resistance.

"Most likely, at this time of the day no Nazi officials will be at the train station. But, don't worry, the one that works there is such a dullard, I doubt if he will even check our papers. But, if he does, your papers are valid documents, so it won't matter. Just act naturally, and cooperate with him. I suggest that we keep any talking to a minimum.

"Also, because it is Saturday, there are only two trains from Krautwiller—this early one and an afternoon train. The problem with the afternoon train is that it's the one all the collaborators and other non-desirables use. That's too bad, because it is more of an express than the one we're taking. I think you Americans would call this train's schedule a 'milk run,' since it stops almost twenty-five times before we get to Thionville."

Weitzman looked to Cantrell, then to Kennedy. "*Merd*, we'll have to stop twenty-five different times?"

"That's what Moses says, Weitzman. Besides, after getting no sleep last night, I think we need to try and get some shuteye. Let's leave the travel stuff up to Brigitte."

"That's a great idea, *Monsieur* Kennedy, because I have already made this particular journey numerous times. Just remember, your documents are valid. If we are stopped—and I don't think we will be—remember, we're in Vichy France. The Germans own the place. But they leave most of the day-to-day stuff to the French Quislings—of which there are thousands! So if you act a little put-out, okay. But be respectful, and they will think you are just another pissed-off Frenchman."

Cantrell was tiring of the conversation, so he asked Brigitte to describe their itinerary.

"The first big city we'll be going to is Saverne. There, we'll transfer to the train that goes to Freyming-Merebach. From there we go west to Metz, then we transfer to a train that goes north to Thionville. Now, for the record, Thionville is around one hundred-ninety kilometers from here, but with all these stops and delays, we probably won't get to Thionville until late this afternoon."

"Beats the hell out of walking," Cantrell said, as he swallowed his last piece of *baguette.*

Brigitte added, "Tomorrow is Sunday. No civilian trains run on Sunday."

"Is there much of a Resistance movement in Thionville?" Silky asked her.

"Well, if there is, I can't really say, for the obvious reasons. But, just so you'll know, the last time there was any Resistance in Thionville was when the *Boche* came through there in the last war."

"That's not good," Kennedy chimed in.

"Not to worry, though, the people we're staying with are true patriots. Unfortunately, I can't tell you who they are, right now... just in case we're captured by the Huns. But I can say they have been personally cleared by Jean Moulin."

"I don't have the foggiest idea who he is, but if you say they're okay, then they're okay with us, too." Kennedy stated the obvious. "And, as for us, if we're captured by the Huns, don't worry about us spilling the beans, because if the Germans catch us in civilian clothes they'll shoot us on the spot, as spies."

Brigitte looked at Kennedy and smiled, "So I guess it's up to me, to not get you shot!"

After a muffled laugh, the four started toward the barn's door. They were met by Brigitte's father, Jacque LaFoche.

"Good morning, gentlemen. Are you ready for a wagon ride?"

Cantrell answered, *"Monsieur, je monterais un chariot pàr l'enfer si j'arriverais de nouveau en Angleterre."* ["Sir, I'd ride a wagon through Hell if I thought it would get me back to England."]

KRAUTWILLER TRAIN STATION, KRAUTWILLER, FRANCE
SATURDAY MORNING, 23 OCTOBER 1943, 0645 HOURS, LOCAL

Just as Brigitte had suspected, the only one at the train station this early in the morning was a ticket agent, who not only knew Brigitte but also was a member of the Resistance.

As the quartet approached, he smiled at Brigitte and asked to see her ticket. He gave it a cursory once-over, then asked the other travelers for their tickets, which were produced. After giving the men a glance, he waved them toward the waiting train.

The four passengers found a section of seats that was open in second class, walked in, and sat down. The train started moving shortly afterward.

Although the three American aviators were utterly exhausted by their ordeal up to now, they found themselves fascinated by the scenery outside the windows, war or no war. They passed through the small towns of Hochfelden, Wilwisheim, Dettwiller, Gerieth and Monswiller, without a hitch. When they began to approach the city of Saverne, the train's ticketing agent came into their compartment.

Smelling as though he had not bathed in at least a week, the forty-something-year old man coughed, then spoke: "Good morning. Your tickets, please."

The quartet handed their tickets to the agent without saying a word. He looked at them briefly, then told Kennedy that the train they would be transferring to usually ran a half-hour late, and if they wanted one, there was a small café close-by the train station that served a descent breakfast. Just as he was about to leave, the man added, "And, should you go there, tell my brother Patrice I will be back this evening."

Answering in flawless French, Kennedy thanked him and said they would deliver his message if their train was late. The agent departed their compartment.

Within five minutes, the train began to slow.

"We're approaching the station. Get your luggage together, and try not to say anything to anyone at the station. This is a bigger city, and most likely the collaborators have it staffed with Nazi sympathizers." Brigitte quickly picked up her small bag.

"*Merd*!" Brigitte said as she looked out the compartment. The ticket agent was coming back their way, and with him were two brutes who looked like they would gladly kill their own mother for a *sous*.

"I wonder what the fuck he wants now?"

Before anyone could answer Brigitte's question, the ticket agent opened their door and stepped inside.

"I just checked with the engineer. Your train is on time this morning, but thank you for offering to deliver a message to my brother."

The agent then excused himself and started out the compartment. As he left, he mumbled, "Now, if I could find something to do with these two morons. Damned brother-in-law, anyway, expecting me to try to find these two dumb-asses jobs. The fucking army didn't even want them!"

After the door to their compartment closed, Weitzman started to laugh, saying that this incident was one he would surely write about when—and if—he got back to Miami.

The others broke out laughing with him, and they departed the train.

So far, so good.

STATION DE TRAIN DE FARÉBERSVILLER, VICHY FRANCE
SATURDAY, 23 OCTOBER 1943, 1805 HOURS LOCAL

Even though the calendar said it was late October, the temperature was still in the mid-sixties and the sunset was spectacular. The steady clickety-clack of the train had become so monotonous that it lulled Kennedy and Cantrell off to sleep.

Weitzman busied himself, looking out the train's windows at the bucolic scenery that was so prolific in this part of the Alsace-Lorraine area of France.

He longed for a corned-beef-on-rye sandwich, with a glass of ice-cold Falstaff beer. Sol began to chuckle quietly, thinking that after the war was over he would invite his mother, and the two of them would explore this region in true Weitzman style—first class, of course!

The train began to slow as it approached Farébersviller. The conductor walked through their car, and announced that this would be the last stop before they reached Freyming-Merlebach.

In French, Cantrell asked Brigitte how far Freyming-Merlebach was from their next stop. She replied that it wouldn't matter, as they were getting off at Farésbersville.

"Can I ask why?" Kennedy quizzed.

Taking command, Brigitte stated, "No. Just get off the train at separate intervals. Mr. Kennedy, you are my husband tonight, so you carry my luggage. You two," she said nodding at Weitzman and Cantrell, "are to follow about one hundred yards behind.

"Once we leave the station, follow us east down the *Rue du Moliere*, turn right and go east for two blocks to 414 *Rue du Dragon*. Remember, if anyone stops you, your papers are legitimate. Even if they take you to the local *Securité* office, be insistent about visiting your sick uncle in Calais. Got that?"

The airmen followed Brigitte's instructions precisely. When they'd arrived at 414 *Rue du Dragon*, the door opened and they stepped inside the two-story building.

A grey-haired woman wearing a tattered blue dress and a bluish shawl met the four inside the building. Quietly, she put her index finger to her mouth and motioned for them to follow her upstairs. On the second floor, the lady turned right, walked down two doors, and unlocked the room. Once inside, she closed the door quietly, walked over to her wireless, and turned it on. After a short period, the music of Mozart could be heard wafting throughout her flat.

"Now you may speak. But, please, take off your shoes and try not to walk around too much. I suspect the man who lives directly underneath is a stoolie for the collaborators."

Silky Cantrell took his shoes off, and reached out for Sol Weitzman's. After securing them, he walked softly over to the front door and set them down. Sean Kennedy sat on a divan and began unlacing his shoes.

"I'm afraid if I take them off I'll never get them back on," he said, standing up to place his shoes next to those of his compatriots.

Oddly, Brigitte took the shoes from him and put them down with the other soldiers' shoes.

"Thank you, but that wasn't necessary," he said, sitting down on the divan.

"What? A wife can't look after her husband?"

Kennedy looked puzzled until Brigitte reminded him that, tonight, they were "married."

Kennedy laughed and quipped, "Too bad that doesn't include a trip to the bedroom."

Sol Weitzman was shocked by Kennedy's comment. Sure, Brigitte was a babe, but for God's sake, there was a time and a place for everything, and he doubted very seriously if this was either.

However, Brigitte's answer stunned both of them. "Talk to me tonight, after we've eaten and had a glass or two of wine!"

Cantrell's right eyebrow nearly jumped off his face.

Damn! I think ol' Kennedy's gonna get laid tonight!

The old French woman re-entered the conversation. "Gazelle, can you wait until I have fed these men before you start carrying on so?"

Brigitte smiled. "Of course, Lioness."

The Lioness turned to Sol Weitzman. "Come to the kitchen with me, *monsieur*, and I'll tell you a thing or two about those bastards, the collaborators."

As Weitzman headed into the kitchen, the Lioness picked up a wine bottle and corkscrew and handed them to Cantrell. "Could you open this bottle of red I've been saving for a special occasion?"

Grinning, Cantrell replied, "I didn't learn too much from my father, but one thing I did learn was when a good-looking woman asks you to open a bottle of wine, you do as she says."

The Lioness smiled at Silky. "Save your bullshit for the whores in Paris, you handsome devil!"

Cantrell showed he could give as well as take. "You know, if you were just twenty years younger…."

The old lady guffawed at his offer. "If I were twenty years younger, it would take all three of you boys to take care of me. So, open the bottle of wine and let's drink up. Good God—a woman could die of thirst around here!"

With both Weitzman and Cantrell now in the kitchen with the Lioness, Kennedy moved closer to Brigitte. "You know, in America when a woman makes an offer like you just did, a man takes her up on it. Were you really serious about wanting to be together with me?"

Brigitte just smiled and said, "Since the minute I first saw you, back in Rottlesheim."

Kennedy pulled Brigitte closer to him and whispered to her, "I haven't been with a woman in over a year. But I can't think of anybody else in the world I'd rather change that with, tonight."

414 RUE DU DRAGON, FARÉBERSVILLER, VICHY FRANCE
SUNDAY, 24 OCTOBER 1943, 0445 HOURS LOCAL

After finishing off her "special" bottle of red wine, the Lioness found five more bottles and all of them proceeded to get tanked. Somewhere between the fourth and fifth bottle, Brigitte LaFoche and Sean Kennedy made their way out of the small flat and down the hall to another room whose tenant was away on business.

Later, after an evening spent in white-hot lovemaking, Sean Kennedy was exhausted. As he lay in bed next to Brigitte, Kennedy wondered just what was going to happen to him and his aircrew.

"Brigitte?" he asked, "What's next?"

Brigitte giggled. "*Monsieur* Kennedy, we've tried every position I know. You tell me."

Kennedy laughed. "Listen, even if I wanted to try it another way, I'm done for. Besides, what I meant was, what's next in getting us back to England?"

Mademoiselle LaFoche reached over onto a small dresser next to the bed, took a cigarette from a package and lit it up. After taking a puff, she said, "After breakfast we are going to start our journey to Calais in earnest."

"Are we getting back on the train?"

"No, even though the *cheminots* [French railway workers] are some of the most ardent supporters of the Resistance. It's just too risky in this part of Vichy. You see, just two months ago, French railway saboteurs blew up trains in Marseille, Saint-Amour, and Mâcon. My God, they blew up ten trains, many of them full of ammunition and troops. Along the Channel ports the Germans risk their lives, just being around a train.[1] But, that said, the Boche are checking the trains all the more. Therefore, for now we are going a different way. We try to change the route each time, to not set up a routine. You understand, don't you?"

"Sure I do," Kennedy admitted. "But that still doesn't answer my questions about what we're going to do today."

Brigitte took another drag off her smoke. "After we eat breakfast, we are going to be visiting a series of farmhouses. We will start with a short walk to Seingbouse, a small village just west of here. From there, we are going to

---

1. For an intensive study of the French Resistance during WWII, read *Soldiers of the Night – the Story of the French Resistance*, by David Schoenbrun, E.P. Dutton, N.Y., 1980. This information is found on page 319 of Mr. Schoenbrun's book.

catch a cart to Macheren. We will proceed northwest to a place called Saint-Avold. Our contact has arranged for an auto to Servigny-lès Sainte Barbe. Once we arrive there, we will then head up to Argancy, where we will spend the night at a nunnery operated by the Sisters of St. Chertienne."

"A nunnery, you say?"

"*Oui*, a nunnery. It has been around since 1807, and for some reason the collaborators have never questioned anything that has gone on inside its walls. So, once we get to Argancy, we are headed for the nunnery. There, we will be fed and given a place to sleep."

"I have to hand it to you, Brigitte, you surprise me every day."

"Good. I will make a deal with you, then. You surprise me once more with your manliness, and I will do my best to get you back to England by the first of November."

"*Mademoiselle*, your wish is my command!" Kennedy took the cigarette from Brigitte and inhaled deeply from it, then crushed it out in the ashtray. He began kissing and fondling Brigitte's breasts, passionately.

Fifteen minutes later, an exhausted Brigitte LaFoche sighed, and exclaimed, "You win! I will always remember your surprise."

Little could she have realized that night, the true significance of her words about Sean Kennedy's "surprise." For Brigitte LaFoche was now pregnant with his child. Nor could either have suspected that four decades later the pair would meet again—and that the next time it would be under much different, and far less turbulent, circumstances.

AN HOUR LATER, ON THE ROAD TO SEINGBOUSE

The walk over from Farébersviller to Seingbouse took less than thirty minutes. It was uneventful, but for the roads being slippery from the rain that had arrived the previous evening.

Looking off to the west, Sol Weitzman noticed the steeple from a small church in the middle of a village the quartet was nearing.

"I take it this is Seingbouse, Brigitte?"

"*Oui*, it is," she answered. Brigitte suddenly stopped walking, then motioned for them to come closer to her, a gesture Weitzman thought overly-cautious considering they were the only human beings within a quarter-mile. Once they were close, she began speaking. "Now, listen to me," she said, sitting on a two-tiered fence alongside the road. "We are going to enter the town in three groups. Silky, you go in first, and then Sol. Sean and I will meet you in front of that Catholic Church. Initially, we make eye contact only, no talking. Then you two strike up a small conversation. You know—the weather, *et cetera*. While you two are doing that, Sean and I will find the farmer who is going to give us a ride over to Macheren.

"In a half-hour, you two start walking out of town. It should take us no longer than half an hour to find the farmer. We will catch a ride with him, and when we see you on the road, he will stop and ask if you want a ride, saying, 'The ground is too wet to be walking this early in the morning.' From there, ask for a ride and then get in. Do not talk too much. All the old man knows is that I am in the Resistance. He will not know you are downed American pilots, and there is no need for him to find out. This way, if everything turns to *Merd*, he might be able to escape being tortured by some collaborating sonofabitch."

As it happened, the foursome ended up walking all the way to Macheren. Almost too late, Brigitte discovered from her contact that the farmer who was to give them the ride was in fact a collaborator, himself!

When she and Kennedy caught up with Weitzman and Cantrell, she was fuming.

"That collaborator son of a bitch! Hell is too good for him!"

Weitzman deadpanned, "I take it the lady is a wee-bit upset?"

"Upset? Hell no! I am fucking furious!" the former airline stewardess replied in street vernacular.

Then she continued, "If it hadn't been that *Monsieur* Kennedy needed to relieve himself, we would have been turned over to the *Securité* by that swine! God, we came so close."

Kennedy wiped the sweat from his brow. "It's true. I had to make a stop along the road, and piss. Apparently, because we weren't where we were supposed to be at the prescribed time, the old farmer took off, maybe figuring we had been tipped off, or something. Then, Brigitte scouted around and found another contact who told her the farmer had been collaborating with some of the Quislings at the *Ministère de sécurité* for the past year-and-a-half!"

"Needless to say, he will be dealt with by nightfall!" Brigitte spewed.

"So what's next?" asked Silky Cantrell.

"Give me a minute, let me think," LaFoche said, as she fumbled around in her bag for a cigarette.

After finding one and lighting it, she continued, "Saint Avold is about five miles from here. Are you men up for an extended walk on this beautiful fall morning?"

"Lead the way, princess," Cantrell said, as he relieved Brigitte of her cigarette and took a long drag from it.

"I didn't know you smoked, or I'd have offered you one," she replied.

"I don't, but I'm thinking about taking it up. Might calm this old Cajun's nerves."

"*Monsieur*, there is only one thing that will calm your nerves, and I am spoken for," LaFoche quipped, as they started walking northwest to the small burg of Saint Avold.

As the foursome approached Saint Avold from the east, Brigitte stopped suddenly.

"There's a problem up ahead."

"How do you know that?" asked Sol Weitzman.

"Without going into details," Brigitte said, "The Resistance has left me a message."

"They did?" Kennedy queried.

"Yes. Look at that cross alongside the road, on the right." Brigitte pointed to a small white, wooden cross about thirty feet from where they were standing. It was being propped up by a few small stones.

The three American soldiers stared at the cross.

"Okay, it's a cross," Cantrell said.

"True, but I can tell by the placement of the stones that we have been compromised."

Weitzman shook his head. To him, this cross was just like the others they'd seen on numerous occasions during their trek. Sol assumed that someone had died there, in either an auto accident or some other kind of mishap. He had no idea, whatsoever, that it was being used as a method of sending messages to members of the French Resistance. Apparently, the Germans did not either.

Brigitte moved closer to the cross, and examined the stones' placement very carefully.

"We continue our walk, but at noon we stop to eat at the *Café Orleans*. That will take an hour. Order simple food, and show no joviality, as we are going to mourn a family member who is being buried this afternoon at a cemetery outside town. The funeral procession will pass by the Orleans. When it does, we will get up and walk with it."

"You think that is going to fool those traitors in Saint Avold?" Weitzman asked.

"It's been done before," Brigitte replied, but offered no details.[2]

SAINT CECELIA'S CATHOLIC CHURCH
SAINT-AVOLD, FRANCE, 1300 HOURS, LOCAL

It was almost as if God ordained it. No sooner had Sol Weitzman slurped down his last teaspoon of chicken soup and eaten his last morsel of *baguette*, than the "funeral procession" passed right in front of the *Café Orleans*. As the retinue of mourners passed by, Brigitte hurriedly reached into her blouse and grabbed a few francs. She tossed the money on to the red-and-white checkered tablecloth, then covertly motioned the others to join her in the procession.

Weitzman was struck by the sincerity of the mourners. They were carrying on as if the entire charade was real.

These people should get an Academy Award for their performance!

At first, Brigitte kept her distance from any of the mourners. But out of the corner of her right eye she recognized a fellow compatriot. Gradually, she worked her way over to the older man. Keeping their voices very low, they appeared to get into an animated conversation.

As they talked, the look on Brigitte's face became more serious. Kennedy, Weitzman and Cantrell stayed back and kept to themselves. Soon, however, Brigitte beckoned them over, so the trio gradually made their way over to where she was walking. Once there, Brigitte said, "We have been double-crossed. This man is the farmer we were supposed to meet back at the village. He informs me that, just before we get to the cemetery, we are to be picked up by the *Securité* forces."

"How do you know he's telling the truth?" Cantrell asked pointedly.

"Because he gave me a codeword from the Great Dane himself."[2]

"Who?" Kennedy asked.

"One of France's finest freedom fighters, a man I would die for," Brigitte replied. "*Monsieur* Léon, here, gave me a password that he could only have got directly from the Great Dane."

"So, what do we do now, Brigitte?"

"We are going to drop out of this funeral procession when it turns right. Follow *Monsieur* Léon, and say nothing as you leave this funeral."

About fifteen feet farther down the road, *Monsieur* Léon made an abrupt turn down an alley. Silky Cantrell followed, then Sol Weitzman. When Ken-

---

2. Weil-Curiel, an early French Resistance leader, escaped in such a manner in 1940 from a house in Brittany that was being watched by the *Gestapo*. D. Schoenbrun, page 111.

nedy started to make the turn, Brigitte pulled on his left sleeve with sufficient strength to keep him from following his comrades.

"Why did you do that?" Kennedy asked indignantly.

"Insurance," Brigitte replied.

"What the hell?" Kennedy said, miffed over Brigitte's act.

He was just about to call her on it again, when she opened the door of a house and pulled him inside after her. Kennedy was determined to find out just what the hell was happening. He was about to say something, when Brigitte pulled a switchblade from her stocking and snapped it open.

"Go out that back door and see if everything is alright with your friends," she commanded.

By now, Kennedy figured there must be some method to her madness. So he stepped outside. There he met the three men. Nothing seemed out of the ordinary. Then Brigitte exited the house, while covertly stuffing the switchblade back into her stocking.

"Is everything alright, *Mademoiselle?*" asked *Monsieur* Léon.

"*Oui.*"

As the old farmer stood there, a smile came across his face. "I guess one can never be too careful, when it comes to the Quislings one must deal with."

"Sorry, but I can't be too careful," Brigitte answered.

"That is a good thing, *Mademoiselle*," Léon said, then added, "And no offense taken, either."

Kennedy walked over to Brigitte. "Sorry for doubting you. I should've figured out by now, that your only desire is to get us back to England alive. I guess my problem is that you don't tell me your plans. But, now that I think about it, I realize you can't!"

"Sorry, Sean, but you're right. The Resistance is so infiltrated with traitors and pro-fascists that one simply cannot trust anyone."

Now Silky Cantrell came into the conversation. "I know you speak the truth, Brigitte, but it sure doesn't say much for Frenchmen. I mean, one would think that all Frenchmen would be working overtime to rid France of the Krauts."

"Perhaps, one would think…," Brigitte replied. "But, look… Vichy is cooperating with Berlin as if they were cousins. My God, look who Pétain appointed as the Minister of Justice—that pig, Raoul Alibert! He is more of a fascist than Mussolini! And Pétain is no better, because he has allowed Alibert to bring up Paul Reynaud, Léon Blum and Edouard

Daladier [former French premiers] and Army commander Gamelin, on trumped-up charges." [3]

Monsieur Léon added, "I will go you one better. My wife went to school with a girl named Germaine Tillion. Germaine and her mother were involved with the patriots at the *Musée de L'Homme*, until Gaveau sold them out. After that, the two continued to work for the Resistance until last August. And do you know who turned them in?"

"No idea," Kennedy admitted.

"What if I told you it was none other than the vicar of the parish of la Varenne—Abbé Alesch, himself!"

"Are you saying their parish priest turned them in?" asked Sol Weitzman.

"Not to worry," the old farmer answered, adding, "Once the *Boche* are gone, we will deal with that 'man of the cloth.'" [4]

"I have no doubt you'll do that," Cantrell said. "And, if you need any help to tie the noose, I'll gladly volunteer."

"I appreciate your offer," *Monsieur* Léon replied, "but the truth is that we won't need help to take care of all Quislings and collaborators once this war is over.

"But, back to my story. The mother of my wife's friend was sent to some German hellhole. As for Germaine, she is tough, and if anyone survives this war, I am sure she will. But her mother? I doubt it…. [5]

Weitzman came back into the conversation. "It's hard for me to believe that your friends were sold out by their own priest."

"Yes. But what is really sad, is that the Catholic Church has dozens of vermin just as bad as the Abbé. Germaine did her best to try to secure the release of some prisoners. In doing so, she went to the archbishop of Paris, and got nothing! In fact, she came away believing that the man was a raving lunatic.

"But, the corruption within the Catholic Church does not stop there, as the man in charge of the Catholic Institute, Cardinal Baudrillard, is a *Nazi*-sympathizing swine. He has appointed a sadistic sonofabitch named Canon Tricot as his secretary!

"It seems there is always another bastard willing to sell out France for thirty pieces of silver. Some day—God knows when—I will piss on their

---

3. Schoenbrun, page 65.
4. Schoenbrun, page 121. The Abbé was captured after the Liberation, tried and executed for his treachery.
5. Germaine Tillion survived the war; however, her mother did not.

graves!"

Weitzman and Cantrell looked at the old man. "I guess we know where *Monsieur* Léon stands, when it comes to traitors!"

Brigitte put out her cigarette and glanced toward the four men. "We can not stay here. But I know of a barn that we can stay in, that is very close. We will use it for the night. Once we are settled, *Monsieur* Léon will go out and buy some food. Later this afternoon, I am going to attempt to make contact with someone in the Resistance.

"I do not wish to alarm you, gentlemen, but it seems that the traitors are getting too close for comfort. It is true, we are in great danger. But enough is enough. I am going to try to contact someone with a radio, to see if the British have an aeroplane available."

"Do you think that's possible, Brigitte?" inquired Sean Kennedy.

"I will find out. Otherwise, we have to keep moving toward Calais."

IN A BARN NEAR SAINT AVOLD, VICHY FRANCE
MONDAY, 25 OCTOBER 1943, 1855 HOURS LOCAL

"Any sign of her yet?" Weitzman asked, as he walked over to the barn door and peered out through the cracks.

"Not yet," Silky Cantrell replied, scratching the back of his neck.

"I hope nothing has happened to her...." *Monsieur* Léon licked his spoon from dinner, and sat down on a bale of hay.

"She'll be here," Kennedy said, as he hoisted the bottle of red wine *Monsieur* Léon had purchased earlier that afternoon in the village. "But if you ask me when, I wouldn't be able to say. But, knowing Brigitte, she'll be back."

"Not to worry," Cantrell said quietly. "She just jumped off a wagon and is walking down the road toward Saint Avold."

"Why is she walking toward Saint Avold, for God's sake? We're over here." Weitzman felt stupid after asking the question. "Damn, I wouldn't be for shit in the spy business. She's obviously going toward town to make sure nobody's following her. I suspect she'll be back in a few minutes."

The old French farmer laughed. "Weitzman, you of all people should not question her ability to find a location. Hell, didn't your people wander around the Sinai Desert for forty years before you got to Palestine?"

"Yes. But there's more to that story than the fact the Jews wandered around for forty years, you know."

"I do. And I also know that the only two who got to go to the Promised Land were the ones who trusted God," Léon answered, giving a little tug at Weitzman's shirt collar.

Sol sat down on a bale of hay and looked the old man in the eye. "What do you say to having dinner with me in Miami, after this war is over? I know a great Cuban restaurant there."

"You got a deal, Weitzman. Dinner for four in Miami, after the war. Let's say, one year after the Nazis surrender?"

"Four? How do you get four?"

You and your wife, and me and my wife—that's four of us!"

Weitzman laughed. "Guess I'd better find a wife as soon as I get home, then."

"What? Are you telling me you are not married? I cannot believe that. A Jewish man who is not married. Why, it's the Eighth Wonder of the World."

"My mother says the same thing," Weitzman said, scratching the top of his head. He looked over at Kennedy. "God, I desperately need a bath, a shave and some descent sleep. You, too?"

From the back of the barn, Brigitte said, "Hold that thought, *Monsieur* Weitzman. With any luck at all, by this time tomorrow you should be in England."

Kennedy rushed over to Brigitte and kissed her. "How in the hell did you manage that?"

"State secret. But I made contact with some people in the Resistance, and, as it turns out, the Americans are dropping an agent in a field two miles from here. All we have to do is to walk there and hide out in the woods until 0230 hours."

"I don't get it, Brigitte," commented Silky Cantrell. "You say the Americans were dropping in an agent in the morning. That means by a parachute. How the hell are we going to get to the plane?'

"My contact was able to reach his contact in London via the wireless. The London contact verified his call signs, and the packages to be delivered. According to my contact, London planned to get you out via the Normandy coast. But that area is swarming with *Nazi* agents, so they decided to go ahead and 'land their cargo' and pick you boys up."

"Can you believe that, Kennedy? Weitzman asked. "We're getting the hell out of here, tonight!"

"So, I guess all we need to do now is to gather our things, say goodbye to *Monsieur* Léon, go for a short walk and wait for our transportation," Kennedy said as he dropped Brigitte's hand.

"Not quite so fast," Léon said. "You don't get rid of me until I see your plane in the air."

"This is how we're going to do it," Brigitte said. "This time, Kennedy and *Monsieur* Léon will go first. Then Weitzman, alone. Cantrell and I will come last. There is a small clump of trees at the north end of the field. That is where we will gather in three hours. We will meet some other Resistance people there. Let me do the talking. You three stay in the shadows. No one needs to know you are there. The only thing they'll need to know is that there are some outbound passengers waiting."

AT THE NORTH END OF A FIELD JUST OUTSIDE THE VILLAGE OF SAINT AVOLD, VICHY, FRANCE TUESDAY, 26 OCTOBER 1943, 0200 HOURS LOCAL

One might think that, at this hour of the morning, with the temperature down in the low forties and the area crawling with traitors and collaborators, that SFC Sean Kennedy would be more concerned about his personal safety than his desire for a cigarette. However, now it was all he could think about—smoking a cigarette. He debated asking Brigitte for one, but that was impossible because she was meeting with a group of partisans on the other side of the field.

He also knew better than to light up a smoke, because a cigarette could be seen for hundreds of yards on such a clear night.

Inwardly, he was glad that Brigitte was with the partisans—it would make saying goodbye much easier. He thought she must have planned it this way. The truth of the matter was that Brigitte was having a very intense argument, although a quiet one, with the local leader of the Resistance. She was demanding that they come up with a better system of getting downed pilots out of France.

Her counterpart kept saying that she had exposed this local cell to an inordinate amount of danger, just by bringing the three Allied airmen there.

LaFoche was doing her best not so slap the woman with whom she was talking, but her arrogance was too much.

"Do you think I planned it this way, Collette?" Brigitte asked firmly.

"No, of course not, but the *Boche* and the traitors are everywhere."

"I know that! Hell, we've almost been caught three or four times over the past few days. So, do not lecture me. Remember, I am the point of contact to get these men back to England! Or have you forgotten that?"

One of the older men in the group came over to where the two women were standing.

"Ladies, let's not fight over this. We are here to receive the 'package' from England and the supplies he's bringing—and to get these three brave airmen back home."

"You're right, Henrí," Brigitte said, as she apologized to her counterpart. "But after this mission is complete, let's all get together somewhere and work on other ways to get these downed soldiers back to England."

"You have my word on it, Brigitte," Henrí replied, as he pulled his collar closer in an attempt to keep out the night's bitter chill.

Across the field, Silky Cantrell was having a very quiet conversation with *Monsieur* Léon. Cantrell told him about his experiences growing up in the bayou country of Louisiana, about alligator hunting, fishing for catfish and his love of Dixieland jazz.

"After we rid France of the *Nazis*, the missus and I would like to come and visit the States," the farmer proposed.

"*Monsieur* Léon, you tell me when, and I'll make the arrangements. Come and stay for as long as you want. But you must leave your wallet at home."

"You don't have to do that," Léon protested.

"To do otherwise would be an affront to Southern hospitality. But I have to warn you—my family does not speak any kind of French that you'll understand."

"What do you mean?" the old man questioned. To him, French was French. He had never heard of any variation on the language.

"Well, my family was booted out of Arcadia after the French lost the Seven Years War.[6] They were sent down to Louisiana, where, in order to survive, they took up fishing, hunting alligators and making whiskey. They were the 'salt of the earth,' so to speak.

"As it turns out, the Americans down there couldn't pronounce 'Arcadians,' and started calling them 'Cajuns.' The French they spoke eventually gave way to Cajun French—a combination of "colonial" French, Acadian French and Creole French.

"When I took French in high school, I had to start all over. Every once

---

6. The terms of the Treaty of Paris (1763) specified that the French had to leave Nova Scotia. Upwards to 75% were shipped to Louisiana. It is known as the Great Expulsion.

in awhile I do slip up, though."

"I noticed that, a couple of times. But I didn't say anything, as I didn't want to draw attention to you."

Now Léon began looking up at the sky.

At first, Cantrell wondered what the old farmer was doing. Then, he heard what he thought was an airplane engine in the distance.

Could it possibly be?

Monsieur Léon looked at Silky Cantrell. "I think you Americans would say, 'the cavalry has just arrived.'"

"Oh, Sweet Jesus!" Silky almost shouted. He walked over to where Weitzman was sleeping, leaned down and touched his comrade on the shoulder.

"*Qu'est-ce que c'est cette connerie?*" ["Who the fuck is that?"]

"*Un telle langue!*" ["Such language!"] Silky half-scolded his friend.

"*Aller à l'enfer!*" ["Go to Hell!"] Weitzman replied, reluctantly awakening from a deep slumber.

"*Alors, vous prendriez l'Angleterre?*" ["Would you prefer English, instead?"]

Switching to English, Sol Weitzman said, "Is that what I think it is?"

"If by 'that' you mean an airplane, Sol—well, I believe you're right!"

Uncharacteristically, Weitzman announced, "Let's saddle up."

Léon looked at Silky Cantrell. "See, I was right!"

Silky walked back to the old French farmer. "Remember—when this damned war is over, come see me."

"How will I contact you?"

"Everybody in New Orleans knows my family. We're the biggest liquor distributors in all of Louisiana—Cantrell's Beverages."

The old farmer hugged the two airmen. He had tears in his eyes.

"Go with God, gentlemen. We will see you when this war is over!"

Kennedy walked over to where the trio was standing. He was about to say something when he noticed a dozen or so figures scampering onto the field. Soon there were ten small fires burning—marker fires, to guide the plane in to a safe landing.

As Kennedy looked up, he saw a signal light blink three times.

"It's coming in!" He saw Brigitte running across the field. She was breathless.

"That plane should land about a hundred meters from where we're standing. As soon as it stops rolling, you three run like hell and get inside.

This area is swarming with traitors."

The plane was an American Beech C-45. Known as the "Expeditor," it was a common utility transport used by the Allies for just such missions as this.

As the plane touched down, the fires that delineated its runway were instantly extinguished. It stopped rolling about a hundred-thirty meters from where the men were standing. The moment the side door swung open, the three soldiers began running with all their might toward it.

As they did, bullets started flying from a grove of trees on the other side of the field.

"Sonofabitch!" Kennedy swore, as a round pierced his right leg. He staggered a step or two, then fell to the dirt.

At the sound, Cantrell and Weitzman turned. Seeing their comrade down, they ran back to where he was lying.

"Leave me here! Get on that plane!" Kennedy ordered.

"With all due respect," Weitzman answered, "Fuck you, Kennedy, you're coming with us. We're not leaving you here to play house with Brigitte! So get your ass up, and come on!"

Kennedy couldn't help but smile, despite the pain, the blood and the flying bullets.

"Okay. Let's get the hell out of here!"

The two men reached down, pulled Kennedy up off the ground, and started half-dragging him. Stumbling along, every time Kennedy's right foot hit the ground, pain shot through his body.

As the three moved rapidly toward to the C-45, it began turning into the wind.

"No you don't, you sonofabitch!" yelled Weitzman.

"You can't leave us here, you bastard!" Cantrell screamed.

As soon as the plane had swung around and had a clear path for takeoff, the pilot began gunning its engines.

The trio limped and ran with all the strength they could muster.

More bullets came zinging in their direction.

Cantrell was winged in the right arm. He dropped Kennedy to the ground.

"Leave me," Kennedy said. "Go!"

"Screw you, you're coming with us!" Cantrell shouted.

They were now only about twenty yards from the plane, when a crew-member stuck his head out the door and shouted, "Hurry the fuck up, we can't wait all night!"

At that, all the adrenaline the three men had left exploded. With one last, mighty effort they dashed to the airplane and dragged themselves inside.

The instant the side door was slammed shut, the pilot applied full power to the plane's twin 450-horsepower, Pratt and Whitney R-9865-AN-14B Wasp Junior engines. After a harrowing, bone-jarring takeoff run down the rutted pasture, the C-45 took to the sky and soon it was out of range of the Vichy collaborators' guns, winging its way over coastal France and across the English Channel.

As the plane banked and climbed, the crew chief broke out the plane's medical equipment. He managed to stem Kennedy's bleeding, gave him a shot of morphine, and not long afterward SFC Kennedy surrendered to unconsciousness.

Cantrell was patched up and given a welcome shot of bourbon.

The three grateful but thoroughly exhausted American flyers slept soundly the rest of the night. On waking the next morning, they were met by an ambulance on the tarmac at Headquarters, 305th Bomber Group, 8th Air Force, Chelveston, England.

CHAPTER NINE

All the Axis are hearing is the tolling of the bells, and we are doing the rope pulling....
—attributed to Admiral "Bull" Halsey, U.S.N.

AT THE DINING TABLE OF MR. & MRS. SEAN KENNEDY, SR.
VOLCANO ROAD, SUTTER CREEK,
AMADOR COUNTY, CALIFORNIA
THANKSGIVING DAY, 1991. 10:30 P.M.

After Mr. Kennedy had finished relating his story, Sean Ohara looked over at Brigitte LaFoche and said, "Obviously, you survived that ambush. How long did it go on, and how did you avoid getting killed or being taken prisoner?"

The Frenchwoman held Sean's hand a moment before replying.

"The shooting lasted for almost twenty minutes. Before it was over, we lost two partisans killed and three wounded—*Monsieur* Léon being one of them. He almost died, but we got him back to the Sisters of St. Chertienne and they nursed him back to health.

"The next day the *Boche* came into the town, and executed ten villagers in retribution."

"Bastard *Nazis*!" the teenager said, as he slammed his right fist into the palm of his left hand.

"I won't argue with that," Brigitte replied, "but the truth of the matter is that the *Nazis* did that sort of crap all the time. Before the weekend is over, have *Monsieur* Dannenberg tell you what they did at Oradour. If I could, I would. But every time I think about what they did there, I get so worked up that my blood pressure goes through the roof."

All the guests agreed, and started to make their way to their respective bedrooms. As they were walking, Colonel Ohara stopped Mr. Kennedy. "When I was in Vietnam, I thought your son told me you made it back from the Schweinfurt raid okay, but that you got shot up pretty badly on another raid three weeks later."

"He must have mixed up Schweinfurt with another mission," Kennedy responded.

"You were back up flying in three weeks?" the teenager asked.

"Yes. Actually, we were back up flying in ten days."

"Ten days?" Sean Ohara eyes were bulging in disbelief.

"We made our first flight ten days after getting back to England. It was on the third one back that the shit hit the fan. We lost two of our crewmembers, who got pretty shot up during a raid over Berlin."

"Were Cantrell and Weitzman with you on that raid?" Colonel Ohara asked.

"Yes, they were. Amazingly enough, neither one of them received a scratch. In fact, after that particular raid, General Jimmy Doolittle sent them both home to sell war bonds. Neither ever flew in combat again.

"Sol Weitzman moved back to Miami, married and taught French at the University of Miami until a few years ago. He has since passed away.

"Silky Cantrell moved back to Louisiana, took over his father's liquor distributorship, got married to a fiery, red-headed Catholic girl, and had five children. He and *Monsieur* Léon became the best of friends, each traveling to the other's county until the old man passed on in 1976."

Brigitte looked at her son. "Jean-Pierre, are you ready to call it a day?"

"Mother, I think I will sit out on the porch for a few minutes longer, and smoke a cigar."

Dexter Dannenberg spoke up immediately, "Did someone say—'cigar?'"

"Guilty as charged, *Monsieur*," the Frenchman replied.

"Mind if I join you?" Dexter asked.

"Not at all. In fact, I have a couple of Cuban cigars I'd like to share with you."

"Lead the way, young man," Dexter said, grabbing the bottle of cognac and two snifters.

THE DINING ROOM OF MR. & MRS. SEAN KENNEDY SR.
THE NEXT MORNING, 9:30 A.M. LOCAL

After yesterday's adventure in gluttony, this morning most of the guests at the Kennedy breakfast table went easy on the food, despite the fact that

Chloe Ohara made eggs Benedict that were to die for. Most of the guests were satisfied with just one serving of Mrs. Ohara's *piece d'resistance*, accompanied by a cup of regular coffee.

That is, with the exception of Dexter Dannenberg, Jean-Pierre LaFoche, and his mother, Brigitte. Each ate ample servings of the eggs Benedict, along with two cups of coffee, and were now preparing to swill down a few bloody Marys.

At first, Colonel Ohara was surprised by Dexter's quaffing of alcoholic beverages at such an early hour, but as he thought more about it, he 'understood.' Last night's story had been a catharsis of sorts for all concerned. Now that the tale of Brigitte LaFoche's wartime tryst with Mr. Kennedy had been brought into the open—and most of all, accepted by the others—it was time to move on.

Colonel Ohara waited until everyone was finished with breakfast before asking CSM Charlie Wilkes a question.

"Command Sergeant Major?"

"Yes, Colonel?"

"So far, we've heard how you and Sharon got married, and how Mr. Kennedy and his colleagues won World War Two. Now, we'd like to hear about your experiences with the engineer battalion during the Normandy Invasion. Are you up for it?"

"It's a long story, Colonel," the senior enlisted man demurred.

"Well, with the exception of my son, Sean, all of us are either retired or on vacation. So, I guess we have the time."

The CSM looked around the dining room, then said, "If I start to bore you, you won't break my heart if you get up and leave."

"Such modesty, Charlie," said Dexter Dannenberg as he took a sip from his bloody Mary.

"The question is, where do I start?"

Dannenberg spoke up. "Why don't you start at Camp Bowie, down in Texas?"

"Works for me," the retired senior NCO said, as he picked up his cup of coffee and began speaking.

CAMP BOWIE, BROWN COUNTY, TEXAS
SATURDAY, 19 SEPTEMBER 1942, 4:00 P.M. LOCAL

Named after Alamo martyr and namesake of the legendary fighting knife, James Bowie, the Army's second Camp Bowie was built in 1940 at Brownwood, Texas as an infantry and artillery-training center. It was garrisoned by the 111th Quartermaster Regiment of the Thirty-sixth Infantry Division, the 113th Cavalry of the Iowa National Guard, the Eighth Army Corps comprising the 174th and 142nd Field Artillery groups, along with its headquarters, and troops of the Third Army under General Walter Krueger composed of special troops of the Seventh Headquarters Detachment, medical units ranging from the Second to the Seventeenth, engineer companies, signal battalions and chemical companies. In August 1943, a prisoner of war camp with a capacity of 3,000 Axis prisoners was established within the post.

By Corporal Wilkes' telling, Camp Bowie was far worse even than Camp Roberts. At least Roberts was relatively close to San Luis Obispo, and the Pacific Ocean, whereas Bowie was a nothing place in the middle of nowhere. Its only redeeming quality was that cold beer was plentiful and the local Texas belles friendly, although since he got married he had more-or-less had given up whoring as his chief form of off-duty entertainment.

The truth of the matter was that Charlie did not get too many opportunities to dip his wick in Texas, as no sooner had he and many of the men from his old unit in California unpacked their gear and reported to the 51st Engineer Combat Regiment, than they were transported *en masse* to Plattsburgh Barracks, in New York.

"What was that like, Sergeant Major?" Colonel Ohara asked.

"Plattsburgh Barracks went back to the War of 1812. In fact, our British friends built a siege battery just north of the mouth of the Saranac River during that war. It has been an Air Force base since World War Two.

"But, enough of the history lesson. If I keep talking, you're going to think you're still listening to Dannenberg."

"Hey, I resemble that remark!" Dexter quipped.

"Anyway, in March of 1943 the 51st Regiment split into the 238th and 51st Engineer Combat Battalions. We did basic training in April of that year and finished our unit training in July, whereupon we got orders to pack up. Scuttlebutt had us going to the Pacific, but that turned out to be a bunch of bovine fecal matter. Instead, we went on some god-awful maneuvers down in Elkins, West Virginia. When we finished that, we trained some more until we got orders to go to North Africa.

"But, before we get to North Africa, I have to tell you a short story, because it pertains to someone you already know about—and he's a key player in the upcoming events.

"It was New Year's Eve. Ian Henry and I were assigned to assist with a detail to go downtown after midnight, and pick up any of the men in the unit who needed a ride back to the barracks. We were freezing our drawers off. The temperature had to be somewhere around thirty degrees, with a light snowfall. As we were coming out of some dive named 'The Fife and Drum,' on Margaret Street, we ran into none other than Sergeant Ernie James. Now, in case you cannot remember who I am talking about, he is the soldier wc pulled guard duty with the night we spotted the Jap sub off the California coast.

"At first I thought I was dreaming. But, sure as hell, there he was. Only, he was no longer Sergeant James, but a butter-bar lieutenant! How the heck we hadn't run into each other before New Year's Eve is still a mystery to me. It was freezing cold out, so we cut our bull session short. Besides, the only reason we were downtown in the first place was to round up newly arrived recruits and get them back to the base before they froze to death. I mean, hell, they were wearing khakis! And that's hardly the proper uniform for Plattsburg, especially during the middle of the winter.

"We shot the bull for a few minutes. Then Lieutenant James told us that he and his running partner were headed up to Jeru's Bar. That bit of news really piqued my interest, because I'd heard that Jeru's was the road to per-dition—and for the life of me, I couldn't figure out what a straight-laced guy like James would be doing in there. And after hours, no less!

"Even my mackerel-snapping buddy from New Hampshire, Ian Henry, knew about Jeru's. Henry told me he'd heard that the owner of the tavern could pass for Clark Gable's double, which Ernie James later confirmed when we were on the boat to Oran, Algeria. As it turned out, James and his fellow officer had been set up with a couple of twins and they were running late. And, in 1943, nobody kept a lady waiting! If he did, he risked another GI stealing her away.

"James was no idiot, so he and his *amigo* high-tailed it the heck out of there in short order. Henry and I went about our business of rounding up all the newly arrived soldiers who were freezing their butts off. As it turned out, one of the twins that James was introduced to was named Faith. To make a long story short, James married Faith after the war, and today they live in Sacramento."

Sean Kennedy Ohara looked perplexed. "Are you telling me that Lieutenant James married a woman he casually met in a bar, and they're still together? How is that possible? I know kids whose parents dated for years before they got married, and for them it lasted five minutes—if even that!"

CSM Wilkes laughed. "Sean, the truth is that a lot of that sort of stuff went on back then. Hell, look how I ended up with Sharon! If you had told anyone in Villisca on Memorial Day weekend, 1939 that I would be married to Sharon Eddy Roberts today, they would have probably called up Sheriff Wilkes and had you arrested for smoking hemp-weed! But I did—and we're still married."

"It must have been the war," Colonel Ohara's son suggested.

"That's part of it, sure. But things were just plain different back then...."

Dexter Dannenberg returned to the conversation. "Sergeant Major, I think I've finally met someone who wanders around more in telling a tale than I do. Would you please get back to your story? At this rate, I doubt we'll get through Operation Torch by kickoff time at the Rose Bowl."

Because Dannenberg had brought up the upcoming Rose Bowl game, the conversation turned briefly to college football before returning to the events of the 238th Engineer Combat Battalion during World War II.

"Over the next few months the unit completed basic training, and by April we did our unit training. That ended in July 1943. We then packed up and went to West Virginia for more training. Mercifully, that was completed soon enough, and on October thirteenth, we embarked from Hampton Roads for Oran, Algeria. We got to North Africa on November second, but didn't do anything worth mentioning. When the Army got tired of us being in North Africa, they shipped us to the U.K., arriving there January 20, 1944.

Once there, we trained out behinds off in preparation for Operation Overlord—the Allied invasion of Normandy—which of course took place on June 6, 1944.

PRELUDE TO D—DAY

Well men, this is the real thing!
—Captain Edward J. Blumenstein, Commanding Officer
Company B, 238th Engineer Combat Regiment

CANTONMENT AREA, 238TH ENGINEER COMBAT REGIMENT
CAMP STOVER, NEAR NEWTON ABBOTT, ENGLAND
THURSDAY, 1 JUNE 1944, 0:530 HOURS, LOCAL

As Lieutenant Ernest C. James sat in the briefing tent waiting for the meeting of craft commanders to begin, he felt a chill run down his back. Everything the men in his unit had been training for the better part of a year-and-a-half was about to be put to use. Nobody had to tell him or any of other men in the smoke-filled tent, that the next few days could very well decide the entire future of World War II.

Have we done everything we could?

Have we forgotten anything?

Seated next to James was George A. Worth, another first lieutenant. Worth was deep in thought, going over everything, repeatedly in his head.

We'll have fifty-eight men from our battalion and eight from a colored trucking company, plus four from a heavy steel treadway bridge company. First Lieutenant Lawrence Cane from Connecticut is the only other officer onboard my craft. Does he know what to do in case I don't make it? Are we ready? Have we done everything we can?

"Briefing starts in two minutes, gentlemen, so finish up your smokes…," someone shouted from the back of the tent.

Worth looked over to Lieutenant Cane, who at the moment was taking a sip from his canteen cup of hot coffee. He nodded his head, and Cane returned a grin and a thumbs-up.

Hell yes, he's ready! Cane fought the fascists in Spain for two years! If there's anyone in this tent who knows about the Nazis, Larry Cane does!

Worth remembered the first time he met Cane, and how fast they had become the best of friends. He also recalled how much Cane loved his wife, who now was expecting yet another child.

"Atten-hut!" someone in the back of the tent yelled. All the officers gathered there stood, until told to be seated by Major Massoglia.

"Well men, this is the real thing! Immediately after this meeting, you will have your respective companies marched down to their awaiting transportation. After departing the cantonment area, you will proceed in a convoy down to the docks and load up in your boats.

"From there, we'll wait until SHAEF gives us the go-ahead," Massoglia said, as he took time to look around the tent. Scanning their faces, he nodded to an officer here and there, and then said, "Good luck, men. And—Godspeed."

Massoglia hollered, "Dismissed!" and everyone quietly walked out of the tent to begin a journey that would end either in their death, or with the defeat of Adolf Hitler. Each of the men felt it, all the way down to their very souls.

Thirty Minutes later...

The road down to the harbor was about as bumpy a ride as any soldier in a deuce-and-a-half truck could expect, given the fact, the roads were cobblestone. But none of the soldiers in Lieutenant James's vehicle seemed to mind, as all seemed lost in their private thoughts. James, who had a knack for observing different types of buildings, looked out the window of the truck from his shotgun position. To his right stood the Imperial Hotel.

From the looks at that old bugger, I would say it was built around 1890....

As his truck drove by the majestic hotel, James thought about the magnificent gardens that had abounded on the hotel's grounds before the war.

I'll bet this Torquay area was quite the place to go, before Hitler....

"Sir, we're coming up on the marina," CPL Wilkes shouted.

James looked up. His LCT [Landing Craft Tank] was immediately in front of him.

"Thanks, Wilkes. After you drop us off, drive this truck back to that parking lot we just passed. You'll be going back for the rest of the men after checking in with the Motor Pool sergeant." Ernie James grabbed his helmet and carbine and opened the truck's door.

"Wilkes?" James said as he stood on the truck's running board. "See you aboard."

"Yes, sir," Wilkes replied, trying not to think about the upcoming events.

As James watched his men assemble in formation, he checked his timepiece and made a mental note of the scene taking place in front of him.

Each platoon commander was assigned a craft filled with somewhere between sixty to seventy men, plus six to eleven vehicles. The vehicles had long since been loaded, and now the men were boarding their craft. From there, each commander would be responsible for his men and their equipment until they arrived on the shore of Utah Beach.

In the back of James' mind, he could hear Massoglia shouting, "Make damned sure each of your men has a life jacket on when they're in the boats, and that all weapons are unloaded until the proper time...."

James cleared his throat and looked over toward T/4 Jesse R. Winkles, from Carroll County, Georgia, who now was perched atop one of the overloaded vehicles in Landing Craft 2331. He was holding a pair of field glasses to his eyes.

"What're you looking at, Winkles?" Lieutenant Worth hollered.

Winkles put the glasses down for but the slightest of time, and replied, "Not much sir, just those other crafts over on the shoreline of Brixam Harbor. Just wondering where they're going, sir."

"Let me know if you see anything exciting, Winkles," Lieutenant Worth stated, as he walked over to another one of his men. The private was named William C. Agnew, Jr., a Mississippian with a powerful faith, and he was spending his last few moments in England cleaning and oiling his rifle.

From his left, James heard someone calling him. It sounded like PFC Ian Henry. He turned around and sure enough, that's who it was. Henry was loaded down with various types of demolition gear. Out of breath when he came up to James, Henry saluted and asked Lieutenant James if he had seen PVT John E. Tyminiski.

"I haven't seen him yet, but I know he's on Lieutenant Worth's LCT. Why don't you try over there?" James said, pointing in the direction of Lieutenant Worth's landing craft.

Just as Henry started to walk toward LCT 2331, he spotted the Polish-American soldier from Queensbury, New York. Tyminiski didn't look too impressed.

"Henry, what in the hell's taken you so long? I was beginning to think I was going to have to take the Atlantic Wall down with my bare hands."

"Sorry, Tym, but these damned explosives somehow got packed in another truck. Their CO knew they were yours, so he gave them to me to deliver to you."

Tyminiski relieved Henry of the explosives he was carrying. Then he cracked a joke that pertained to Irishmen and alcohol, and departed the area.

Ernie James walked over to where Lieutenant Worth was supervising the last bit of packing of equipment on board his LCT. James noticed the eight colored soldiers from the dump truck company. They looked ready to go. Then he looked around the harbor. What he saw there overwhelmed him. There were literally hundreds of boats on the horizon, each one flying an American flag.

As James lit up his pipe, he reflected on the scene before him.

You're a helluva long way from Ord, Nebraska, soldier.

Later that day, 1700 hours local...

Corporal Charlie Wilkes was the last man on board James' LCT. After convoying troops to the harbor for the majority of the day, the drivers were given a hot meal made from the Army's new ten-in-one rations. Consisting of a well-planned, balanced diet that could be eaten either hot or cold, the drivers wolfed them down in record time. Then they too were loaded on the waiting trucks and driven down to the docks.

"Good to have you onboard, Corporal Wilkes," James said as he pointed to the aft section of the LCT. "All the men are back there. Make yourself at home. Word has it we're out of here within the hour."

"Thanks, sir. I'll go back and check in with my platoon sergeant." Wilkes dropped his gear on the LCT's deck, and began walking.

ON THE OPEN SEA, HEADED FOR FRANCE
THURSDAY, JUNE 6TH, 1944, 0515 HOURS, FOGGY

They had been at sea, for what seemed to be an eternity. More than half the men on board were seasick, and Corporal Wilkes was about to make another trip to the rail. It was no use, as he had long since thrown up all vestiges of food. As he stumbled his way to the railing, he bumped into PFC Ian Henry.

"You look like shit, Charlie."

"If I look half as bad as I feel, you're being too kind. I have to look worse than shit," Charlie replied, retching.

Henry tried to comfort Charlie the best he knew how. But he knew the only thing that could stop Wilkes' seasickness was good old *terra firma*. Unfortunately, the only *terra firma* they were going to be landing on had thousands of German soldiers waiting to kill them. Nevertheless, Ian Henry suspected that Wilkes would prefer being shot to being as sick as he was.

Charlie sat down on a box of ammunition and put his head between his legs. Ian tried to get Charlie's mind off his misery. In his unmistakable Yankee accent, Ian began his tale. "Yeah, Charlie, every summer we'd all go down to my aunt's house up in Maine. She lives in the port town of Arundel. It's great lobsta country. My Uncle Cassidy would take us out when he went to check his lobsta traps. The first time I went out on his boat I tossed my cookies, too, but after a while, I got used to it. You might even say I was a regular swashbuckler."

Charlie had heard enough. "Ian, you crazy fucking Yankee! First of all, how the hell can you go 'down' to your Aunt's house 'up' in Maine? Secondly, I don't have the slightest idea whatsoever what the hell a 'lobsta' is, but the mention of anything edible right now isn't a good plan. So do me a favor and shut up. Or shoot me."

"For crissake, Charlie, all I was trying to do was to take your mind off your troubles. You don't have get a case of the ass on me now."

"Well, if you wanted to take my mind off my troubles, Ian, you'd tell me this tub is going to make it to shore. Or, haven't you noticed that there's nearly three inches of water sloshing around in the floorboards? At this rate we're going to have to swim to France!" Charlie looked up at his friend.

"Charlie, in a few minutes, the United States Navy is going to cut loose with a barrage to wake those Nazi bastards up."

Corporal Wilkes felt the urge to vomit again, but managed to suppress it. "In the mood I'm in I feel sorry for those Nazi bastards, because by the time I get through with 'em, hell will seem like a vacation."

Smoking a pipe while looking off toward the shore, Lieutenant James came upon the soldiers.

"You two ready to hit the beach?"

"Sir, if we don't get ashore pretty damn soon, we're going to have to swim in," Ian replied.

"Well, if it makes you feel any better, I asked the British chap who's piloting this tub if he thought we were going to have to swim for it."

"What did he say, sir?"

"He talked it over with the commander of Company A, and they've requested permission for us to go in early. Otherwise, I'm afraid our choice is a wet one," James said in a lowered voice.

"Sir?" Now a PFC named Eric Duncan, from Keller, Texas, joined the conversation. "This might be a fucked-up time to bring it up, sir, but I can't swim."

James looked at the nineteen-year old Texan. "Private, I'll bet you a month's pay that you're not the only one on this tub who can't swim. And, the last time I looked around, ain't none of us can walk on water. So, I guess the best we can hope for is that His Majesty's Navy gets us within wading distance of France. Once there, it's up to us."

Although he felt like vomiting again, Wilkes managed to speak. "Lafayette, here we come!"

Lieutenant James checked his watch again, and then said, "I just hope all those airborne boys did their jobs."

"How so, sir?" Wilkes inquired.

"From what I remember of the plan, H Hour is at oh-six-thirty. We are supposed to hit the beach at oh-six-thirty-one. Two minutes later, the demolition guys start clearing sixteen, fifty-yard paths through the mines.... By ten-thirty hours the half-tracks are due...."

James looked at his watch again, and then toward the shore. It was approaching 0540 hours. Not coming from a seaboard state, James was unfamiliar with estimating distance on the water. But, to the best of his thinking, he figured they were still a good distance from the French coast.

Hell, we're already behind schedule.

He was about to say something, when what sounded like all five thousand ships in the invading force cut loose with a barrage. The noise was beyond deafening. Yet, to a man on the LCT, no one felt sympathy for the intended targets.

The Krauts started this mess, and now it's time for some pay-back!

"Sounds like the Navy is battling it out with some shore batteries," Duncan said to nobody in particular.

"Don't know about that, Eric," Henry said, as he looked to starboard. "But for sure, somebody is giving, and somebody else is catching hell."

Suddenly, there was a horrific explosion in the distance.

"Sounds like the Krauts got lucky," Duncan muttered absently.

What he didn't know was that the Norwegian destroyer *Svenner* had just taken a German torpedo into her boiler room. And, with it, thirty Allied service personnel had been instantly killed.

Miles to the rear, Lieutenant General Omar N. Bradley, U.S.A., grabbed his field glasses and watched the invasion force make its way toward Omaha Beach. Bradley was filled with doubts, as Allied intelligence had informed him just before leaving England that the 1st Division and the 29th Division were headed right smack-dab into the throes of some of *Herr* Hitler's finest: the 352nd Division. It was too late now to do anything.

Those men would have to overcome the Germans, or die trying.

CHAPTER TEN

*When you have secured an area, don't forget to tell the
enemy.*
—Murphy's Law on Combat

IN FRONT OF THE RESIDENCE OF
MR. & MRS. SEAN KENNEDY, SR.
VOLCANO ROAD, SUTTER CREEK,
AMADOR COUNTY, CALIFORNIA
FRIDAY, 23 NOVEMBER 1991, 1:00 P.M. LOCAL

"Well, gentlemen," CSM Charlie Wilkes said as he turned to walk
over the small bridge that led to the Kennedys' private residence, "Most of
my unit hit Utah Beach somewhere between oh-seven-thirty and oh-eight-
hundred hours. Now, I say 'most of my unit,' because two of our LCTs
developed engine trouble and returned to port on June 5th. But, stuff happens
on the battlefield. That's why you prepare for any eventuality. Because I can
tell you, if there ever is a case where Murphy's Law prevails, it's out on the
battlefield."

"Why do you say that, Sergeant Major?" Sean Ohara said as he set his
walking stick down on the porch.

"Well, I gotta tell ya, things didn't look too good that morning! Not
only were the Germans shooting at us, but the guy who was supposed to be
leading us, Colonel McMillan, was still back in England."

"How did that happen?" the teenager asked.

"His landing craft sprung a leak, and had to head back to port. It happened
on another one of our unit's boats, too. So, with McMillan out of the picture,
command of the 238th was turned over to Major Martin Massoglia. The
good thing was that, if I'd had to pick someone else to fill the battalion
commander's shoes, I doubt if I could've picked anyone better than Major
Massoglia. You'll see, as this story unwinds, that he was more than capable.
But, that's way down the line. Let's get back to Utah Beach.

"It's been said that the Americans achieved their greatest success on Utah Beach, because the Fourth Division was able to get farther inland than their counterparts. Thus, the impression is that it was a damned cakewalk. Nothing could be further from the truth. For whatever reason, the Krauts didn't murder us when we first came in, so the Fourth was able to come ashore along with its support elements, the 238th being one of them. But don't for a minute think we were unopposed, because there were plenty of Krauts trying to ruin our day.

"By nightfall, the 4th Division was six miles inland from Utah Beach, and amazingly enough, we didn't have one casualty on D-Day. All that back-breaking training had paid off, except for one soldier, and our luck was holding."

"You want to explain that one, Charlie?" Dannenberg inquired as he sat on the porch.

"Sure, Dex. You see, we lost one soldier in Oran, a Private James M. Anderson from Jacksonville, Florida. He was a good soldier… and a helluva nice guy. Jim was Swedish, and when word came down that there was a Swedish ship in the harbor, he went down to visit it. While there, he got a load on, and apparently was jumped by some of the local talent and murdered. It was a shitty way to go…."

"How do you remember their names, Sergeant Major?" Colonel Ohara's son inquired.

Command Sergeant Major Wilkes was about to say something, when his wife, Sharon, walked outside and onto the porch. She looked the young man in the eyes and said, "Charlie remembers their names, Sean—because he can't forget them."

Sean Kennedy Ohara looked over to the sergeant major to see if he would agree with his wife. What he saw instead was the CSM wiping away a tear. It was an awkward moment, but one he would not soon forget.

Noting that Charlie Wilkes wasn't immediately able to continue, Colonel Ohara suggested that they belly up to the bar, get some fresh Dominicans and eat some of their hostesses' world-class mincemeat pie.

After demolishing the pie, it took another few minutes for the men to get settled down again. When they did, Command Sergeant Major Wilkes began to give more details of his unit's landing on Utah Beach.

Looking over at Colonel Ohara, Wilkes asked Ohara if he remembered his comment about Lieutenant James' wondering if their LCT would make it ashore.

"Yes," the colonel replied, as he sat down on a rocking chair and took a sip from his Wild Turkey on the rocks with a twist of lime. It was an odd concoction, but the colonel had started drinking it as a young soldier in Vietnam. He'd never really given them up, although he no longer swilled them to the degree he did during his days in the 1st Signal Brigade in Nha Trang, South Vietnam.

"Well, obviously we made it ashore. But I have to tell you, it was a sonofabitch in doing so. Our LCT was taking on water and the only way we were able to stay afloat was to put our engineer's water pumps into use. It got down to the point where the Brit driver called whoever in the hell was coordinating the landing, and got permission for us to go in ahead of schedule. You talk about a 'Charlie Foxtrot'—this was one in the making.

"In fact, it gave new definition to the acronym 'SNAFU,' a World War Two term that literally means 'Situation Normal, All Fucked Up'."

At that, everyone listening to Wilkes' story laughed, even though all had heard the definition numerous times.

Before he could continue with his story, Dexter Dannenberg asked CSM Wilkes if he might interject something.

"Go right ahead," Wilkes answered, as he lit up a cigar.

"Without going into all the sordid details," Dannenberg said, taking a sip from a cocktail, "When you guys hit the Normandy coast, I had been working for Wild Bill Donovan for quite some time. We'd been up to our knees in dirty tricks and special operation missions within occupied France. It certainly was a great time. There we were—fighting for our very existence, using every nasty deed we could come up with, in an all-out effort to defeat Hitler. Needless to say, we pulled out the stops to trick the Huns into believing that we were coming in at the Pas-de-Calais. There was that business with Patton and his 'dummy Army,' too, although the OSS had nothing to do with that. Apparently, Ike made that decision early-on in the game.

"We did everything known to man to convince the Krauts that the second front was landing at Calais. But in the end, whether or not the German High Command fell for it didn't matter. I say that, because the 'Austrian Corporal' was convinced we were coming in at Calais. Hell, that's why Hitler refused to cut General von Salmuth's 15th Army loose to assist Rommel!

"And it's well known that nobody on the German OKW, including Keitel, dared to argue with *der Fuhrer*. But there were other things that played into the picture, too. For instance, the weather had been so crappy that the *Luftwaffe* was unable to fly, so the lack of good intel hurt them. That, and the fact that the Germans were—pardon the expression—as fucked up as Hogan's goat when it came to overlapping commands, and their complete stupidity for not decoding all the messages from the French underground that had been sent the night before, were just frosting on the proverbial cake! Yes, the war gods were smiling on us that night!

"Oh, I could go on for hours. But nothing I'm saying is what you haven't already heard about or read about. So I guess I'll just cease and desist for a bit, and let the good Command Sergeant Major continue his version of how the 238th Combat Engineer Battalion won World War Two." Dannenberg then feigned a salute to his fellow Midwesterner.

CSM Wilkes was about to continue with his story, when he looked up and saw a Jeep Cherokee arriving in front of the house. An Army lieutenant colonel and a good-looking woman in her late thirties got out of the vehicle. Mr. and Mrs. Kennedy went outside to greet their son and his wife, who had driven up from Fort Ord. Wilkes looked around the room.

"I think VE-Day is going to have to wait until the morning, gentlemen."

All present agreed.

While the Kennedys were outside getting caught up on the latest news in their youngest son's Army career, Colonel Ohara asked his own son if he had any plans for the next day. The youngster replied that he had agreed to tag along with Command Sergeant Major Wilkes for an hour or so, while he drove over to the nearby Shenandoah Valley to pick up a few cases of wine.

"Why don't I go along, too? Our wine cellar could use some replenishing. Besides, the way these two guys are dragging their stories out, I wonder if we're going to get Charlie on the shores of France, before the first snow falls here in Sutter Creek."

CSM Wilkes laughed. "Okay, Michael, I get the point. But you've got to understand something, Colonel—Dexter and I don't have too many friends we can talk to about it, anymore. Most of our Army buddies have gone on, and the ones who are alive damn sure don't want to discuss it. Not that any anyone else who might come along would get it, anyway."

Ohara laughed. "You're probably right. Why don't you guys continue with this saga in the morning? I'm going back in the house to watch the football game."

MONTEVINA WINERY, 20680 SHENANDOAH SCHOOL ROAD
PLYMOUTH, CALIFORNIA. SATURDAY, 24 NOVEMBER 1991, NOON.

"Well, considering there isn't any more room in either car, I think we're about done wine shopping," said CSM Wilkes as he closed the door to his Chrysler minivan. He looked over at Colonel Ohara.

"Colonel Mike, what do you think? Are eight cases of wine going to last me the rest of the year?"

"Command Sergeant Major, if I didn't know that six of those cases were for Trinity Church's annual Christmas party, I'd almost be tempted to call the WCTU," joked Ohara as he put case of Barbera in the trunk of his '65 Ford Mustang convertible.

"Got time for a Dominican?" Wilkes asked, pulling two Punch Robusto cigars from their canister.

"Between you and Dannenberg... my heavens... one could get addicted to these things," Ohara said, as he helped himself to the treat being offered.

"Truth of the matter is, Colonel, if I were as young as you I'd be worried about the number of cigars I smoke. But, since I'm already way past seventy, I don't think it matters."

"No—if he were any younger I'd take the damned things away from him!" Sharon Wilkes said as she took a sip from her can of soda.

They walked over to a picnic table, where the colonel's son was sitting. He had just finished his soda and was in the process of crushing the can when the trio approached.

"Mind if we blow some smoke in your face, young man?" Wilkes asked as he pulled out his lighter and cigar cutter.

Even if I did, would it matter? the teenager thought. Instead, he replied, "No problem."

Wilkes fumbled with his cigar for a few seconds, then said, "Well, then, what do you say I get my unit ashore and start winning World War Two?" He grabbed a can of Coke and pulled the tab.

"As I recall we were about to land on Utah Beach...."

UTAH BEACH, NORMANDY COAST OF FRANCE
JUNE 6TH, 1944, APPROXIMATELY 0730 HOURS LOCAL

As Lieutenant Ernest C. James looked ashore, he knew that all the best-laid plans of Eisenhower's SHAEF HQ staff were already in the toilet.

This current has dragged our sorry butts at least a half-mile from where we're supposed to be, and the smoke from that naval bombardment has screwed up any chance for us to actually see where the hell we're supposed to be landing!

As the Army officer from Nebraska attempted to come up with "Plan B," another hellacious explosion went off in the distance.

The way this tub is leaking, there's no way we'll be going in on the fourth wave!

In the background, James could hear PFC Ian Henry carrying on.

"Shit! The fucking Krauts just got another one of our landing boats!"

Henry stood up ever so slightly, stuck his head up to eye level and tried to see whose LCT was no more. Corporal Wilkes leaned over to where Henry was stooped, and shouted, "We're all ate-up, but I think it's going to work in our favor."

Henry gaped at his comrade in disbelief. "You crazy bastard! The battalion commander's back in England, we're at least a half-mile from where we're supposed to be, and you think it's going to work in our favor? I've heard about people being foggy, but hell, you're beyond foggy!"

Henry was about to say something else, when the LCT went aground. The British ensign piloting the LCT shouted, "This is as close as I can get you chaps!"

Lieutenant James and Captain Reichmann scrambled over to the forward ramp and peeked over it. They were joined by a warrant officer named Knapp from the motor section. Reichmann spoke first. "To my way of thinking, we're about a hundred yards out." He looked at Lt. James. "And unless we plan on sitting here like a great, big target, I think we're going to have to swim to shore."

"We don't have any other options," James admitted, as he pointed to a German pillbox on shore.

James was about to respond to Reichmann when he saw PFC Duncan advancing toward him.

"Private Duncan, come here."

"Yes, sir."

"Find Corporal Wilkes. I want you two to work your way through the boat and find out just how many men we have onboard who can not swim. Then report back to me immediately," James said, as he bit down on his pipe stem.

Within a few minutes Duncan was back, reporting to 1LT James. "Sir, the best we could come up with is that we got us about fifteen men who can't swim a lick."

"Thank you. Good job."

James looked to Reichmann. "We might as well get started. I'll follow you."

Reichmann turned and addressed the troops. "Okay, men, listen up. For those of you who can't swim, Lieutenant James and I are going to take you ashore. Get your gear and follow us. And don't worry, we're all wearing Mae West lifejackets. They should keep you afloat. Now, for those of you who can swim, you're about get off this miserable tub and get your first European bath."

Muffled laughter could be heard in the background. Reichmannn continued, "The main thing is not to panic. We are going to get ashore, and we're not losing anyone. Got that?"

"Yes, sir!" the men shouted in unison.

"Gentlemen, we're going ashore, and we're going kick the Krauts all the way back to Berlin!" Reichmann shouted, as he went forward to disembark from the LCT.

Lieutenant James was the first officer in the water. He took two men with him. Once ashore, James made sure they were able to fend for themselves, then went back out into the surf to gather up more engineers. He was met by Captain Reichmann, who had two soldiers in tow. James briefly waited for Reichmann. As the two officers swam back to the LCT, small arms fire sprinkled the area.

Damn, one would've thought the Navy would have taken care of those bastards by now! Hopefully, Collin's 4th will take care of them.

Back on the LCT, Warrant Officer Knapp was putting the final changes on his plan to get the 238th's equipment ashore. He looked over the ramp.

Captain Reichmann and Lt. James were directing more enlisted men into the cold Atlantic waters. "Jump in men, your Mae West will keep you afloat," James said as he swam toward an enlisted man from Missouri.

Soon, four more enlisted men joined Reichmann and James in swimming toward Utah Beach. Before they got too far away, Knapp hollered to Reichmann, "Sir, while you're out there taking your morning bath, T5 Kreager and I are just about ready to drive the R-4 'dozer in. We already have the snorkel and air intake hoses deployed."

"Good luck, chief, see you in a few," Reichmann said, as he continued ferrying another group of non-swimming enlisted men to the French shore.

Knapp looked at Kreager. "You once told me you've been driving 'dozers since you were twelve. If anyone here can get this dozer in, you're the soldier who can do it. Good luck. I'll see you onshore."

Kreager proceeded to rev up the R-4's engine and put it in first gear, and just like that—SPLASH! Even though Kreager was standing, he was up to his neck in salt water. But the 'dozer was still moving toward the shore. As he made his way forward, an artillery shell from a nearby artillery battery exploded close-by, accompanied by small arms fire.

Back on the LCT, Knapp oversaw the operation of marrying the men with their equipment. That was accomplished with relative ease. Surprisingly enough, in the waist-high surf Kreager's 'dozer was still running, so he hooked up a towline to the landing craft and was able to pull the LCT far enough inward so the men could drive their trucks and equipment from the LCT directly onto the beach. Once ashore, they busied themselves with filling in the gaping shell holes made courtesy of the battleship *Texas'* sixteen-inch guns. Next, they gapped minefields and set out a reconnaissance patrol. So far, nobody had been hit.

Major Massoglia was in complete command of the unit. In fact, he discovered that the aggregate used by the *Nazi*s in building their so-called "impregnable" Atlantic Wall hadn't been thoroughly cleaned, and thus hadn't set up properly. The unit's 'dozers went to work, and soon were able to punch a whole in it large enough to drive as many vehicles through as were needed.

Having finished ferrying their non-swimming engineers to shore, 1LT James, CPT Reichmann and CWO Knapp were gathered around the hood of James' vehicle when Massoglia approached.

"James, I need you to do something for me," Massoglia said without going into detail.

James motioned for his driver, Private Plover, to get their vehicle ready.

Plover did as directed, and went over to start his truck. As he was doing so, a German 88mm shell landed within spitting distance, exploding. Plover was knocked on his ass. Without warning, another shell hit the vehicle, which was loaded with tons of explosives. Fortunately for all, the second shell was a dud. 1LT James jumped onto the back of the truck to see why the shell hadn't exploded.

"Damn! That shell hit a primed satchel charge, but the nitro starch didn't go off."

"Goddamn good thing, or we'd all be with Jesus," an enlisted man volunteered from the ground.

Wilkes couldn't resist. "That's assuming Jesus needs engineers!"

Because a medic wasn't readily available, PFC Henry checked out PVT Plover.

"It doesn't look like he's hit, sir, but for sure he's out cold."

More men came over to see their wounded comrade. "Probably just a concussion," someone offered.

"If that had happened to me, you'd be changing my underdrawers!" Charlie Wilkes quipped to nobody in particular.

Just then, a German pillbox opened up. Fortunately, their aim was off.

Everyone ducked for whatever cover they could find. Reichmann shouted to First Sergeant Freck, "Sergeant, get a squad over there with a bazooka and take those bastards out!"

JUST OUTSIDE THE VILLAGE OF
LA MADOLENE, TWO HOURS LATER

After checking his map to verify their position, CPT Reichmannn directed the men to listen up.

"You men remember your training. We're going into La Madolene. Everyone stays in single file. If there are any Krauts in there, let's don't let them kill all of us on the very first day!"

CPL Wilkes was in charge of six soldiers. He checked their equipment as they each marched by, then ran to the front of the column. The pace was moderate. He could hear gunfire off in the distance. As they approached the village, PFC Henry, who was walking directly behind Wilkes, tapped his immediate superior on the shoulder.

"I don't like it, Charlie. Something ain't right."

Wilkes turned to face his buddy. "I don't, either. But the last time I saw a map, Berlin was in this direction."

A soldier named PVT Alberto L. Rael, from Arroyo Hondo, New Mexico, checked his rifle yet another time.

"There goes Alberto, checking his equipment again," said PFC Harold Miller, from Blanchard, Oklahoma, as he too checked his weapon.

"Hell, you should've been standing by him back on the LCT. Jesus, if he didn't check his life vest a hundred times, he didn't check it once," PVT

Julius E. Webb cracked in his Tennessee accent.

"All right, guys, cut the crap and pay attention," CPL Wilkes said, as he too wondered what lay ahead of them on the road to Berlin.

PHEWWWWW! PHEWWWW!

What the fuck is that?

Before Wilkes could ask anyone what the whistling was all about, he found out. A couple more German 88s exploded.

"Hit the ditches!" someone shouted from the front of the single-file column. Nobody had to be told twice. Soldiers scrambled into the ditches along the country road.

Covered with of mud, Wilkes looked up from behind the patch of weeds he was lying in. He saw a group of American infantry troops standing around and not taking cover.

Are they out of their fucking minds? They should be looking for cover, not standing around with their fingers up their asses!

Suddenly a German shell landed in their midst—and just like that, the GIs were gone. The Germans continued firing for approximately ten minutes.

Seeing the soldiers die unnecessarily made Henry become nauseous. He looked at Wilkes. He heard another loud explosion in the distance. Then nothing. Just silence.

"All right, men, on your feet!" CPT Reichmann shouted. "We're going in. Remember—single file."

The engineers regrouped, and continued their trek into the village of La Madolene. As they walked by, they passed the spot where the eight soldiers had been standing. Charlie Wilkes counted seven dead. In the background he heard a medic say he thought one of them might survive.

Training, Charlie—training. It's going to save your ass!

D-DAY +1. NEAR ST. MARIE DU MONT, 7 JUNE 1944, NOON

Since the wee hours of this morning, the engineers from H&S Company had worked on opening a water point, the first one on Utah Beach and, therefore, the first one in France. Their next task was to rehabilitate cratered roads U-5 and T-7. Then, they were to open a road designated S-9, as it was under water for nearly a mile. They fixed the problem by gathering rubble and road expedients along the way, performing their duties while intermittent artillery shells landed in their midst. At night the *Luftwaffe* came out and harassed them, making sleep nearly impossible. Everywhere the soldiers looked, they saw remnants of crashed gliders.

Once the CP was established, CPL Wilkes ran the radio while PFC Henry was put on a detail with PFC Gordie D. Hall, from Apalachicola, Florida and PFC James C. Harrell, from Vicksburg, Mississippi. SGT Jack Harrison, a Texan, was the NCOIC. They were out looking for any survivors inside the gliders. So far, there hadn't been any.

"Shit the bed," Henry said, as he looked at a glider a hundred or so feet in front of him. It was busted all to hell. Henry took a deep breath and approached the wreckage.

What he saw inside startled him. The glider had been carrying a jeep in the rear, and the sudden stop on impact caused the jeep to slam forward, instantly killing all onboard.

What a fucking waste!

"Mark the spot, Henry, and we'll notify graves registration," SGT Harrison said, shaking his head.

"Hey, SGT Harrison, I think I see some paratroopers hanging in that clump of trees," one of the soldiers in the detail shouted.

"Well, what the hell are you waiting for, soldier? Run your ass over there and cut them down!"

But the American paratroopers were dead, hanging in their parachute harnesses. All had been machine gunned.

"Shit, between that fucking swamp and these fucking trees, they didn't stand a chance," Ian Henry said as he started gathering dog tags.

Harrison was behind him. "Henry, these men knew the score before they left England."

Ian Henry misunderstood what his NCO had said. He thought Harrison was glossing over the men's death. He was about to say something that probably would have landed him in the brig, when Harrison continued, "and yet, they climbed aboard that paper airplane and came in here, anyway. I guess that's what makes them paratroopers and us engineers. What a sorry waste of brave men."

After marking the places where the soldiers had been killed, PFC Henry and a few other men worked their way over to a bypass. There they were greeted with another huge shell crater, courtesy of the USS *Texas*. One of the men stopped and lit up a Camel, and the other soldiers soon joined him. Henry found a large boulder and took a load off his feet. He gazed off into the distance and thought he recognized 1LT James approaching.

Being the ranking man on the detail, Henry told the men to continue taking their break while he went over to see what was on the lieutenant's mind.

"Good afternoon, sir," Henry said, with a half-assed salute.

Lieutenant James wasn't impressed, "PFC Henry, are you trying to get me killed?"

Henry knew immediately that he'd messed up. He'd been told by the Army from Day One that you did not salute an officer if there was even the slightest chance of any Germans being around. He got flustered.

"Aw, shit, sir, I fucked up. Sorry. It won't happen again."

Lieutenant James wanted to laugh at the young man, but didn't. "That's okay, soldier. But I have to ask you something."

"Do you think you could express yourself without cussing every other word.?"

Henry's face flushed red with embarrassment. He attempted to apologize, but in the process dug his hole deeper. "Oh, fuck, sir. I mean, shit. Dammit, sir, I don't know what's come over me. Ever since I've been in this engineer unit, my vocabulary has gone all to hell."

LT James wondered why he'd brought up the topic in the first place. For as long as he could remember, he'd heard enlisted men use obscene language. He decided to drop the matter, and reached into his uniform pocket for his pipe to buy some time. While he was doing that, he noticed some American paratroopers approaching. They had a small contingent of German prisoners with them.

A staff sergeant, covered with sweat, blood and cuts, presented himself to James.

"Sir, do you know where we're supposed to take these Krauts? We caught them a half a mile from here. They were shooting our guys, who got hung up in the trees last night."

"Yes, take them back to the beachhead, sergeant. They're gathering the POWs there."

"Could your unit take them, sir? We gotta get back to the fighting."

"Normally, I'd say 'yes,' but I really can't spare anyone at the moment," James replied while he lit his pipe.

The NCO spat a stream of tobacco juice, then told his men to gather up the four German captives. The group started walking back toward the beachhead.

James and Henry continued their conversation briefly. Suddenly, they heard what sounded like a Tommy gun let loose. Ian Henry suspected the paratroopers decided they had better things to do, than to wet-nurse a bunch of murdering, bastard Krauts. He knew it was against every rule in the Geneva Convention, but he also understood what must have gone through the minds of every one of those paratroopers after catching the Germans killing their buddies.

Henry was about to say something to Lieutenant James, when his suspicions were confirmed. The paratroopers returned alone. As they filed by, one of them offered, "They tried to escape."

The rest of the afternoon went by rapidly. Around 1700 hours the men called it a day and headed back to their bivouac area to set up a perimeter and eat. Their dinner was good old-fashioned Army C rations. But that didn't matter to Ian Henry, as he still hadn't regained his appetite.

About the time they finished eating, Henry's platoon sergeant, Staff Sergeant Marion P. Davis from Sheffield, Alabama, got up and started reading the names, times and locations of where the men were to pull guard duty that evening. Physically and mentally exhausted, Henry hoped he would get guard duty from 2000 to 2400 hours.

I still got enough piss and vinegar in me to do that.

Henry gathered up his gear, and reported to SSG Black.

As he approached SSG Black, the NCO said, "I just want to tell you that you done good today, Henry."

"It was kind of rough, sergeant. I keep thinking about those paratroopers, and how shitty it is that they didn't even make it to the ground."

"That's good, Henry. You keep remembering them. And when you come onto some Germans, you'll know exactly what to do. In the meantime, tomorrow we got us a mission to go out and reconnoiter some more roads. I want you and PFC Duncan to come along. I'm going to teach you how it's done."

"Any reason for that?" Henry asked.

"Yes, because when I tell you something, you listen. I do not have time to teach some of these other men. I will clear it with First Sergeant Freck. Our job is to recon the roads, and see what kind of condition they're in. We are going to head out right after morning chow. In the meantime, try to get some rest."

Three hours later...

It just didn't seem possible. PFC Henry checked his watch. Certainly, the soldier waking him up was mistaken. How could three hours gone by that fast?

Shit! 1945 hours, right on the button!

"Okay, Mac, just as soon as I crawl out of this fart-sack." He thought how good a hot cup of coffee from the corner drugstore in his hometown would taste just about now.

"My name ain't 'Mac,' Henry. It's Corporal Dwight Long," the junior enlisted man replied in an accent that clearly said "Oklahoma."

"What's up, corporal? Anything I should know?"

"Yep. The Jerries are probing our lines. Keep as quiet as possible. If you hear a noise, it is probably some Kraut trying to breach our perimeter. Challenge him with your toy cricket. If he don't reply properly, kill him."

Ian Henry prayed to God that he wouldn't have to kill anyone tonight. He knew there would be a time for that; he just hoped it wouldn't be tonight. That business back there in the gliders was enough of a test of his Catholic faith for one day.

He picked up his M-1 and made his way over to the foxhole. As he dropped down into the ground, he discovered another Yank in it. On close examination, he discovered that his guest was none other than Corporal Charlie Wilkes.

In a barely audible voice, Henry asked Wilkes why he was there.

"Couldn't sleep."

Henry couldn't believe his ears. "You can't sleep? How's that possible? I'm fucking exhausted."

"That's understandable, 'cause you've been bustin' your ass all day. As for me, all I've been doing is running a radio."

"Well, enjoy it, Charlie. Tomorrow's another day."

Wilkes was in a talkative mood. "Hey, Ian. I heard James ripped you a new ass over your vocabulary today."

"Sure did. And you know what? Now I swear worse than you do, Charlie. I never did that before I met you, you know."

"Piss off, Henry," Wilkes said as he climbed out of the foxhole. After he crawled a few feet he turned his head and whispered, "And stay the fuck awake. This place is crawling with the Jerries. Remember, we're one day closer to Berlin!"

With Wilkes gone, Henry wanted to do something that would take his mind off the GIs in that crashed glider. He tried to look up at the stars, but the weather was too crappy for that. Soon his head was filled with the scene of the dead soldiers—their faces distorted, their twisted bodies, and the smell of death. The scene kept repeating itself, over and over, and his forehead began to drip with sweat. He reached into his pants pocket for a handkerchief to wipe his brow.

You're gonna go Section 8 if you don't forget about that shit, Ian.

The sound of a cricket brought him back to his foxhole.

As if by rote, Henry clicked his toy cricket and then blurted out the night's password, "Betty Grable."

Hesitation.

Henry chambered a round in his rifle.

This motherfucker better say "Dagwood sandwich" pretty damn soon, or he's gonna be dead!

After what seemed like an eternity, the soldier coming in through the lines finally responded, "Dagwood sandwich."

"Step forward and be recognized," Henry said, keeping his finger on the weapon's trigger.

When the soldier came forward, Henry recognized him as one of the paratroopers he had seen that afternoon with the "escaping" German POWs.

"A word of advice, Mac," Henry said in a lowered voice, "You'd better be a bit quicker with the password, or somebody here's gonna shoot your ass."

The paratrooper looked as scared as Ian Henry felt. Henry quietly questioned him as to what the hell he was doing wandering around so late at night.

"We were out on a recon and I got separated from my squad. I remembered there was an American unit back here, somewhere."

"Well, I don't think it's safe to be wandering around. You should probably stay with me tonight, and in the morning we'll deal with getting you back to your unit."

From the look on the other soldier's face, Henry realized he had said the magic words.

"Now get in this foxhole, and stay awake," he added, matter-of-factly.

About a minute later, Ian Henry realized he had just given orders to someone who outranked him. The paratrooper was a corporal.

Whispering, Henry asked him his name and hometown.

"My name's James Swenson. I'm from Iowa."

"Where about?"

"You probably ain't never heard of it—Stanton."

"You gotta be shitting me."

The corporal looked strangely at Henry.

Most Iowans didn't even know where Stanton is, so how in the hell does this guy? I mean, hell, he's gotta be from Boston.

Henry snickered. "Old Charlie Wilkes ain't gonna believe his eyes in the morning!"

The paratroop leaned back a bit, and looked at Henry again. "I used to know a guy back in Iowa, from Villisca. Name was Charlie Wilkes. We played football against his school every year. As I recall him, Wilkes was a real pussy-chaser. Are you telling me he's in this unit?"

"He sure is! He's the CO's driver, and a radio operator."

"Well, if that ain't the cat's whiskers! I come all the way to Normandy just to run into Charlie Wilkes."

From the next foxhole Henry heard someone say, "Would you two shut the hell up? You can kiss each other's ass in the morning. In the meantime, keep your eyes open and your mouths shut!"

D-DAY +2, NEAR ST. MARIE DU MONT
8 JUNE, 1944, 0600 HOURS LOCAL

From the way Corporals Wilkes and Swenson carried on during the morning meal, one might have thought they were long-lost brothers. The serendipitous nature of their encounter practically overwhelmed them. Both took it to be a good omen, although the truth of the matter was all they could remember was trying to kill each other on the gridiron twice a year.

After a half-hour of "catching up" time, during which Charlie explained how Randy Robert's widow, Sharon, had visited him at Camp Roberts and that they'd got married, CPL Swenson asked Wilkes' help in finding his unit.

"They're gonna think I'm either a deserter, or that I'm dead—neither of which sounds like a good idea to me."

Now Ian Henry entered into the conversation. "I doubt it, at least not today. Now, in a week from now, who knows? Things are so screwed up—hell, there are units in places they ain't supposed to be, and there are other units supposed to be in certain areas and they ain't there. If that makes any sense."

"I guess it does," Swenson replied, as he tried to figure out just what it was the soldier from New Hampshire just said.

Charlie Wilkes could see that his fellow Iowan was confused, but knew better than to try to straighten out Ian's misuse of the King's English. Instead, he remembered what he was supposed to have already told CPL Swenson.

"Swenson, I talked to my platoon leader, Lieutenant James, about you. He said he'd take your situation up the chain of command. But, with things being as ate-up as they are, that might take days. In the meantime, you're going to become an engineer."

"I don't know shit about engineering," Swenson admitted.

Not known for his subtlety, Wilkes replied, "Well, that's okay, you big fucking Swede, because the name of this unit is the 238th Engineer Combat Battalion. And the last time we talked, you were familiar with that combat MOS."

"Yeah," Swenson replied, "I'm so good with that MOS that I managed to get separated from my unit on the first day of the invasion."

"Stop pissing and moaning," Charlie said, a bit disgustedly. "It really doesn't matter where you are, James will get that crap straightened out eventually. Right now, our job is to kill these fucking *Nazi*s. The more we do that, and the faster we do that, the faster we'll get back to our families and the States."

Swenson knew he had screwed up, and admitted it. "Wilkes, to be honest with you, I ain't much of a soldier. I didn't want to be in the Army. In fact, I tried my best to get out of it. I went to Chicago to try and get hired at a factory where the guys don't have to fight because they're critical of the war effort. But, it didn't work out that way, so here I am."

For a fleeting moment Charlie felt sorry for Swenson, and chose to ignore his guilty admission.

"Well… let's put that aside for now, and let's go see if we can find another cup of coffee."

At just that moment, CPL Duncan came over to where the two Iowans were sitting. He was carrying a canteen full of hot coffee.

"Is there any more of that?" Charlie said, pointing at the canteen.

"Not officially," Duncan replied.

"Just what the hell does that mean, 'not officially'?" Swenson asked.

"I was out at the shitter, and ran into Henry. He told me the CP had some coffee, so I mooched a canteen from him."

Charlie Wilkes desperately wanted some hot coffee. He looked at

Swenson, then grabbed his sidearm and stood up. "Grab your rifle, you dumb-fuck Swede. Let's go get us a cup of joe."

Swenson stood up, grabbed his M-1 and replied, "Lead me to the war, Corporal."

As the two men walked toward the command tent, Wilkes imagined the look on his wife's face when she read his letter saying that he'd met up with James Swenson, from Stanton, Iowa, during the invasion of Normandy.

When the two GIs got over to the CP, Ian Henry happened to be standing outside the tent. "Hey, you got any more of that coffee?" Duncan asked quietly. Henry said they did, went inside the tent, filled his canteen and came back out. He then gave each soldier a half cup of the steaming, black liquid.

As the two swilled down the coffee, Henry told them about an incident that occurred during the night that cost a Pentecostal chaplain from the 1106th his life.

"Apparently the padre went out to relieve himself and forgot his cricket. When he returned back to his unit, someone shot him by accident."

"That's the shits," Swenson replied, knowing that Henry was also lecturing him for being too slow last night in returning the password and countersign.

"Yeah, and from what the scuttlebutt says, that chaplain was a helluva good preacher man."

Henry stopped talking and pointed to a group of soldiers twenty or so feet away.

"You've been assigned to that three-striper, Staff Sergeant Jack Harrison. He's from Oklahoma. The other men are PFC Gordie D. Hall, Private James C. Harrel and Private Kenny Miller."

Sergeant Harrison waved Swenson and Wilkes over to where he was standing, having recognized Swenson from their brief encounter the previous afternoon. Looking at the paratrooper, he said, "Lieutenant James is working on getting you back to your unit. In the meantime, you're assigned to me. We're going out to recon some roads today. You being a paratrooper, I'm assuming you know something about infantry tactics…."

After getting my sweet ass lost yesterday, you mean?

"Yes, sergeant," Swenson answered.

"Good. Keep your eyes peeled, and follow me. We're going to recon some road designated S-9. It shouldn't be too big of a deal. The rest of the unit is busy grading three other roads. With any luck whatsoever, we could

finish early. And, if that's the case, I am in favor of a full night's sleep."
Sergeant Harrison's desire was fulfilled that evening.

D-DAY +4, 10 JUNE, 1944
NEAR THE VILLAGE OF LE GROSILLIERE, 1630 HOURS LOCAL

For the past twelve hours, PFC Henry and Corporal Swenson had been
detailed to assist the supply section in the distribution of supplies. Both men
were exhausted, and feeling not the least argumentative when the NCOIC
advised them they could return to their squad. As a means of thanking them
for their hard efforts, the supply sergeant told them where they could get
some freshly-brewed coffee. He ended his remarks by saying, "But I don't
think you should go back to Harrison without taking him one."

The pair immediately left the area, grabbed their canteen cups, and
headed for the mess tent. Once they had their precious brew, they sought out
SSG Harrison—who, as it turned out was only fifty or so feet away.

Henry reported in to Harrison, and handed him the cup of hot coffee.
Harrison thanked him. But his 'thank you' seemed distant.

"That's fresh from the mess tent, sergeant," Henry said as he sat down
to savor the wonderful smelling brew in his canteen. PFC Gordie D. Hall
and PVT James C. Harrell joined the three enlisted men.

When the two were seated, they heard Henry say to Swenson, "It looks
like the entire unit's now in-theater, since those last platoons from the line
companies and Colonel MacMillan arrived, doesn't it?"

Swenson wondered aloud, "How the hell does that affect us? I ain't an
engineer, but from what I see, you guys have done just fine without them."

SSG Harrison looked over to Swenson, but said nothing. However,
from the look he shot Swenson, the soldier from Iowa knew he'd screwed
up. "Sorry, sergeant. Some day I'm gonna learn to keep my big Swedish
nose the hell out of other people's business."

SSG Harrison didn't reply, just nodded his head. Then he opened the
subject that was bothering him.

"I heard-tell that Sergeant Weeks from Company A got killed back on
the 9th. Apparently, he was out reconnoitering for a bridge over the Douve
River, just north of Carentan, when some Kraut machine gun opened up on
him. Two other Able Company soldiers were wounded in the same fight.
Turns out that Company A's aid man, a private named Brown, managed to
get them the hell out of there while the Krauts were still shooting at them.

Reichmann says he's being put in for the Silver Star."

"I don't know what I'd do under those conditions," Ian Henry admitted.

"Ain't nobody does," Harrell replied.

Henry thought about what Harrell had just said, and changed the subject.

"Well, the good thing, is that four hundred-eighty-foot steel treadway bridge across the Douve River is finally done."[1]

PVT Gordie Hall reflected briefly. "You know, they didn't teach us about building bridges in that fast of a river current, nor did they say anything about the tides. Man, I would bet the water level rises more than twelve feet there."

The other soldier, a private named Kenny Miller, from Muskogee, Oklahoma, was cleaning his rifle. He walked over to where the men were standing and added, "But the fact remains… that the bridge done got built. And, we while we was building it, we were waitin' fer a massive German counterattack. You know, Lieutenant James done wrote up the report, and he said it was the first major bridge constructed in-theater."

Miller then spat a stream of tobacco juice, and sat down again.

SSG Harrison rose. "Before you guys break your arms patting yourselves on the back, just remember the Germans haven't counterattacked yet. In addition, to my way of thinking, that ain't going to last forever. And, remember—Berlin is still a helluva long way from here."

"Shit, sergeant, we were just making conversation…," said Ian Henry.

"Well, talking time is over. We got us a mission. So everyone gather around and listen up," SSG Harrison added, as he reached into his pocket for a small map.

He resumed speaking. "As you all know, we're attached to the 101st Airborne now, and they want us to continue with laying more anti-tank mines and putting up more double aprons of barbed wire."

"More fucking barbed wire?" Henry muttered.

SSG Harrison had had about enough of soldiers complaining. He had a job to do, and all the bitching and complaining wasn't helping.

"Henry, I didn't start this damned war, and I don't know if I'll live to see its end. But, one thing's for sure, I'm not going to listen to you men complain every time we draw a mission. So from now on, keep your mouth shut unless you have something to say that actually contributes to the

---

1. This was the first major bridge constructed in France by U.S. forces during WWII. James, *238th Engineer Combat Battalion in Action in WWII*, pg. 42

mission—okay?"

"Yes, sergeant. I was out of line."

"Good. Now the rest of you, listen up. This afternoon, when we were out there putting the finishing touches on that treadway bridge, Lieutenant Chalfort made contact with the V Corps at some place called Isigny. Now that that's been done, Utah and Omaha Beach are hooked up. So that's one for the good guys. But, let's not get too cocky. I'm sure the Krauts aren't going to take that one lying down. More than likely, there will be some serious fireworks in that area over the next few days.

"As for tonight's mission, we're going to assist in ferrying some 101st Airborne Division troops across the Douve River, east of Carentan. We're going to use assault boats and floats. It looks like there will be plenty of Germans in the area—so expect lots of small arms fire and artillery. Now, this ain't gonna be a picnic. Private Miller is right: those tides are close to thirteen feet. But we've been given a mission, and we're gonna do it right. And without losing anyone. Got that?"

"Yes, sergeant," the young GIs replied.

SSG Harrison stood up. "Alright, let's get this show on the road. Berlin is that way."

D-DAY +5, 11 JUNE 1944
NEAR THE VILLAGE OF CARENTAN, 1400 HOURS LOCAL

Lieutenant James and Captain Reichmann had been out on patrol for the better portion of the day, when their squads came upon another hedgerow. Reichmann gave the hand signal to his men to get down and use the hedgerow for protection.

The captain leaned over to his senior noncom, and spoke. "Have the men conceal themselves in that depression that's covered with trees and brush. If the Krauts start shelling us again, it should provide us with cover."

"Yes, sir."

Reichmann saw Lieutenant James off in the distance, and rose to make his way over to discuss the situation with his counterpart. Just as the two officers were about to make contact a German 88mm shell landed no more than five feet from them!

THUD!

"Holy shit!" one of Reichmann's soldiers yelled, "It's a fucking dud!"

"Good damned thing it was," said a junior enlisted man, as he crouched down as deep as he could into the French farmland.

"Well, Ernie, I say we get the hell out of here," Reichmann yelled, getting up and starting to run toward his men.

When the two officers got over to where their men were now digging in, Lieutenant James looked over at the next field.

"I don't believe it," watching a seventy-year old French woman stacking hay with a pitchfork.

Speaking to nobody in particular, a GI wondered aloud where the French men were.

"Hopefully, they're busy fighting the Krauts," added another soldier.

PFC Henry was taking it all in. While he didn't appreciate having a German 88 almost ruin his day, he did have to laugh when he saw Lieutenant James walking over to snap the old woman's picture.

"Hey, everybody," he said. "Check out Lieutenant James. He's going to take her picture."

Corporal Swenson couldn't believe his eyes, either. "Leave it up to the L-Tee. I mean, who else but James could come up with a camera in the middle of a battlefield?"

Looking at Corporal Swenson, Henry joked, "Now just think about it. If you were still in the airborne, you would have missed all this...."

Now SSG Harrison spoke up. "Alright, break time is over. Let's get back on patrol. Everyone except Henry, get up on your feet and keep your eyes peeled."

Henry looked to his NCOIC for guidance. Harrison supplied it. "You probably should get back to the CP and relieve Wilkes. He requested you to assist him with radio operations, and the Old Man approved it. So run your butt back to the AO and report in to the first sergeant."

Ian Henry was relieved. This patrol business was too much like being a soldier to suit him. He turned around, and headed back to the area of operations.

Swenson picked up his rifle and started walking toward the next hedgerow. As PFC Henry walked away, he watched Lieutenant James trying to photograph the French woman. For some reason or another, she had disappeared temporarily, having gone back into her hovel.

Maybe she doesn't want her picture taken?

A few moments later the old lady reappeared. But, this time she was wearing a very colorful feathered hat—obviously, it was her pride and joy.

"Damn," thought Swenson, "it's going to be a long war!"

CHAPTER ELEVEN

*Our landings in the Cherbourg-Le Havre area have
failed to gain a satisfactory foothold and I have
withdrawn the troops. My decision to attack at this
time and place was based upon the best information
available. The troops, the Air Forces and the Navy did
all that bravery and devotion to duty could do. If any
blame or fault attaches to the attempt, it is mine alone.*

—Statement prepared by Gen. Eisenhower, which would
have been issued in case the 1944 Normandy Invasion
failed

LIVING ROOM, THE RESIDENCE OF
MR. & MRS. SEAN KENNEDY, SR.
VOLCANO ROAD, SUTTER CREEK,
AMADOR COUNTY, CALIFORNIA
FRIDAY, NOVEMBER 23RD, 1991, 5:00 P.M. LOCAL

"That was quite a tale, Sergeant Major," Colonel Ohara said as he got
up from the sofa.

"Yeah, I thought he was never going to get out of Normandy," Dexter
Dannenberg added.

"After what happened on June 14, I didn't either," replied Charlie
Wilkes.

"Before you go into that story, Charlie, I'd like to fill in the lad on the
battle for Carentan." Dannenberg said.

"I didn't know you were there, Dexter?" inquired Colonel Ohara.

"I wasn't, of course. But it doesn't mean I didn't have access to the
battle reports that came through to us at The Park. Now, my memory might
be faulty, but the way I remember it, V Corps was up to their asses in
alligators. So was VII Corps. Both were bogged down, and the Krauts were
turning up the heat.

"It was one of the few times I actually saw Eisenhower up close and personal. I can remember taking over some Ultra traffic to SHAEF. I was in the process of delivering them to my contact when General Eisenhower came into the room. Don't ask me how the hell he knew who I was, but he did.

"As soon as my contact had logged in the traffic, Ike picked up the messages and began reading them. Now, the normal procedure was that after the traffic was logged, a courier would take them over to Eisenhower. As far as I knew, he never came over and got them himself. The fact that he did, told me things were not going well across the Channel.

"Of course, as things turned out, Ike's concern was justified. It looked like the Germans were about to break through both corps—which would have been an absolute disaster. The truth of the matter is that, had Hitler released his reserves, he might have been successful. But, the 'Austrian corporal' had been completely duped into believing that the Allies were coming across the English Channel at the Pas de Calais, and, as such, he refused to give Keitel permission to move any troops.

"In order to counteract the German attack, Ike turned to his old friend, Bradley, who then ordered V Corps to take Isigny. He also directed VII Corps was to take Carentan.

"The brunt of the mission fell upon the 101st Airborne Division—which, at the time was bogged down on the southern flank of Utah sector. The 101st commanding officer attempted to explain his situation to Collins, who then took his concerns to Bradley. Bradley responded by telling Collins to reinforce the 101st, if necessary. In short, Bradley didn't want any excuses. He wanted Carentan taken—end of discussion.

"A helluva battle took place. As I recall, the 506th Parachute Infantry, along with the 501st Parachute Infantry and the 1st Battalion of the 401st Glider Infantry, fought this one. But the 'fit hit the shan' on the Carentan highway, when the Krauts counterattacked.

"It was a SNAFU of the first order. Hell, the Krauts damn near overran the 3rd Battalion during one of their many counterattacks. One time, they got within one hedgerow! But the GIs held, and finally on the 8th of June the Screaming Eagles were able to establish a position on the southern flank of VII Corps.

"Another problem we had was that our intelligence was all screwed up. We didn't think Carentan was well defended, because we had planes fly over the city and our pilots reported the Germans had flown the coop. That wasn't true, of course, and the battle became one intense sonofabitch.

"Hell, here's another incident I remember. It sort of tells you just how tough this battle was. During the course of the fight, word came down that the Krauts wanted a truce. Well, our guy, General 'Nuts!' McAuliffe, the commanding officer of the Screaming Eagles, went along with it. He wanted to get his wounded out. He sent in his surgeon to talk to the Jerries. The Krauts refused to let him see their general, and in fact used the time to reinforce their lines.

"As soon as the doc got back to his unit, the Jerries opened up with every damned type of weapon they had in their arsenal. It was a shitty thing on the Germans' part, but in the end, our guys won the day. In fact, the historical significance of this battle is often overlooked. Hell, had the Krauts been successful we could have lost the beachheads, and God only knows what kind of a disaster that would have been. We might have had to come to some sort of rapprochement with Hitler!"

"So—what happened then?" Sean Ohara inquired.

Dannenberg looked over at CSM Wilkes. "Charlie, they're playing your song."

"Well, while that was all going on, the 238th went to work building bridges. The first one spanned forty feet over the DeVire canal, which is just east of Carentan. The second one we built was eighty feet long. In both instances, the Germans were shooting at us. It certainly made for an interesting experience," the CSM said as he picked up his cocktail. After taking a sip, he continued, "But I gotta tell you, the worst was yet to come. We were attached to the 101st, and bivouacked at Le billionerre near Carentan. Orders came down for us to lay a double-apron barbed wire fence in the front of the entire division. We'd been doing that for some time, when either someone dropped an armed mine or a truck from B Company hit a mine—which caused the truck's entire load of mines to go off."

"Ouch!" Colonel Ohara commented.

"We lost nine good men."

"That must have kicked the snot out of your unit," replied Colonel Ohara.

"It did, but at the time there wasn't much one could do about it, except to mourn the loss of our comrades. Remember, we were ass-high in Krauts. But I still can recall every one of those men's names. The enlisted men we lost were Corporal Miller, T/5s Camano and Willis, PFCs Hardy and Dunam, and Privates Cias, Webb and Weiss. Lieutenant Wise was also killed. Of course, those nine men were the ones who were killed. That's not counting any of the men who were severely wounded."

Colonel Ohara and his son could see that CSM Wilkes was struggling to continue his story. Ohara was about to suggest they turn on the television to see what football game might be playing, when Wilkes abruptly laughed.

"The damnedest thing was that ol' Lieutenant James lucked out again. You see, his platoon had been laying mines about three hundred yards away when the accident—or whatever the hell it was—happened. Amazingly, the only thing James got out of it was a giant concussion."

"So, what came next, Sergeant Major?" asked Sean Kennedy.

"Well... PFC Wilkes ran his fanny back to the AO, and reported in...."

THE 238TH COMBAT ENGINEERS AREA OF OPERATIONS NEAR THE VILLAGE OF CARENTAN, FRANCE 14 JUNE 1944, 1620 HOURS, LOCAL

After reporting in to the OPNS tent as directed by SSG Harrison, CPL Wilkes began to instruct PFC Henry on how to log in messages. Henry busied himself at the task while Charlie worked the radio.

Ian Henry admired how his friend Charlie could remember everyone's call signs, and how proficient he seemed at working the net. As he waited for Charlie to instruct him in another task, Ian picked up a rough draft of an after-action report that Captain Reichmann had begun writing.

"Reichmann says we've been up to our ass in Krauts all morning."

Finished with passing messages, Wilkes answered, "You needed a report to know that?"

"No, I'm just making conversation," Henry replied.

"Headquarters has probably figured that one out by now," Wilkes commented. "But, sure as hell, they're going to want a full report on that business out in the minefield."

"I sure am glad I don't have to write that one," Henry added.

Wilkes picked up his canteen and took a sip. He promptly ejected its contents.

"Shit! Some miserable bastard used my coffee cup to spit out his tobacco juice!"

Ian Henry wanted to laugh, but knew better. Instead, he said, "When you find out who did it, why don't you piss in his canteen?"

"I'll take your suggestion under advisement," Charlie said, as he looked around for something to wash down the disgusting taste in his mouth. As he was searching for something else to drink, he spotted his canteen.

"Damn! Do I feel like an ass? Look what I found! Charlie picked up his own canteen cup and showed it to Henry.

"Aw, shit, Charlie—how did that happen?"

"I don't know. Chalk it up to the 'Fog of War,'" Wilkes replied disgustedly.

"What the hell are you talking about, Charlie?"

The truth was that Charlie had first heard about Carl Maria von Clauswitz's treatise on warfare just a few days before, when he'd overheard Lieutenants James and Worth discussing a friendly-fire mishap that occurred on D-Day. But the phrase seemed to fit his circumstances, so Charlie used it.

Knowing nothing more now than he did before Charlie answered his question, Henry gave up and went outside the tent. But not before flipping Wilkes off.

Ian longed for sleep, but quickly gave up that idea when he saw SSG Sergeant Marion P. Davis, PFC Duncan and CPL Swenson approaching him.

"All right, Henry, break time is over."

"Come on, sergeant, I just got off work," Henry objected.

"You've been on a break since we got to France!" Davis replied half-heartedly.

"With all due respect, staff sergeant," PFC Henry replied, "I ain't exactly got any calluses on my butt."

Overhearing the conversation from within the OPNS tent, Charlie Wilkes came outside and blurted, "Henry, the only place you have calluses is on your hand, and we all know why!"

SSG Davis roared with laughter. Then, nodding toward Ian Henry, he said, "Grab your rifle, you're going out on a patrol with my squad."

"Anywhere in particular, sergeant?" PFC Duncan asked, as he lit up a smoke.

Davis used his right foot to clear a spot of dirt of debris. Then he used his finger to draw a line.

"We're here." Now he drew another line about four inches away. "These are the woods over yonder. G-2 thinks the Krauts are over here," he said, making a small mark in the dirt about an inch from the wooded area.

"Our job is to go out there and find out if the *Nazis* are where the Intel boys believe them to be."

Swenson, who up to this moment had been silent, asked, "What are the rules of engagement, sergeant?"

A smile came over Davis' face. "Damn, I love it when someone asks a smart question. The ROEs are real simple—we're to verify where the Krauts are, all the while not letting them know that we're in the area. In short, we are not to engage them, if possible. Does everyone understand that?"

Henry reached into his fatigue jacket and pulled out a stick of gum. It was his last one. Ian wondered if he should save it for another time.

What am I saving it for? Berlin? Besides, who says I'm even going to live to see Berlin?

He extracted the gum from its wrapper, and then licked the paper. It was an odd thing to do, but he had done it since grade school. As he grabbed his rifle and prepared to move out, he heard what sounded like a jeep approaching.

He turned his head and took a glance: sure as hell, it was a jeep. But, not only was it a jeep—it was a full-blown command staff car. Ian caught the eye of CPL Swenson, and nodded his head in the direction of the oncoming vehicle. Initially Swenson looked at him strangely, because he hadn't heard the jeep approaching. When he finally figured out what Ian's head nod was all about, he expressed himself accordingly.

"Fuck me! This don't look good."

Forty feet away from where Henry and Swenson were standing, corporals Robert M. Harding from Detroit, and Lonnie Hood from Sanderson, Florida, were cleaning their rifles and pretty much not paying attention to what was going on. At that moment, however, Hood looked up and saw the staff car.

Then he heard an officer in the background say, "Shit, this don't look good."

Once PFC Duncan had put all the pieces together, he nudged PFC Henry.

"Do you think we ought to inform the brass in the Operations Tent that a four-star general's in the area, or should we let them get caught with their drawers down?"

"It might be fun to see them jump through their assholes. But, after whoever's in that Jeep departs the area, we'll be in for the reaming of our lives. So I think I'll run my happy ass over to the operations tent and tell them life is about to get interesting."

"Do that, and do it fast," Duncan replied.

Henry hightailed to the tent. When he got inside he noticed it was full of officers. He quickly told them that a four-star was rapidly approaching, then got the hell out of the tent as fast as he could.

When he got back to the group of soldiers preparing to go out on patrol, he heard the first sergeant holler, "Attention!"

Inside the tent, all of the officers and enlisted men looked up and saw none other than General Maxwell Taylor, commanding general of the 101st Airborne Division, standing in front of them. And he did not look amused.

"Good afternoon, general," Major MacMillan said.

"Are you in charge here, Major?" General Taylor asked.

"Yes, sir."

"Then you stay, and the rest of you people leave."

Nobody had to be told twice to get the hell out of the operations tent. Taylor and MacMillan stayed inside for ten minutes. Even though Charlie Wilkes was a good twenty feet away from the tent, he could hear everything that was going on—and he could tell that General Taylor was livid.

"Major, are you aware that we are expecting a major counterattack tonight?"

"Yes, sir." MacMillan replied.

"And are you also aware that a minefield was to have been laid to prevent the Krauts from overrunning our positions?"

"Yes, sir."

"Then will you please tell me, major, why that has not been done?"

MacMillan could not produce an answer adequate enough to satisfy the 1922 graduate of the United States Military Academy. And he knew better than to try to snowball Taylor, as it was common knowledge that Taylor's first job in the Army had been an engineer.

"Major," Taylor said in his West Point voice, "I am going to get to the bottom of this debacle. And when I do, heads are going to roll."

Taylor did a one-eighty and walked out of the tent, got back into his command vehicle, and drove away.

General Taylor made good on his word as soon after leaving the 238th operations tent. He discovered that the task of laying the mines had been given to Captain Reichmann. Why the mines had not been laid puzzled him, as Reichmann was considered a top-notch officer. He wondered why the junior grade officer had refused to lay the six hundred mines needed to stop the German counteroffensive.[1]

Of course, the encounter between General Taylor and Major MacMillan quickly became the *topic du jour* around the 238th AO (Area of Operations).

Corporal Wilkes had never really taken a liking to his unit's commanding officer. Charlie didn't know why he didn't care for Major MacMillan, but he just didn't. On one occasion he'd given it some serious consideration, and attributed it to the fact that he had gotten along so well with this commanding officer at Camp Roberts. But Charlie doubted if Major MacMillan even knew his full name.

Of course, if Wilkes had really been fair and objective about the matter, he would have remembered that he'd been Captain McDonald's driver, and that on any typical day he and the captain would spend at least three or four hours together, while MacMillan knew him only as a radio operator and occasionally as his driver.

As General Taylor's vehicle departed the AO, Wilkes looked at the other enlisted men, then whistled under his breath.

"I think the shit just hit the fan."

"How so?" Duncan asked.

"When a general orders a minefield to be laid and it doesn't get done—heads roll. Mark my word on it."

"He'll get over it," Henry added, as he started to apply camouflage paint to his face in preparation for the evening's patrol.

"Bullshit!" Wilkes replied. "I'm sure heads are gonna roll over this one."

Henry ignored Wilkes, but Duncan didn't. "How in the hell did you come up with that one? It was just a minor screw-up. It'll all blow over."

"Yeah, and Hitler is going to surrender to Churchill tomorrow morning. Listen, you stupid ass, General Taylor just doesn't 'drop in' on his commanders to have tea."

"I know that. But it don't mean Taylor's gonna can MacMillan's ass over it, either," Duncan replied.

"Eric, under most circumstances, I'd say you're right. But these ain't

---

1. Reichmann felt that in good conscience he could not order the task down without some protection. To his way of thinking, to do so would have been negligent and unnecessarily endangered his men's lives. Once Taylor understood Reichmann's position, he ordered the necessary protection, and the minefield was laid.

normal circumstances. Besides… I'm beginning to think that the brass believe there's more to that supposed leak on Mac's LCD when we were coming across the Channel, than we first thought.

"And, as for his not being here on D-Day… that one just won't go away."

"You're imagining crap, Charlie," Duncan replied.

"Listen, jackass, I ain't the only one who thinks something wasn't right about what happened back on June 5th, in regard to our good major and his 'leaking LCT.'"

"I think you're full of shit, too, Wilkes." Swenson added.

Charlie was getting frustrated. After all, he was the one who spent ten to twelve hours in the operations tent every day. And, by God, the way he figured it, if anyone in the entire 238th Engineer Combat Battalion should know what the hell was going in the unit, it was him!

Lowering his voice, he looked directly at Swenson. "I shouldn't say this, but I've overheard some of the officers talking behind Mac's back, and I'd say that not too many of them would miss him if he was relieved."

"I ain't buying it, Wilkes. If the Army fired everyone who fucked up, nobody would have a job."

Wilkes was too weary to put up with any more of his Iowa neighbor's hard-headedness, and was about to resort to knocking the crap out of him, when he looked over and saw that Swenson had an ear-to-ear grin on his face.

They've been jerking me off this whole time! Well, don't you feel like a fool? Good thing you didn't shoot off your mouth, Charlie.

Much the wiser, Wilkes joked with his old high school nemesis for a few more minutes. Just about the time he decided he needed to go back into the OPNS tent, he remembered something he'd seen in the afternoon distribution.

"By the way, Swenson, I've got it on pretty good authority that you're being permanently assigned to the 238th Engineer Combat Battalion."

Swenson was incredulous. He had been sweating having to go back to the 101st, but now his prayers were answered. He was staying put. However, he was pissed, anyway. He reached inside his fatigue jacket and grabbed a smoke. As he fumbled for a match, Charlie asked him when he'd started smoking.

Ignoring him, Swenson blurted out, "Fuck you, Charlie. Answer my question: when did you find out I wasn't going back to the 101st?"

Charlie could see that his fellow Iowan was in no mood for grab-ass.
"Your transfer order came in with the afternoon mail."

"Mail?" Swenson shouted. "You bastard, we got mail in, and you didn't tell us?"

Wilkes realized he'd used the wrong word. He'd said "mail," but meant "distribution." He corrected himself immediately, and Swenson backed off.

Corporal Swenson could not have been more pleased. Even though he didn't know his ass from Page 8 when it came to 'engineer stuff,' he knew his being in that career field at least gave him a better-than-average chance of going home to his wife when the war was finally over.

"Well, thanks for letting me know, Charlie. I guess I owe you one."

"Don't thank me. Thank Lieutenant James. He put in a good word for you to Major Massoglia, and Massoglia put in a request to brigade. I guess your unit bought off on it. Either that, or they figured you weren't worth a fuck as an infantryman and decided to dump your ass on us."

Swenson knew Charlie was screwing with him. But inwardly he knew that Charlie was right on target, so he decided to ignore that last comment. Instead, he looked at his watch and tapped its face. In doing so, he brought Ian Henry and Eric Duncan back into the conversation.

"I'd say it's time to get off our lazy asses and get back to work. After all, ain't we being paid to win this damned war?"

His comment brought chuckles from both Henry and Duncan as they started to walk toward their platoon sergeant, SSG Harrison, who was discussing something with Lieutenant James. While Charlie Wilkes strolled back to the OPNS tent, he looked up and saw that the sky was full of some rather ominous-looking clouds.

If I were in Iowa, I'd say we're in for a helluva storm.

Suddenly, he laughed aloud.

Charlie, my boy, in case you haven't figured it out—this ain't Iowa!

Once inside the tent, Charlie Wilkes was greeted by some wonderful news: apparently, a cow had "strayed" into the line of fire of an M-1 and had paid the ultimate price for doing so.

We're having steak tonight!

As it turned out, Wilkes was correct in his weather prognostication. A major storm came through the area and completely decimated the ports on Utah and Omaha beaches, severely hampering the Allied supply effort.

During the next few weeks the 238th moved to Chef DuPont, where they remained until the 20th of June. During that time, they constructed an eighty-foot DS Bailey bridge over the Douve River near St. Sauveur Le Vicomte. The unit was under constant shelling and machine gun fire, but they completed their missions, securing and repairing roads in support of the 79th and 90th Infantry Divisions, as well as the 82nd Airborne Division.

CHAPTER TWELVE

It is wrong to mourn soldiers who have died in battle.
Rather, we thank God that such men lived.
—General George S. Patton
in a speech given six months before he died

THE LIVING ROOM OF MR. & MRS. SEAN KENNEDY, SR.
VOLCANO ROAD, SUTTER CREEK,
AMADOR COUNTY, CALIFORNIA
FRIDAY, 29 NOVEMBER 1991, 6:15 P.M. LOCAL

Sean Kennedy Ohara was absolutely exhausted. Every muscle in his body hurt. He was sitting in a Lazy Boy recliner, pondering whether he had the *cajones* to ask his father for a shot of Jack Daniels or some other suitable adult beverage that would make him forget he'd spent most of the afternoon chopping firewood.

His dad walked over to where the teenager was sitting and handed him a couple of aspirins, then thanked him for helping the Kennedys get in the last bit of wood needed for what was sure to be a rough winter.

"I was thinking about asking you for some Jack Daniels…."

"Hand me back the aspirin, and I'll pour you a weak one," his father replied, as he got up and walked back into the kitchen.

Dexter Dannenberg sat on the other side of the Kennedys' living room. He had his head firmly planted in a book, a thick one at that. Without lifting his head from the book he was reading, Dexter spoke.

"You worked your butt off today, young man. I'm sure the Kennedys are deeply appreciative. In fact, I was thinking that after Christmas I'd like to have all of you down to my condo in Palm Springs. I have a ton of things that need your brawn to complete, and it would afford me an excellent opportunity to have your father show me how to play golf. Your mom could, of course, spend her time shopping and hanging out at some of the many day spas we have nowadays."

The young Ohara knew that his father would accept that invitation in a New York minute. After all, Dexter had just said the magic word—golf.

"I'd love to, Mr. Dannenberg. And I'm sure my mom and dad would want to spend some time with you in Palm Springs, too."

"Did I hear the word 'golf'?" Colonel Ohara said, as he walked back into the room with a small glass of Jack-in-Black on the rocks.

Dannenberg looked up at the colonel. "What do you say, to you and your brood coming down to Palm Springs after the bishop cuts you loose from your duties at the cathedral? Say, the 27th or so of December?"

"It sounds great to me, Dexter. And I'm sure Chloe would want to come down."

"Then, you're on. In the meantime, why don't I fill you in on what was going on back in London while the 238th was winning the war on the Continent?"

Dannenberg put down his book and began speaking.

CABINET WAR ROOMS,
KINGS CHARLES STREET, WESTMINSTER
LONDON, TUESDAY, 13 JUNE 1944, 11:30 P.M. LOCAL

Winston Churchill was in a foul mood. But, because his personal staff was small to begin with, and the fact was that most of them had gone home, there wasn't anyone to bully. He reached for his brandy snifter and walked over to the davenport and sat down.

Today has been a dastardly day. That Austrian corporal has unleashed some new type of weapon against England, and the only person who seems to know what in blazes they are is in the men's room washing his hands! Damn!

Churchill reached for his lighter, and took another sip of brandy.

Come on, Attlee! How long does one need to wash his hands before they're clean?

Clement Attlee approached Churchill, although too slowly for the prime minister's satisfaction.

"Come on, Clement. What have you got for me?

Attlee looked down at the PM and began speaking.

"Well, Winston, from what the Homeland Security chaps tell me, the Huns have begun launching some form of rocket at us.

"One of the blokes over in the West End reported that these 'buzzing bombs' are about twenty-five feet long and carry somewhere in the neighborhood of two thousand pounds of explosives."

"That's going to be bloody-damn rough on the civilian population," Churchill replied, as he took a long draw from his torpedo cigar.

"Winston," said Attlee, as he tried to find a place where Churchill's cigar smoke wasn't overwhelming to his nostrils, "these flying bombs have a tremendous capability to destroy the entire city of London. Why, the report from West London—Staverley Road, to be exact—said that some folks were quietly having breakfast when all the sudden their neighbors' homes disappeared."

Churchill did not respond. He was lost in thought. Attlee continued talking.

"I can only hope that our Royal Air Force boys can find out where they are coming from—and damned soon. Otherwise, I hate to think of the damage these weapons are going to wreak upon London. The psychological toll these buggers could inflict is staggering."

Churchill took a long draw from his smoke. Attlee correctly surmised he was gathering his thoughts. Suddenly, the prime minister spoke again.

"You know, when Chamberlain resigned and the Huns attacked Norway, I told the British people that 'I have nothing to offer but blood, toil, tears and sweat.' But these weapons, as ghastly are they are, in reality are the last hurrah of a desperate man leading a desperate people. We will surely defeat them."

"I have no doubt you're right, Mr. Prime Minister. Certainly, it's only a matter of time before we gain complete air superiority over the Continent. And, as such, *Herr* Hitler will have no place in which to hide his new 'miracle weapons.' But the question remains: what can we do in the next few days to counteract this latest development of *Herr* Hitler?"

"Clement, with a little luck, with God, and the Eighth Air Force and the R.A.F. on our side, we shall stamp out this bunch of vermin and cast them into the abyss."

Attlee looked at his watch, then said, "Why don't we set up a meeting with Ike and General Doolittle's flyboys from Wycombe[1] [WWII headquarters of the Eighth Air Force] in the morning, and see what our American friends can do to assist us?"

---

1. The 8th Air Force was organized on 1 February 1942 at Langley Field, Virginia. It was designated as VIII Bomber Command. On 23 February 1942, the VIII Bomber Command was moved to England. Ironically, its Headquarters was established at the Wycombe Abbey School for girls.

Churchill picked up his brandy. He took a sip and said, "Make the call."

THE LIBRARY OF SEAN KENNEDY, SR.
VOLCANO ROAD, SUTTER CREEK,
AMADOR COUNTY, CALIFORNIA
FRIDAY, 29 NOVEMBER 1991, 6:30 P.M. LOCAL

"What happened after Attlee made that call, Mr. Dannenberg?" Sean Ohara asked, reaching over for a piece of Mrs. Kennedy's fudge.

"Well, southeastern England and Belgium caught hell. It didn't take long before we found out that the *Nazi*s were launching their buzz-bombs from "ski-jump" launch sites in the Pas-de-Calais area, and along the Dutch coast. They did so until our armed forces overran them in October 1944.[2]

By war's end, the Krauts had launched over eight thousand missiles against England. Hell, if my memory serves me right, they shot over twenty-three hundred at London alone! The worst thing about them, was the psychological effect they had on the civilian population."

"I can't imagine the terror those V-1s and V-2s must have caused in the English people," Sean Ohara said, as he took a sip of his liquor.

"But, as strange as this might sound, Sean," Dexter answered, "when I think back to those dark days I'm filled with pride, because I can recall that every time one of Hitler's 'miracle weapons' bombed London, the Brits' resolve became stronger. The caricature of that English bulldog was accurate. The general consensus amongst the English populace was that, come hell or high water, they would defeat the Nazis—miracle weapons or not!"

The young Ohara was about to speak again when CSM Wilkes came into the room.

Nodding at Dannenberg and then looking toward the teenager, Wilkes quipped, "Hasn't the old guy run out of gas yet?"

"No, Command Sergeant Major. Mr. Dannenberg was telling me about living in London during the V-1 and V-2 attacks."

"Well, I tell you what—let me grab some of my stash of Old Fitzgerald Kentucky Straight Bourbon Whiskey, and an ice cube or two, and I'll

---

2. William C. Story, Jr. wrote a definitive article on ballistic missiles, which he presented to the faculty of Advanced Airpower Studies at the USAF Air University, located at Maxwell AFB, Alabama in 1994. It is available at http://www.fas.org/man/eprint/story.htm.

continue from where I left off."

While Wilkes was fixing his drink, Dannenberg and Sean were joined by Colonel Ohara. "Mind if I listen in?"

"Not at all, colonel. As a matter of fact, it might be a good idea if you were to sit in for a while, as Charlie continues with his story of how he won World War II," Dannenberg joked, knowing that CSM Wilkes was about to re-enter the library.

"Listen Dexter, I haven't said one thing that's not one hundred percent true…."

"Calm down, Charlie," Colonel Ohara said as he winked in Dannenberg's direction, "Nobody's accusing anyone of being Audie Murphy here."

CSM Wilkes sat down in his recliner.

"But, you know what? There was one day I felt like I could give that soldier from Kingston, Texas a ride for his money."

Dexter Dannenberg's eyebrow shot up. "Charlie, you've never told me this story, have you?"

"No."

"Then by all means, do."

"It was June 18th. As you'll recall, I wasn't just the commo guy in the operations tent, I was also Major Massoglia's driver. And on this day, Massoglia ordered lieutenants Reichman and McClure to reconnoiter the main road to Cherbourg. As it turned out, Reichman's driver had gone on sick call that morning, probably with a case of pneumonia. So that meant I had to drive for both officers.

"We were about three miles south of the city, when we ran into a barrier that was put up across the road. Massoglia had been specific: *Do not* make contact with the Krauts. So, after a brief discussion, Reichman ordered me to turn the staff vehicle around. It was right then—when our vehicle was dead in the middle of the friggin' road—that the Germans lambasted us with every damned '88' they had left in their arsenal. I thought we were dead meat. And, sure as hell, when we were right smack-dab in the Kraut's crosshairs, one of those sonofabitches got lucky. They creamed our vehicle. But the war gods were with us, because nobody was hit.

"As we were busting our asses getting the hell out of the area, we crawled through ditches and depressions. Just about the time I thought we were home free, the Krauts opened up with mortars. But the damnest thing about it, was that not one of us got so much as a scratch! What we didn't know at the time, was that we'd actually entered the outer defenses of Cherbourg."

Sean Ohara looked at the old soldier and shook his head. "I'd say you were pretty darned lucky, Sergeant Major."

"I ain't gonna argue with that. But... I didn't exactly tell you the whole truth about our injuries."

"How so?"

"When we got back to the AO, I reported in to SSG Black. I must have looked like hell after all the crawling around in the mud, but that didn't seem to bother him. All he did was look at me, laugh, and ask if I had another uniform.

"I told him I did, and his response was classic: "Then put it on, because you've crapped in that one!"

Ohara's son nearly fell out of his chair with laughter, which caused everyone in the room to laugh, too. Wilkes took it all in good stride, as he knew he had lived through a skirmish that by all rights should have punched his ticket.

238TH OPERATIONS TENT,
SOMEWHERE NEAR QUETTETOT, FRANCE
22 JUNE 1944, 1945 HOURS LOCAL

Having just finished the paperwork on the construction of a thirty-three foot timber trestle bridge over the Seye River near La Valdecie, Lieutenant James was sorely tempted to call it a day and turn in for the night. Tomorrow, the 238th was scheduled to build a fifty-foot timber bridge over the same river, near Rauville La Bigot. But he also yearned to write a letter to his girl back in the States.

Sitting on an upended ammo box, James reached into his fatigue jacket and pulled out his pipe. Then he found his bag of tobacco, grabbed his kit and began writing:

June 22, 1944
Faith:
My letters are obviously getting irregular. Wish I could tell you what we are doing, but cannot. You can read about it in the papers, for we are in the thick of things. It is rough, little sleep and poor food. All rations since the sixth have been K or C, except for the steak. Tonight we had stew from vegetables the French gave

us.

Did you read the news article where a soldier said the French did not celebrate when we moved in? Wrong. I was out all day in a jeep, and people everywhere were out waving at us. In many places, families stood out in the road and stopped us, offering us a drink of cognac or wine. We had a whole jeep load of flowers that people had thrown at us. They were happy people. If there were any Germans around, they would call the first soldier and turn them over. How do people back home take what we are doing? After seeing those here, I think it may be worth it.

I am tired. I can hardly keep my eyes open.

No mail yet, but we are looking for it every day.

Some old mail came, none of which I have answered.

Yours,

Ernie

LT James put down his pen and sealed his letter. He then walked over to his cot, lay down and took off his glasses. He was exhausted, but his mind was fully alert.

During the month of June, the people of the Contentin Peninsula have endured many hardships. They've been occupied by a defensive German Army, been subjected to severe aerial bombardment, an aerial infantry assault and an invasion of their coast. Their farms have been ruined, their livestock killed, and many of them haven't lived through the siege. Yet, they still welcome us as liberators. Hopefully, we can continue to return that feeling.

THE 238TH BIVOUAC SITE NEAR QUETTETOT
24 JUNE 1944, 0430 HOURS LOCAL

Even though none of the officers in the 238th Engineer Combat Battalion had slept more than four hours, every one present had been in-country long enough to know that this morning's briefing was destined to be more than a list of bridges needing to be built and mine fields to be cleared.

The battalion had sent down the OIC of G-2 to brief them personally. Mercifully, the mess steward had provided them with hot coffee.

Captain Reichman and Lieutenant James were sitting toward the rear of the tent when Major Massoglia called the tent to attention.

The colonel from G-2 quickly told the men to remain seated. After a short introduction, he began his briefing.

"Gentlemen, first of all, let me thank you for all the great work you've done in the area south of Carentan. I especially want to thank you for the roads you've built and the others you've repaired. You have been heavily engaged for over a month, and without much rest.

"I would like to tell you that you're going to get some rest, but that's not the case. As you know, we have come up against some heavier than expected resistance in the St. Lo area. The Krauts have virtually stopped our advances. We have men dying out there for a few yards of ground. I'm here to tell you that it's going to change as of today, so listen up while I explain the order of battle."

Pointing to a map, the colonel continued, "Army Air Corps is about to lambaste this area here. Then the artillery boys take over. At H-Hour our forces are going to move forward through the hedgerows—taking out the Krauts' main line of resistance—which will allow for everyone's favorite general, George S. Patton's, newly-formed Third Army to break out and head toward the Brest Peninsula."

A smattering of laughter broke out at the mention of their "favorite" General Patton, which the colonel permitted for a few seconds. Then he continued his briefing.

"Now, I have to tell you, my sources say that General Bradley had a helluva time getting this one through SHAEF. It seems that the folks at Army Air Corps want to drop their ordnance perpendicular to the Krauts' line. Which, in this case, is the St. Lo-Periers Highway. Air Corps says that would be the safest way to do their bombing runs, as otherwise it would give the Jerries too much time to get our planes in their crosshairs.

"General Bradley fought this tooth and nail, because–as you can see–" the colonel said, moving his hand on the board to where the American soldiers would be ready to jump off, "he thinks it's too risky for our boys on the ground.

"Anyway, a real Donnybrook ensued, as Bradley insisted that the flyboys come in from an east-west direction, one that's parallel to the aforementioned highway.

"H-Hour for this operation is set for 1130 hours local time. As far as we know, ol' Georgie Patton is chomping at the bit, now that he's been let out of Ike's doghouse."

There was more snickering from the officers in the tent. Then the G-2 officer continued his remarks.

"A couple hours before all hell breaks loose, our guys will be pulled back some twelve hundred yards, as an insurance policy in case of errant bombs from the flyboys. What comes next is truly impressive. At last count, we have over fifty battalions of artillery ready to unload on our German 'friends.' In short, it's going to be Omaha Beach all over again. But this time, we don't have to take the beaches!

"If all goes according to plan, Georgie Patton should be in Brest before the week is up.

"Now, where does the 238th come in on this battle? The plan calls for us to move to Beaumont, where we will drain the Douve River Basin. By doing that, we will be able to regulate the locks at La Barquette. After that, we're going to support the 83rd Division southwest of Carentan. They should be holding the same positions that we prepared for the 101st back in June. Our primary job during this time will be to remove any mines in the area. You know—the ones you recently laid."

Again, laughter rippled though the tent.

The colonel stopped talking and looked at the assembled officers, taking the time to look each officer directly in his face. When he had finished making individual eye contact, he said, "If this works, we're on our way into Berlin."

Major Massoglia sensed the O-6 from G-2 was done speaking, and called the men back to attention. As the soldiers stood up, Massoglia made his way over to the military intelligence officer, assisting him out the door and back to his vehicle.

THE DINING ROOM OF THE SEAN KENNEDYS
VOLCANO ROAD, SUTTER CREEK,
AMADOR COUNTY, CALIFORNIA
FRIDAY, 29 NOVEMBER 1991, 7:30 P.M. LOCAL

"So, how did the battle of St. Lo go, Sergeant Major?" Sean Ohara asked.

"God, it turned out to be a total 'Charlie-Foxtrot'! The units on the ground had no more than fired their red smoke shells when the wind picked up, causing the smoke to drift back toward the grunts on the ground."

"Why was that a problem?"

"The problem was that our flyboys were coming in under radio silence, meaning that hundreds of P-47s and nearly fifteen-hundred heavy bombers were about to drop their payloads on our troops! Not only that, they were coming in perpendicular to the Germans' main line of resistance. Whatever sonofabitch changed those orders should've been shot!

"God, we lost a bunch of good men that day—and for what?"

"Why didn't someone get on the radio and wave them off?" the teenager asked.

"We couldn't wave them off, because we didn't have any such thing as ground-to-air liaison yet. Needless to say, those poor bastards in the 30th Division were creamed! And that the scheduled H-Hour went to hell in a hand basket.

"Mind you, the entire purpose of this engagement was to get the Allies moving, and cluster-fuck or not, we had to go back the next day and do the same thing. Only, this time, it was half an hour earlier. As if that was going to make things better. Hell, it was damned near impossible to fill in the ranks with new troops, and re-supply everybody on the ground.

"We did what we could. But when morning came, the same thing happened. As soon as the smoke was popped the next morning, the breeze started coming in from the right! God Almighty, this time it was a catastrophe. If my memory serves me right, we lost sixty-plus more men KIA, and hundreds were wounded."

"Was the attack cancelled?"

"How could they? We'd already told the Krauts we were coming. No, it went ahead anyway. But I have to tell you, we didn't hurt the Germans as hard as we thought. Consequently, we ran into a friggin' buzz saw.

"We also lost General Leslie McNair. He was sent up there to monitor the situation, but instead was killed by one of our own bombs."

"I didn't know anything about this," Colonel Michael Ohara commented.

"Not many people do," explained the senior non-commissioned officer. "It wasn't something we wanted to broadcast. But, I can guarantee you one thing—those brave men in the 30th Division who survived that day, sure as hell remember it."

For the next few minutes the topic of the conversation changed from the D-Day invasion, to the friends' planned invasion of some local Sacramento area malls early the next morning. The rest of the evening was spent watching television and preparing to depart the Kennedy compound in the morning.

During breakfast the following morning, Charlie and Sharon Wilkes asked if it would be okay for them to join the Oharas on their shopping spree.

"The more the merrier," Colonel Ohara said, sipping on his coffee. "But I'd have thought you already sent your sons' presents, considering they're both in Europe."

Sharon Wilkes smiled, first at her husband and then to Colonel Ohara.

"Actually we're planning on flying to Europe to see them and their families after the first. But I'm of the opinion that we'll still need to send the kids something for Christmas morning."

Wilkes entered the conversation. "Actually, colonel, we mailed all the boys a ton of presents a month ago. But my wife always has to go after that 'last present' for God-knows-who."

Colonel Ohara was about to reply, when he noticed his wife giving him "the look."

"I plead the fifth, your honor."

Mrs. Ohara sat up straight, and smiled. "Actually, my husband is just cheap."

"And your point is, Chloe?" Charlie asked.

Now Dexter, too, came into the conversation. "So, while all of you are spending yourselves into bankruptcy, I think I'll mosey on over to the Ohara's villa in Granite Bay and prepare dinner for us."

"An excellent offer, Dex," the colonel replied as he picked up his coffee cup and headed for the door.

Mrs. Ohara looked over toward the Kennedys.

"I guess his holiness has decided we're leaving for Sacramento."

CHAPTER THIRTEEN

If any question why we died, tell them because our fathers lied.
  —Rudyard Kipling

COLONEL AND MRS. MICHAEL BRANDON OHARA'S RESIDENCE
LOS LAGOS, GRANITE BAY, CALIFORNIA
SATURDAY, 30 NOVEMBER 1991, 5:00 P.M. LOCAL

From the moment Colonel Ohara drove his SUV onto their property, he suspected that Dexter Dannenberg was up to something, as he did not recognize one of the late-model automobiles parked in the driveway. Looking to Chloe, he said, "I smell a rat."

Chloe, a mistress of English understatement, observed, "Rat might be too strong of a word—but I'd be willing to go 'furry thing.'"

As he pulled his car into its parking spot, a light in his head clicked. "I'd bet that old rascal has invited Ernie James up here."

"I wouldn't put it past him," Mrs. Ohara answered, as she broke into laughter.

Now Colonel Ohara had it figured out: their entire trip to Sacramento had been planned as a diversionary tactic, to get him away from home long enough to bring the retired Ernie James and his wife, Faith, to their residence.

Ohara looked at his wife, and said," You were in on it, weren't you?"

"I couldn't help but go along with it, when Dexter asked me what I thought about asking Major James up for the night. I mean—after that stunt he pulled back at Congressman Banks' home this Labor Day past, I just had to go along with this little caper."

Colonel Ohara began to see the humor in Dannenberg's prank, and he too began laughing.

"I should've expected something like this, considering his *modus operandi* in Vietnam." He turned off the engine and exited the car. As he began walking toward the house, Dexter Dannenberg came outside to greet them, accompanied by a very tall, grey-haired man and a small woman of about the same age.

Just about the time Dexter started to introduce Major James (USA, retired) and his wife, Ohara extended his hand and spoke up.

"Ernie James, I presume?"

"Yes, colonel. And this is my bride, Faith."

"Pleased to meet you, and Mrs. James," Colonel Ohara responded. He motioned for the entourage to follow him inside.

For the next thirty minutes, Ohara and his wife whipped up cocktails and snacks for their guests, while son Sean made a fire in the fireplace. During that time both he and CSM Wilkes joked with Dannenberg about his cunning ways, none of which seemed to bother the former CIA agent. After a few minutes Dexter looked at his watch and excused himself.

"I have things to accomplish in Mrs. Ohara's kitchen. So, if you all will excuse me, I'll leave you in Major James' capable hands. Doubtless, he will agree to fill you in on some more of exploits of the 238th."

Ernie James toyed with his pipe, but didn't light it. He'd given up smoking it years ago, but he still fiddled with it when recalling the events of World War II. After a few minutes of hearing about where Wilkes had left off, James began telling his story.

"As Charlie told you, the battle for St. Lo was vicious. Because, after taking Caen, Montgomery knew that if he captured Falaise, the Krauts would be encircled. The US was in the south, and we were kicking the snot out of them in 'Operation Cobra,' while the Brits and Canadians were hitting them in 'Operation Totalize.'

"Now, Monty had been promising for weeks that his troops were going to take Caen. But, like everything else Montgomery said, it didn't happen the way he wanted it to happen. SHAEF's plan was for us was to break through the German's lines while protecting our flank, and by doing so we'd encircle the Krauts in front of Montgomery near the town of Falaise.

"My unit witnessed it from atop a hill above the city. It was from there on the 24th of July that we watched the tremendous Allied force of fighters and light bombers, followed by heavy bombers, fly over. Wave after wave was strafing and dropping their payloads. You could look up and see bomb bay doors open, and bombs lazily falling out of the belly of the aircraft.

"Then the entire front exploded. The Krauts' anti-aircraft opened up. Several British and American planes lost their wings, or exploded in the air, all the while spiraling down to an explosive crash and a plume of smoke. Sometimes there were parachutes. But most of the time there weren't any. Many of their bombs fell short and killed a lot of our own troops.

"Of course, the Germans didn't sit idly by—they threw in their very best armored units against both us and Montgomery. When Montgomery finally attacked, it was near Caen. But it wasn't until thirteen August that the Brits succeeded in capturing the town, which meant that thousands of the Huns were able to escape—and that we'd see them again!

"We were assigned to Combat Command B, which was part of the 2nd Armored Division, with the 1st Division riding on our tanks. We broke through St. Chiles, which is near St. Lo. Company C was under command of First Lieutenant Wong, and most of the time they fought as 1-1 Bravos [infantry]. The rest of the 238th was a mile or so behind. It was no cakewalk, however, as Wong ran into a Kraut counterattack. But Wong's boys held their section of the line, and slugged it out toe-to-toe with the Germans' armor and infantry column.

"As I recall, a whole lot of Wong's warriors earned Silver and Bronze Stars in that battle. One platoon received the French *Croix de Guerre* and the Presidential Citation. We did, however, lose a few good men. PFC Scenna, Sergeant Smith and Corporal Hood were killed, and a bunch of our guys were wounded."

Major James paused briefly for a sip from his cocktail before continuing.

"When we finally caught up with Wong, we witnessed something that I shall never forget—all the dead soldiers, who'd been crushed to death by tanks. It was one bloody damned mess."

Taking another sip from his drink, James continued with his story.

"While all that business was taking place, some of Lieutenant George Worth's men from B Company were busy constructing a bypass for the field artillery boys from Pont Herbert to St. Dennis le Gast. No small feat, when you consider it was over thirty miles in length. I'm of the opinion that we wouldn't have been nearly as successful, had it not been for T/4 Brown. He pushed his D-7 'dozer hard that day, keeping up with the armored unit the whole time.

"As for the rest of the 238th, they were strafed by our own planes, which was disturbing, considering that we all used the same daily codes of colored panels and smoke. Lieutenant St. John's platoon got the worst of it. They were bombed by our pilots during the preparation for the breakthrough, and many of his men were injured.

"Back on the battlefield, everything was shot to hell. The best way to describe it would be to compare it to the surface of the moon. But the damnest thing about it, was that there were some Krauts who'd actually survived that attack. Now, they weren't what you'd call combat-ready, and some of them wandered right into our lines. Our troops pretty much ignored them, because they were so shell-shocked. Instead, our battalion cleared the roads of mines, built some airstrips, and by-passed enemy pockets of resistance while performing various other infantry and engineering tasks.

"For our efforts, the commanding general of the 2nd Armored Division wrote the battalion a letter of commendation for its performance."

"You know, Major James," Dexter Dannenberg said as he took a seat on the sofa, "I remember the battle of St. Lo as if it were just yesterday. Could it possibly be that it actually occurred forty-six years ago?"

"Afraid so, *Monsieur* Dannenberg," Chloe Ohara said, as she winked at their chef of the day.

"Well, my body tells me it was forty-six years ago, but my brain tells me it was just yesterday," Dannenberg lamented.

"So, what was Bletchley Park up to during this time?" Colonel Ohara asked Dexter.

"It was pretty damned exciting."

"How so?"

"As you know, colonel, it was right about this time that Colonel von Stauffenberg and company attempted to kill Hitler during a strategy meeting at *Wolfsschanze* [the Wolf's Lair]. Most Americans know about this one, because it nearly worked. But what they don't know is that it was just the last of seventeen attempts on Hitler's life.

"It was also the culmination of six years of covert work by more than two hundred German Army officers, diplomats, civil servants and politicians, who wanted to rid Germany of the 'Austrian corporal.'

"Hell, after the war was over, Allied intelligence found out that back in 1938, during the Sudetenland crisis, the German OKW organized a strike force to take Hitler out. The reason they didn't, was because they found out that the Brits wouldn't stand up to Hitler, which would have made them look like they were merely in it for a power grab. Had they done so—who knows? Maybe Hitler would have been disposed of, along with the rest of the anti-Semitic thugs from the *Nazi* Party."

"Wouldn't that have been a gift from God?" Major James added. "But…

it didn't happen, and so the 238th continued its march toward the Siegfried Line."

"Save that for the dinner table, Ernie," Dexter Dannenberg said, as he offered to freshen Major James' drink.

"I will," James replied, "but make the next one very weak…."

"That's exactly what Charlie said you'd say," Dexter said, pointing to the dining table.

THE DINING ROOM OF THE OHARA RESIDENCE
LOS LAGOS, GRANITE BAY, CALIFORNIA
SATURDAY, 30 NOVEMBER, 1991, 6:00 P.M.

The dining room of the Ohara's home was fit for a prince of Tuscany. Measuring thirty feet in length and twenty in width, the window-laden room buttressed up against the veranda that overlooked the back lot of the Ohara's California oak-studded property.

Sean Ohara often wondered why the three-story house hadn't collapsed, given as much glass as was used in the home's construction. The truth of the matter was that the Oharas had hired a structural engineer to design their home, and an architect to build it.

Sean always sat in the same seat—the one with the best view of the back yard. He'd done so ever since the first time he saw a family of deer traipsing across their property. From that time on, he'd claimed the chair as his. There was one problem with it, though: it was the closest seat to the refrigerator, which meant that whenever anyone wanted anything from it, he was the one who had to fetch!

But it's a small price to pay for this view!

After everyone had feasted on Dexter's gastronomical delight of garlic shrimp and scallops, Major James made a comment which caused everyone at the table to laugh heartily—except him and his wife. Innocently taking a sip from his coffee, he said, "I don't know if you know it or not, but thousands of Poles fought with the Allies during WWII."

Afterward, Ernie was curious about what he'd said that was so funny.

"Major James, with the exception of you and your wife, everyone else here spent the last Labor Day weekend in Iowa, listening to a hair-raising story about Dexter Dannenberg and a Polish spy named 'Thomek.'"

Dannenberg came to the man's rescue. "Ernie, I'm booked up for New Year's Day, but if you and Faith would like to come down to Palm Springs sometime—say, in February—I'll be glad to fill you in on it."

Faith James glanced over at her husband. "Ernie! I could get in a few sets of tennis…."

Ernie James smiled at his wife of forty-plus years. Then, looking back at Dexter, he said, "Okay, Dex, we'll be there."

"Great!" answered Dannenberg, as he excused himself to go to the restroom.

Now Major James picked up his story from where he'd left off earlier.

"The Poles were a courageous lot. What they lacked in equipment, they made up in bravery. Case in point: their armored division didn't have diddle when it came to artillery, so the boys at SHAEF teamed them up with some Canadian units."

Looking across the dining table, James could see the younger Ohara had an odd look on his face.

"Do you have a question, Sean?"

"Yes, as a matter of fact. How did they communicate with each other?"

"Well, I'm glad you asked. Since most of the Poles spoke French, and of course the Canadians did, it worked pretty well. Take Hill 262, for instance. With perhaps only a bit more than a thousand troops, they were up against some of *Herr* Hitler's finest SS and *Panzer* divisions. The *Nazi*s knew their goose was cooked if they didn't break out of the noose the Allies had put around their necks. They had to make it back over the Seine, or surrender.

"After studying the situation they decided that the weakest spot in the Allies' line was Hill 262. So they attacked, and in short order occupied most of the hill. But the Germans hadn't counted on the heroic actions of a Polish colonel named Sevigny. At the height of the engagement, with shells flying everywhere, Sevigny determined he needed to know how the Krauts were keeping the Allies from advancing. So what did he do?

"He grabbed a passel of hand grenades and crawled out of his tank on his belly until he found the German anti-tank gun emplacement that was creaming the good guys. Ignoring his personal safety, he braved withering machine gun fire and tossed his grenades into the midst of an entire gun crew, thus turning the tide of battle.

"While that was going on, the 238th was in direct support of the 2nd Armored Division. Companies A and B had established and defended a ten-mile barrier line east of Barenton, through the small town of St. George de Rouelle.

"And that brings me to my next story. It's interesting, because when I think about this next tale, I chalk up my actions to having too much testosterone.

"You see, word had come down that we needed to blow up several German-held bridges along the Orne River. After we talked it over among ourselves, we decided to load up a truck and a jeep with explosives. Our plan was to drive to a site overlooking a bridge. From there we'd plan the demolition, then load the explosives on the jeep and drive hell-bent-for-election to the bridge. We hoped we'd be able to set the charges, ignite them, then tear-ass back to our site before the Jerries could zero in on us.

"Now, for the poor dogfaces who had to rebuild those bridges—well, I can't imagine their task, given how thoroughly we'd blown them up."

"Why were you blowing up those bridges in the first place, Major James?" Sean asked.

"According to G-2, the Krauts were expected to launch their counterattack in that rural area. But with those bridges blown, and all the Cain our own infantry troops raised, the Germans didn't attack."

At this point in the conversation, a smiling CSM Wilkes added, "Why don't you tell them what happened the next day, major?"

James grinned at his former subordinate. "You mean 'the Midnight Ride of Tilley and James?'"

"That very one, sir."

Laughing, the retired army major continued. "The next day I was given a mission to gather some intelligence on the Krauts. We were not, exactly sure where they were, so it was my job to sniff them out without engaging. My driver Tilley and I piled in a jeep and headed out. We soon came on a small town, and while we were trying to get our bearings, what showed up other than a Jerry tank! Well, needless to say, before that Kraut tanker could zero us in, ol' Tilley made tracks—we skedaddled our fannies back to our AO. Of course, we caught a lot of razzing from our compatriots, but the point wasn't lost on them that we had indeed found the enemy."

Now Wilkes continued, "It was shortly thereafter that Company A was relieved by the 4th Cavalry group, and Company B was relieved by the 22nd Infantry Regiment. An officer from the 4th told one of our GIs that he'd gained newfound respect for the Engineer Corps.

"When asked why, the officer replied, "I don't know of many infantry units that could hold five miles of line. But you guys did it. Good show!""

"So what happened after that, major?" inquired Sean Ohara.

"After the battle of Falaise Gap we busied ourselves constructing roadblocks for the 3rd Battalion, 8th Infantry Regiment, which was attached to the 2nd Armored Division. Company B built roadblocks and bypass roads around Barenton for the 67th Armored Infantry Regiment. We also removed mines, cleared, maintained and posted roads, and, believe it or not, conducted training when we weren't working."

CSM Wilkes came back into the conversation. "As I recall, that's when Corporal Camerisi of Company C was killed, when his weapons carrier ran off a bridge in the dark."

"I believe you're right, Sergeant Major," James replied.

"He was a good man," Wilkes added.

"They all were," James said, as he glanced at Colonel Ohara.

Looking at Major James, Wilkes decided to lighten up the conversation.

"If my memory serves me right, this was about the time Tilley scored some 'white lightning.' How did you describe it, major?"

"It was the vilest concoction I ever drank. It tasted like a shot of the most rot-gut tequila, mixed with sulfuric acid and molten metal. God help us, if the *Nazis* had ever got hold of the stuff for their rockets at Peenemunde!"

"Did I hear someone say 'Peenemunde'?" Dexter Dannenberg asked as he returned from his bathroom "errand."

"Ernie was talking about some 'white lightning' his driver scored. He compared it to the Germans' rocket fuel," Colonel Ohara answered.

"Before you continue with that story, Ernie, I'd like to share some first-hand information about Peenemunde."

"By all means, Dexter, please fill us in," Chloe Ohara asked.

"Churchill wanted Peenemunde put out of action in the worst way. We'd been trying to clobber them since mid-August 1943, but we hadn't had much luck. Anyway, I remember coming home from a Tuesday afternoon shift out at Bletchley Park. The reason I remember it was a Tuesday, was because Tuesdays were my Friday nights.

"By that, I mean I had the next day off, and I was thinking about my upcoming visit to see a bloke I'd met in 1939. You know—the chap from the Claridge Hotel, over on Brook Street in London's West End.

"Anyway, back to Peenemunde. As my motorcar passed the local airfield, I noticed there wasn't a plane within sight. Of course, one had to be delicate when snooping around as to where the planes were. But, a couple of days later, I saw an ULTRA message concerning the bomb damage our planes did on a raid over Peenemunde, and the number of planes the Germans claimed to have shot down.

Our pilots' estimates weren't too far off, either. The reason the Krauts hit so many of their targets was attributed to the fact that there wasn't a cloud in the sky on the night of the raid, thus making our bombers perfect targets. We launched over five hundred planes that night."

Major James interrupted Dannenberg's tale.

"You know, Dex, the good command sergeant major and I have some rather interesting stories to tell about some of those German rocket scientists at Peenemunde. Especially that anti-Semite, Werner von Braun."

Dannenberg nodded in agreement. "I didn't know it at the time, that von Braun and his boys were a bunch of damned *Nazis*—none of us did. Nevertheless, I can tell you for certain that it didn't take too long for us to figure it out. Of course, after the war it was glossed over, because the German scientists we'd captured were playing such an instrumental role in our own rocket program."

"Ah, yes. It is the same old story: politics make for strange bedfellows. The truth of the matter is that Ike was a pragmatist. The Russians were kicking our butts in the space race, and our government needed those German scientists. So, *viola!* their *Nazi*sm is covered up, and as a result we ended up on the moon first."

All those present who were old enough to remember the origins of the U.S.-Russian space race nodded their heads in agreement. They all knew that what Dannenberg had said was true.

But none were proud of it.

CHAPTER FOURTEEN

Where is he? Here he is.
He is hanging here on this gallows....
That night the soup tasted of corpses.
—Wiesel

COLONEL AND MRS. MICHAEL BRANDON OHARA'S RESIDENCE
LOS LAGOS, GRANITE BAY, CALIFORNIA
SUNDAY, DECEMBER 1ST, 1991, 8:15 A.M.

As their guests were sitting around the dining room table, sipping freshly brewed coffee, suddenly Sean Ohara asked his mother if he could borrow her Jaguar later that afternoon. His request caused Colonel Ohara to stop what he was doing at the counter and look over toward his teenage son.

"The Jag?"

"Sure, dad. After church I want to go shopping with Sarah Worthington."

"Sounds serious," Mrs. Ohara commented.

"Not that serious, Mum," the teenager replied. "But I do want to make an impression on her, and everyone up here in Los Lagos has an SUV...."

The senior Ohara gave his wife the 'it's your call' look. She agreed to loan her prized automobile to her son, with the proviso that he be back home by five p.m.

At that point, Mrs. James looked at the young man and began asking him about his girlfriend. Before anyone realized it, Sean Ohara and Faith James were absent the dining room table and out on the veranda, where they remained for almost a half hour. When they returned, Faith made an announcement.

"Colonel Ohara, I'd say your son has great taste in girls. Before you know it, he'll be getting married to a fine young woman."

Major James spoke up. "If Faith approves of this young girl, Sean, I'd say you better stake your claim, young man."

"Wait a minute," Sean pleaded, "all I am doing is taking her shopping...."

To which Colonel Ohara replied, "Son, all I was doing when I met your mother was looking for a telephone...."

That comment clearly flustered the colonel's son, so everyone decided to back off from any more discussion of his love life. After a few awkward seconds passed, the teenager looked to Dexter Dannenberg and said, "Can you help me out here, Mr. Dannenberg?"

Dexter took a sip from his cocktail, and then dryly replied, "I'm afraid I am not the right person to ask for help when it comes to women."

That brought the house down with laughter.

When order was finally restored, Colonel Ohara agreed to let Sean borrow their new Jaguar, but only if he promised to invite the young lady and her parents up to dinner during the upcoming holiday season. The young man agreed.

Now CSM Wilkes continued telling his story.

IN A BIVOUAC AREA AT ST. MAXINE, NEAR ALACON, FRANCE TUESDAY, 22 AUGUST 1944, 9:00 P.M. LOCAL

PFC Ian Henry was dog-tired. The last few days had been a physical nightmare. On the first two days of last week the unit had bivouacked at Le Bois Richard, put up road blocks for the 3rd Battalion, 8th Infantry Regiment [which was attached to the 2nd Armored Division] and built roadblocks and by-pass roads around Barenton for the 67th Armored Infantry Division.

When they moved from St. Maxine to Ferriere Bochard, they heard that the French Resistance in Paris had risen up and was in the process of giving the retreating Huns a run for their money.

Sitting around a now-doused fire, CPL Wilkes looked over to PFC Henry.

"From what the radio says, the French Resistance is really giving the *Nazis* and all their collaborators holy hell, for the way they ran Paris the last five years."

"Screw 'em!" Henry said. "Every *Nazi* they kill is one less we have to."

"They certainly got a right to do it," CPL Erickson said, lighting up a smoke.

"Ain't anybody denying that," Wilkes said, "especially after what happened to those poor bastards in Obradour.

"Obradour, who?" Erickson asked.

Wilkes looked at him as if he had two heads. "Ain't you heard what those fucking Krauts did to the folks at Obradour, yet?"

"Guess I ain't," Erickson replied. "It ain't like I get the Des Moines *Register* every day."

"I know that, shithead," Wilkes replied. "But I thought by now everybody'd heard what those sonsabitches did."

"Well, I ain't heard of it, either, so tell us…," Ian Henry said, joining the two GIs' conversation.

"G-2 reports that a bunch of SS assholes surrounded the village of Oradour-sur-Glane. The Kraut in charge ordered everyone in the town—I think somebody said it was over six hundred-fifty people—out into the town square. They suspected the townsfolk were hiding explosives. He had all their papers checked and, then, when that was over, had everyone in town locked up—the men in barns, the women and children in a church.

"Well, you know what those fuckers did? They burned the entire town, and shot everyone with machine guns.

"Intel says they killed over two hundred women, and about the same amount of kids. Nearly that many men were massacred, too. A Catholic bishop found the charred bodies of fifteen children in a heap behind the burned-out altar inside the church."

Henry spit into the fire. "The bastards who did that are just a bunch of fucking barbarians. Hell is too good for 'em!"

"That's sorta how I see it, too," Erickson commented, taking a long drag off his smoke.

Henry raised his eyes up toward the roof of the tent, and said, "God—I know you ain't gonna let any of them bastards in heaven, who murdered those women and children. And, just to show you how much it pisses me off, I'm personally gonna to kill as many of those motherfuckers as I can find. The way I figure it—I'll kill 'em, and you can send 'em on their way to hell!"

Shaking his head, Charlie looked over at Erickson and laughed.

"What's so damned funny, Wilkes?" Ian asked.

"That has to be the most fucked-up prayer I ever heard," Wilkes answered, as he picked up his weapon and headed off to his sleeping bag.

Ian knew what he'd just said went against every grain of his Catholic faith. But the visceral feeling he got when he thought of the atrocity the

Germans had committed against those innocent civilians in Obradour, caused him to unload his thoughts even further.

"Charlie, you and I both know them bastards don't deserve any better that gettin' killed. So, as far as I'm concerned, I'm doing God's work."

Suddenly he felt the urge to vomit. He excused himself and walked away from the almost-extinguished fire. Then Ian Henry retched.

Erickson stood up and looked at Charlie. "Did you ever meet Mr. Swenson, at Clarinda High School?"

"Once or twice," Charlie admitted. "Not socially, just at football games."

"He told us once that Napoleon said, 'God was on the side of the army with the best artillery.'"

"In which case—we win!" PFC Gordie Hall stated, as he walked by where the two men were standing.

"Where you headed, Hall?" Erickson asked.

"I got guard duty until twenty-four-hundred hours."

"That sucks."

"It sure as hell beats having it from twenty-four-hundred to oh-four-hundred hours."

"Ain't gonna argue with that one. By the way, who does have it, then?"

"That's what I was coming over here to tell you, Erickson—you do."

"Crap!"

FIFTY FEET FROM THE OPERATIONS TENT, LIEUTENANT JAMES PUT DOWN HIS PIPE AND RE-READ THE LETTER TO HIS BELOVED FAITH.

22 August 1944

Dear Faith,

I haven't written the last few days, for the usual reasons. Things are looking up. Someday, I'll be able to write every day. I have acquired some souvenirs recently: .25 and .38 caliber pistols, under some gruesome circumstances.

We were going through a new part of the country, and the people welcomed us with open arms. They lined the roads for miles and threw flowers and bottles to us, full! France gets more beautiful by the day.

I encountered the cutest little French girl I've ever seen. She has long,

brown curly hair, big blue eyes and a musical laugh—in short, a knockout!
She liked me and kissed me. Of course, I came out with the inevitable bon-
bons. She sat on my lap and we had a long talk. Her name is Georgette, and
she was a refugee from Paris. She is very ticklish and when I pinched her
knees, she squealed. We have a date for tomorrow night. Some day, fourteen
years from now when she's eighteen, she's going to wow the boys.
    Yours,
        Ernie

In the tent next to Lieutenant James', Major Massoglia and Captain
Reichmann were discussing events concerning the fall of Caen. Both men
were exhausted, from having been working for the last eighteen hours. Yet
they somehow managed to carry on a conversation.

CPT Reichmann reached over to take off his boots. "The first time I
heard the G-2 guy brief everyone on Operation Neptune, I knew we were
in for one helluva fight."

"How so, captain?" Massoglia wondered aloud.

"There was no way the Krauts were going to just roll over and let us
have the Orne River and the Caen canal. I mean… hell, if they could keep
us from those two bodies of water, there's no way in God's creation we
could gain access to Caen's roads."

Massoglia agreed. "Yep, if we didn't take them away from the Huns,
they would've had free reign to travel anywhere they wanted. You add
that to the fact that the Army Air Corps wants part of it turned into an
airfield…."

"Hell, major, the British 3rd Army Division has been slugging it out
with the Huns since D-Day," Reichmann added.

Massoglia took off his helmet and laid it on the ground. Then he sat
down on his cot and looked over at Reichmann. "You know, captain, the
Canadian 2nd Corps went up against at least five armored divisions."

"I heard that," Reichmann responded.

"Well…." Massoglia said, as he closed his eyes, "I read a message
today that estimates our Canadian Allies have lost somewhere in the
neighborhood of fifteen hundred men."

Reichmann lay down on his cot, and said, "They better hope to God
they don't have too many more fights like Caen. Canada can't afford to
lose that many soldiers."[1]

"The odd thing is," Massoglia said, trying to stay awake for a few

---

1. The Battle for Caen would deal the Canadians their worst loss of life during the Battle of Normandy.

more seconds, "Caen dates back to the Middle Ages—and it's been fought over ever since, constantly."

"Hopefully this will be the last time...." Reichmann said, as he fell asleep.

"Yeah—right. In your dreams, captain."

THE BIVOUAC AREA AT LE MARIAS
NEAR PONT LE BERG (SOUTH OF PARIS, NORTH OF CORBEIL)
THURSDAY, 24 AUGUST 1944, 0600 HOURS LOCAL

"What the heck are they waiting for?" Private James Harrell asked his relief driver. "I mean, we've been sitting here for twenty minutes already, wasting gas. Let's get this show on the road."

"Hold your horses," SSG Marion Davis said in his Alabama accent. "Massoglia is on the radio to somebody upstairs. As soon as he's done with that, we're outta here."

"Where we going, staff sergeant? Harrell wondered out loud.

"Scuttlebutt says were being attached to both the 1st Infantry Division and the 3rd Armored Division."

"That don't answer my question, sergeant. Where are we headed?"

"Germany, you dumb-ass," Davis answered, as he walked away to make last-minute checks on the vehicles ahead.

Harrell looked at his co-driver. "Ain't the sergeant a piece of work? I'm glad he told me we're headed toward Germany. All this time, I though we were heading to friggin' Hollywood."

The young man from Nebraska spit tobacco juice out the window, and replied, "You're the piece of work, Harrell. I mean, I ain't been in the Army too long. But I do know that the chances of a staff sergeant knowing where we're headed is just about as likely as a congressman knowing what the hell *he's* doing."

Harrell looked at his co-driver and laughed. "Yeah. Besides, the longer we're here means the less time we spend messing around with the Germans."

Spitting out the side of the window again, the Nebraskan replied, "I imagine there'll still be some of them bastards around, when we get to where-ever-in-hell it is we're going."

Fifteen or sixteen vehicles ahead of Harrell's three-quarter ton pickup truck, Major Massoglia was finishing his conversation with the assistant division commander, Major Poe.

"Roger your last transmission. We will now proceed to the proscribed locations and set up operations from there. Out."

Looking to his driver, Massoglia said, "As soon as I get back from briefing Major Dawley on that radio message, we'll leave."

"Sir," the GI driver said, "Major Dawley headed out really early this morning to Corps Headquarters."

"That's news to me," Massoglia admitted.

"Sir, I thought you knew…."

"Nobody tells me crap, son. But, if that be the case, let's get this show on the road!"

"Just as soon as you tell me where the hell we're going, sir."

Massoglia glanced over at the driver with a puzzled look. "You mean you don't know where we're headed?"

"No sir, nobody told me a damned thing."

Massoglia laughed aloud. "In that case, let's drive toward Berlin!"

Now the major's driver was truly bewildered. He looked at Massoglia and asked, "Really, sir, I do need better directions than that—'Berlin.'"

Massoglia laughed again. "Last century, there was a real famous newspaperman who said, 'Go West, young man.' Well, I'm not famous, but I'm telling you the opposite: 'Go East, young man.' And if you find that paper-hanging sonofabitch from Austria, shoot him! Then we can all go home."

The enlisted man shook his head, turned the truck's ignition key, and put the vehicle into first gear. All he knew was that his unit was heading toward Berlin.

The 238th Engineer Combat Battalion would be on the road for the better part of September. They would act in support of the 1st Infantry Division and the 3rd Armored Division, in their dash across France and Belgium into the Siegfried Line defenses of the Third Reich.

Along the way, they constructed a 528-foot steel treadway bridge across the Seine River at Evry Pont le Berg, near Corbeil. The bridge was completed in six hours. When finished, the men peeled off their uniforms and dove in. There was very little German opposition to their construction now as the enemy was retreating so fast he didn't have time to fight.

On August 27th they built a 568-foot floating Bailey bridge across the Seine. While in Corbeil on 29 August, the unit came upon trainloads of destroyed German fighter planes, which were loaded on cars and intended to be sent back to Germany for parts—testimony to the Allies' air superiority.[2]

When General Dwight David Eisenhower's Supreme Headquarters starting planning for the invasion of France, numerous options were discussed. But the plan they decided on was one put forth by Lieutenant General Sir Frederick E. Morgan, COSSAC [Chief of Staff to the Supreme Commander Allied Forces]. The eventual plan would run hundreds of pages long, and everything from which unit was going to be given the job of scaling Pont du Hoc, to which unit should have the honor of liberating Paris, was included.

The story of how Eisenhower "selected" the 2nd French Armored Division to liberate Paris is particularly interesting because, as the invasion progressed, Eisenhower actually considered bypassing the City of Light.

Commanded by Major General Philippe Leclerc, the 2nd French Armored Division had been sent to North Africa by General de Gaulle in 1943. Leclerc, a captain at the time, was told by de Gaulle to raise an army—which he did in short order. By French standards, Leclerc's soldiers were good. Good enough, at least, to beat the Italians!

Having now proved himself in combat, Leclerc's soldiers were next assigned to protect the left flank of Montgomery's Eighth Army, a job they did with vigor.

Because Leclerc was so good on the battlefield, he sailed through the officer ranks. But he had one drawback—he irritated the hell out of his superior officers. Under most circumstances, that would have been the end of him. But it was not to be, because in late 1943 de Gaulle asked him to get an army together to assist the Allies in liberating Paris.

Leclerc jumped at the chance, and took his men to Algeria for training. Once trained, the unit was moved to England to prepare for Operation Overlord.

Two months after the Normandy Invasion, Ike and de Gaulle met. The purpose of their meeting was for Eisenhower to tell the Free French Army leader that he planned to bypass Paris.

De Gaulle was furious, because he feared the communists would make inroads into the post-war French government, and told Eisenhower. Ike did not buy the French general's argument. At that point, de Gaulle "suggested" that unless Eisenhower got on with the liberation of Paris, that he, Charles de Gaulle, would send General Leclerc's 2nd Armored Division into Paris to do the job. Ike caved, and on the 23rd of August, Leclerc's soldiers approached Paris from the north, while the U.S. 4th Infantry Division came in from the south.

Realizing that Paris was about to fall to the Allies, *Herr* Hitler ordered General Dietrich von Choltitz to "defend to the last soldier," leaving the Allies nothing but "…a field of ruins." Choltitz "obeyed" Hitler's order, insofar as he had his engineers lay down explosives in Paris' landmarks. But he refused to give the actual order to destroy Paris.

Initially, the French forces ran into heavy resistance. But by the 25th they had either put down the German units or chased them out of Paris. Thirty-five hundred German soldiers surrendered, and General Choltitz was captured soon after.

Paris was once again free from Nazi oppression.

THE BIVOUAC AREA NEAR VILLENEUVE LE COMTE
THURSDAY, 28 AUGUST 1944, 0:430 HOURS LOCAL

CPL Charlie Wilkes couldn't believe someone was shaking his leg. That could only mean one thing: it was time to get up. He grabbed his flashlight, turned it on, and pointed its beam at his watch.

Sonofabitch! It's four thirty. I don't have to get up for another hour and a half. This damned well better be important!

Wilkes shined his flashlight toward the soldier who was shaking his foot.

"Tilley?"

"Bigger'n crap," the GI replied.

"What's up, man? I don't have to get up for another hour-and-a-half."

"Actually," Tilley replied, "that's true. But Lieutenant James wants to know if you're interested in 'liberating Paris.'"

"What the fuck?"

Tilley laughed. "Lieutenant James and me are driving into Paris today, and he wants to know if you want to come along!"

Charlie shook his head. "I thought the French were supposed to liberate Paris."

"They are. But from what we hear, the Krauts have cleared out and the city is wide open. You want to go? Last chance, Charlie…."

"Well, as long as I don't have to drive, okay. I'll go."

"Good, grab your weapon and steel pot, and follow me."

Wilkes hurriedly got dressed and picked up his rifle. Then he looked at Tilley.

"Hey—how the hell did I get chosen for this one?"

"Dunno, the L-T just told me you two had a 'history,' and let it go at that."

As Charlie Wilkes stumbled out of his tent, he was greeted with the fresh smell of France in the fall—the sweet smells of close-by fields, a sky full of stars, and a fresh cup of hot coffee. His thoughts turned to his wife, Sharon, and his two little sons.

Someday, sweethearts, I'll bring you here.

With Tilley driving, and Lieutenant James holding down the shotgun position, Charlie Wilkes knew he was in for breezy ride sitting in the back of the jeep.

Tilley had been driving Lieutenant James since the invasion. Both he and the lieutenant seemed to know exactly where they were going this morning. Tilley started the engine, let it warm up for all of about ten seconds, then spun the vehicle around and headed east. Tapping Lieutenant James on the shoulder, Wilkes asked the 0-2 how far it was to Paris.

"According to this map, it's around forty-five kilometers. We should be there within an hour."

"Well, I gotta say this," the enlisted man seated next to Wilkes said, "never in my wildest dreams did I think I'd ever get to see Paris, France."

"We're not there yet," Charlie reminded him.

"I know, but it's still pretty damned exciting for this old farm boy," the GI admitted.

THE OUTSKIRTS OF PARIS, FRANCE
28 AUGUST 1944, 8:15 A.M. LOCAL

As the foursome approached the outskirts of Paris, Charlie thought he heard gunfire. Looking over at the soldier next to him with a quizzical look on his face, he was about to say something when Lieutenant James told Tilley to slow down a bit.

"Tilley, did you hear that?

"Sure did, lieutenant. What do you want to do—go back?"

James looked around the vehicle. As an officer he knew that ultimately he was responsible for the lives of the three men who were with him. He did not detect any desire to turn around. Looking back to the driver, he said, "There's only one thing that's going to keep me from the Champs Elyssees, and that's a bullet from a German rifle. Drive on."

Charlie looked at the soldier next to him and gave the" thumbs-up" sign.

The GI responded with a smile and an outstretched hand. "Name's Shelby. Matthew Shelby, from Indiana."

"Charlie Wilkes, here. I was raised in Iowa, but I live in southern California with my wife and two boys."

"No shit? You live in California?"

"Yep."

"I've always wanted to see California. What do you say, that after this war is over we meet at your house, an' have a beer or two?"

Charlie was amused. Here they were, less than ten miles from downtown Paris, and the dogface next to him seemed more impressed with just the mere fact that he lived in California.

"Okay, pal, you got a deal. Let's get together the first Fourth of July after this sonofabitch is done with."

"You're on," the soldier said, as he reached in his pocket and pulled out an envelope. On the back of it he wrote, "Southern California—July 4, 1946."

Charlie looked at the envelope and then tapped Lieutenant James on the shoulder. When James had turned around, Charlie pointed at PFC Shelby and said, "Lieutenant, the farm boy here says this war'll be over by July of 'forty-six. What do you think, sir? Is he right?"

"Wilkes, the way the Germans are running back toward Germany, I'd say he's probably right. But, you have to remember this—even if we were to defeat the Krauts by next May, we're not gonna get to go home right away. No way. We'll more than likely be doing some kind of duty here for one helluva long time."

"But, sir," Shelby said, "ain't they going to cut us loose after the war? I mean, my draft papers said 'duration plus six.' I thought that meant six months, not six years."

James laughed. "Shelby, Uncle Sam probably has a couple million soldiers here now. It would take some time to get us home within six months, under the best of conditions. No, I'd say we'll be here for almost a year afterwards. Then, the professional soldiers will take over."

Shelby looked at the lieutenant with a puzzled expression on his face.

"But, lieutenant, I thought *you* were a lifer."

James burst out laughing. "Shelby, I have to finish up some work at Cal Berkeley to become an engineer. I also have one heck of a swell gal waiting for me back in the States. So, no. When Uncle Sam cuts me loose, he won't have to ask me twice—I'll be down the road and on my way back home."

"Speaking of women, lieutenant," Tilley said as he slowed down the jeep, "look at them over there."

James, Wilkes and Shelby looked over to the side of the road, and saw four young women running toward their vehicle. They were laughing and smiling.

"I suppose we ought to stop and see what they need," James said with a twinkle in his eye.

Once the jeep stopped moving, the four Frenchwomen began smothering them with kisses, exclaiming, "*Long vivent l'armée américaine!*" ["Long live the American Army!"]

Charlie Wilkes, who now wished he'd paid more attention in his high school French classes back in Iowa, blurted out, "*Juste m'appeler Lafayette!*" ["Just call me Lafayette!"]

The girls roared their approval, and began kissing the GIs in earnest.

Lieutenant James managed to break away from one of the girls clinging to him. He walked over to an older woman on the sidewalk who was approaching their jeep.

He started to say something, but the woman spoke first.

"Thank you, lieutenant, for everything you and your men have done for France."

James was taken aback by her command of the English language, and asked her where she learned to speak it so well.

"I used to teach English at a Catholic school before the *Nazi*s showed up."

James looked at her and smiled. "Well then, *mademoiselle*, I suggest that tomorrow you go back to that school, and tell them you are again available."

"I will do that, lieutenant! But that leaves me in a quandary."

"How so, madam?"

"What am I going to do tonight?"

Damn, she certainly doesn't mince any words!

Ernie James smiled at her, saying, "If I weren't on a vital mission for the war effort, *mademoiselle*, I'd take you up on you kind offer. But, I think if you wait here a few more minutes, you might find another American officer who will jump at the chance to spend some time with such a lovely woman. But… alas…I have to be somewhere in two hours."

The Frenchwoman smiled and said, "In any case, lieutenant, thank you once again for your efforts to defeat the Fascists."

James nodded his *adieu* and walked back to the vehicle. Now it was surrounded by nearly ten young Frenchwomen, all in amorous moods.

As James sat in the jeep, he glanced at Tilley.

"Start moving very slowly, so none of these girls gets hurt. And don't stop until we're at the Eiffel Tower!"

Tilley did as he was ordered, and the jeep began to move forward.

Undaunted, the girls continued kissing them. Then they got down off the jeep, to wait for the next vehicle full of handsome American liberators!

CHAPTER FIFTEEN

Cease firing, but if any enemy planes appear—
shoot them down in friendly fashion.
—Admiral "Bull" Halsey

NEAR MONS, BELGIUM
TUESDAY, 5 SEPTEMBER 1944, 1900 HOURS LOCAL

Since August 28th, the 238th Engineer Combat Battalion had traveled approximately three hundred-five kilometers (190 miles) northeast, to an area just outside Charleroi, Belgium. In the process, Company B repaired a concrete arch bridge over the Marne River at Trilport, and erected a thirty-six foot steel girder bridge over the Marne south of Meaux (this bridge involved extensive welding). They also repaired a four hundred ninety-five foot bridge at Eably over the Marne, and repaired a three hundred-sixteen foot timber trestle bridge across the Aisne River, near Soisson, France.

On August 31st they repaired a two hundred foot timber trestle bridge across the Oise Canal (southwest of Chavignon) and improvised a bypass by placing plank treadway on rails on a bridge over the Aisne River near Soissons, France.[1]

As the war progressed, Eisenhower began making decisions to reflect the changing battlefield situation. Therefore, General Omar Bradley was able to give General Patton's Third Army more gas and ammunition, which enabled Patton to capture Metz, France.

To get to Metz, Old Blood and Guts' soldiers had to cross the Marne, Vesle, Aisne, Meuse, and the Moselle Rivers. Under normal circumstances, these waterways would have presented tremendous difficulties, but the Germans were so disorganized and scattered that Patton's soldiers crossed the five rivers without encountering much resistance.

The XII Corps seized Chalons on 29 August and then established a bridgehead on the Meuse on 31 August. The only thing that kept them from going further was the lack of supplies.

---

1. *238th Engineer Combat Battalion in Action*
in WWII, James, pages 62-65.

The rout became apparent to everyone at SHAEF, as well as General Omar Bradley in the field. Bradley took advantage of the situation and ordered the First Army, under General Hodges, to turn his direction of advance from northeast to north. In doing so, the First Army captured 25,000 of *Herr* Hitler's finest soldiers.

It was at this point that the European Theater of Operations' (ETO) supply problems ground the campaign to a halt. It took the "Red Ball Express" to break the logistical logjam.[2]

TUESDAY, 5 SEPTEMBER 1944
IN A CONVOY HEADED TOWARD MONS,
BELGIUM, 21:15 HOURS LOCAL

Kaboom! Kaboom! Kaboom!
Off in the distance the entire landscape erupted with fire. The ground shook, and death followed.

In a classic "Fog of War" situation, the 3rd Armored advance guard somehow met the point of the German column near Mons, Belgium. Soon, the American tanks and other vehicles found themselves commingled with the German enemy! The 3rd's tankers were the first to figure out the convoluted situation, and one hell of a firefight ensured.

The suddenness and the ferocity of the ensuing battle between American tankers and German *Panzers* caused CPL Charlie Wilkes to spill an entire steel cup of hot coffee down the front of himself, burning not only his chest but his groin area, as well.

"Fuck!" he shouted, as he tried to think of something other than killing PFC Ian Henry for his erratic driving.

With his New England accent, Henry shouted, "Calm down, Charlie. I can't see a fucking thing in this dark, and with all that racket going on in the distance…."

Once the scalding hot coffee began to cool, Wilkes was able to gather his thoughts.

"What in the hell's going on up front, anyway, for God's sake?"

"I dunno. It sounds like *our* tanks have found some of *their* tanks."

"Either that, or Jesus Christ just showed up!" Charlie responded, covering his eardrums.

"I doubt that, Charlie," Henry yelled back. "But, I tell you what—

---

2. See http://www.army.mil/cmh-pg/brochures/norfran/norfran.htm for complete details.

whatever the hell is going on up there, somebody's getting their ass kicked. I just pray to God it's our boys kicking their boys' asses, and not the other way around. I've never heard such a racket in all my life."

The vehicles in the convoy began to slow, then came to a complete halt. Major Massoglia, who was riding in the vehicle in front, jumped out and ran back to Charlie's jeep.

"Get me on the net, Wilkes. I've got to find out what the hell's going on...."

Charlie picked up the radio's handset, "Eagle, this is Jean. Come in, please."

No answer. Wilkes tried again.

"Eagle, this is Jean, come in please."

Still no answer.

"Try it one more time, Wilkes, and then try Able Company," the major demanded.

"Eagle, this is Jean, come in please."

"Jean, this is Eagle, go ahead."

Charlie handed the major the handset. "They're on the line, sir."

"Eagle, this is Jean. What the hell is going on at coordinates oh-six-four-niner-five-four?"

"Roger, Jean. Initial reports are that our guys have run into a pack of Krauts, and all hell is breaking loose. Jean."

"How do you want us to proceed, Eagle?"

"Negative, Jean. Do not proceed until you are cleared from this end. Roger my last transmission."

"Eagle, this is Jean. Will not proceed until cleared from your end. Eagle, this is Jean, out."

As Major Massoglia passed the headset back to Wilkes, he said, "If you boys know any good prayers, now might be the time to get them into action. From what Group tells me, our boys are in one helluva fight, and the outcome is uncertain."

"What do you want us to do, sir?" Wilkes inquired.

"Go back and find the first sergeant, and get him up here immediately."

CPL Wilkes started to go look for the first sergeant, but Massoglia called him back.

"Wilkes, you stay here. I might need you to operate the radio."

PFC Henry took the hint, and got out of the jeep and started running toward the back of the convoy. He did not have to run too far. He had gone no more than a hundred yards when he was met by First Sergeant Freck.

"What's the hold-up, Henry?" the senior enlisted man asked as the GI approached.

"First Sergeant, the shit has hit the fan up front, and Major Massoglia wants to see you immediately."

"Okay, I'll run up and talk to him. In the meantime; you get everyone out of their vehicles and set up security according to S.O.P."

Since the first sergeant was a stickler for training, Henry did not have to ask what security procedures needed to be taken. Nor did anyone else in the unit and within five minutes every man who was supposed to be manning a weapon was, and every man who was supposed to be digging a hasty fighting position was doing so, also.

NEAR MONS, BELGIUM
WEDNESDAY, 6 SEPTEMBER 1944, DAWN

For the past ten hours, the men of the 238th Combat Engineer Battalion had been waiting for the battle between the Germans and the tankers from the 3rd Armored Division to let up.

Try as he could, neither CPL Wilkes nor PFC Henry had managed as much as two winks of sleep. Irritable, they were. But awake they were, too.

From the distance, Henry thought he heard airplanes. He looked up, and the sky was filled with American fighter planes headed toward the now petering-out tank battle.

For the next hour, all hell broke loose. And then there was silence.

Major Massoglia was just about to call Group when Major Poe, the assistant division commander, called and told him to get his troops moving again.

"Okay, men, mount up. We're back on the way to Berlin," the major said as he jumped into his jeep.

Under the usual circumstances, PFC Henry would never speak to an O-4 without being addressed, but this time he asked him how long he thought it would take until they actually got to Berlin.

Massoglia thought about it briefly, and then replied, "No idea, son, but I have a feeling that the 3rd Armored Division and the 8th Air Force just shortened our arrival date by a few days."

Within three miles of Massoglia's comment, CPL Wilkes spoke up. "Holy Fuck! Look at this mess!"

Although not eloquent, what CPL Wilkes was describing was the total annihilation of a German armored division.

As they passed through the carnage, Lieutenant James wrote in his diary.

Devastation was as far as the eye could see; destroyed vehicles and arms, dead horses and men. In one place you could have waked over an entire field without missing an enemy body.[3]

The rest of that day was spent clearing the roads of the debris left over from the battle. The men of the 3rd Armored Division busied themselves by taking prisoners and with mopping up.

James finished his comments this way: *The cream of what Hitler had left, with which he planned to man the Siegfried Line, was destroyed. (The) warehouses in Charleroi were overflowing with 250,000 prisoners. It was a long day.*[4]

THE OPERATIONS TENT, 238TH ENGINEER COMBAT BATTALION NEAR NAMUR, BELGIUM WEDNESDAY, 6 SEPTEMBER, DUSK

CPL Wilkes was exhausted. His lack of sleep the previous night, added to the eighteen-hour workday he had just finished, had taken their toll. Nor did he know how he was going to pull a six-hour shift on the radio after First Sergeant Freck finished with the briefing he had just started.

He took a sip of his now-cold coffee, sat up on the ammo box, turned around, and listened in on what the senior NCO was saying.

"Okay, I'll say this again, just to make sure everyone knows what he is supposed to be doing in the morning. Tomorrow, we're going to take a train to Namur and build a bridge across the Meuse River.

"I don't have to tell you, that all the Krauts aren't out of Namur—so be on the lookout for ambushes. Also, there are Belgian citizens in Namur, too, so I don't want to get any reports of us killing innocents. However, if you can kill some of Hitler's thugs, be my guest!"

With that last remark, everyone knew the first sergeant was done with his briefing. He called the tent to attention, then walked out. As he did, all the non-commissioned officers present picked up their steel pots and rifles, and headed outside, leaving CPL Wilkes and PFC Henry alone in the tent.

---

3. *238th Combat Battalion in Action During World War II,* James, page 67.
4. *Ibid.*

Henry looked at Wilkes.

"Looks like it's more of the same tomorrow."

Wilkes yawned. "Henry, it looks to me like it's going to be more of the same until we kill that bastard, Hitler."

Henry reached over and picked up his steel pot. "We might not have to, Charlie. Maybe the German High Command will be successful the next time they try to rid us of that 'Austrian corporal.'"

Charlie spat out his stale coffee. "Ian, after that last debacle, I doubt if there'll ever be anyone in Germany that tries to kill that motherfucker again. I think we're either going to have to do it, or the Reds."

As Ian Henry walked out of the tent, he wisecracked, "I don't know about you, soldier, but I don't give a damn who kills him—as long as somebody does it, and soon. Maybe then, we can get some sleep."

While Henry and Wilkes were trying to figure out how they were going to make it the next few hours without falling asleep, Lieutenant James was putting the final changes on a letter to his parents three tents away.

September 8, 1944

Dear Mom and Dad:

Here's another family letter. The time element is getting worse and worse. The war is moving quite fast and when we move, it's a "pick up and go affair." I was recently in one of the biggest messes I've ever seen. Jerry got in a massive traffic tie-up, and our armor and planes spotted them—they had a field day.

Our job was to make the roads passable after the carnage.

Imagine pushing thousands of mixed and assorted automobiles, artillery, equipment, horses and dead Germans off to one side with a 'dozer. Wish I could go into a lot of detail about it, but you'll hear about it later....

I had another close one. One night, about 15 Jerries crawled up on us. One of our men fired quickly, later saying, "I knew damned well it wasn't a Yank, so I shot."

Fourteen German soldiers came out yelling, "Komrade." I got a Luger [pistol] out of the deal and a beautiful bayonet; chrome with bone handle. I also found a honey of a Jerry camera F3 w/lens and range finder, a 35mm job.

You ought to see these Germans give up—shoot a gun into the woods and they start coming. It's nothing to see a couple GI's bringing in a hundred at a time....

As James continued writing, Captain Reichmann came into his tent. Ernie put down his pen and looked over to where his counterpart was standing. When not in front of the enlisted men, Lieutenant James always referred to Reichmann simply by his last name.

"What's up, Reichmann?"

"I was just putting the final touches on tomorrow's mission, and thought I'd stop by to coordinate the effort with you," the O-3 said as he sat down on an old ammo box.

"Go ahead, what's up?"

"You know about the bridge we're supposed to put up tomorrow over the Sambre River near Namur, don't you?"

"Yes. Major Poe says we'll probably have to put in a hundred-fifty foot TS Bailey bridge, plus Group also wants a five hundred-fifty foot steel treadway on the Meuse near Liege."

"I knew about those," Reichmann admitted. "But, you know we're also going to have some of the boys repair a T-hinged arch bridge over L'Ourthe River at Liege. Plus, there's a ton of other jobs in that area, too."

Reichmann took a deep breath, "When does it stop, Ernie? The men are exhausted. And, after that mess back there at Mons... well, it's taken its toll."

Lieutenant James reached down to his makeshift table and grabbed some pipe tobacco. He proceeded to clean out the bowl of his pipe and put some fresh mixture in. Then he lit the pipe, and looked back at Reichmann.

"I know. I've been trying to write this letter for the past hour, and, at this rate, it won't be done until the war is over."

Reichmann laughed. "Well, the truth of the matter is that, the way these Krauts are surrendering, I doubt if this mess goes on past Christmas."

"I hope you're right, captain," James said as he took a draw from his pipe.

"But, knowing our friend, Hitler, who knows? That SOB's one clever fellow. Who knows what he's got up his sleeve?"

"I wouldn't be surprised that, after we kill the bastard, we find the Devil himself up his sleeve," Reichmann said, as he stood up and made his way out of the tent. As he let down the tent's flap, he added, "See you at the officers' brief at oh-seven-hundred hours."

Lieutenant James sat back down on his cot, lay his pipe down and took off his glasses. He would try to get a bit of shuteye before he was to report for officer of the day (OD) duty in forty minutes.

During the next few days, the 238th Combat Engineer Battalion continued their march toward Germany. On 14 September 1944, they crossed the Siegfried Line in support of the 3rd Armor and the 1st Division. Their first job inside Germany was clearing a blown bridge two miles southwest of Aachen.

Located a few miles east of where the Netherlands and Belgium buttress up against Germany proper, Aachen was the first major German city to fall to the Allies. It was a hard-fought battle, as Hitler had given orders that it was to be held until "the last man."

Eisenhower believed the best way to win the war was to destroy every bit of Germany's war-making ability. Aachen was renowned for its industrial capacity. Called the "Broad Front" strategy by SHAEF, Ike wanted the Allies to go on the offensive everywhere in Western Europe.

The British disagreed with Eisenhower; they called for a narrow thrust into Berlin. But, because General Dwight D. Eisenhower was the Supreme Allied Commander, it didn't matter what the British wanted. Ike was going to destroy anything and everything that could produce war materiel for the *Nazi*s.

Colonel Gerhard Wilck, German commander of the city of Aachen, surrendered himself and his troops at 1200 hours on 21 October 1944. Two American prisoners of war belonging to the 1106th Engineer Group were released by Col. Wilck to make contact with the outposts of "C" Company, 238th Engineer Combat Battalion. Wilck was then taken to the 26th Infantry, 3rd Battalion command post for interrogation.

Afterward, Col. Wilck was granted permission to address his soldiers. Wilck's speech to his men must have been a difficult one to make, for the proud commander of the once invincible *Wehrmacht*.

This is a painful occasion on which I must speak to you. I have been forced to surrender, as ammunition, food and water are exhausted. I have seen that further fighting would be useless. I have acted against my orders, which directed that I would fight to the last man. At this time, I wish to remind you that you are German soldiers and to ask that you will always behave as such. I wish you all the best of health and a quick return to our Fatherland when hostilities have ceased, so that you may help in the rebuilding of Germany. The American commander has told us that I cannot give you the seig heil *or* Heil *Hitler, but we can still do it in our hearts....*[5]

PREPARING TO ENTER THE OUTSKIRTS OF AACHEN
FRIDAY, 29 SEPTEMBER 1944, MID-AFTERNOON

Every soldier in the 238th knew something big was up. For the past two days, they had been busy making sure every piece of equipment they possessed was ready for use. This meant that all vehicles had been serviced and all crew weapons cleaned.

The officers contributed to the belief of an impending holocaust, but constantly advised all the enlisted men to get as much sleep as possible, always ending their admonition by saying, "You never know when you'll be able to rest, so take advantage of the opportunity now."

For CPL Daniel Erickson, the notion of having to be reminded to sleep was plain crazy. He was so tired, that he had literally fallen asleep while standing up the previous day. At the moment, he was fast asleep inside a three-quarter ton truck.

Next to him lay PFC Ian Henry, also sound asleep.

Neither man was impressed when CPL Wilkes began shaking their boots.

"Okay, you two rise and shine. This damned war's gonna be over soon, and you guys will have slept through it!"

Both soldiers responded in like fashion: "Fuck you, Charlie!"

"We ain't got time for romance, you two. Lieutenant James wants both of your sorry asses in his tent in ten minutes. So wake up, clean up, take a piss or whatever else you have to do, and get your butts over to see the L-T within ten minutes."

Ian Henry sat upright and looked at Wilkes.

"What's up?"

"We've been attached to the 1st Infantry Division again. The first sergeant says we're going to move into the positions the 1st took from the Krauts. We'll also be reinforcing the 2nd Battalion, 18th Infantry Division on a thirty-five hundred yard front, about a mile south of Aachen."

"No shit? Aachen?" CPL Erickson asked.

"No shit, son. We're headed into Aachen—right into *Herr* Hitler's industrial heartland."

"Well," Erickson said. "Now we're getting someplace."

---

5. 1st Infantry Division G-2 Periodic Report, 21 October 1944.

"Yep," replied Wilkes. "With any luck at all, we just might be in Berlin by Christmas."

"In that case," Erickson said, tucking in his blouse and grabbing his weapon, "let's get a move on. I have a honey waiting for me back in the States."

Two Hours Later...

As the 238th's convoy approached their rendezvous site, Lieutenant Wong raised his right arm to signal the vehicles behind him to stop.

"What's up, L-T?" his driver quizzed.

"According to my map, we should be coming up on American troops very damned soon."

From out from nowhere, an American soldier stepped from behind a rock outcropping and raised his right hand. The GI looked like hell. He needed a shave and it appeared as if he had been through a meat grinder.

"You from the 238th?"

"Yes," Wong said, as he tried to make out the soldier's rank.

"Welcome to Aachen, sir," the enlisted man offered.

"You look like hell, son. When was the last time you had some hot food and rest?"

"Hell, sir… that would depend on what day of the week it is."

"Well, we're not infantry, but I believe we'll make a good accounting of ourselves," 1LT Wong said as he handed the soldier his coffee cup. "It's cold, but at least it's coffee."

The enlisted man took the officer's cup and drained its entire contents.

"Damn, that was good, sir. I owe you one."

When the soldier turned a bit, Wong saw a private first class stripe underneath the soldier's filthy uniform.

"Where's the rest of your unit, private?"

"They're out here somewhere, sir. But where—I don't know. The only thing I do know is that we've been killing a helluva lot of Krauts and they've been killing a helluva lot of us. However, if you want to talk to somebody in authority, you might send someone down that trail over to my right. I believe there is a staff sergeant over there. But I couldn't guarantee it."

"How many men do you think you have left in your unit, private?"

"It's hard to say, sir. I would guess somewhere around thirty… maybe thirty-five."

As 1LT Wong turned around he saw 1LT James approaching.

"What've you got, lieutenant?" James asked.

"Ernie, this private tells me his unit has been pretty chewed up, but that there might be some non-commissioned officers over to our right."

James motioned CPL Erickson over to where he was standing. "You come with me and this private. We're going to find out what the hell's going on out here."

Looking back to 1LT Wong, James said, "I have our guys setting up a perimeter. When I get back, we'll get the men fed, set up a CP and get patrols out."

"Got it, Ernie." With that, Wong started back to his vehicle.

1LT James and CPL Erickson hadn't walked more than a hundred yards when they came up on a master sergeant and four junior enlisted men, eating C- rations.

The master sergeant stood up and approached James.

Without saluting, the MSGT asked James if he was from the 238th Engineer Combat Battalion.

"Affirmative," James replied.

"I'm Master Sergeant Tucker, and these men are what's left of my first platoon."

Erickson shook his head in disbelief. Did he just say these four men are all that's left of an entire platoon?

James bit down on his pipe. "Where is your battalion, master sergeant?"

"I'm it. There are no officers left in this battalion."

Over the next few days, the men of the 238th would learn that their fellow soldiers in the 1st Division had suffered horrific losses in the battle for Aachen, and that ranking non-coms taking over command of a unit was the norm for them because most of their officers had been killed in action.

As for the Germans, they figured that the western boundary of Aachen was the logical route for the Americans to attack, and as a result they had heavily fortified the area.

For the next month, the 238th fought as infantry—patrolling when necessary, and leading advances. On 2 October 1944, the 1st Division turned the line over to the engineers, leaving them with 3,500 yards of front to defend. They had Free French soldiers to their left and an almost exposed flank.

This position was on the reverse slope of a wooded hill. As a result, the Krauts were able to look directly down upon them from their positions less than one hundred-eighty meters away.

The 238th occupied the German's Siegfried Line, taking over their pillboxes and battle encampments. The unit was spread out in this manner: Company A, then Company B, with Company C further on down the line.

THE SIEGFRIED LINE, AACHEN, GERMANY
WEDNESDAY, 4 OCTOBER 1944, 10:00 A.M. LOCAL

Having just got off his all-night shift working the radio in the operations tent, CPL Wilkes was bone-tired. There had been incidents of German probes all night and, as a result, nobody in the unit had got much sleep.

Charlie was just about to sit down underneath a tree and try to grab a few minutes worth of sleep, when he heard someone yell, "Here they come!"

No sooner had the GI yelled those three words that all hell broke loose. A platoon-sized element of *Wehrmacht* soldiers was approaching their location in an all-out attempt to overpower the Americans.

But the engineers stood their ground. When the shooting died down, the Americans had killed one German soldier and captured six more.

At the time of the initial contact, 1LT James, Private Nesbit Wilson (a big, muscular man who seemed to have an allergy to attaining any rank above private) and an enlisted man named Jack Rollins got pinned down and were unable to extricate themselves from their untenable position.

Hiding as best they could from the German soldiers, the three GIs found themselves trying to be invisible by standing next to a tree. Unfortunately some German machine gunner had their position locked in and was blasting away at both them and the pine tree.

"If we don't get that sonofabitch pretty soon, sir," Wilson said as he pulled a grenade from his web gear, "He's going to screw up our entire day!"

Had it not been for the precariousness of their situation, 1LT James would have probably made some wise comment. But levity would have to wait.

More bullets poured into where the three men lay, causing Wilson to lose his temper. This went on until suddenly Wilson stood up and threw his grenade. His aim was stupendous! He hit the German foxhole dead center.

The firing stopped.

Ernie James pulled out his pistol, preparing to go forward to make sure all the downed soldiers were dead. As he left the CP, he said, "That was a mighty good throw."

Wilson followed Lieutenant James, holding his weapon at the ready. On seeing his handiwork, Wilson mentioned, "Well, hell, sir, I used to be a pitcher in the minors before Uncle Sam drafted me."

"Well, God bless Abner Doubleday!" Lieutenant James exclaimed as he dusted himself off.

After searching the dead German soldiers for anything of intelligence value, James and Private Wilson made their way back to the pillbox that had been converted to a command post. Wilson looked at Lieutenant James.

"I don't get it, sir."

"What's to get?"

"Well, the Germans have to know they're getting their asses kicked, yet they keep coming. And every time they do, we tear them up. I mean, look, we got us a field of fire so tight that ain't nothing gonna get through it. And, that ain't counting Lieutenant Trowell's new 81-millimeter mortar platoon. Hell, we can zero in on the Krauts with deadly fire, just by picking up a field phone."

1LT James did not respond at that moment. But he too wondered how many more young German soldiers were going to be gunned down by him and his men before they got the point: Germany is finished! Go home!

James and Wilson had been in the CP for about ten minutes when Wilson noticed Captain Reichmann approaching.

Private Wilson moved over so the captain could fit in the pillbox. Once settled, he said, "I just wanted to let you know that we now have commo with the flyboys."

"How did you arrange that?" James inquired.

"I didn't, Group did. They want the Air Corps boys to attack from the east, toward us. I guess the idea is, they want to make sure if the Huns attack they aren't going to be able to withdraw."

"Makes sense to me," James admitted. "We might as well kill them here and now."

"Yes, and with the communications system we've set up, I don't think the Germans are going to be able to take this real estate back."

For the next few minutes, 1LT James and CPT Reichmann discussed the war, the communications system and when they thought the next liquor ration might come in. They were disrupted when the field phone in the CP rang.

Private Wilson picked up the phone.

"Jean CP."

A soldier from another pillbox began speaking. "This is Dawkins, let me speak to the L-T."

Handing the phone to Lieutenant James, Private Wilson said, "It's Dawkins, he wants to talk to you, sir."

James took the phone. "This is Lieutenant James. What's up, Dawkins?"

"Sir, one of our lookouts just spotted a German patrol about three-quarters of a mile from here."

"Whereabouts, Dawkins?"

"By the tree line, sir."

"I'll take care of it, Dawkins. Tell the man who spotted the Huns he did good. James, out."

Lieutenant James handed the phone back to Private Wilson. "Get me those artillery boys on this thing, pronto!"

Wilson complied, and in less than thirty seconds Lieutenant James was talking to the commander of an artillery unit.

Recognizing James' voice, the commander asked him where he wanted the "mail" to be delivered.

"The tree line in front of OP number 4, sir," James replied.

"Wilco, lieutenant, mail's on the way," the artillery captain replied, as he directed his artillery batteries to "fire for effect."

Within seconds, the entire horizon exploded.

"How's that?" the artillery officer asked, still on the field phone.

"That barrage landed about thirty feet in front of us, sir. But the Huns are ten feet in front of that. So bring it in ten feet more."

The artillery officer issued the orders and his artillerymen adjusted their fire accordingly. Within seconds, more shells landed within twenty feet of the American observation post. This time, the barrage landed right on top of the oncoming German soldiers, killing them all instantly.

It was over within two minutes. The final score? Americans—none. Germans—dozens!

After the artillery barrage was over, James looked over to Reichmann.

"Well, captain, the artillery boys earned their pay today."

Rubbing his eyes, CPT Reichmann replied, "We all did, lieutenant. We all did."

TWO NIGHTS LATER, DUSK
COMPANY B DUGOUT
OVERLOOKING THE GERMAN LINES

Lieutenant James had just got back from a trip to the woods to relieve himself when the field phone rang again. PFC Henry picked it up.

"Dugout 6, over."

The soldier on the other end of the line was excited.

"Henry, let me speak to the L-T"

Henry immediately recognized the other voice as SGT Creel, and handed the headset to 1LT James. "It's Creel, sir, he wants to talk to you. He sounds excited."

James took the headset, and spoke. "Go ahead, Creel."

"Sir, it's the damnedest thing ever."

"Calm down, Creel. What is it you're calling about?"

"Sir, believe it or not, there's a Kraut soldier walking this way. Somehow he's made it through our anti-personnel mines, and he's heading this way."

"Creel... stay low! Whatever that Kraut is up to, he'll probably try to blow himself to hell in a minute or two," James replied.

"And what if he don't, sir, what do you want me to do with him?"

"I doubt if that's going to happen, sergeant. But, if it does, capture him then blindfold his butt and bring him to me. Maybe he's got something of intelligence value."

A few moments later the soldier was standing directly in front of where Creel was crouched. With lightning speed, Creel reached out, grabbed him by his foot, and pulled him to the ground. It was obvious to the other GI who shared the dugout with Creel that this German soldier had seen the elephant once too often. He offered no resistance whatever.

Creel immediately blindfolded him, tied his hands behind his back, and pulled him over to where Lieutenant James and PFC Henry were keeping guard.

As soon as the enemy soldier was pushed into James' dugout, Creel reported that he'd searched him and found a camera. James took it and gave it to PFC Henry.

"Henry, get Major Massoglia on the radio. Tell him the situation. Ask him to send some of those freeloaders back at the CP over, to retrieve us of ol' Hans here and his camera."

Within ten minutes, three enlisted men approached 1LT James' dugout. James recognized two of them. Looking to the other soldier, James asked, "Who are you?"

"Staff Sergeant Miller, from G-2. I'm new, sir."

"So, sergeant... you just happened to be out on an evening constitutional?"

The E6 laughed. "Actually, sir, that's pretty accurate. I just got in from the States and wanted to see what was going on out here...."

James took a draw from his pipe, and said, "I wouldn't be too anxious, sergeant. This war has a way of biting you in the butt."

The staff sergeant's ears turned red.

He got my point. That tells me he's got a brain!

"Well, take ol' Hans here back with you, and do it quickly. It'll be damned dark in a few minutes. If you don't get back to the CP pretty quick, you might get you and your troops' asses shot off."

The staff sergeant started to salute, but one of the lower enlisted men stopped him. "Don't do that! You want to get the best L-T in the 238th killed, for crissakes?"

The soldier from G-2 apologized, picked the German soldier up by the scruff of his collar, and spoke to him.

"Auf deinen Füßen, Soldat. Wenn du lustiges alles versuchst, schicke ich persönlich dich zur Hölle!" ["On your feet, soldier. If you try anything funny, I'll personally send you to hell!"]

Lieutenant James was impressed with the GI's German. "Where did you learn to speak German like that, sergeant?"

"Coon Rapids, Minnesota, sir. My family emigrated from Germany after the last war. There are quite a few German-speaking dairy farmers up there—mostly Lutherans, of course."

"Well soldier, take care of Hans there, and keep your head down. We always need fluent German-speaking soldiers around here."

After an hour of interrogation, the now-surrendered soldier told his inquisitors of the location of an officer's mess hall in Aachen. Acting on that bit of intelligence, the next day around noon the 238th dropped a 4.2 millimeter mortar on the coordinates the German soldier had given them.

No smoke.

Another round was launched. Again, no smoke.

The order was given to fire for effect. A few days later the men discovered that the first two mortars had gone right down the steeple of the building—thus no smoke!

However, the Germans' *Mittagessenzeitmahlzeit* (lunchtime meal) was cut very short.

SATURDAY, 7 OCTOBER 1944, 2:40 A.M. LOCAL

The long and short of it was that, ever since the Allies crossed over the Siegfried Line, the *Nazis* had been doing their best to push them out of Germany. Beginning around dusk every evening, enemy combat patrols were sent out to probe for possible weaknesses in the Allied lines.

On one night alone, Company C withstood three heavy assaults on their position. The final time, a GI named Smolkowicz was forced to call in artillery fire in on his own position.

The next night, Company A called for 4.2 mortars a few feet from their outpost line. Unfortunately, one of the shells landed right on top Lieutenant Draganza's dugout. Seeing the damage to a fellow officer's position, Lieutenant James, with CPL Erickson and PFC Henry, ran over to see if anyone was still alive.

As the men stood there, they heard Lieutenant Draganza's voice. The two enlisted men jumped into the debris and began pulling away some of the timbers that were used to fortify the position. Within a few seconds, Lieutenant Draganza said something in Yugoslavian, and climbed out.

"You okay?" James inquired, hardly believing that his comrade was still alive.

In an example of classic understatement, the Yugoslavian-American officer said, "Yes, but I need to see a medic."

As the lieutenant was being helped into a jeep, James looked at him. "Now I know just how tough you *Mahalvitch* guys are."

The young, second generation Yugoslavian-American replied, "Strong enough to beat Tito!"

As the medics were helping Draganza with his seatbelt, Ernie James offered a suggestion.

"Well, let's finish this war before you start another."

CHAPTER SIXTEEN

Therefore, take the whole armor of God that you may be able to withstand in the evil day, and having done all, to stand.
—St. Paul's letter to the Ephesians

COLONEL AND MRS. MICHAEL BRANDON OHARA'S RESIDENCE
LOS LAGOS, GRANITE BAY, CALIFORNIA
SUNDAY, 1 DECEMBER 1991, 5:00 P.M. LOCAL

For the past three hours, CSM Wilkes and Major James had been relating all that had occurred to the 238th Engineer Combat Battalion since they left the Aachen area and moved east to Eischweiler. James told of the total destruction that the 1st Division wreaked upon the *Nazis* and how the battlefield was strewn with bodies and destroyed equipment. Major James was now finishing the story.

"Eischweiler is on the Aachen-to-Cologne Autobahn. We were awed by those superhighways, as there wasn't anything like them back in the States at the time. However, what struck us is how they had skimped on materials, as the concrete was often of poor quality, and with evidence of inept workmanship.

"During the slack times we trained with many weapons, shooting into a large open-pit mine. We used excavation machinery, and the buildings in the mine were utilized as targets. Our guys fired bazookas, rifle grenades, 37mm antitank guns, machine guns and just plain, old grenades.

"By the last week of November, Company C was busy repairing a one hundred-fifty foot steel truss over the Inde River west of Eischweiler. The weather was absolutely dreadful," James said, as he picked up a glass of water.

At that point, CSM Wilkes again entered the story.

"I still get chills when I think about how damned cold we got during that winter. And, especially I remember December 12."

"Are you referring to Lieutenant McClure?" James asked, as he put his glass down on the dining room table.

"Yes."

"It was horrible, what happened that day. I can remember it as if it were just yesterday," James admitted.

"Mind if I tell it, Ernie?"

"Better you than me."

"The afternoon had been one cold sonofabitch," Wilkes began. "It was dreary, wet and miserable. We'd been working on roads all that morning. First Lieutenant Eugene McClure and his men had come up on a German mine field.

"Our S.O.P. stated that the engineers were required to explore it, and to mark it for other troops. Major Hudson, from Group HQ, and 1LT McClure went out to make the inspection. Now mind you, McClure was new to the commissioned ranks, having been given a battlefield commission a few weeks earlier. Therefore, it would be fair to say that he was still green.

"Well, sure as hell, while the two men were out there, Major Hudson stepped on a shoe mine, which is a small wooden box anti-personnel mine that contained about a quarter-pound of explosives inside. The blast took off his foot just above the ankle.

"Then McClure stepped on a shoe mine, which caused him to fall on his belly. While crawling to get out of the field, he set off another mine. This time, his body was blown apart. All the while, Captain Reichmann was getting ready to hightail it over to a bath point to get the day's mud and filth off. On his way over, McClure's driver came in to report that his OIC was severely wounded.

"Reichmann got hold of Lieutenant Draganza, and the two headed out into the minefield. When they got there, they discovered that a medic and the battalion doctor, a man named Zimont, were already on the scene. Reichmann and Draganza went out into the field to rescue Hudson, who, by that time, had been out there for over half an hour.

"Almost every time they put their bayonet into the ground, they found a friggin' German mine. One of the damned things exploded when they threw it aside. Reichmann pulled Hudson onto the stretcher by his collar, and as he and Draganza were lifting the stretcher, Reichmann stepped on a shoe mine. He was blown several feet into the air, and he too lost his foot at the ankle.

"To compound the situation, he suffered shrapnel wounds from hell to breakfast. His eyes were hit, his face and hands—they were all bleeding profusely. Draganza started digging out the shoe mines and tossing them to one side; however, one apparently hit a non-metallic mine and caused it to explode. The force from the explosion almost cost our young Yugoslavian-American lieutenant his neck! It knocked him senseless."

Now Major James came back into the conversation.

"I remember that day, too. I was just arriving back from the command post from a work detail, when I got word that I was to go out with my platoon. I found my medic and T/5 Ward, a truck driver. They agreed to come out with me.

"When we got there, Draganza was incoherent, yelling like a crazy man. We got hold of some mine detectors and a couple stretchers, and then we entered the minefield. It didn't take but a second or two for me to figure out that the mines the Krauts had put down couldn't be detected by our mine detectors. So we tossed them.

"What we did next, was to pull out our bayonets and begin probing the ground in front of us with them. When we found a mine, we carefully put it aside. While we were out there all the men in the field were yelling for us to hurry up. After what seemed like an eternity, we finally did reach Hudson and Reichmann, and we put them on the stretchers. T/5 Ward picked up the front of Reichmann's stretcher and I picked up the back. Draganza, who was back on his feet now, took the front of Hudson's stretcher and another medic carried the back end. We carefully wove our way back to our lines, making sure we only walked where we knew was safe.

"Our hands were numb from the cold. To make matters worse, Reichmann's ankle was jabbing me in the stomach. Draganza was practically in tears, knowing we were almost out of the field. When we got out of that hellhole, the ambulances were there waiting to take the men to the nearest field hospital.

"When that was over, I made my way back to the Eischweiler battalion command post, and I'll be damned if some half-assed colonel didn't want me to go back out to the minefield and retrieve Lieutenant McClure's body.

"I couldn't believe my ears, and asked that sonofabitch if he was giving me an order. He replied in the affirmative. At that point, I asked for some medics to come with me in case my luck didn't hold. Well, Dr. Zimont absolutely refused to risk his medics on such a mission and went over to see the colonel, who eventually withdrew his order. The next day Captain Smith took a half-track out there and recovered the lieutenant's remains."

Now CSM Wilkes rejoined the conversation.

"If that wasn't enough excitement for one day, when we got back to the unit we were ordered to build an eighty-foot, class 40 double Bailey bridge on the Autobahn over a railroad line at Luchen."

"Yes, and I recall the artillery fire was so intense that we had to call it a day, and wait until the next day to go back and finish that job," James added.

"You are so right. It was one s-c-r-e-w-e-d up day, if you ask me." Wilkes said, as he picked up a cup of coffee.

Major James added, "But not as screwed up at the Battle of the Bulge."

"How so?" Sean Ohara inquired.

James paused briefly, and then said, "I had to think about it for a bit. Let's begin on December 15, 1944. The battalion commander, a colonel, was giving a briefing."

BATTALION COMMAND TENT, NEAR EISCHWEILER, GERMANY
FRIDAY, 15 DECEMBER 1944

"Before I get started with this briefing, gentlemen," the colonel said, "I'd like to call Private Henry and Corporals Wilkes and Erickson forward."

PFC Henry looked puzzled. As far as he knew, he had not screwed up anything lately, nor had he heard of any fuckups Erickson might have done. But — Charlie Wilkes? Hum... as far as he knew, Charlie had been too busy working the radios and pulling guard duty to get into anything too brackish.

When all three men made their way to the front of the tent, the first sergeant called the room to attention, "Attention to orders. Private First Class Henry, you are hereby promoted to the rank of corporal, effective date, 1 November, 1944." Ian Henry started to smile, but thought better of it. Instead, he bit down on his tongue. The first sergeant gave him a set of corporal stripes.

"Henry, you've done a great job around here, and the colonel wanted you promoted as soon as possible. Unfortunately, we haven't had the administrative support to get this promotion completely through the system, but you'll be getting all your back pay one of these days."

There was laughter in the tent, as "one of these days" could be translated to tomorrow or two weeks from now—or never—and all the men knew it.

The first sergeant repeated his call to attention, and then said, "Corporal

Erickson, you are hereby promoted to the rank of sergeant, effective date 1 December, 1944. Thank you for a job well done!" He then handed the now-beaming Erickson three stripes. Erickson took the stripes and saluted the colonel.

What occurred next came as a complete surprise to all the men inside the 238th command post tent, except for the colonel and the first sergeant.

The sergeant put the men at ease. Wilkes was confused, big time. His two friends had been promoted... so, why not him? As soon as the colonel began to speak, he figured it out.

"Gentlemen," he began, "the next soldier we are going to promote is our battalion radio operator and driver for Lieutenant James. However, before we do that, I'd like to say a few words. Like most of the men in this unit, Corporal Wilkes is a fine soldier. In fact, if you ask me, I think he should make a career out of the Army." There was a bit of laughter in the tent, which the colonel ignored, but he did have a smile on his face.

"The outcome of the matter, of course, is up to Sergeant Wilkes. I'm sure that when this damned war is over, he will make the right decision. In the meantime, I want to express my personal thanks for his tireless efforts in keeping our communications up, and in doing such a fine job keeping Lieutenant James out of trouble."

There was more laughter in the tent, this time with the entire group of officers chiming in. The colonel was on an unusual roll, and he played it to the hilt.

"So, before I pin these three stripes on him, I'd just like to say, Sergeant Wilkes, keep up the good work, and take good care of my lieutenants — even the ones who stray in Paris, when they aren't supposed to."

Sonofabitch, he knows we went into Paris!

The entire tent broke into laughter.

Damn! And, apparently, so does everyone else!

After the laughter dissipated, the first sergeant called the room back to attention and said, "Corporal Wilkes, you are hereby promoted to sergeant, with the effective date of 1 December 1944."

Charlie Wilkes' face was red as a beet. He could already hear all the catcalls and snide remarks from the junior enlisted men, about him being an ass-kisser. Nevertheless, in his heart, he was almost as proud as when his son was born.

Sergeant Charles Wilkes, United States Army. It has a nice ring to it!

The battalion commander directed the men back to their seats. When they once again were seated, the colonel turned the briefing over to Captain Cline, the unit's S-2 officer.

Cline cleared his throat, and said, "Gentlemen, something's up in the Ardennes. I say this because, as I speak, the other half of our old regiment, the 51st Engineer Combat Battalion, is asshole-deep in combat operations with the enemy. Now, what the *Nazi*s are actually up to, we don't know yet. But our intelligence operatives believe that Jerry is up to something no good. What is it? Who knows? All we know is that he is up to something. I tell you this, so you'll be careful. After all, we've come this far.

"Let's try to make it all the way back to the States."

SATURDAY, 16 DECEMBER 1944
VERSAILLES, FRANCE

General Omar Bradley (USA) was in Versailles for a conference with Eisenhower when the messenger came in to give Ike a message from SHAEF. Ike's eyebrow went up ever so slightly. He had given specific orders that he and General Bradley were not to be disturbed. Yet, here he was being disturbed. He waived the young captain forward.

What do you have for me?"

"An urgent message from SHAEF, General."

Ike took the message from the signal corps officer, it read:

OPERATIONAL IMMEDIATE
TOP SECRET
SHAEF 1000 HOURS

FROM: SHAEF G-2
TO: EISENHOWER ONLY

1. *Preliminary reports of a massive German assault this morning at 0530 hours. It began with an artillery barrage on Allied troops throughout the Ardennes region.*
2. *Intelligence reports elements of the 6th SS Panzer Army broke through American lines at 0800 hours.*
3. *In the northern sector Dietrich's 6th SS Panzer Army is attacking the Losheim Gap. It appears they are trying to break through to Liège.*
4. *General von Manteuffel's 5th Panzer Army is attacking in the*

direction of Bastogne and St. Vith.
5. *To the south, General Brandenberger's 7th Army is attacking in the direction of Luxembourg in what appears to an effort to secure the flank from Allied attacks.*

MAJOR GENERAL STRONG, CHIEF OF INTELLIGENCE

When Ike finished reading the twix, he handed it to Bradley, who skimmed it.

Adjusting his glasses, Bradley said, "I think it's a spoiling attack, Ike."

"How so?"

"I think the Krauts are doing it as a ruse to hamper Patton's boys."

Eisenhower thought otherwise. "Brad, this isn't a spoiling attack. Hitler is coming at us full force."

Bradley put the message down on a table and looked at Eisenhower, "Phew, 'Georgie Boy' isn't going to like what Bedell is going to have to tell him."

Eisenhower's uncharacteristic reply let everyone present know that he was very concerned with the German attack that began at 5:30 that morning in the Ardennes.

"Well, tell him that Ike is running this damn war!"

Bradley pondered the situation briefly. He had only two newly arrived and inexperienced infantry divisions, plus two combat-tested divisions available to stop Hitler's Sixth SS *Panzer* Division under the command of General Dietrich, and the Fifth Panzer Army, under General Manteuffel. He stood up from the chair he had been sitting in and picked up his helmet.

"I'll meet with George tomorrow morning in Luxembourg, General."

GENERAL OMAR BRADLEY'S HEADQUARTERS,
VERDUN, FRANCE
SUNDAY, 17 DECEMBER 1944, 1000 HOURS LOCAL

The captain who held open the door for the commander of the 3rd Army to enter General Bedell Smith's office looked all of twenty-five years old.

"Come in, General Patton. General Smith is expecting you."

"Thank you, captain," General Patton said as he walked into

Eisenhower's assistant's office.

Patton was somewhat taken back by the Spartan conditions of the office, but was immediately struck by the markings on the huge map to behind Ike's executive officer's desk.

Patton looked toward Bedell Smith, pulled out a cigar from his blouse, and nodded his head to Ike's assistant.

Smith walked over to where Patton was standing. "George, I feel you won't like what we're going to do, but I fear it is necessary."

"I can read a map, Bedell."

"Ike's very concerned, George."

"As well he should be," Patton replied.

"Whatever the Jerries are up to, we don't fully know yet. But as you can see, he's raising hell with our entire line."

"What do you need, Brad?" Patton asked, lighting his cigar.

"What can Third Army do?"

"I can have two divisions on the move tomorrow, and a third one the day after."

Bradley looked directly into Patton's eyes. "George, what about the Saar Offensive?"

Patton smiled at his former boss. "What the hell, we'll still be killing Krauts! And I can guarantee Ike one thing: I'm going to hit this bastard hard!"[1]

TUESDAY, 19 DECEMBER 1944
GENERAL GEORGE SMITH PATTON'S HEADQUARTERS,
0700 HOURS LOCAL

General Patton's senior command had been waiting for their boss for twenty minutes. When he strode in, they could tell something was up.

"Gentlemen, we're up to our assholes in Krauts. Their raising holy hell all through the Ardennes, and I have to meet with Ike this afternoon. So I'm going to make this short."

After looking each one of his senior men directly in his eyes, Patton said, "I want you to get our logistics wizards to work on three possible plans of attack. Out goal is to stop those lousy Hun bastards at the Meuse—and from there, we'll hold the lines. We will not retreat one foot from there! I'm meeting with Ike in four hours, and I want to be able to

1. *Patton, A Genius For War*, Harper Collins, Carlo D'Este, page 678.

give him something he can hang his hat on."

Patton walked over to a map on the wall, and used his index finger to draw a circle around the location where III Corps was currently engaged in operations. From the look on their boss's face, all men present knew the situation was grim.

"I am assuming that I'm going to be given control of VIII Corps. Once that happens, I'm going to marry them up with III Corps, who will take control of three divisions from First Army. I'll then issue orders to disengage from the Saar."

Looking at his staff plans and operations officer, Patton again used his right index finger to trace out three possible routes of attack. "Have your people draw up operations using these routes. Once I find out what exactly our mission will be, I'll call General Gay to let him know which way he is to start heading. I'll use code words. Are there any questions?"

There being none, Patton picked up his riding crop and helmet and walked out to where his driver was waiting to take him to Verdun.

SHAEF HEADQUARTERS, 1100 HOURS THAT SAME MORNING

To the young military policeman standing outside General Eisenhower's office, there appeared to be more stars sitting around the conference table in the next room than appeared in all of last night's sky. He stopped counting after General Arthur Tedder, General Walter Bedell Smith, General Omar Bradley, General Jacob Loucks Devers, and General George Smith Patton entered into the second-floor office of the French Army barracks.

The twenty-year-old enlisted man from Carmel, California also noticed the looks on the faces of all the senior officers present. They spoke volumes.

You'd better stay awake, sergeant. If anything happens to any of these men, we could lose this fucking war!

Inside the office, Eisenhower the Supreme Commander was speaking. "The present situation is to be regarded as one of *opportunity* for us, and of *disaster* for the Germans. There will only be cheerful faces at this conference table."[2]

General Patton could tell that Eisenhower was worried sick about the quarter-million German soldiers, who were currently wreaking havoc

---

2. D'Este, page 679.

with the Allied troops in the Ardennes. The strain on Ike became all too apparent, when Eisenhower's G-2 and G-3 showed up five minutes late. Looking to Major General Kenneth Strong (G-2) and General Harold "Pinky" Bull (G-3), Eisenhower scoffed,

"Well, I knew my staff would get here—it was only a question of *when*."

Now that all of his senior officers were present, Eisenhower continued with his monologue.

"First thing we have to do, is to stop all offensive operations in the Allied sectors and concentrate on stopping these bastards from coming any further. My plan of action is to stop them cold at the Meuse River. Once we've done that, we will counterattack and drive those sonsabitches back to Berlin."

Ike looked toward Patton. "George, how soon can you attack with six divisions?"

"Give me the word, general, and I'll have my men attack in forty-eight hours!"

Ike wanted a realistic answer, but the commanding officer of the 3rd Army's reply sounded like bravado to him. "Goddammit, George, this isn't the time for theatrics. When can you attack with six divisions?"

Patton held fast. "Ike, I'm serious. I have my staff working on the plans, as we speak. I say we *will* be ready in forty-eight hours! I have my people working on three possible scenarios, each one with a separate code-word. All I have to do is call General Gay, give him the code, and we're on the road!"

Eisenhower desperately wanted to believe him. But he'd known George Patton for a long time, and as such he was all too-aware that the West Point graduate from Virginia was prone to shooting from the hip.

"George, I need an honest estimate! When can you attack? I was thinking you'd be ready by the twenty-third."

Patton stood up and walked over to the huge situation map on the wall. With his right index finger, he pointed to Saint-Vith. "Right here, Ike. Right here at Saint-Vith-Bastogne. I am going to kick those bastards all the way to hell! Just give me the word, and I'll put in a call to General Gay."

Bradley could not believe his subordinate would let the conversation go this far south, and in front of Eisenhower. He shook his head and said, "George, are you telling us that you're going to pull three divisions from the line, turn them north and march them over one hundred miles in this dreadful weather, without sleep and food, and send them into battle against a quarter of a million enemy soldiers?"

A supremely confident George S. Patton replied, "Brad, the Kraut's stuck his head in a meat grinder. And this time, I've got hold of the handle."

Patton's comment brought a few chuckles from around the table. Then the senior officers got down to formulating their plans to halt Hitler's hordes from overrunning the Allied positions. The meeting continued for another hour. As the conference broke up, everyone in the room was fully aware that the Allies were in danger of losing the war. Their only hope rested with George S. Patton, and the men under his command.

Both would perform admirably.

After leaving the conference, Patton had a subordinate call General Gay. He then spent the night in Luxembourg. Over the next three days, Patton made appearances with his front-line units by driving from division to division, corps to corps. His army fought its way to Bastogne, arriving three days after the final major German assault.

According to the German High Command's own calculations, Patton's 3rd Army killed 12,652 German soldiers, wounded another 38,600 and caused 30,382 to go missing.[3] The loss of equipment on both sides was incalculable—the difference being that the Allies could (and would) replace their lost men and materiel.

The Battle of the Ardennes officially ended on 28 January 1945. The German High Command withdrew the German Sixth *Panzer* Army out of the Ardennes and sent it to fight the Bolsheviks on the Eastern Front. By doing so, they left huge gaps in the line against the Allies. For Hitler's soldiers that remained—it was *Götterdämmerung*.

WEDNESDAY, 20 DECEMBER 1944
XHORIS, BELGIUM, 1845 HOURS LOCAL

SGT Wilkes had a difficult decision to make. He could drink another cup of coffee to try to keep warm, knowing that in the process he would become so jittery that he'd never be able to sleep when he got off duty. Or, he could sit there and freeze his butt off.

This friggin' tent is as cold as Iowa in January.

Wilkes had been drinking hot coffee since he went on duty at noon.

---

3. D'Este, page 699.

His nerves were so shot now, that he thought he actually might smack the first sonofabitch who gave him any crap. That is, until CPL Ian Henry entered the command tent.

With his usual New Hampshire innocence, Henry came inside the tent, smiled and asked, "What's up, Charlie?"

"Just sitting here, freezing my ass off. Like everybody else," Wilkes replied.

"Mind if I sit down?"

"What've you got for me?" Wilkes asked, knowing that Ian wasn't supposed to be in the command tent unless he was on official business.

Not having heard a negative reply to his interrogative, Henry sat down.

"I was bringing a report up to the Old Man from L-T James."

"On what?"

"On all those mines the guys laid over in the Inden-Lucherberg area today, in support of the 104th Infantry. James reports that they got the job done, and everyone is packed up and ready to jump to our next A-O first thing in the morning."

"Leave the message on that ammo crate over there. First Sergeant Freck's using it as his portable desk. I'll make sure he sees it, the minute he gets back from his briefing up at HQ," Wilkes said, as he stood up and stretched.

"He's at a meeting this late at night, as cold as it is? Damn— something big must be up."

"Freck's inbound as we speak. He called on the radio about five minutes ago to have me pass the word to our sentries, so none of them accidentally takes a pot-shot at him. I just sent Erickson out to advise all the men on the line. When I talked to him, he said he was about five minutes out from our lines, and that he's coming up the back way."

CPL Henry knew he risked death (or at least a severe ass-chewing) if he were caught inside the command tent without being on official business. But at the moment he didn't give a damn what they did to him, as he was dog-tired. Sitting on an ammo crate, he asked, "What's on the net?"

"From what I've been able to pick up, the 'Battered Bastards of Bastogne' under old General McAuliffe are still hanging on. But I guess frostbite is kicking the snot out of them."

"Well, I can believe that. I tried to take a piss a few minutes ago and couldn't find my pecker," Ian Henry said, laughing.

"I guess I could say 'what's new?' But I won't. I'm too damned tired, but so full of coffee I doubt I'll ever be able to sleep. Guess I'm like the Greeks—I don't know which way to turn."

Henry started to laugh. "Has anyone ever told you, you're one fucked-up soldier?"

"Not within the past four hours, they haven't. But anything longer than that…" Wilkes said, then forgot what Henry's question was and just stopped talking.

CPL Henry looked toward his best friend. He was close to exhaustion.

"Charlie, I wonder if the Huns are as cold and beat-up as we are."

"I hope this is like a weekend in Miami, compared to what those sonsabitches are having to put up with," Wilkes said, as he reached over and took a sip of the bitter coffee sloshing around in his steel canteen cup.

"Because, quite honestly," he continued, "as I recall, that sonofabitch Adolf Hitler declared war on us. So, to my way of thinking—fuck him, his soldiers, that von Braun whore and all the rest of those *Nazi* bastards."

Henry started to laugh. "Charlie, does your wife know you swear and cuss and carry on like you do?"

"Sharon knows," Charlie admitted.

"She doesn't care?" Ian asked.

"Ian, I never said that. If I carried on half this bad around her and the boys, she'd slap the shit out of me and ask if I was gonna eat with this mouth."

Henry smiled. "When we get the hell out of here, you and I got to spend some time together. Who knows, maybe Sharon could find someone back there in Anaheim who would like to marry a grape farmer from San Luis Obispo."

"Are you still on that?" Charlie asked, thinking back to the conversation he and Ian Henry had back at Camp Roberts, right after Charlie's Iowa National Guard unit was federalized in the early part of 1942.

"Hell, yes! What's changed, other than we've slugged it out every friggin' day since Normandy on four or five hours sleep, worked twelve to fourteen hours a day and been shot at every time I fart?"

Charlie Wilkes started to laugh. "So that's it?"

"What?" Henry asked.

"So, you're the reason these Huns keep trying to kill us? Well, hell

— in that case, stop farting!"

"Charlie, you're a piece of work."

Henry looked at his watch. The first sergeant was due in any moment. He figured he'd better hurry this conversation along, and then get the hell out of the command tent before First Sergeant Freck showed up, ready to rip out his tonsils for being inside the tent without a good reason.

"Anything else exciting on the net? Henry asked, as he stood up to go back outside into the bitterly cold evening.

"A couple hours ago, I read some traffic that said General Bruce Clarke's Combat Command B of the 7th Armored Division, and troops the Army grabbed from the 28th and 106th Divisions, are putting up one helluva fight at Saint-Vith. When I showed it to the first sergeant, he told me that the 1st, 2nd, and 99th Infantry divisions are barely hanging on over on the Elsenborne Ridge."

"It don't look good, Charlie."

"Nope. And when you figure in the fact that the 82nd Airborne, under James Gavin, is up to their asses in a shootout with the Krauts—it all adds up to whoever wins that motherfucker, wins this war."

"Why that battle, Charlie?"

"According to Freck, it's a matter of life and death, as the *Nazi*s are ever so close to our P.O.L. [petroleum, oil and lubricants] storage facility in Stavelot. He says we have over two million gallons of gas stored there! But G-2 is under the impression that the Huns don't know they're that close to all that gas."

"Fuck me," Wilkes said, "if those Lugerheads get that gas, they could run our asses all the way back to Normandy."

"Well, I guess ol' Jimmy Gavin's 82nd Airborne is gonna have to keep those sonsabitches the hell away from all that fuel," Henry said, as he sat down on one of the chairs in the tent.

"I wouldn't make myself too comfortable, if I were you," Wilkes warned.

"Yeah, I know. But shit the bed, Charlie, I'm exhausted. I was out in the field yesterday laying mines until I nearly dropped. I don't think I've ever worked that hard in my life."

"Hey, ain't nobody ever said being a combat engineer was easy."

"Fuck, Charlie, you sit here all day on your ass and drink coffee, and you got the balls to tell me I'm a pussy. That's rich, just fucking rich."

SGT Wilkes looked at his friend and said, "Hey, Henry, I'm just giving you a ration of shit. Somebody has to do it! I think it's written somewhere in Army regulations that everybody gets a ration of shit, every day. Hell, if I didn't I could be written up for dereliction of duty."

Just at that moment, 1SGT Freck came into the tent. Henry stood up and started to leave, but was told to remain by the senior NCO.

"Henry, I want you to bring all the officers over here, right now. Tell them I need to see them immediately."

As Ian stood up to make his way to the tent flap, the sergeant said, "And don't forget to wear your helmet!"

THE 238TH COMBAT ENGINEERS COMMAND TENT
FIFTEEN MINUTES LATER

Major Massoglia cleared his throat a bit, waited for the tent to quiet down, then began speaking.

"Sorry to take you away from your duties on this freezing-cold night, gentlemen, but the Battalion CO wanted this information disseminated as soon as I got back here. He sends his regrets that he couldn't attend, but he has some pressing business back at HQ."

There were a few grins on the junior officer's faces, because to a man they suspected their commanding officer had most likely scared up a poker game, and wouldn't be back until the next morning. The truth of the matter was that the colonel had gone on ahead to XVII Corps HQs, to explain the battalion's task.

Massoglia, of course, knew where the CO was. But he did not feel the need to share that information with the present company.

He cleared his throat again and said, "Effective 2400 hours local time, we're being attached to the XVIII Airborne. We'll get our actual orders in the morning, but for right now we're doing a VOCO (Verbal Orders of the Commanding Officer). And this order concerns every swinging you-know-what in the battalion, less company kitchens and administrative echelons of H/S Company. They are to move out to Xhoris and proceed to the crossroads at Manhay. Barrier lines are to be prepared along the roads to Manhay to Bra, Manhay to La Fourche, and Manhay-Grandmenil-LaForge."

Stating the obvious, Major Massoglia added, "These lines are to be designed to prevent the Germans from entering into the area, and to deny them access to the main road [Manhay-Werbomont]. Our mines are to be laid on the ground, but are to be buried, if time permits.

"Company A is assigned the road Manhay to Bra; Company B, the road Manhay to LaFource; and Company C the road Manhay-Grandmenil-LaForge. The battalion command post is to be established at Chene-al-Pierre. Companies A and C are to move out at 0330 hours, and Company B gets to sleep in—they move out at 0445 hours."

There was a brief bit of chuckling among the officers. Then the major continued with his briefing. "Now, as you know, all the roads are a friggin' mess, and we'll have to work around that. But, suffice it to say, we're driving straight through to Verviers, then on to Spa, whereupon we'll turn east just north of My. Remember, our meeting point is to be the intersection near the town of Werbomet—which is about five miles north of the village of Manhay.

"The next part is cloak-and-dagger. Once we're there, we are to meet an unknown person who will then direct us to our defensive positions."

"Ah, Major," one of the first lieutenants said, "I want to reiterate what you just said. We're supposed to meet an unknown person in the dark?"

Major Massoglia scratched his head and replied, "Lieutenant, I didn't make this crap up. Those words are directly from G-2. For all I know, it could be Dwight D. Eisenhower, himself."

From the back of the tent, one of the officers muttered, "If we don't hang on here, it damned well could be Ike."

"Anyway…," Massoglia said, clearing his throat again, "once we meet up with the mystery man, he's going to take us to our new home."

The major was finished with his briefing. He put his helmet down on an ammo box and asked the assembled officers if they had any questions. None were forthcoming, so he looked toward the officers and said, "Make sure our sentries are wide awake tonight—I'll see the men from Company A and C at 0330 hours."

"Thank you, major," Lieutenant James said, as he lit his pipe and sat down on a cot. He had staff duty officer at 2400 hours and wanted to try to get a few hours of sleep before going on duty.

The major looked at Lieutenant James, and said, "And now, unless you men need me for something, I'm going to try to catch some sleep. God only knows how much we're going to get in the next few days."

"Good night, sir," the men said as the battalion executive officer opened up the tent's flap and walked outside into the bitter cold evening.

THE 238TH COMBAT ENGINEER COMMAND VEHICLE
THURSDAY, 21 DECEMBER 1944
IN THE ARDENNES FOREST, 0500 HOURS LOCAL

The convoy had been on the road for less than fifteen minutes, and already SGT Wilkes was already freezing his ass off.

Damn! I didn't think any place could be colder than Iowa in December, but man, was I wrong!

1SGT Freck was trying to drink some coffee without spilling it all over himself, and up until now he had been successful. That is, until SGT Wilkes hit a pothole.

"Damn! I'm sorry, first sergeant, I didn't see that sonofabitch."

"Is that a statement of fact, sergeant, or an observation?"

"Beg your pardon, first sergeant?" Charlie replied, not having a clue as to what the first sergeant said.

"I said, Sergeant Wilkes, are you telling me you're a sorry SOB, or are you asking forgiveness for spilling this entire cup of coffee all over me?"

Wilkes thought about it for a second and then answered, "On both accounts, first sergeant. That is, I'm a sorry sonofabitch for spilling the coffee on you, and that I'm a sorry sonofabitch in general."

1SGT Freck shook his head in agreement, and said, "In which case, drive on."

And "drive on" the 238th Engineer Combat Battalion did. The unit plowed through the Ardennes Forest until it reached an intersection about five miles north of the village of Manhay, Belgium.

Using only the blackout lights on the ¾-ton truck, Wilkes slowed down when he saw the vehicle in front of him stop.

The 1SGT grabbed his weapon and dismounted from the vehicle. Looking to Wilkes, he said, "I'm going up to talk to the XO. Keep the engine running."

"Wilco, First Sergeant," Wilkes replied as he got out of the vehicle to stretch.

CPL Henry was driving the vehicle directly behind Wilkes. When he saw that the convoy was stopping, he decided to stretch his legs and get whatever blood he had that wasn't frozen, flowing again.

Hobbling over toward Wilkes, he asked, "What's the deal?"

"Fuck if I know. Freck says we're supposed to meet somebody here, and that the 'somebody' is going to direct us to our defensive positions."

"Well, one thing for sure," Henry said as he leaned over in an effort to touch his toes, "we ain't gonna get much sleep tonight. Especially if we have to dig defensive positions."

"Maybe it won't come to that," Wilkes replied.

"What do you mean?" Henry inquired.

"Well… it stands to reason that the guys from the Seventh Armored will already have dug defensive positions. With any luck at all, all we'll have to do is get our weapons and sleeping bags out of the vehicles and go to sleep."

"Charlie," Henry said, "That ain't gonna happen, for two reasons. One, because it would just make too much sense, and since when have we ever done anything that made sense? And, two, it would mean that our unit must have coordinated with this unit beforehand. And when has that ever happened?"

"By the way," Charlie asked, "what time is it?"

"Twenty-four hundred hours," Henry replied. "Why do you ask?"

"Because Freck said we're to meet our contact right here, at this very moment."

"I was wondering why in the hell we stopped the convoy," Henry added.

"Well, to be honest with you, I have a confession to make," Charlie replied.

Henry feigned a genuflection. "Lord have mercy, Charlie Wilkes is about to make a confession. The trouble is, Sergeant Wilkes, this damned war'll be over by the time you finish with your confession."

"Screw you, Henry! I wasn't talking about the type of confession you mackerel snappers do."

Henry laughed, and then came closer to where SGT Wilkes was standing.

Wilkes began, "As I was about to say… the first sergeant already told me that once we meet up with this contact, we're going to be taken to our positions, and then we'll be able to get some shuteye."

"Honest to God, Charlie?"

"Honest to the Big Guy, Henry, that's what he said."

Ian Henry was about to say something else, when the first sergeant came back to where the two enlisted men were standing. Captain Smith was with him, along with a man neither Charlie nor Henry recognized.

Addressing the unknown man, Smith said, "So, you don't have the slightest idea where the hell we are?"

"Ain't got the foggiest, captain. All I know is that the Krauts occupy most of the area around Manhay. I was told to have your column drive south, being careful to reconnoiter the roads on both sides."

Smith looked to the first sergeant, "Sergeant Freck?"

"Yes, sir."

"Let's do as this man suggests, and make sure the men keep their eyes peeled for any Germans on the way."

"Yes, sir," Freck replied.

Looking to Ian Henry, the senior NCO said, "Corporal, you heard what the captain said. Pass it on to the drivers of five vehicles, then have the fifth driver repeat those instructions down the line. Once you're satisfied that the fifth driver understands the order, get back into your vehicle and follow us south until we get to our new bivouac area. Once there, come see me for further instructions."

"Yes, sergeant," Henry said, as he ran off to inform the driver behind him of what the details of the unit's movement plan were. The next seven miles went by very slowly, as the 238th sent men out on patrols on all side roads to make sure they were not going through the enemy's lines.

About forty-five minutes later, the column of vehicles came on the village of Manhay. As the convoy approached the village, everyone in the trucks grabbed their rifles, just in case all hell broke loose.

As it turned out, they did not need them, as they were met by a forward unit from the 7th Armored Division. Within an hour, the men of the 238th were able to get some well-deserved rest - about four wonderful hours of rest, in twenty-nine degree weather.

FRIDAY, 22 DECEMBER 1944
XHORIS, BELGIUM, 0610 HOURS LOCAL

SGT Charlie Wilkes could not believe his good fortune—for the past four hours he had been able to lay down in an honest-to-god bed! How that came about was convoluted, but as he opened his right eye and looked at a ceiling instead of the falling snow outside, he simply didn't care.

It happened this way. When the first sergeant had earlier returned to his vehicle with another soldier, he'd looked at Charlie and said, "Hop in the back, Wilkes. Sergeant Sherwood is going to drive us to our housing for the night."

Charlie thought he was hearing things.

Perhaps, he thought, the first sergeant was just so tired that he misspoke when he used the word "housing."

As Charlie got himself situated in the rear of the vehicle, he overheard the NCO from the 7th Armored Division tell Freck, "You're being billeted in private residences tonight, if that's okay with you."

"How do we rate that? Freck inquired.

"Truth of the matter is that the people in Xhoris think they're safer with you guys from the battalion command post staying in their homes."

"Well, quite honestly, I think my men would sleep with the devil, if it meant a night inside out of this damned snow."

It was at that point that Charlie muttered, "Hell, I'd sleep with Hitler if it meant I got to sleep in a bed!"

Charlie looked at his watch.

Damn, I go on duty in an hour.

Wilkes started to get out of bed when the door to his room opened. An older man stepped inside his room. In halting English, he said, "If you would like to clean up a bit, I can bring up some water and a bowl."

Damn—room service too!

"Quite honestly, sir, I would love to wash up. But only if you'll let me go get the water."

The older man hesitated a bit and then said, "I can bring it up. You see, my girls are downstairs and they are not clothed good."

Charlie laughed, "Okay, I'll wait for the water."

The older man then said, "My name is Fritz Mueller."

"Pleased to meet you. My name is Sergeant Charles Wilkes."

"Charles…," *Herr* Mueller said, "I shall return." Turning around to go out of the room, he suddenly stopped, turned back and said, "Just like your General MacArthur, 'I shall return.'"

Charlie could not help but laugh. After all, he had slept on a bed, and now was about to get a washcloth and a bar of soap.

There really is a God in heaven!

Fifteen minutes later

Charlie had just finished dressing when he heard light tapping at the door.

"Sergeant Wilkes, are you dressed?"

"Yes, *Herr* Mueller, please come in."

"Was the water warm enough?" the old man asked.

"It was wonderful. In fact, it was the first warm water I have had for a bath since we left England."

While Charlie was talking, the old man reached into his pocket, pulled out a small, used bar of soap, and handed it to him. "Merry Christmas, Sergeant Wilkes. I am sorry we do not have a new bar of soap to give you."

Charlie was clearly taken back by this man's generosity, and his eyes began to tear up.

The old man continued talking. "My family and I are so thankful for all the young American boys who come to Belgium to run these *Nazi*s out. May God bless all of you."

Charlie reached into his shirt pocket and pulled out a piece of paper. He extracted a small pencil from the same pocket. Then he wrote down his address in Anaheim, California, USA and handed it back to his host.

"After this war is over, if you and your family can make it to America, please come and look me up. My wife and I will put you up for as long as you want to stay."

The old man looked at the paper. "This is true? You live in California?"

"I do now. You see, my wife was given a strawberry farm when her grandfather died, and my wife and family live there now until I get home."

The old man then asked, "How far is this place from Hollywood?"

Charlie began to laugh, and said, "Two hours, or so."

"Oh, my wife would love to see big movie stars."

Charlie could not resist saying, "So would mine."

Charlie's last comment clearly confused his host. But he needed to get downstairs and report in for duty, so he put his pulled the old man toward him and hugged him.

"When you and your family come to California, we will find some movie stars."

"Thank you, Mr. American soldier, thank you for coming to Belgium and running the *Nazi*s back to Germany."

Charlie knew that if he did not get out of this situation soon, he would lose it. So he hugged his benefactor another time, leaned over, picked up his rifle and walked downstairs and into the freezing-cold weather.

From the background, he could hear the old man saying, "Merry Christmas, Mr. Charlie."

One hour later

    As SGT Wilkes walked up to the residence that was serving as the 238th Combat Engineers Battalion headquarters, he spotted Corporals Ian Henry and Erickson standing outside, both with cigarettes in their mouths.
    "What's up, gentlemen?"
    "Gentlemen?" Erickson replied. "Okay, Wilkes, what do you want?"
    "Why would you say that?"
    "Because you haven't referred to me as anything but 'shithead' for the last six months," answered Ian Henry.
    "I'm sorry for that," Wilkes said as he lit a cigarette.
    "Apology accepted. And from now on, you must refer to me as *Corporal* Shithead — agreed?"
    "Yes, Corporal Shithead," Wilkes said, laughing.
    Now Erickson returned to the conversation. "Man, did we draw a shit detail, or what today?"
    "What do you mean?" Wilkes asked.
    "An operation order came down last night, and it looks like the entire battalion is going out to lay as many mines as possible in the next couple of days. The supply guy said he heard we were supposed to lay somewhere in the neighborhood of twenty thousand mines."
    "Which tells me the Germans must be raising hell with our lines, if we need that many," Henry interjected.
    "The way I heard it," Erickson said, "Company C is going over somewhere east over to Grandmenil, and Company A is going over to Manhay. Company B is going to be in reserve here in Xhoris. I guess were supposed prepare all the roads and bridges for demolition, while putting up roadblocks."
    "So, what are you gonna during your spare time?" Wilkes asked, realizing the enormity of the task Erickson had just described.
    "As a matter of fact, according to Lieutenant James, we're to provide security for those sites by digging in our machine guns and antitank guns."
    "Shit, in this freezing snow?" Wilkes attempted to warm up his hands by breathing into his gloves. Then he continued, "Aside from you two, who else is going?"
    "Looks to me as if every swinging dick in the unit—except for a few rear-area types like you, Charlie," Henry added.
    Not wanting to gloat, Wilkes acted as if he hadn't heard Henry's

comment.

"What about Duncan? I've been training him to work the radio as a backup."

"Nope, PFC Duncan, Corporal Long and Private Kenny Miller are all going," Henry replied.

"Damn, two Okies and a Texan! That ought to give Hitler's Huns a headache!" Charlie grinned as he took a drag from his smoke.

Henry laughed, too. "Wilkes, while you're sitting here in a warm house, drinking hot coffee, I'll be out there in the field, with those three derelicts."

Wilkes looked at his watch, "When do you guys leave?"

Looking at his watch, Henry replied, "The truck is due now, and those guys were due here ten minutes ago."

Looking down the road, Charlie spotted a ¾-ton truck coming in their direction.

Pointing to the approaching vehicle, he said, "Well, try to keep warm guys and stay out of trouble. We've all come too damned far for anything to happen to us now."

"Fuck," Henry said, "Where are those three numbskulls?"

The three-quarter pulled right up to where the three GIs were standing. When it stopped, Henry did a double-take. Inside the cab, sitting next to the driver, was none other than PFC Duncan. He rolled down the window and hollered out, "Henry, we gave up waiting for you at the over in the cantonment area, and decided to try here."

Henry looked puzzled, "What the hell are you talking about, Tex? I was told to meet you guys here, ten minutes ago."

"By who — Hitler?" Duncan replied.

Henry looked to Wilkes. "Hell, the inmates are running the asylum again."

"Sounds like a normal day in the United States Army, if you ask me," Wilkes replied as he gave Ian Henry a half-assed salute.

Henry returned the salute, saying, "And by the way, mister, Merry Christmas — in case we don't get back in time for Baby Jesus' birthday party."

Wilkes walked over to his friend and tapped him on the shoulder. "Same to you, and next year, let's do Christmas in Anaheim."

"You're on!" Duncan replied.

"I was talking to Henry, Duncan! But, I tell you what, all of you are invited to my farm next winter for Christmas. My father-in-law makes one hell of an eggnog!"

"You're on, Wilkes," everyone said as the truck began to accelerate away.

TWELVE HOURS LATER,
SOMEWHERE NEAR MANHAY, BELGIUM

On arriving in Manhay, the 238th encountered tanks from the 7th Armored Division. Most of the 7th personnel were asleep, and seemed somewhat surprised to see other GIs. Lieutenant James met with an officer from the 7th Armored Division to set up a plan to reconnoiter their area of responsibility in all directions around Manhay, for existing and proposed defensive barriers and minefields, and then to take up defensive positions in their assigned areas.

Charlie thought Lieutenant James had lost his mind, when he ordered the men in the unit to carry their gas masks with them. James never explained his reasoning (he did not have to — he was in charge), but the men would later find out that, through some rather intense interrogations of a German officer, that there was a possibility of the Germans using chemical warfare.

All the companies busied themselves, preparing their assigned roads with blocks of daisy chains and prepared trees for felling as abates. Selected roads, bridges and culverts were prepared for demolition. Hasty mine fields were laid in preparation for an expected enemy spearhead.

Security was to be provided for these defensive sites and minefields by digging in machine gun nests, antitank guns and bazookas. The men were assigned to pull the daisy chains if attacked.

Late that night it began to snow heavily, subjecting most of the men in the 238th Engineer Combat Battalion to freezing conditions that were to last for several days.[4]

Lieutenant James had just finished making rounds to ensure that all the defensive positions he was responsible for were completed, and the men were ready. He was about to clean out his pipe when he heard an incoming shell.

Too far away from an actual defensive position to do any good, James ran as if *der Teufel* was chasing him around Hell, and dove into a low spot

---

4. *Experiences of Ernest C. James*, prepared for the author, pages 4-5.

in the terrain head-first, holding his hands out in front. As he was diving, a German 88-millimeter shell exploded a few yards away and a hunk of shrapnel hit him, tearing a one-inch gash in his hand. He hit the ground in a foot of snow and landed right smack-dab in a puddle of slush, which actually turned out to be cow manure.

The artillery barrage continued sporadically for the next half hour. When it lifted, the company medic came by and cleaned out his wound. As the medic was wrapping his hand, he said, "You make sure you put in for a Purple Heart, lieutenant."

James was nonplussed, "Just put some of that new drug, sulfa, on it. I'll worry about the other once this war is over."[5]

SUNDAY, 24 DECEMBER 1944, 1600 HOURS LOCAL
XHORIS, BELGIUM

Right after the men finished eating breakfast, German *Panzers* cut loose with an artillery barrage. But all they accomplished was to rearrange the mounds of snow on the ground, because all men in the unit immediately took cover in their fortified fighting positions when the shelling began.

Earlier that morning, the 238th received a shipment of over one hundred tons of mines from a truck company that was commanded by a white lieutenant and a black first sergeant. The unit had over fifty trucks in its convoy. As the black soldiers were unloading crates, one of the officers from the 238th was brain-struck with a brilliant idea: why not ask those soldiers to help them lay the mines?

Recognizing that each truck had both a driver and an assistant, one of the officers from the 238th approached the truck company's commander and first sergeant about having their personnel assist the 238th in uncrating and assembling the mines to be deployed. The white officer did not have a problem with helping out, nor did the first sergeant. If the truth were known, the black NCO was taken aback that an all-white army company would even ask for their assistance. But to the engineers, the only thing that mattered was getting the mine fields laid before an expected German counterattack. They probably would not have refused an offer of help from the Devil himself.

---

5. 1LT James never did receive a Purple Heart for this wound.

The black soldiers readily agreed to help the engineers, and untold hours of labor were saved by the two units working together. With the snow coming down in near-blizzard conditions, the mines did not have to be buried and, as such, the two army units were able to lay thousands of yards of mines in a matter of hours.

The remainder of the day was spent building up defensive positions and guarding the minefields with automatic weapons, rocket launchers and machine guns. Some of the men were relieved, but the commanding officer stayed behind with the idea they would defend their positions until they were either relieved, or killed.

While most of the men of the 238th Engineer Combat Battalion spent their day before Christmas laying mines, CPL Henry, PFC Duncan, and CPL Dwight Long spent their day placing satchel charges of TNT around the bases of trees, making them ready for demolition, if necessary.

CHRISTMAS EVE, 1944
XHORIS, BELGIUM

The snow had been falling continuously all day. For nine men of Company "A" under the command of 1LT Ernest James, it was a mixed blessing, as it covered both the minefield they had laid previously and their roadblocks. Company "B" also had their positions protected, while Company "C" was busy extending their field and roadblocks.

The Company "C" engineer trucks had been off-loaded of construction materials, such as three-by-twelve-inch planks and tool chests prior to their commitment. They were then combat loaded with the materials and weapons required for combat. Unneeded equipment and materials were stored in a farmer's barn and covered with straw. The Belgians who hid the materiel for the US Army risked serious reprisals by the *Nazi*s, if American equipment was found on their farms.

All one had to do, was look at the massacre of one hundred-fifty American soldiers at Malmedy on December 17 by members of *Kampfgruppe Peiper*, to get a general idea of what kind of mood the *Nazi*s were in.[6]

The handful of Belgian civilians remaining at Grandmenil were evacuated to the west toward Huy. With those civilians out of the

---

6. Among the American soldiers who escaped was actor Charles Durning. An American patrol discovered the massacre that night. The memorial at Baugnez bears the names of the murdered soldiers. See website http://en.wikipedia.org/wiki/Malmedy_massacre for further information.

crosshairs, and their positions well dug in, the men of the 238th Engineer Combat Battalion awaited the German juggernaut.

Off in the distance, every man could hear a ferocious battle taking place to the south of their positions near the city of Manhay.

Each platoon in the batallion decided to share their rations with the Belgians, and gave their food to the citizens to be prepared. Before the food was actually cooked, though, the unit was directed back to the minefields. The Germans attacked and broke through the lines, only to encounter the minefields from the friendly side. The *Nazi*s lost five or six tanks in the ensuing battle, and retreated on foot.

The next day, elements of the 82nd Airborne attacked and drove the Germans back, relieving the platoon from Company A that had been surrounded all night.

On Christmas Day, the men were relieved by the 82nd Airborne, and were thus able to return to Xhoris. On arriving back at Xhoris, the men discovered their Belgian hosts had waited for them to return before preparing the food they'd left behind.

Ian Henry put down his plate, and walked over to where a PFC named Long, from Pennsylvania was sitting.

"When was the last time you ate something as good as that?" Henry asked, sitting down on the floor next to the man.

The PFC was not known for his table manners. He wiped his face with his right sleeve and replied, "Not since I joined this fucking Army, I ain't tasted nothin' that good."

Henry was aghast. "For Chrissakes, can you clean up your language around these women and kids?"

The junior enlisted man looked perplexed. "Don't they speak French? How the hell do they know what I just said?"

Henry couldn't help but laugh. "First of all, Belgians speak French and Flemish."

"They do?" Long replied.

"Yes, they do," Henry replied.

"I dunno, French—Flemish—it's all the same to me. But if you say so, I'll go along with you."

"Hey… have you seen Charlie Wilkes?" Henry asked.

"I done seen him 'bout thirty minutes ago. He was outside, pissing on a tree."

Henry just shook his head, and stood up. "I was just wondering if you'd seen him. I heard he was going to get tonight off, too, and thought I'd like to spend Christmas with him."

"You two have been buddies for too long," the PFC replied.

"Yes, we've been buddies since Camp Roberts. I knew him before he was married and had kids."

"He's got kids?" Long asked.

"Three boys," Ian replied.

"Don't he know what causes them?" the young man said, smiling.

"Oh, I think if anyone in this unit knows how babies get here, Sergeant Wilkes *would be* the man. And, if you were to see his wife... my God, she'd give Betty Grable a run for her money."

"Really, she's got big tits like Betty Grable?"

Ian was incredulous. "For God's sake, it ain't right to talk about another man's wife like that. I think you can burn in hell for less."

"No shit? You can burn in hell for wanting to screw someone else's wife? Well, I'll be go to hell. They do that all the time back home in Pennsylvania."

Henry just shook his head. "You're one messed-up soldier. Don't you know it's against the Ten Commandments to commit adultery?"

"Adultery? What the hell is that?"

"When you're married and you screw another man's wife," Henry replied.

The soldier just sat there, not replying for the longest time. When he finally did, he said, "Guess I'll be going to hell, then, because I think I fucked eight or nine married women back in Allentown."

Henry was about to throw in the towel with this soldier and his boorish behavior, but decided to give it one more try. "You know, you can ask for forgiveness?"

"From who, their husbands? Hell no! I ain't doing that. Them dumb bastards can't keep their wives happy and they come around wanting me to give it to 'em. Why, shit! I'd be a damned fool to go around with my dick in my hands and beg forgiveness."

Henry shook his head: "Forget it, let's just say we never had this conversation."

"Conversation? Is that was you call it?"

Henry shook his head again and stood up.

"See you in the morning—you and I got guard duty."

"Okay, and...." the young Pennsylvanian said, and then looked up at Henry. "And, if you find Wilkes, tell him 'Merry Christmas' from me. Charlie's good people. Always done me right."

"I'll do that, and Merry Christmas to you, too."

As Henry started to walk away, he turned and replied, "Hopefully, next year we'll all be home."

"Beats the fuck outta bein' here," the GI replied then said, "Sorry, Henry, guess I'll never get the hang of being a gentleman."

"Well, God loves you anyway, and Merry Christmas."

As Ian Henry was walking into the kitchen, one of the married Belgian women was telling Lieutenant James about how her husband had been taken away to Germany as a prisoner. She had tears in her eyes.

James wanted to change the subject.

"So, Madam Bouvier, why don't you have a Christmas tree?

The forty-year-old Belgian woman's English was rudimentary, at best, but somehow she knew what the words 'Christmas tree' meant.

"*Oui*, we have many Christmas trees, but we have no men to cut them."

James looked over at SGT Davis, and nodded his head toward the door. Davis discreetly left the room. About an hour later he returned with a small Christmas tree, which all the soldiers joined in to help decorate.

Just as SGT Davis was about to put an angel on top of the tree, he heard what sounded like airplanes overhead.

He looked at 1LT James. "Ours, or theirs?"

Before Lieutenant James could respond, a bomb burst nearby. He yelled, "Unless someone in 8th Air Force has f-ed up, I'd say they're Kraut planes."

The Belgian woman of the house ran into the room from the kitchen. "*Monsieur*, in the cellar."

Although the soldiers were in a safer location, the place in which they were now located was freezing-cold. Lieutenant James and SGT Davis each took a couple of the younger children under their coats and kept them warm, until the bombing stopped about a half-hour later.

SOMEWHERE IN THE ARDENNES FOREST
ON A ROAD HEADED TOWARD MANHAY

The jeep in which the battalion commanding officer and CPT Blumenstein were riding also was freezing cold, but it beat having to walk to where the 7th Armored Division was located. He and CPT Blumenstein had just finished off the last of some cold coffee, when Blumenstein noticed a group of American soldiers headed their way in a hell of a hurry. Many were without their weapons.

"Stop the car, driver!" the colonel shouted, as he leapt from the vehicle and ran over to talk to one of the retreating soldiers. Recognizing the patch on one soldier's arm as being from the 7th Division, the colonel demanded to know where in the hell he was going.

"Sir, the area is lousy with Krauts. We were overrun back there."

"Where's your weapon?" the colonel inquired.

"Somewhere back there in the snow. And if we don't get the hell out of there, we too will be in the snow — permanently!"

"Just hold on, soldier! You're not going anywhere, but back into a defensive line. We're going to stop the Germans here. Got that?"

Whether or not the colonel's rank impressed the soldier, nobody knows, but after gathering his breath, the GI from the armored unit began shouting to the men to stop running. Most of them did.

The colonel swung into action and ordered all the engineer troops to form a line, and ordered the rest of those running to get into the battle line and prepare to stop the Krauts. In short, the rout was over; resistance was next.

While the commanding officer busied himself with getting the American soldiers to stop retreating and to fight the enemy, CPT Blumenstein hightailed it to the 7th Division headquarters. Without stopping at the front of the building to clear security, Blumenstein marched right into Brigadier General Robert W. Hasbrouck's command tent.

Under any other circumstances, Blumenstein's behavior would have resulted in a severe ass-chewing, but the truth of the matter was he had been a master sergeant before the war and Hasbrouck knew him.

"What've you got for me, Blum?" the general demanded.

"General, your troops are routed, and running like hell from the enemy."[7]

The general blew a gasket, and all hell broke loose. Within minutes, regiments were on the move. The 82nd Airborne and another armored outfit were moved into position to block the oncoming German attack.

By Christmas night, Manhay was back under the control of the Allies. The commanding officer of the 238th Combat Engineer Battalion was to be

---

7. James, *The 238th Engineer Combat Battalion in WWII*, page 100.

decorated with a Silver Star for his actions.

Photos taken by the news media of the destroyed German Tiger tanks were published in *Life®* magazine.

The fallout from the near-debacle was overwhelming—a few ranking officers in the 7th Armored Division were relieved of command and sent home, their careers in ruins.

When 1LT James and his men got back to Xhoris, they found that the townspeople were as hungry as them. But they hadn't touched the food they'd prepared to eat with the soldiers, before they'd been pulled out to stop the German advance. Instead, the Belgians waited for the Americans who had brought the food to return, and break bread with them.[8]

As a footnote to the Ardennes battle, Company C relinquished its frontline positions intact to the infantry company (and not the engineers) of the 75th Infantry Division. It is interesting to note that not one of the 238th Engineer Combat Battalion's positions had been in German hands or had to be retaken, as was the case in Manhay. They took some casualties (and lost a truck due to shelling), but the company emerged relatively unscathed.

Major James noted in his book, *Information on the 238th Combat Battalion*, that "...historical maps will show a small bump at the western edge of Granmenil, where the 560 *Volksgrenadier* Division penetrated momentarily. This area was outside the Company C defensive area, and that the Germans never made it into Granmenil during the Battle of the Bulge."

James further stated that, "...historians are unsure why the German division turned left and headed for nearby Granmenil on a secondary road, instead of moving directly north toward Hitler's objective: Liege."

Conjecture would indicate that most likely they (the Germans) felt it necessary to defeat or contain the 3rd Armored Division, a tank threat to their left flank if they headed north. They thereby encountered the mine belt and defending troops of Company C, 238th Engineers. Had they boldly pressed north on the main road to Liege, they would have been met with the bazookas and machine guns of Company B, 238th Engineers and the straggler lines that had been organized by the battalion commander, who was personally commended by Major General Matthew

---

8. In an interview with the author on 9 November 2006, Ernie James still said the believed that Christmas Day dinner was the best Christmas dinner he had ever experienced. He said, "Just watching those nearly starved children eat their fill made it the best Christmas meal, ever." Many of the men in the 238th communicated with the citizens of Xhoris, Belgium up until 1990.

B. Ridgeway, commander of the XVII Corps (Airborne) for his actions in the construction of the initial barrier in the vicinity of Manhay.

This was the last organized defensive lines on the road to Liege.[9]

---

9. James, *Experiences of Ernest C. James*, page 18.

CHAPTER SEVENTEEN

A love of tradition has never weakened a nation, indeed it has strengthened nations in their hour of peril; but the new view must come, the world must roll forward.
—*Sir Winston Churchill*

COLONEL AND MRS. MICHAEL BRANDON OHARA'S RESIDENCE
LOS LAGOS, GRANITE BAY, CALIFORNIA
MONDAY, 2 DECEMBER 1991, 5:10 P.M. LOCAL

As Sean Ohara drove into the driveway of his parents' home in Los Lagos, he thought back to the butt-chewing he'd just endured from his basketball coach, and the subsequent laps he and most of the junior varsity team had to run as a result of their gluttonous behavior over the past week. Tonight would be different—no seconds on anything, including his mom's world-renowned pumpkin pie.

Looking up the walkway, he saw CSM Wilkes coming toward him.

"How'd school go today?" the senior retired NCO asked.

"Well, if our basketball coach ever wanted to get out of teaching, he doubtless could get a job in the Army as a weight control officer."

"Put on a few over the weekend, huh?"

Oh, yeah, and he wasn't amused. He made us run ten laps around the track, all the while he was ragging on us."

"Sounds like a purpose-driven man, if you ask me," Wilkes replied.

"That, he is."

"Well, the good news is that we're having shrimp salad tonight, and your mom has put the remnants of her pumpkin pie into the freezer."

"Sounds great," the teenager replied.

"And… they're all at the dinner table, waiting for us."

"Then let's make some tracks," Sean Ohara said, as he quickened the pace.

After the blessing offered by Colonel Ohara, and a bit of small talk, the conversation returned to the plight of the 238th Engineer Combat Battalion as they prepared themselves for a new year and the end of World War II.

Now CSM Wilkes began speaking of the events surrounding New Year's Day, 1945.

THE 238TH ENGINEER COMBAT BATTALION COMMAND POST
CHINE AL PIERRE, BELGIUM
MONDAY, 1 JANUARY 1945, 1415 HOURS LOCAL

SGT Charlie Wilkes was putting the final touches on the morning report. As he hunted for the right letters, he was thinking about the past five days.

"Let's see—since we left Xhoris, Belgium five days ago, we've been working in direct support of the 82nd Airborne Division. We have constructed barrier lines by preparing trees for abatis, bridges for demolition, prepared road blocks and laid mine fields throughout the 82nd's divisional area. In short—the usual combat engineer bullshit."

He stood up in order to stretch, saying, "And why in the name of God am I doing this friggin' morning report? Since when did I become a lousy clerk?"

"You became a clerk because I said you are…." 1SGT Freck said, as he entered the room.

Wilkes was clearly embarrassed. He was complaining about being inside a somewhat heated room, having to work ten hours a day at the most, and was getting three meals a day—one of which was usually hot.

"Sorry, first sergeant, I guess I've been in the Army too long," Wilkes said as he handed the senior NCO the now-completed morning report.

Freck liked Wilkes, so he let his grumbling pass. He sat down on a upturned ammo crate to check the morning report.

After he finished reading, the 1SGT looked over to where Wilkes was working.

"Any word on Lieutenant Latchaw, or those four other men who were hit by that mortar?"

"I talked to the medic a few minutes ago, first sergeant, and from what he said, the lieutenant tore up his guts pretty bad—but somehow he managed to walk into the collection station. When the medical facility came under fire, the lieutenant made his way into a ditch, where he remained until the medics scooped his ass up. From what I gather; they're operating on him as we speak."[1]

"That kid's got balls… hell, he gets the living hell shot out of him, and still he manages to walk into the aid station. Sure tells me just how tough these men have become since we left Plattsburg. Hell, I almost feel sorry for those *Nazi*s out there," the first sergeant said as he handed Wilkes his canteen cup.

"Could I ask you to put about a half cup in this?"

"No problem, first sergeant, I'll run over to the mess tent and get you some fresh coffee. There's an ugly rumor running around, that the mess steward actually got some fresh coffee and real meat in on that last delivery. I was about to go check it out before you came in," Wilkes replied.

"That's not a rumor, Sergeant Wilkes. We're having beef stew for dinner tonight."

Wilkes stopped walking and looked toward his superior NCO. "First Sergeant, I may be new to the Army, but if we're having beef tonight, the Germans are finished."

"How do you figure that?" Freck wondered aloud.

"We've been fighting the biggest battle of this friggin' war during the past two weeks—and we have fresh meat, along with being supplied with thousands of mines, bullets and all the other stuff that an engineer unit needs. Well, the way I figure it, Hitler is *fucked*, lock, stock and barrel. In short, he needs to pack it up, because we're going to be in Berlin before the Fourth of July and this fucking war is—o-v-e-r!"

Freck was tired, and Wilkes' last sentence made no sense grammatically. Yet he understood.

"Just get me some coffee, Wilkes. And leave the war planning to the boys at SHAEF."

"Yes, First Sergeant, I guess I am rambling…."

Ten minutes later...

When SGT Wilkes walked back into the tent with the first sergeant's coffee, the senior NCO was talking to 1LT James.

"Any news on Wong's boys, sir?"

James took the pipe from his mouth, "No, sergeant, but I believe that's because Wong's men laid so darned many mines down, to stop them dead in their tracks. That, and the fact that they built some pretty solid defensive

---

1. In April 1946 Ernie James and his wife, Faith, were near the Campanile on the UC Berkeley campus, when from nowhere, he saw Latchaw. After 15 months of agonizing recovery treatments, the Army officer was about to enter the UC system in pursuit of a BS in Engineering. He graduated in 1950. Captain Wong also attended CAL after the war. He majored in architecture.

positions, which undoubtedly have slowed down the Krauts."

As Wilkes handed the first sergeant his coffee cup, the NCO told the lieutenant about Charlie's belief that Hitler was finished, and what the junior NCO had based his reasoning on.

James looked at Wilkes. "He might have something there, sergeant. But, instead of this war being over by the Fourth of July, I'll say Hitler throws in the towel by Memorial Day."

"Sounds like we got ourselves a friendly wager," Freck said, as he took a sip of the freshly-brewed coffee.

James took in the first sergeant's comment, and ran with it. "Well, of course it's against Army regulations to gamble. But I'm willing to go this far: if this war isn't over by Memorial Day, I'll give SGT Wilkes a shot of scotch."

Wilkes smiled. "I'll take that deal, Lieutenant. And, if I'm right, I'd be willing to give you a shot of some of that rot-gut that Private Miller calls whiskey."

James looked to the first sergeant. "I'd say we have a deal."

James put his pipe back in his mouth, and lit it.

Ain't no way I'm going to lose that bet—Hitler is finished!

Having finished his business in the command post, 1LT Ernest James excused himself and walked outside into the bitter cold afternoon. His thoughts were of Faith, and how they had met exactly two years ago this very day, at that dive of a place called Jeru's Bar, back in Plattsburg, New York.

Man, it's been two years! In some ways, it seems like a million… and, then… in some ways it only seems like yesterday.

James knew he couldn't spend too much time thinking about the woman he wanted to marry. If he did, he risked not staying focused on the mission ahead and, more practically, it served no purpose whatever!

As he left Faith and Jeru's Bar in his mind, James' thoughts turned to the events surrounding an evil poker game he'd been involved in, a year ago this very day.

God, that was one helluva night—back there in Oran.

James continued walking back to his tent. As he approached it, he smiled.

Oh—screw it! I'm going back to my tent and toast the new year. That is—if I still have some scotch left!

As it turned out, Lieutenant James did have some scotch left. *Exactly one shot.* He savored every sip, then crawled into his sleeping bag.

Well, it could be worse. You could have officer of the day, and be up all night!

Although there hadn't been much of his "adult beverage" left, from which to partake, it took its toll on the junior officer from Ord, Nebraska. Wifteen minutes of putting his head on the makeshift pillow, Lieutenant Ernest C. James was out, cold!

SATURDAY, 6 JANUARY 1945
NEAR STOUMONT, BELGIUM, 1900 HOURS LOCAL

For the past five days, 1LT James' platoon had been out in the elements. Every day they had been subjected to freezing cold weather, and guard duty at all the bridges and other installations in the area south and east of Manhay.

While he too was freezing, his thoughts were of the letter swirling around in his head that he wanted to write to the woman he planned to marry.

James glanced at his watch, and thought that he had just about enough time to walk to the next three posts, before some other troops were scheduled to come in and relieve his men of their duty for the night.

Having received some mail within the past two days, James' supply of Prince Albert was now replenished. So he thought nothing of reaching into the pocket of his fur-lined trench coat and extracting his pipe. After filling its bowl, he walked over to a small clump of trees, crouched down low, covered the pipe's bowl, and lit up.

There… that wasn't too bad…. And—oh my God, does this tobacco taste wonderful!

James stuffed his hand back into his fur-lined glove and stood up. He continued walking toward the next guard post. As he walked, he thought to that afternoon back in Aachen, and how it had come about that he'd ended up with the only fur-lined trench coat in the engineer battalion, that he knew of.

One afternoon in Aachen while checking on his men and the perimeter, he'd come on a partially-destroyed farmhouse. James carefully ventured inside, hoping to find a bottle of cognac. Instead, he'd discovered something vastly more useful than a bottle of schnapps: a fur-lined coat.

He immediately picked it up and tried it on under his trench coat. While not a perfect fit, he was much warmer with it on. From then on, he wore it as if it'd been issued by the supply section.

The way he figured it, the devil be damned—it was friggin' cold out there, and this jacket just might keep him from being a frostbite casualty. A few days later, James came upon an old Belgian woman who must have been in her eighties. When she saw him wearing the fur coat, she asked him to leave it with her until his next time in the area.

He did, and when he went back, the old woman had cut up the fur coat and lined both his trench coat and a pair of his leather gloves.

James was so affected by the woman's generosity, that he took her picture.

As the lieutenant kept walking, he made a mental note to tell his men to continue making anyone and everyone give the password before they were allowed into the cantonment area. There had been numerous reports of infiltrating German paratroopers coming through Allied lines and raising hell behind the lines. With all that going on, James knew he had to reiterate the policy he had stated three days ago: "You have a password—use it. Trust nobody!"

One night, some of Lieutenant James' engineers stopped the commanding general of the 82nd Airborne Division. When the general could not give the proper response to the password challenge, he was held up for almost an hour. At the time, the general was furious. But when his temper cooled, he commended those men for paying attention to their orders.[2]

"Halt! Who goes there?"

What the hell?

James looked up, and saw CPL Duncan pointing an M-1 carbine directly at him.

Damn, I was so lost in my thoughts I damned near got my ass shot off!

By now, CPL Duncan had recognized his platoon leader and was about to tell Lieutenant James to advance, but had second thoughts. He decided to play it by the book.

"I say again—who goes there?"

"Rosebud."

In his Texas accent, Duncan said, "Step forward and be recognized."

James took two steps into the snow, and got a good look at CPL Duncan.

"Well, you ain't Orson Wells," Duncan said, "but you'll do. You may advance, L-T."

---

2. James, *The 238th Engineer Combat Battalion in WWII*, page 102.

Lieutenant James came forward a few paces.

"I see you guys have been busy building more guard stations. Hell, this one's so well hidden, I didn't see you."

"Well, sir, with all those Krauts infiltrating, we decided it might be a good idea to move around a bit, Just in case those sonofabitches try anything stupid."

"Good job, corporal," James said as he entered the newly-made roadblock.

"What's the word, sir? Are moving tomorrow?" Duncan asked, as he sat on a log.

"I think we're going to be working out of this area until the eighth, and then scuttlebutt has it that we're moving to someplace called My for a few days in support of the 83rd Division."

"We have a lot of bridges to build, sir?"

"I heard we're scheduled for a hundred-foot Bailey bridge at Lansival, over the Groumont River. But I'm also told the area is lousy with Krauts. So, I guess we'll have to keep our rifles by our side as we work."

"We always do, sir," Duncan declared.

James took another draw from his pipe, rubbed his eyes, and looked toward the enlisted man who shared the guard post with CPL Duncan.

"How about you, PFC Miller? How's the Army treating you tonight?"

"Sir, when did I get promoted?" the soldier from the Sooner state asked.

"What do you mean, Miller?" James replied.

A smile came across Miller's face. "Sir, I ain't a PFC, I'm a private. Been one since we left Oran."

James remembered how it was that the young man sitting next to him was still a private, when nearly everyone else had had at least one promotion since they left North Africa.

Damn! Him and that Arab woman! What a helluva mess that one was!

James decided, right there on the spot, that Miller had probably paid enough for his indiscretion with an Arab woman—and her daughter. He advised Miller that he'd been promoted back to private first class, effective 1 December 1944.

"Damn, that's good news, Lieutenant, that's more money to send home."

James almost wanted to laugh. The difference between a private and a private first class could not be more than eight bucks a month. But as he thought about it, to this young nineteen-year-old from Muskogee, eight dollars was probably a lot of money.

"Well, PFC, I should have told you before. But with all that's been going on... guess I just forgot."

PFC Miller looked at the lieutenant. "Well, sir, thanks for telling me, now. I'll make sure I write home to my momma and tell her I got my stripe back."

"You do that, PFC. Write home, and tell her tonight. We have a truck going out in the morning, and I'll make sure your letter gets on it."

"That's great, sir. With any luck it'll get there before my momma's birthday."

"And when's that?" CPL Duncan asked.

"February 14th. Valentine's Day."

238TH ENGINEER COMMAND CENTER, ESCHWEILLER, GERMANY
SUNDAY, 25 FEBRUARY 1945, 0800 HOURS LOCAL

For the past eight weeks, the 238th Engineer Combat Battalion had been bivouacking in Eschweiller, Germany, in support of the 104th Infantry Division. For the most part, they spent their days training, repairing roads and building bridges in the area west of the Roer River. They did this as a means of preparing for the next big push by the Allies—the crossing of the Roer River. The XVII Airborne Corps had been unsuccessful in their attempts to capture the many upstream dams, but that did not stop them from trying.

Like the men of the 238th Engineer Combat Battalion, the divisions inside the XVII Corps spent their time reconstituting and being re-supplied with armaments and equipment that was lost during the Battle of the Ardennes.

Some of the men in the 238th not actively engaged in the effort to cross the Roer were given leaves to visit the Verviers region of Belgium. When SGT Charlie Wilkes was offered a three-day pass to visit the area, he readily accepted. The way he figured it, any town that had been around since Roman times had to beat the hell out of some town in southwest Iowa.

Years later, while taking a history class at USC, he would learn that Verviers was called "Virovirus" by the Romans, and that in 1651 the prince-bishop of Liège gave the burg a charter and changed its name to Verviers. By

1830, the town had grown to a respectable twenty-thousand, which topped out in 1900 with a population of fifty-three thousand-plus citizens.

But none of that mattered to SGT Wilkes, as the deuce-and-a-half he and CPL Henry were riding in slowed down and then finally stopped in the main square of the old Belgian town. A huge smile came across Henry's face.

"My God—a Catholic Church. We have to go in it."

"What do you mean, 'we'?" Wilkes asked, as he climbed out of the vehicle.

From the look on Ian Henry's face, Charlie could tell he had committed some sort of a sin. Whether it was a cardinal or venal, he neither knew, nor cared. He was about to say something when Henry blurted out, "Aw for God's sake, Charlie, you don't honestly think you've made it this far without me praying for you every night. Do you?"

Wilkes looked at his comrade from New Hampshire, and raised one eyebrow.

"Really, you've been praying for me?"

"Is the pope Catholic?"

"Of course he is, but what does that have to do with me?"

"Charlie Wilkes, listen to me. Do you honestly think that you've lasted this long in the war, without me and everybody in my family praying for you every night?"

"You have?" Charlie replied in near-disbelief.

"Of course I have, you damned fool. Somebody has to pray for your sorry ass. You surely don't."

Wilkes reached into his blouse pocket, found a pack of cigarettes, and lit one. After taking a draw, he said, "That's pretty nice of you, Ian."

"'Nice' ain't got nothing to do with it, Charlie. I do it because at the end of the day I need to talk to someone who can keep this mess straight. And I only know one person—God."

Charlie started to give some smart-assed reply, but decided that discretion was probably the better part of valor. So he said, "Well, thanks for doing that. And… I guess you're right, I should pray more often. But I don't think God has the time to waste on me."

Ian shook his head, and asked, "Charlie, ain't you got no faith at all?

Wilkes did not reply right away. Instead, he allowed his mind to wander to his mother's death, this "father's" suicide, his girlfriend's death after the botched abortion in Omaha. And his best friend Randy's death, at Pearl

Harbor."

Charlie began slowly, "No, Ian, I guess I ain't got much of a faith. Too much shit has happened to me. Guess I lost it somewhere on the way here."

Henry looked at his best friend. He could tell that his friend was baring his very soul, so he took it easy on him.

"Charlie, it's true you've been dealt cards from a stacked deck, with your momma being murdered and all, and your girlfriend dying like that back in Omaha. But, look at it this way—sure, life's been tough. But look at you now. You're a sergeant in the United States Army, married to a wonderful woman who, if the truth were known, probably has more money than you'll ever be able to spend. And you have three wonderful boys, all waiting for you when you get home. So, just maybe... if it was me, I would talk to the 'Big Guy' every night, and ask him to make sure that somehow you get home in one piece so you can raise that family. It sounds reasonable. To me, at least."

Ian Henry leaned over to tie his boot.

Charlie knew his friend was right, and decided that he too should spend a few minutes each night talking to God.

"Okay, but I ain't becoming a Catholic."

To which Henry replied, "I don't think it matters to God, Charlie. And, for that matter, I don't think you'd be worth a damn speaking Latin, anyway."

"Now, I'll agree with you there. I barely scraped by with Ds in my Latin class back in Villisca High School."

Henry started to laugh. "Well, if my memory serves me right, your church doesn't require you to speak Latin."

Charlie looked toward his friend, Ian, and shook his head slowly. As the minutes passed, he was overwhelmed with memories of his wife's first marriage. It was a marriage he had intimate knowledge of, because her husband had asked Charlie to stand in as best man for his older brother, who was off playing football at Princeton.

"You know that Sharon's first husband, Randy, was the Episcopalian. She was a Methodist when they met, but they got married in the Episcopal Church in a small town twelve miles away, because that was where Randy's parents attended church.

After he died at Pearl, Sharon moved to Anaheim, gave birth to Charlie Jefferson Roberts—our middle boy—and then married me. We were married by an Episcopal priest three days after Master Charlie was born. So… I guess that makes me an Episcopalian, sort of."

"Well, Charlie, it works for me, and if you think about it, I don't think God really gives a rip as to what denomination we belong to, just as long as we don't break his rules."

Charlie took a long drag off his smoke and sat down on a nearby bench. Ian joined him.

"So what got you talking about religion, anyway, you crazy Yankee?"

"I don't know why I brought it up today. But, I can tell you, it's been on my mind for a long time," Henry admitted.

Charlie looked his friend directly in the face. "So you really do pray for me every night?"

"Honest-to-God, Charlie, every night."

Charlie shook his head up and down and then replied, "Well, I guess I should get off my pathetic butt and talk to the Baby Jesus once in a while."

Ian laughed, then said, "You do that, Charlie."

For the next five minutes the two GIs sat on the bench and finished their cigarettes. After Henry finished his smoke, he began to field strip it, which caused Charlie to laugh.

"So, I wonder if you'll keep doing that after this friggin' war is over."

"Who knows? The only thing I do know is we better get off our butts and go over to the reception area and check in, just like Lieutenant James told us to do. And remember, if any of those military police types give us any crap about our uniforms, we're to tell them we're from a combat unit, and as such don't have to have a Class A uniform handy."

Ian looked toward his friend. "Just let's not be smart-assed about it, or we might find our happy behinds on a deuce-and-a-half headed back to Eschweiller."

"God—for a minute there, I almost forgot about dear, old Eschweiller," Charlie admitted.

The two soldiers reached over, grabbed their overnight bags and began walking toward a building with a sign in front that said, "Allied Reception Point."

As the two men approached the building, CPL Henry stopped dead in his tracks and said, "Charlie, would you look at those girls over there in the park! My God, the one with curly brown hair is absolutely beautiful."

Charlie stopped walking and looked toward the young women his friend was staring at.

"Ian, ahh... those girls look mighty young. Hell, they can't be more than sixteen years old."

"Well, hell, Charlie, I ain't but twenty-three, myself."

"Ian, I'll say this one more time... they can't be more than sixteen years old."

Henry stopped walking toward the reception area. Instead, he made a forty-five degree turn and began walking over to where the teenage girls were standing. As he approached, the girls began to giggle.

Jesus, God! Do I feel like an ass!

Henry decided to walk past the girls, and act as if he was going somewhere else. His act fooled none of them. As he walked by, the one he'd been intrigued with nervously said, "May we help you to find something?"

Henry chuckled to himself at the girl's stilted use of the English language, but quickly got over it when he thought how much better her English was in comparison to his French. But, crappy French or not, if he wanted to get to know this brunette's name and particulars he was going to have to make more of an effort than he had so far.

What the hell, give it a shot, Ian.

"Hello. My name is Ian Henry. I'm from New Hampshire, U.S. of A. What is your name?"

The young brunette smiled, gathered her thoughts, and replied, "My name is Genevieve Pelletier. I am a student here at St. Mary's School for Young Ladies."

Henry couldn't believe his good fortune in finding such a pretty girl, who not only was Catholic but who spoke English. But he didn't want to make a fool of himself, so he decided his best course of action was to go very slowly.

"Your English is very good. Did you learn to speak it at St. Mary's?"

"Actually, I knew English before my mother and I moved here two years ago. Right after I was born, my father took a job in London. We lived there until 1939, when my father was asked by the government to come home to help set up a civil defense system. He did so, and received a commission to the rank of colonel. After we surrendered, my daddy was taken prisoner."

"I am sorry to hear that," Ian replied.

"We say the rosary for him every night, and my momma believes with every bone in her body that daddy is still alive and that we will see him again after the *Bosch* are defeated."

One of the other two girls with *Mademoiselle* Pelletier suddenly came into the conversation. "Corporal Henry, who is your friend?"

Henry was so engrossed in getting to know Miss Pelletier that he had completely forgotten about Charlie Wilkes, who as this moment was walking in his direction.

"I will introduce you to my friend, after I know all your names," Ian said laughingly.

At that point the oldest girl of the trio replied, "My name is Nicole Saenz, and this young lady is Denise Cavalier. We also go to St. Mary's School for Young Ladies."

Now Charlie Wilkes stepped into the conversation, "Please call me Charlie."

Nicole Saenz started to laugh. "And you are as tall as Charles DeGualle, but a far-sight better looking."

"Oh, don't say that girls, he's already in love with himself," Henry joked.

Wilkes decided to play along, "Well… when you are this perfect—why not?"

Charlie's comment drove the girls to hysterics. When they stopped laughing, Nicole said, "Charlie, do you remember what happened to the last man who was perfect?"

Wilkes was clueless. He didn't have the foggiest idea that the young teenager was referring to Jesus Christ.

"Oh, la-la," Denise replied, "Don't let Sister Sarah hear such a thing! It would send her into shock!"

"And who is Sister Sarah?" Charlie asked.

From across the street, Charlie could see a Catholic nun walking their direction.

"Did someone call my name?"

Smiling, Charlie asked, "If you are Sister Sarah, I am the guilty party."

The nun smiled at Charlie and replied, "My name is Sister Sarah. I am the lead instructor at St. Mary's School for Young Ladies here in Verviers. And you two are….?

Wanting to impress Genevieve, Henry jumped into the conversation, "Sister, my name is Ian Henry. I attended Holy Rosary Church, in Hooksett, New Hampshire."

Having satisfied her curiosity as to CPL Henry, the nun looked in Charlie's direction.

"And you would be who?"

"My name is Sergeant Charles Wilkes. I am from Villisca, Iowa, a small town in the southeastern part of Iowa. But my wife and family live in Anaheim, California."

Still smiling, the nun said, "I am sorry, I didn't catch the name of your parish."

Charlie was having a great time playing along with this woman. He knew she wanted to know what Catholic Church he attended, and, since he did not attend a Roman Catholic Church, he decided to string her along as far as he could. That is, without risking damnation.

"That's because, Sister, I didn't say which church I attend."

"Well, you do attend, don't you?" the nun shot back.

"My wife goes for me," Wilkes admitted.

A smile came across the older woman's face. "What is it with you men anyway? You think you can save yourself by having your wife say the rosary for you. You know, it doesn't work that way, don't you?"

Wilkes couldn't stand it any more, "Sister, I'm pulling your leg. My wife and I are Episcopalians."

The nun laughed, "Oh, so what you are telling me is that neither you nor your wonderful wife passed Latin in high school."

"Actually," Wilkes said, becoming serious, "Latin wasn't one of the subjects they taught at the Methodist Church my momma attended before she died."

A saddened look came to the nun's face, "I am so sorry to hear that, Sergeant Wilkes."

Charlie knew he had to change the subject, and fast.

"Sister," Charlie said as he looked over to Genevieve, I came over here to rescue this beautiful young lady from my friend here, Corporal Henry."

Sister Sarah laughed, and replied, "Sergeant Wilkes, if anyone needed being rescued from the United States Army, I would say it would be these girls from you!"

Her comment caused Charlie to snicker and say, "Well, I guess in the grand scheme of things you're probably right. But I swear, Sister, since I married my wife, I haven't fooled around with any stray women. Honest to God, I haven't been doing that."

Sister Sarah walked over to where Genevieve was standing, and said, "Young lady, why don't you and the girls gather up a few more American servicemen and bring them up to the school? I'll go ahead and see if there is still some of that brandy we put away when the *Bosch* showed up. I think Sister Maria could be coaxed into cooking something up for them."

Genevieve was taken aback by the sister's comments, as she had always thought her instructor to be somewhat of an old curmudgeon.

"Sister Sarah, I don't think we'll have a difficult time finding some young American soldiers who would like a home-cooked meal and a bit of brandy." Looking at her two friends, she asked, "You don't either, do you?"

One of the other girls said, "If they are anything like my older brother, Francois, I doubt it."

Within fifteen minutes, the three Belgian teenagers had found three more young American soldiers who were thirsty and hungry—and talkative. Once they introduced themselves, the GIs discussed everything from their hometowns to their girlfriends and wives.

Not surprisingly, all the men who took a few hours out to break bread with the nuns and talk to the young high school girls, found that morning to be one of their most pleasurable during their entire tour of duty.

For Charlie Wilkes it was a beginning step in a long journey back to church and the practice of his newly-found Episcopal faith.

Ian Henry would remember this as the day he met his soul-mate and future wife.

ALONG THE ROER RIVER
SUNDAY, 25 FEBRUARY 1945, 1400 HOURS LOCAL

The road back to the 238th's Command Post was a slippery mess, so the U.S. Army convoy was moving slowly. At first, neither CPL Henry nor SGT Wilkes could have given a darn how long it took to get back to their AO. But, as the time on their passes began to run out, they wished the lead vehicle would speed up a bit. That is, until the noise from an artillery bombardment kept getting louder. Initially, CPL Henry was able to put it in the back of his mind, as he was still in a state of bliss over meeting Genevieve. But, as their convoy approached their AO, he looked over to Charlie Wilkes and said, "Sounds like ours."

"It sure as hell better be, or we're screwed. It hasn't let up for the past twenty-five minutes."

A PFC named Bill Donaldson, from the 238th Combat Engineer Battalion, joined the conversation. "The artillery boys started up that crap at

0230 hours on the 23rd. They've been blasting the shit out of everything that walks, talks or moves from Jülich, [near Aachen] to Duran, in the south."

"How do you know that? Weren't you down in Verviers, too?"

"I was, got there yesterday on what was to be a three-day pass. But word's come down that we're going to cross the Roer River soon, and all passes were cancelled."

"That sucks," SGT Wilkes said as he started to light a Camel.

"From what I gather, everybody's busting their butts back at the unit. I heard that companies B and C, commanded by captains Blumenstein and Wong, have started to build a Class 40 M-2 steel treadway bridge at predetermined sites—and both are constantly being shelled by the Germans.

"From what one of the GIs told me, more than once the partially constructed bridges were hit by German artillery. Because of all that crap, the acting commander of Company A, First Lieutenant James, was asked if he could build the one-hundred-forty foot Bailey bridge under fire.

"According to my source, James told them, 'Why, hell yes we can, but we'll have to do it during the night.'"

"Sure as hell, Company A went out after dark and were there all night. So were the 327th Engineers. I heard-tell they're constructing an infantry support bridge a few yards upstream. Unfortunately, artillery and mortars hit it, but that didn't stop James' Bailey bridge from being started. In fact, they were ready a day before they were supposed to be."

SGT Wilkes looked over to CPL Henry, and kicked his boot, "You hear that? Ol' Lieutenant James is kicking some ass."

"From what Donaldson says, James didn't have to kick too hard. All of his men went out and worked their butts off. All James had to do was to go out with them. Remember, these men are engineers!"

CPL Henry started to laugh, then said, "Listen to yourself, Donaldson. You're sounding more like a recruiter every day."

"Bullshit," Donaldson replied. "All I'm saying is that everybody in the 238th Combat Engineer Battalion is one tough sonofabitch. We have been slugging it out since Utah Beach. Lots of our guys bought the farm, but we're keeping on, keeping on."

The truck the men were riding in slowed and came to a complete stop.

"What's up?" SGT Wilkes asked the driver.

"This is where you guys get off."

"The hell you say," Wilkes replied.

"Listen, Mac, I don't make the rules. Your outfit is up that road to the right. They can't be more than five hundred yards north of here, in a small village."

"Then why don't you haul our sorry asses those fifteen-hundred yards?" Wilkes inquired.

Clearly frustrated with all the questions coming his way, the driver replied, "Because if I turn down that friggin' road, every Kraut artillery piece in this sector will open up on me! And, quite honestly, I don't feel like dying today. So, sorry if you guys have to walk a few hundred yards, but you having to walk a few hundred yards beats the shit out of me dying today. You got that?"

Wilkes nodded his head up and down. "Not only do I got it, but you have our permission to get the hell out of here. And, just so you won't think we engineers are a bunch of ungrateful sonsabitches, thanks for the ride. And, see you in Berlin."

With that exchange, the truck driver gave Wilkes the "V" for victory sign and began to turn his truck around.

SGT Wilkes, CPL Henry and PFC Donaldson picked up their gear and began walking toward a small village down the road.

In order to stay warm, Wilkes walked very fast. After a few hundred yards, Donaldson shouted up to him, "You in a footrace to Berlin, Charlie? Damn, you always walk this fast?"

"Not usually, but by my watch, we're already an hour late."

Donaldson and Henry both looked at their watches ad then quickened their pace, too.

As they walked, Henry said, "All I know is, the faster we get across that damned Roer River, the faster we'll be in Berlin and then I can get back to Genevieve."

Charlie Wilkes laughed. "Damn, you sure got it bad for her, don't you?"

Smiling, Ian Henry answered, "Mark my words, Charlie, I'm gonna marry her, and we'll live happily ever after on my winery in Paso Robles."

Wilkes smiled. "I'm beginning to believe you will, Ian. All we got to do now is to not get our asses shot off."

Twenty minutes later...

As the three GIs got back to their AO, they reported in at the HQ

Operations Building. As Wilkes picked up a pen to sign in, he saw 1SGT Freck looking at him.

"I'm sorry we're an hour and a half over time, first sergeant. It won't happen again."

Freck accepted Wilkes' apology. "After you get squared away, report back here, as I'm sending you three men, along with some others, to relieve some of the men at the bridge site where 1LT James was working. And yes, all three of you should have been here ninety minutes ago... but, let's just say my watch wasn't working."

"Works for me, first sergeant," Donaldson said.

"Me too. And, thanks, first sergeant," added Ian Henry.

Having finished his talk, the senior NCO said, "Well? If you three stand around here much longer, instead of going over to the mess tent, you're going to be mighty hungry when you get back here in the morning."

An hour later...

As SGT Wilkes and CPL Henry climbed off the truck at the bridge construction site, Wilkes noticed a full-bird colonel from the Army Corps of Engineers standing there. For a brief moment Charlie wondered why such a high-ranking officer was in attendance—so far as he knew, Lieutenant James' men were fully competent.

From a distance, Wilkes heard someone say, "Are you gonna stand there all afternoon with your finger up your ass, or are you going to give us a hand so we can finish this motherfucker before the war ends?"

Ian Henry wondered who would have the balls as to address him so brusquely. Turning, he recognized the voice as CPL Duncan's.

"Tex, if it was anybody but you talking to me that way, I'd have to kick his ass."

"Henry, you'd better pack your lunch, you're going to be at it for awhile."

Henry walked over to CPL Duncan and shook his hand. "Hey, what's O-6 doing here?"

"He's been on site most of the day," Duncan responded. "I don't have the foggiest idea of why in hell he's here. He ain't said much... in fact, it seems to me he's a one-man glee squad. All he's done is pay us compliments. The men kind of like him, but what he's actually doing here—well, your guess is as good as mine."

Having stood around as long as they dared, Wilkes and Henry made their way over to where Lieutenant James was working.

"Good morning, Lieutenant," Wilkes said as he drew near.

"Oh… Wilkes—good to see that you and Henry are back. I was hoping I wasn't going to have to take off and go to Verviers to rescue your two sorry behinds from the MPs."

"Sir," asked Ian Henry, "What was the deal with those pricks anyway? My God, they were hauling in soldiers who weren't in Class A uniforms! As if any of us have one of those…."

James took the pipe from his mouth, turned it upside down and tapped it with his hand. "Most likely they are just following the orders some garrison rat drew up. But, the good news is that you're here."

"Sir, can I ask you what the colonel is doing here? Don't they trust you to get this bridge built? I mean…. how many bridges have we built so far?"

James pulled a small packet of Prince Albert from his jacket and filled his pipe. "He's got his orders, too. In the meantime, I want the two of you to go over and relieve those four men working on those far bearings. We're almost done here, which is a good thing, because every few minutes the Krauts open up with some artillery. And be careful, because this area is reportedly lousy with German armor."

"Well, then, that explains why you have only put up the ramp on this side, doesn't it?" Wilkes asked.

"Actually that was the colonel's idea."

As Wilkes looked up, he saw an enlisted man running in their direction, his hands waving wildly in the air. When he reached the men, he reported in. "Sir, the guys down-stream say a column of Kraut tanks is headed in this direction."

James looked toward SGT Wilkes. "I'd say it's time we knock the bearings out from under the bridge and let our armor go get those Jerries. You and Henry run over to Private Black and have him take care of that!"

Wilkes and Henry ran as fast as they could, to where the engineers were working. When they got there, Wilkes immediately recognized Private Black. Normally, a private was not put in charge of such a major project. But Private Black had been recently reduced in rank because of an error he made during a reconnaissance he'd conducted. Yet LT James knew he was the most competent man he had. So he'd appointed Black "acting sergeant," and all the men followed him as such, even if he didn't really have the stripes to back up his position of authority.

"Black, we gotta drop this bastard's bearings," Wilkes shouted.

"On whose authority?" one of the other engineers asked.

Before Wilkes could reply, Private Black heard the German armor approaching. He turned, looked out across the Roer, and yelled to his men, "Let's drop those bearings and get the hell out of here!"

What occurred next went as smoothly as a well-choreographed musical on Broadway. The engineers knocked the bearings from the bridge with sledges, dumped the nose over the side and put on one ramp section up. As soon as that was complete, a group of American tanks that had been hidden in the wooded area behind them sped forward and crossed the newly-completed Bailey Bridge, engaging the Germans as they crossed.[3]

238TH COMBAT ENGINEERS BRIDGE GUARD HOUSE
SUNDAY, 25 FEBRUARY 1945, 2055 HOURS LOCAL

After all the excitement at the river that morning, SGT Wilkes and CPL Henry were more than pleased to be back in the comfort of a commandeered house and a warm fireplace—albeit one filled with smoke from a never-ending poker game that they'd heard about while eating their evening meal. One of the soldiers from Company A told Wilkes that there was talk of a small game of poker later on that evening, in the guard's temporary quarters.

About an hour into the game, Wilkes had lost all he dared to lose and, although Ian was actually ahead a fin or so, he too wanted out of the game.

Gazing around the room, Wilkes saw a PFC who looked like he wanted to try his luck. Charlie nodded in the soldier's direction. "Hey, I gotta go take a dump, and I'm losing my ass off. You want in?"

"Always glad to take other people's money," the GI from Idaho replied.

Wilkes looked at the other players at the table. "Well, if none of you mind, I'll relinquish my seat to the gentleman from the great potato state."

The four other poker-playing soldiers all nodded their assent to the change.

After Charlie took care of his nature call, he and Ian got into a conversation that seemed like it was never going to end.

---

3. According to James - *238th Engineer Combat Battalion in Action in WWII*, page 115 – this bridge that crossed the Roer River was built in three hours and forty-five minutes, and was probably the only Bailey Bridge built during WWII that was erected by the US Army engineers on a river crossing while under assault conditions.

In his New Hampshire accent, CPL Henry said, "I swear to God, Charlie, I heard that her tits were thirty-six-and-a-quarter inches."

"If her tits are thirty-six-and-a-quarter inches, I'm Winston Churchill! Nobody's tits are that big!"

"Ask any enlisted man in the unit, Charlie. They'll tell you that Betty Grable's tits are thirty-six-and-a-quarter. Now, I know that, because I saw her picture in a pin-up a few months ago, and I swear that article said her boobs were thirty-six-and-a-quarter inches."

Henry then reached into his pocket for stick of gum. Once he had the gum in his mouth, he continued, "Charlie, for God's sake, people can't make up crap like that—Betty Grable's boobs are thirty-six-and-a-quarter inches!"

Henry's comment nearly brought Wilkes to tears with laughter, which resulted in Ian becoming mildly irked at his best friend.

"And, just what the hell is so funny?"

Charlie began to ramble. "You… me…. Here we are, talking about some woman's tits that neither one of us will ever be able to play with, in the middle of this friggin' war. I don't know, it just seems like a pretty dumb thing to be talking about. Especially since I'm married, and know that Mrs. Wilkes wouldn't be amused in the slightest by this conversation."

Henry stopped chewing his gum briefly and looked his best friend, "I guess it just proves that St. Barth was right."

"St. Barth? Who in the hell is he? Is he one of *your* saints, or both of our saints?"

"By 'your,' I'm assuming you mean Catholic, and 'both' means that both you Episcopalians and we Catholics revere him as a saint. Yes?"

"Yes, that's what I meant," Charlie admitted.

This time it was Henry's time to chuckle.

"What the hell's so funny?" Charlie inquired.

"Well, two minutes ago we were talking about the size of some Hollywood starlet's tits…. And now, it's about St. Bartholomew and whether our respective churches revere him as a saint."

"Yes, that's it, Father Ian," Wilkes said as he did a half-assed genuflect, which caused Ian Henry to get angry.

Seeing that he had clearly irritated his friend, Charlie backed off. "Ian, I was just dicking around. I wasn't trying to piss you off. I meant it as a joke."

Charlie reached into his field jacket pocket for a smoke. He had one left.

"Damn this war, anyway," Charlie said as he went through a litany of complaints. "The food sucks, the weather sucks, the Germans suck and I'm down to my last smoke."

Ian countered, "Hey, look at it this way: if it sucks this bad for us, and we're winning this fucking thing, think of how bad this war must suck for the Jerrys."

"I know you're right, Ian. But, for the life of me I can't feel sorry for these *Nazi* bastards. Hell, Hitler declared war on us on December 8th, not the other way around. So screw 'em—all of 'em."

Before moving on to another subject, Ian Henry returned to his previous point. "So, do you want to know about St. Bartholomew, or not?"

"Sure, Padre!" Wilkes said, and then regretted it.

Henry ignored his friend's comment, and began talking. "St. Bartholomew was one of the twelve disciples, Charlie. If my Catholic schooling doesn't fail me, I think he is the same as the 'Nathanael' mentioned in the Gospel of John. He was from Cana. Sister Sarah said he preached in India and in Greater Armenia, where he was beheaded. So, in answer to the original question, is he a saint in both the Episcopal and Roman Catholic churches? I'd say yes!"

"But I don't get it. Why did you say he was right?"

"In a nutshell? St. Bartholomew said—and I'm paraphrasing him—that 'men were just no damned good!'"

Charlie took a drag from his smoke, and replied. "Well, if that's what he said, I'd be inclined to agree with him. And…."

Before Wilkes could finish his sentence, an enemy artillery shell landed on a building they'd both been in, just a few short hours ago.

Then another shell hit in the area. Then another. Both soldiers dove for the dirt and covered their heads with their helmets.

Debris from the now partially-destroyed building flew in all directions. Wilkes and Henry were struck with pieces from the building, causing both soldiers to bleed. Charlie was losing blood at a higher rate than Ian Henry.

"Shit! I'm hit!" Wilkes said as he felt, then saw the blood gushing from his right hand.

"Don't feel like Mother Goose," Henry replied. "The bastards got me too!"

Lifting up his head to reconnoiter what was going on, Wilkes could see that the building his comrades were in, had actually withstood the pounding and was still standing.

He stood up, kicked Henry in the butt, and said, "Let's get those men outta there!"

Henry immediately jumped up, and they ran in the direction of the now burning building.

From a distance, someone yelled, "Get down, the artillery ain't over yet!"

Both Henry and Wilkes ignored whoever was doing the yelling, and rushed into the building where the card game had been in progress.

With all the activity, Charlie's hand was now flowing hard. Ian looked at it, reached into his pocket and pulled out a handkerchief. "Wrap your hand in this, and put your glove on. That should be enough pressure to get it to stop. While you're doing that, I'm going inside to see if anybody made it."

"I'll be right in, Florence Nightingale," Wilkes said as he began wrapping his hand.

Henry came upon a door that was blocked. He heard moaning on the other side. He stood back, and kicked that door with all the might he could muster. Unfortunately, he couldn't budge it.

"Fuck!" Henry screamed, as he started to kick the door again.

"Gonna have to wait on that one, Ian," Wilkes yelled, as he and Ian gave the door another hard kick. This time, it moved. Pushing hard to get it open, Wilkes and Henry scrambled in and began pulling out the five wounded soldiers inside.

After tending to the soldiers' immediate medical needs, SGT Wilkes, CPL Henry and the guards were driven to a medical aid tent.[4]

On the way to the tent, Wilkes looked over toward Ian Henry.

"St. Bartholomew was right—people are no damn good!"

Throughout the night, the *Nazi*s continued to shell and bomb the three bridge sites. One of their shells knocked out several floats on the bridge that Company C was working on. The floats were immediately replaced, as they were critical to the Roer River crossing. Without those three bridges, none of the men who crossed the Roer in assault boats would have had the use of any vehicles or armored vehicles. That meant the Roer River crossing would have been an abject failure. As it was, the 238th received many letters of commendation from the commanding generals of the VII Corps and the

---

4. As it turned out, those five wounded soldiers would be the only casualties the 238th Combat Engineer Battalion would sustain in the crossing of the Roer River. Years later, Ernie James visited the site, which had been turned into a pub for young Germans. After a few drinks the patrons figured out why Mr. James was in the bar.

104th Division for the part they played in defeating Hitler.

The sister unit of the 238th—the 237th—constructed a two-hundred-sixty-four foot infantry support bridge near Duran, which the Germans zeroed in on, post-haste. So much so, that it had to be abandoned. The engineers then went downstream and built another bridge.

For many of the men in the adjacent minefields leading to the newly constructed bridge, the war became particularly vicious. Many had their feet blown off. There they lay, dying, screaming for a medic to rescue them.

For the men of the 238th, it was a vision of hell, as they had to ignore their comrades' pleas for help because their first obligation was to finish the bridge over the Roer, so that American infantry and armor could continue their march toward Berlin.

NEAR THE OUTSKIRTS OF COLOGNE
HQ BUILDING, 238TH COMBAT ENGINEER BATTALION
SATURDAY, 3 MARCH 1945, 1300 HOURS LOCAL

For the past hour, there hadn't been a soul in the communications room. SGT Charlie Wilkes was bored. In order to pass some time, he thought about doing a traffic check. But after reading the radio log, he decided against it.

Damn, I just did that seventeen minutes ago!

As he set the clipboard down onto a desk, he heard someone walking down the aisle. He looked up and saw CPT Smith.

"Welcome back, sir. I heard you were being released today."

CPT Smith downplayed his wounds and subsequent trip to the field hospital. "Thank you, Sergeant Wilkes. I guess the medics thought I'd milked my wound about as much as I could, so they gave me the boot."

"Well, sir, you might want to say that to some of the other troops. But, remember that CPL Henry and I were the ones who drove you to the field hospital. And, as I recall, you were badly wounded."

CPT Smith smiled, then asked Wilkes if he knew where 1LT James was currently working.

Wilkes looked at his watch and said, "He went back over to Horrem early this morning, sir. He wanted to check on that eighty-foot DS Bailey Bridge that the Huns bombed and strafed. I could raise him on the radio, if you want."

Just as SGT Wilkes began walking over to the radio set, 1LT James came into the communications room.

When the two officers had finished exchanging their greetings, James got down to business by filling the company commander in on the activities his unit had been involved with, since Smith was wounded.

Wilkes decided to make himself useful and go drum up some hot coffee for the two officers, knowing that James had been out in the rain all morning. When he returned to the communications room, James was finishing up with his litany of completed projects. He then began talking about their next objective: Cologne.

"When we tidy up all those projects, captain, our next objective is Cologne. We've been clearing mines from the roads leading into it for a couple of days now. I've also got a detail of men scheduled to reconnoiter bridge sites across the Rhine.

"Also, some of our guys are currently occupying several of the buildings along the west bank of the Rhine. These men report they can see Krauts on the other side, but that it's too far for rifle fire. And artillery fire is out of the question, as nobody wants to accidentally hit the dome."

"I can understand that," Smith replied. "After all, I think we're probably within two or three months of defeating the Germans, and it makes no sense whatsoever to blow up a cathedral that took them six hundred-plus years to build. There's no sense in deliberately pissing them off. God knows, an occupation army is going to have its hands full, as it is."

James reached into his field jacket and pulled out his pipe. Then he nodded his head toward the captain. It was his way of asking (without asking) the captain if it was okay for him smoke. Smith nodded back and James lit up his pipe.

"Sir, you said you thought this fun-filled adventure would be over in two or three months. Are you basing that on some intelligence, or just a gut feeling?"

"While I was lying around in the field hospital, mending, I talked to a lot of guys from infantry outfits. To a man, they all said that Jerry is through. The reasons they gave were pretty much the same across the board—the Germans are down to cannibalizing for spare parts, gas is non-existent, and the quality of the soldiers they're seeing—well, most of them are way too old or way too young. No—I'd say the Nazis are about through."

"That would be great, captain. I'd sure like to get back to where I left off with Faith."

CPT Smith laughed a bit, and said, "So you're going to marry her, huh?"

"Sir, the minute I can, I'm going to do that."

"Well, good luck with it, lieutenant. But don't forget—there still exists the small fact that the Japanese haven't surrendered yet!"

James replied, "Well, hopefully General MacArthur's boys will have done to them what Georgie Patton's Third Army has done to the Krauts, by the time we're ready to be shipped over there."

"Amen to that!" SGT Wilkes said, as he walked out of the room to go relieve himself.

1LT James and CPT Smith looked at each other, then Smith said, "I didn't know he was religious."

"Sir, he seems to have gotten very religious, since February 25th."

"February 25th?" inquired CPT Smith.

"It's a long story, sir."

"Well, I have time," answered CPT Smith, as he began walking out into the hallway.

Observing that SGT Wilkes hadn't yet entered the commode, CPT Smith called to him.

"Yes, sir?"

"After you're finished with business in there, get someone to relieve your duty."

"Is there a problem, sir?"

"No problem, sergeant. Just get someone to relieve you. I want you to go over to the motor pool and draw out a vehicle, then meet Lieutenant James and me back here. I want to get out into the field with the men—plus I want to hear about what it took you to get some religion."

"Yes, sir," Wilkes replied as he walked into the bathroom. *Now what the hell is this all about? Me? Religious?*

NEAR A STEEL STRINGER BRIDGE AT NIEDERAUSSEM
LATER THAT AFTERNOON

"The men are working on a steel stringer bridge down there, sir," 1LT James said as he pointed off to the west.

"Drive us down there, Wilkes."

Charlie Wilkes did as ordered, driving the two officers down to the construction site. There, they got out of the vehicle and walked to where the engineers were finishing up their work.

"Well, look who's here," one of the enlisted men said, as James and

Smith got within a few yards of the bridge.

Most of the men kept at work on the project. But a few of them came over and welcomed back their commanding officer.

"Heard you boys have been busy," Smith said, covering his eyes with a hand to block the sun shining in his face.

"As busy as bird dogs in hunting season, sir," one of the enlisted men said as he wiped his brow.

"Well, you know what the Good Book says: 'Idle hands do the devil's work,'" 1LT James added with a grin.

The next few minutes were taken up by the captain going around and more-or-less "checking-in" with his men on the site. It wasn't that he felt the need to check in with the troops, it was more about a gesture to let each enlisted man know that he was back, and that he appreciated all the hard work they'd been doing in his absence.

While CPT Smith was out looking around, an E6 came over and talked to 1LT James. "Sir, do you remember that four-hundred-yard bypass that Company A built through that factory at Horrem to the autobahn?"

" Yes. Why do you ask, sergeant?"

"Well, sir, as it turned out, after that coal we tried to use for a bedding for the tanks went south, the men went out on a reconnaissance patrol and 'liberated' a bunch of clay pipe from some old German, who had an enormous case of 'the ass' when we left him."

"Yes, that was damn good engineer work, sergeant. But, why do you bring it up now?"

"Well, one of the men said that the old Kraut showed up at headquarters the other day, demanding payment for the pipe we took."

"Who did he talk to?" James inquired.

"I think Massoglia, sir."

James reached into his field jacket for his pipe, and lit it.

"Well, if anything comes of it, I'll tell Massoglia that it was an exigency of the service and have him refer the matter over to headquarters, and let them straighten it out."

"But, lieutenant, Massoglia doesn't know shit about none of this stuff," the E6 responded.

James took a drag from his pipe. "In which case, strike one up for the U.S. Army, as it's the first time since we landed in Normandy that somebody isn't going to make a buck off Uncle Sam."[5]

---

5. As it turned out, Massoglia did not have any knowledge of the incident and told the factory owner that the bill was most likely never paid.

TWO DAYS LATER, IN FRONT OF
THE HEADQUARTERS BUILDING

CPL Henry about wet his trousers when SGT Wilkes told him that he'd been chosen to drive 1LT James and their commanding officer to reconnoiter bridge sites across the Rhine.

"You ain't jerking me off, are you Charlie?" Ian Henry asked as he picked up his helmet and rifle to head over to the operations tent.

"I ain't got time to bullshit people, Henry. The Old Man and James are going into Cologne, and you're driving them. There will be three or four other vehicles going as back up, just in case everything turns to shit and you have skedaddle the hell out of there."

"Man, Charlie, do you think we'll get to see the inside of the dome?"

"What the hell are you talking about? What dome?"

CPL Henry chalked up SGT Wilkes' lack of knowledge of cathedral terms to the fact that he was, at best, a half-assed Episcopalian—and at worst, an outright heathen. Nevertheless, he kept his smartass remarks to himself and simply explained to his superior NCO that the most northern European countries referred to the largest church in whatever burg as "the dome."

Charlie listened to his comment, then asked a question that nearly floored CPL Henry. "So, what's the big deal about this church, anyway?"

"I ain't never been in it, but I can remember seeing pictures of it when I was taking German at St. Mary's back in New Hampshire."

"Wait a minute—are you telling me you speak German?"

"Well, I don't think I could sit in on chemistry class at Heidelberg University and understand what in the hell is going on—but, yes, the where's the toilet' type questions, I do understand."

"And why doesn't anyone else know that you speak German and French?"

"Beats the crap out of me, it's in my personnel folder," Henry replied.

"Ah… the Army! What an organization," Wilkes replied, adding, "I'll keep that bit of information stored in the back of my brain. And, rest assured, your German-speaking ability won't be shared with anyone."

"I don't care if everyone knows I speak German. I mean, hell, with my red hair and Irish Catholic upbringing, I don't think anyone's gonna confuse me with any of these *Nazis* running around."

"It ain't that, numb-nuts," Wilkes said to his best friend. "How long do you think you'd be in this unit if anyone knew you were fluent in German?"

"Charlie, I ain't fluent, I just understand enough German to get some food and some pussy."

"You just made my case, soldier. Now get your butt over to the motorpool and draw out a vehicle. Cologne awaits the 238th Combat Engineers Battalion!"

"Your wish is my command," Ian said, as he scooted out of the area and made a dash to the motor pool.

As he walked, he thought about all those painful hours he'd endured in his German classes, that his father had insisted on Ian taking when he was in high school.

Maybe I can finally put them to use. But which do I want first? Food, or pussy?

Hell, Ian, you've been hanging around too many GIs!

IN FRONT OF THE HOHE DOMKIRCHE ST. PETER UND MARIA THE MAIN CATHEDRAL IN COLOGNE

"Phew, I guess the boys from the Eighth Air Force had a few go wild," 1LT Ernie James said, as he got out of the jeep he'd been riding in for the past hour. After the other three vehicles in the recon group were stopped and a perimeter was set up, 1LT James, CPT Smith, CPL Henry and James' driver, PFC Plover, grabbed weapons and made their way over in front of the church that the people of Cologne started building in 1248 A.D.

As the two officers surveyed the damage to the house of worship, Henry and Plover started to make their way toward the church's main entrance. Before they were inside, they were met by a German priest.

The cleric spoke first, "Good afternoon, gentlemen."

CPL Henry looked at the man.

"*Irgendein Tag, daß der Krieg ist durchaus ein guter Tag.*" ("Any day the war is quiet is a good day.")

The priest again spoke. "Your German is excellent, young man. Are you German, yourself?"

"Actually, I am one hundred percent Irish."

"The devil you say," the cleric replied, looking at CPL Henry again.

Henry took off his helmet and genuflected. "You might find this hard to believe, Father, but many Americans study German. Some do it because they *are* German."

"But with you, you are Irish."

"Yes, my father insisted that I learn German. He said it's the language of scholars, scientists and intellectuals."

"That used to be true, young man. But I am afraid that kind of went away, in 1933."

"Ah, yes, the year *der Fuhrer* came to power."

"Yes, the year Adolf Hitler came to rule Germany," the priest reflected on, with sadness.

"It will be that way again, Father."

The priest started to look around to see if anyone was watching him. Then he laughed. "Hopefully, this will be by the end of the year."

"Well, if General Patton has anything to say about it, it will." Henry replied.

After a brief, albeit uncomfortable pause, the priest asked Henry what his purpose was. In short, were the men there for army-related reasons, or were they interested in having their religious needs met.

From behind Henry, CPT Smith said, "We have completed the business part of this mission, Padre, and some of the men would like to see the cathedral. Is that possible?"

"That is possible, *Herr Hauptman*" (captain), the priest said, recognizing the rank on Smith's collar.

"Well, then, come in. God's House is open to all."

"Thank you, Father," CPT Smith said. "But, before we take the tour, I wish to have each man introduce himself to you."

"That is not necessary," the priest said, then continued, "I am sure God knows who everyone one is, and that is all which is important, yes?"

Having said that, the priest began his tour. "I regret that I will not be able to show you the entire dome, due to the bombing. [Although Allied pilots tried their best not to hit the cathedral, it was hit fourteen times. Fortunately, though, it did not collapse.]

"We regret that, Padre," 1LT James said, stating the obvious feeling of his troops.

"I know these things happen during war. But, for the grace of God, the building has not collapsed. Hopefully this war will end soon, and it can be rebuilt back to its original glory."

"We all do, Father," Ian Henry added.

With such unpleasantness now aside, the priest started to give the soldiers a short tour. "Work first started on this church in 1248, and was finally completed in 1880, when Emperor Wilhelm I himself came to officially dedicate this church, that was built to honor St. Peter and the Virgin Mary...."[6]

IN THE GRAND ROOM OF COLONEL & MRS. MICHAEL BRANDON OHARA'S RESIDENCE, LOS LAGOS, GRANITE BAY, CALIFORNIA MONDAY, 2 DECEMBER 1991, 8:00 P.M. LOCAL

We are not interested in the possibilities of defeat. They do not exist.
—Queen Victoria of England, 1889

After CSM Wilkes had finished his story about the Catholic priest who gave the men of the 238th Engineer Combat Battalion a short tour of Cologne's ancient cathedral, the conversation returned to the present.

The visitors had all moved into the grand room of the Ohara residence. How the room had acquired its name was in itself, humorous. One would think that after seeing the Steinway grand piano sitting near the west wall of the room, that it had been named after the piano. In fact, nothing could have been further from the truth. The reason the room had been christened "Grand Room," was that during the building of the Ohara's residence, this room had cost an extra fifty grand. Thus, the name!

After dinner was finished and the dishes had been cleared away, the party moved into the grand room where, for the past two hours, CSM Wilkes and Dexter Dannenberg had been relating the events that took place between January 1 and the middle of March, 1945.

Knowing that V-E Day occurred on May 8, 1945, Sean Ohara suspected that his father's friends would finish their tales about the Great Crusade in the next hour or two.

But, before they resumed, there were a few questions he wanted to ask.

"Sergeant Major, could you tell me what it was like in March, 1945?"

"What do you mean, Sean?"

"Well, you had to have known that Hitler was finished. I mean, from

---

6. Ernest James stated in his book, *238th Engineer Battalion in Action in WWII*, page 119, that, "...they [the priests] were afraid that the troops would take artifices from the church, but there was no need for fear. No one would knowingly desecrate such a beautiful structure." The priest gave 1LT James a small piece of stained glass, probably hundreds of years old.

what I've read, by that time everyone had pretty much concluded that Hitler had shot his wad in the Ardennes, and that the war was lost.

"Weren't you worried that you would end up like Paul Baumer?"[7]

Taking a sip from his glass of sherry, the retired senior NCO replied, "Of course we were, but just like Paul Baumer, we still had a job to do, and the plain truth was that Hitler wasn't completely finished. And there was all that talk of the '*Wunderwaffen*' (wonder weapons). But, none of us really knew how long that dreadful conflict would continue. And, as far as the so-called 'miracle weapons' went, it wasn't until Stalingrad fell that everyone at SHAEF knew Germany's goose was cooked, no matter how many times that *Nazi* idiot, Joseph Göebbels, claimed that Germany's *Endsieg* (Final Victory) was right over the horizon."

Dexter Dannenberg came into the conversation now.

"Hell, I was a 'nothing' at Bletchley Park, but after seeing some Ultra traffic that described how Germany's industrial production had peaked in forty-four, I knew that no matter what Albert Speer attempted, no matter how many Jews he starved, how many Poles he murdered in his factories, it just didn't matter—Hitler and his bunch of bastards were done-for!

"It's not to say that we didn't all pray to God every night, that the *Nazi*s would surrender, or that another Count von Stauffenberg would come along and actually be successful and kill Hitler, but it was not to be so."

CSM Wilkes took another sip of sherry, then asked Mrs. Ohara if he might have some more.

Sharon Wilkes looked toward her husband, and said, "Good thing we're not driving tonight, honey."

Wilkes smiled at his wife. "You're right, I should knock it off. But you know the rest of the story, and if I'm going to get through it, I'll need one or two more glasses of this fine Spanish sherry."

Mrs. Ohara looked to the senior NCO as he held his glass out to be refilled.

"How far, CSM?"

"All the way to the top, young lady. And, if you would, please leave the bottle close-by."

Sean Ohara thought, *if this old warhorse, who has every friggin' award except the Congressional Medal of Honor, needs to be plowed to finish his story, guess I'd better grab onto my hat and hold on!*

After taking a long sip of wine, Charlie Wilkes began the last installment

---

7. Paul Baumer is the main protagonist in Erich Maria Remarque's great WWI epic, *All Quiet on the Western Front.*

of the wartime exploits of the 238th Engineer Combat Battalion with a story about the First Army's bridgehead on the Rhine River at Remagen. He called it, "The Door Hitler Failed to Lock."

NEAR THE OUTSKIRTS OF BERGHEIM, INSIDE A TENT LOCATED
AT THE 238TH COMBAT ENGINEER BATTALION'S
AREA OF OPERATIONS
SATURDAY, 17 MARCH, 0930 HOURS LOCAL

By any stretch of the imagination, CPL Ian Henry should not only have been exhausted, but furious. But not today, even though he'd pulled twelve hours of guard duty the previous night after working fourteen hours. As he lay in his cot, he became giddy.

How can this be? Could it possibly be that, at around 0300 hours this morning, I realized I'm hopelessly in love with that young Belgian girl, Genevieve Pelletier?

The soldier rolled over in his cot, knowing he had to get some sleep— beautiful Belgian babe notwithstanding.

Ian, snap out of it, you just met her. How could I be in love with her? Hell, for that matter—do I even know what love is?

Pulling the covers over his face in an attempt to block the morning sun shining in his eyes through a small opening in the tent, Corporal Ian Henry, of the United States Army, decided to turn the matter over to God. After he genuflected, he began to pray:

Hail Mary, full of grace. Blessed art Thou amongst women.
Father in Heaven, thank You for another day of life.
Father, I am exhausted, so I am going to get right to the point.
Lord, I know you already know my innermost thoughts and, as such,
I pray for forgiveness, if I am wrong on this matter, but
I believe that You hath made known unto me this beautiful
girl, Genevieve Pelletier, because it is Your desire for me to marry her
and for us to have many children who will be disciples of Your Holy
Catholic Church. If this be true, Heavenly Father, please send me
some sign that I will understand.
I also ask you to watch over Mom and Dad,
my brother, Joseph, and my sister, Cecelia.
And, Lord, I beseech you to give the words to bring

Charlie Wilkes into Your fold. I know he's a louse, Lord,
but I think he is worth the effort. Honestly, I do.
These things I ask, Heavenly Father, knowing that we are unworthy of
Your grace, but Thou O Lord, are the Father of our
Salvation and therefore I beseech You to grant these prayers.
That I ask in Your son's name, Jesus, the Christ.
Your faithful, but sinful servant, Ian Henry.

Three hours later...

Ian Henry was dreaming.

As Charlie Wilkes stood in front of the massive doors to California's Mission San Miguel, he thought back to the many times he and Ian had attended church there during their days at Camp San Luis Obispo, during those dark days following Pearl Harbor.

He smiled at his best friend, Ian, and straightened his tie for yet another time.

"Charlie," Ian said in his inimitable New Hampshire accent, "How many times are ya' gonna straighten that thing?"

"Gotta look good when I go in to see God, Ian. You know that."

"Stop it. God is everywhere, not just inside this church," Ian responded.

"Yeah, I know it, buddy."

"Just because Genevieve and I are about to get married doesn't mean you can jerk me around...."

Charlie Wilkes laughed. "Yeah, it does. And don't think that just because you two are getting married that Sharon and I don't expect to see you every July 4th. Or, for that matter, any holiday you feel like coming down to the strawberry farm in Anaheim."

Ian wiped his brow, and looked out toward the Nacimiento River that flowed off in the distance. He remembered the first time he'd seen this part of California, and how many times he'd thought of this valley's golden, rolling hills while he was in Normandy.

He cupped his right ear with his hand to see if they were still there.

Yes, right there, he thought, as he felt a slight breeze in the air. He strained his ear and then he heard that familiar buzz of the honeybees.

Just as I remembered it.

He breathed in deeply and could tell that autumn was on the way.

He briefly savored the moment. As he turned around, he felt Charlie shaking his right shoulder. He turned, and started to smile at his best man.

As it happened, when CPL Henry woke up, he did see his best friend, Charlie Wilkes' face, but he wasn't asking Ian to come with him into the chapel to marry Genevieve. Instead, he was yelling, "Henry, wake the fuck up and get your ass dressed and get outside in three minutes, because that's when we're all headed out."

Shaking his head and wiping his eyes, CPL Henry leapt out of bed and started to dress, even though he hadn't heard a word Wilkes said. By now, he was conditioned to do what he was told and to ask questions later, if at all.

Two minutes later, CPL Henry was outside his tent and dressed, with his weapon at his side and wondering what the hell was going on. Everyone in the unit was running around as if Attila the Hun was knocking at the front door.

Ian reached into his pocket for a smoke, but came up bare. He looked at the GI sitting next to him to ask if he had a smoke.

"Don't look at me, pal, I done smoked my last cigarette yesterday."

"That sucks, but I guess I'll get over it. Can you tell me what the hell's going on?"

"You ain't heard?" the private replied.

Henry shot the GI one of his 'so, if I knew the answer to that question, do you think I would have asked you in the first place?' looks. What CPL Henry didn't know, was that behind his back many of the soldiers in his unit did not care for him, because they thought he was too "uppity." That is, all of them except SGT Charlie Wilkes. The way Charlie looked at it, Ian Henry didn't suffer fools lightly. And that suited him just fine!

"Come on, pal," Henry replied, "I just woke up after getting three hours sleep after a twenty-six hour shift. No, I ain't heard what the hell is going on."

As the two-and-a-half ton truck started to pull away from the 238th AO, the GI next to Ian said, "What is it that we've been trying to do since we left Cologne?"

"What's this—twenty questions?" Henry shot back.

"Come on, Henry, lighten up. You'll have plenty of time to be a prick when we get to Remagen."

"Remagen? Where in hell is Remagen, and what the hell is so important about it?"

Smiling while drawing out his answer, the GI replied, "Oh—other than capturing a bridge a few miles south of Bonn, that crosses the fucking Rhine River?"

"Phew, you're shitting me. Who did that?" Henry responded, knowing that if the soldier sitting next to him was correct, then the last barrier into the very heart of Germany's industrial Ruhr area had been breached.

"So, all those plans to cross near Wessel [a small burg north of the Ruhr] are for naught…. And we done got us a bridge still standing. Holy Shit! That's great news, because, trust me, we've all heard that every friggin' bridge we've come onto was blown up the minute we got there."

"That's true," the private replied. "But scuttlebutt has it that an element from the 9th Armored Division was able to fight their way across this bridge that starts with the letter 'L.'[8] Apparently, the Krauts were able to set off a few of the demolition charges and destroy parts of it, but I guess the Germans' biggest explosives didn't go off and, as a result, we done got us a bridge!"

Henry was about to respond when the truck hit a pothole so big that it rattled his teeth. He yelled up to the driver, "Hey Mac! Slow down, my Irish ass ain't gonna make it another mile, the way you're driving."

Instead of slowing, the driver ignored Henry's comment and put the pedal to the metal, which pissed Henry off even further. He was about to say something, when he noticed the driver's left arm extended out the window and his middle finger standing upright.

Henry was livid, and commented to the soldier sitting on his other side, "Remind me when we get to this Remagen place to kick that asshole's butt."

"Better pack your lunch, Mac. That is, unless you think you can kick Sergeant Wilkes' ass."

"That's Charlie driving this sonofabitch? Why is he driving so crazy?"

The GI replied, "You know that Lieutenant James's men have been going up and down the Rhine, looking for a place to cross?"

"Yeah, he's been doing that for a couple days now."

"Well, from what I heard, a few days ago elements of the 9th Armored Division captured a bridge in this Remagen place, during something called Operation Lumberjack.[9] And, while this-here bridge ain't in the best location for transporting troops and all, we've still managed to push thousands of

---

8. The name of the bridge was the Ludendorff Bridge, named after Paul Hindenburg's Chief of Staff, General Erich Ludendorff.

GIs over it into Germany."

"That still doesn't answer my question."

"Yeah, and to be truthful, I ain't got the foggiest idea what the hell the rush is all about. Especially, if we're shoving troops across the river. I don't make no decisions that count, and ain't nobody asked me lately what my opinion was, or wasn't. So, screw it, all I know is that the 'big boys' at SHAEF put out an 'all call' for every swinging dick combat engineer-type to get up there to that Remagen place. And that explains why Wilkes is burning up the road to get there."

"Well, I'll be go to hell," Henry said aloud. "We've crossed the Rhine...."

Henry's comment caused the soldier next to him to start laughing. "Yep, you done been hanging around that Wilkes character too long. He says the same thing about his sorry ass going to hell—but, in his case, he might just be right."

For the next few hours, every time the American convoy came to an area where they could see across the Rhine River, the Germans on the other side shot at them. Once they arrived at Remagen they found that a bridge was under construction. They were then directed to work with the 237th Combat Engineers to build the second bridge across the Rhine.

Since the Ludendorff Bridge had been damaged, 1LT James took his platoon across the completed first bridge and immediately secured a beachhead, in the process clearing out whatever Germans remained in the area.

A few days later, they received orders to move east to the interior of Germany. General Lawton Collins' VII Corps, consisting of, among others, the battle-hardened 1st and 104th Infantry Divisions and the 3rd Armored Division, again led the way for the First Army.

The 238th Combat Engineers moved many miles a day with relative ease, covering the territory through Paderborn, Kassel, Halle and Leipzig to the Elbe River in little more than a month. They were then assigned to the 104th Division, following within hours of the advancing 3rd Armored Division. Their mission was to open as many roads as possible, and to build as many bridges as necessary, so the advancing units could move unimpeded.

It was during this period that the men in the unit began to encounter the

---

9. Soldiers from the 27th Armored Infantry Division captured the Remagen Bridge on 7 March 1945. It was learned after the war that the German military disobeyed orders to destroy it because they believed the war to be lost, and therefore it made no sense whatsoever to destroy a bridge what would be needed in the rebuilding of Germany.

German slave labor camps. Lieutenant James was among the first to figure out that the local farms and factories utilized this type of labor. He noticed that the human slaves were housed in buildings near their work areas, and that to the casual observer the men and women did not appear to be severely beaten, or tortured.[10] It didn't mean that they weren't ill-treated by their overseers, though, because they were. James also noted that none of them looked like they were being over-fed.

THE 238TH BIVOUAC AREA, AT BAD DRIBURG AND GEHRDEN
MONDAY, 9 APRIL 1945, 0430 HOURS LOCAL

For someone who had just pulled a twelve-hour shift at the operations tent, the previous day, plus a six-hour shift as sergeant of the guard last night, SGT Charles Wilkes should have been exhausted. Under usual circumstances, he would have barely been able make it to his cot before he fell asleep, exhausted. But not today.

He tossed and turned a bit, rearranging his pillow for the third time. As he closed his eyes, he thought back to the previous evening's BBC broadcast. The one story he vividly remembered, was the one that reported that Allied units were in the process of clearing the northeastern Italian city of Vicenza. According the reporter, the GIs involved were involved in a brutal door-to-door battle. It was a downright slug-fest. The good news was the BBC report that Italian soldiers were surrendering by the thousands.

Hell, look how long it took those bastards to conquer Emperor Haile Selassi!

As Charlie tried desperately to turn off his brain and go to sleep, he thanked God, albeit not in a formal prayer, that he had been spared from fighting in the battle currently being waged in Vincenza. He then pulled his sleeping bag over his head, in a futile attempt to gather some much-needed sleep.

However, sleep was not to happen. Instead, his mind kept spinning. He kept recalling a message that somehow had been routed through the 238th communications center. Classified "Secret," the message went into detail about someplace called Orhdruf.

The message stated that the concentration camp had been liberated by

---

10. During one of the many interviews conducted by the author of Major James, the question came up as to why James's men failed to do something for the slaves. James stated that they could tell that all of the slaves were malnourished, but given their mission (build bridges and clear roads) there really was not a thing that he or his men could do for them. That job was to be left for the soldiers to follow.

the 4th Armored Division of the 3rd Army, back on April 4[th.] As it turned out, soldiers from the 89th Division reached the abandoned camp that same day, after finding some escaped prisoners who had been hiding since SS troops massacred somewhere between sixty and seventy following roll-call two days earlier.

The message went on to give details of the living conditions within the camp. Just the paragraph that detailed the buildings in which the prisoners were held, sickened Charlie almost to the point of wanting to upchuck. He tried to forget the words of the message, but it was no use. They all came back, verbatim:

Approximately one hundred by thirty feet long, these quarters were all without heat and housed anywhere from two hundred to two-fifty men. American servicemen have been forbidden to enter into them because they were rife with typhus-bearing lice. According to one of the prisoners, there had never been bathing facilities, and the clothing from the dead was simply reissued to other prisoners. None of the survivors had anything that even resembled a pair of shoes.[11]

As Charlie lay there, he shook his head, trying to get last part of the message to leave his brain. It seemed that this shit-hole did not even have a crematorium. So, when the SS thugs left the place, they had stacked up dozens of dead Jews in-between railroad ties and set them afire.

How the hell could a civilization that produced Bach, Beethoven, Göethe and Schiller come up with something as depraved as this?

Charlie decided right then, that if he were ever going to get any sleep he was going to have to take Ian Henry's advice: he needed to start talking to God on a daily basis. So he closed his eyes, and searched for the "right words." It was odd, but once he started to pray, the words just seemed to flow:

Heavenly Father, I come before You as a simple man—a woefully sinful man. Yet, my mama told me that You have always used men like me to do Your work. I guess, that is what we are doing here—Your work, but I pray for a quick resolution to this miserable business, as every day brings forth some newly

---

11. According to www.Scrapbooks.com/Ordruf?ordruf02.html, nothing remains of this Nazi death camp, as it was burned to the ground after the war.

*discovered form of barbarism that defies reason, like Orhdruf. I
ask You how it is humanly possible to do such hateful things to
another human being. I plead with You to watch over the men
in the 238th for the duration of this horrible war, and that You
bring the rest of us safely home to families. For those fallen, I
ask You to raise them to into your presence. Before I close, I ask
you to watch over my wife and children, to comfort them and let
them know that when this task is over, I will be home.*
       This I ask in Your Son's name, Amen.

Ten minutes after he finished his prayer, SGT Charles Wilkes fell sound
asleep. When he awoke six hours later, Charlie thought of his long-deceased
mother. A smile came to his face as he thought, *Mama, I think I have finally
talked to God. Thanks for not giving up on me.*

Later that morning...

Had it been anyone other than CPL Henry shaking his cot and asking
if he was going to lay in his fart-sack all day, SGT Wilkes probably would
have hopped out of bed and knocked the crap out of the perpetrator. As it
was, Charlie opened his right eye, then his left one, and focused on a piece
of paper that looked strangely like an envelope being held about six inches
from his face.

"You can, or you can't, get your sorry ass out of bed and read this letter
from Mrs. Charlie Wilkes, from Anaheim, California. You decide, soldier."

"Fuck you, Ian. Give me that letter."

"No thanks to the first offer, and yes to your second one."

Charlie sat up, took the envelope from Henry, held it under his nose
and sniffed.

God, I love this woman!

"The mail clerk did the same thing, Charlie."

"Remind me to break his neck when I see him next, will you?"

"I don't think you're going to get a chance today, Tiger, because as
soon as you get your pants on, we're driving via convoy to some place
called Einbeck."

"As long as it's toward Berlin, I don't give a damn where we're going.
Because, the sooner we get to Berlin...."

Ian had heard Charlie say what was coming so many times, that he finished his sentence for him, "...the sooner you can get back to Sharon and the boys."

Charlie ignored Ian Henry, and carefully tore open the letter from his wife.

March 19, 1945

Darling:
Just a quick note to let you know that all is well here—the boys
are getting so big that I dare say you won't recognize them when
you get home— which we hope is by this Christmas!
From the news stories here, it looks as though Hitler is about through.
At least that is what I heard on NBC radio last week.
As for the farm, Dad says we're going to have another bumper crop
of strawberries, and the Army has promised to buy all that we can grow.
Dad is excited about such a big crop, and worries constantly about
getting enough laborers. Somehow he manages—although last Friday
all of us picked berries for six hours in order to get enough berries for
the fruit stand that Dad opened up a few weeks ago.
How is that for Iowa work ethic? As if he doesn't have enough to do
around here as it is, now we have a fruit stand, too!
Dad says it will give the boys something to do this summer...
The weather has been wonderful—temperature in the low 70s.
I can tell you one thing, this ain't Iowa.
But I think you'll fall in love with the farm and Southern California.
We all miss you so much.
The boys and I pray for you every night.
Kisses, Sharon

Later that afternoon...

SGT Charles Wilkes had been on duty by himself for the past two hours, and he desperately needed to run to the men's room or risk wetting his pants. The problem was that he simply could not leave the communications center unattended. To compound his difficulties, the chatter on the radio had been relentless.

From the sounds of it, the entire German front is collapsing, and every unit is calling in requesting combat engineers. As if we have any to spare!

He walked over to the doorway and looked out in both directions. He was trying to find someone of authority who could talk to a unit down-range about some *snafu* over materials needed for yet another Bailey bridge.

Damn! I wish someone would show up and talk to this jackass, and while they are at it, relieve me so I can go talk to a man about a horse.

Wilkes looked to the unit's "tote board." It was a chalkboard that had been purloined from some rear area unit. It was completely filled with missions in progress, missions to be completed, when the expected of completion was, and who the OIC was for that project.

I don't think the 238th Combat Engineers could possibly spare any more men for anything else, other than maybe to shoot Hitler.

He read the scrawl on the board. *Let's see, we have guys working on the Bailey Bridge near the Weser River. We've just about wrapped up that three-hundred-twelve foot steel treadway job at Beverrungen. Now, that was a piece of work—the boys actually built that damned thing in total darkness!*

Then, the guys from Company A constructed a three-hundred-twenty footer for the infantry over the Weser River, while the Krauts dropped artillery every fifteen minutes. I wonder why none of those shells hit any of our guys. It ain't like they didn't have ample opportunities to do so.

And then we've got an eighty-foot number going in over at Northeim, near the Leine River, along with a seventy-footer near Katlenburg, over the Rhume River.

Ain't there any more combat engineers in this whole friggin' theater, except us?

In his headset, he heard the following message: "Jean, this is Leap Frog, I need to talk to Six, if possible. If not, Three would do, over." [Six was the codeword for the battalion commander.]

"Leap Frog, this is Jean. Six not available at this time, nor Three, but will advise as soon as either becomes available, out."

With that transmission on its way, SGT Wilkes decided he was out of options. He abandoned the communications center for a minute and ran down to the latrine—or stand there and piss himself. Ripping the headset off, he ran down the hall toward the latrine, unbuttoning his trousers as he moved. He barely made it to the head, before the urine started to fly.

Damn, if I'd have waited another second, it would've been too late! What's the deal, anyway—ain't there anyone around, or what?

For the next minute and a half, Charlie Wilkes urinated. Just as he was finishing, he heard what sounded like a gaggle of soldiers walking down the hall.

Shit! Me in here with my dick in my hand, and the radio room empty... that ain't gonna work!

He quickly washed his hands and ran back to the now-full communications room.

Charlie looked around. There were lots of officers present, but he didn't know any of them except for 1LT James, who at the moment was fiddling with his pipe.

"Lieutenant James?" he said, as he walked toward the officer from Nebraska.

"Yes, Wilkes, what do you need?"

"Leap Frog just radioed in a few minutes before I went to the latrine. He needs to talk to the Colonel, but he said an 0-3 would do."

"Give me the headset, Wilkes, and I'll call him."

"Thanks, sir," Charlie said, as he picked up the headset and handed it to Lieutenant James.

An old hand around the radio, James got right down to business. "Leap Frog, this is Jean, come in please."

Charlie started to walk away. But, before he got too far, James called him back.

"SGT Wilkes."

Turning, Wilkes replied, "Yes, sir. Is there something else I can do for you?"

James just laughed, "Yes—button your trousers!"

His face now beet-red, SGT Wilkes stammered, "Damn, I was in such a hurry to get back here, I plumb forgot."

SATURDAY, 10 APRIL 1945
NEAR HERZBERG, GERMANY, 1400 HOURS LOCAL

For the past two hours, many of the men of the 238th had been partaking in an activity they lovingly referred to as "hunting." It was not that the mess hall had broken down, nor was it because they needed rations. The truth of the matter was that the engineers were "hunting" bypassed Jerries, and there were thousands of them.

It all began when somebody (no one knew who) suggested that they go out and round up some of the German soldiers that had been brushed aside on their way to other objectives. The rationale for this "hunt" was that there were literally thousands of Krauts wandering around the forest like the lost tribes of Israel, albeit, everyone agreed that they probably should not make that particular comparison to someone wearing an SS uniform. Not that anybody expected to take one of those bastards alive. Even CPL Henry said he would shoot them on sight!

The difference about today's hunt was that Wilkes had placed a small wager that he would bring in the most Krauts. CPL Henry thought that gambling on the lives of other human beings was over the top. But, the more he thought about it, the more he realized that unlike other times when they ran into German soldiers, they probably would not have to kill them. Instead, the Krauts would throw down their rifles, throw up their hands, ask for an American cigarette and thank God that their duty to the Austrian corporal was over.

Ian also believed this activity sure beat the hell out of sitting around back at the AO, wondering if he would ever see Genevieve again.

The only drawback was that the spring thaw had begun and everywhere he stepped it was slicker than cat shit on linoleum. He'd fallen on his ass twice already.

"So, Eric," said Ian Henry as he lit a cigarette, "did you hear about that concentration camp called Buchenwald that was liberated a few days ago?"

"Nope, sure didn't," said CPL Duncan, as he spit tobacco juice.

"One of the guys from G-2 was down yesterday, and he was talking to some of the brass. Turns out that this place is near Weimar—whereever the hell that is."

"From what the G-2 type said, our guys liberated the place right after the Krauts began packing up their crap. Apparently, the prisoners organized and took over the place to prevent atrocities by the retreating camp guards.

The G-2 weenie said there were over twenty thousand prisoners there, and that the living conditions were unbelievable."

Duncan spit more tobacco juice, then said, "You know, when we first got here, I sorta felt sorry for the Krauts. I figured they were just poor bastards like us. Their government fucked up, and they had to put their ass on the line to bail it out. Nothing more, nothing less. But, the more I hear about these sorry sonsabitches, the less sympathy I feel for them."

"You know me, Eric. I'd give anyone the shirt off my back if they needed it. But I too am getting to where you are. There are just too many of these stories floating around for them not to be true.

"I mean, hell, I read Hitler's book a few years ago and thought the guy was off his rocker, then. But I honest to God didn't think the German people would allow that crazy sonofabitch to start another world war. Nor did I think they'd do half the crap they're being accused of now."

Duncan reached in his pocket and pulled out a can of tobacco. He offered some to Henry.

"Nah, that shit's nasty. Besides, I think you have to be from the South to chew it. Why, if I came home chewing tobacco, my mother would slap my face into the middle of next Tuesday."

"She would?" Duncan asked incredulously.

"Bigger than shit, she would," Henry replied.

"Hell, my momma chews the stuff her own damned self!" Corporal Duncan's comment stopped Henry dead in his tracks.

"You lying sonofabitch, telling me your momma chews! Ain't no way in hell that's true."

"Bullshit, Henry, my momma does chew tobacco!"

Damn, I guess I won't ever get on my momma again for passing gas in public.

CHAPTER EIGHTEEN

Against enemies who preach the principles of hate and practice them, we set our faith in human love and in God's care for us and all men everywhere.
—Winston Churchill, 1942

ON THE VERANDA OF COLONEL & MRS. MICHAEL BRANDON OHARA'S RESIDENCE, LOS LAGOS, GRANITE BAY, CALIFORNIA WEDNESDAY, 4 DECEMBER 1991, 4:30 P.M. LOCAL

When Sean Ohara drove up into his parents' front driveway, CSM Wilkes did a double-take.

"I thought you'd be getting home much later. No basketball practice tonight?"

"Not tonight. All the teachers had to attend some sort of a meeting, so the coach told us to hit the road."

"That's great, because the missus and I have to head on back to Nevada City tomorrow, and I want to finish telling you how my unit won World War II," Wilkes replied as he lit an Upmann cigar.

"Let me grab a cold one, and I'll meet you on the deck," Chaplain Ohara's son replied.

"A cold one, you say?" Wilkes asked, wondering what the teenager was planning to grab out of the refrigerator.

A few minutes later, as Sean Ohara strolled out to the back verandah, Wilkes pointed to the bottle of Snapple® in his hand and said, "I was wondering what you meant by a 'cold one.' Guess I know, now—you meant a bottle of peach iced tea. I should have known."

The younger Ohara laughed a bit, then replied, "Hey, my dad is pretty liberal about alcohol with *his* friends. But, to date he's never offered any of my friends anything other than wine at communion."

CSM Wilkes nodded his head in agreement, and added, "Tell you what, I would trade that, any day, compared to how my teenage years were spent."

Remembering the story Dexter Dannenberg told when the Ohara family visited the congressman who Colonel Ohara had known when they'd been enlisted men during the Vietnam War, the teenager nodded in agreement, and smiled.

CSM Wilkes sat down next to Sean. "I guess by now, you've figured out that I'm not the most religious person in the world."

"So you have implied quite a few times over the past few days, sergeant major."

For a few seconds, the retired non-commissioned officer sat quietly. Sean Ohara briefly studied his weathered face and wondered what it would be like to be a man with CSM Wilkes' worldly experiences.

After a brief interlude, Wilkes came back to their conversation. "I could blame my lack of religiosity on my childhood, but that would be bogus. That's the common cop-out of every hoodlum in the penal system today. So, I'm not going to go that way. Instead, I'll just say that I'm just one hard-headed Irishman who needs his proverbial Episcopalian ass kicked."

At that precise moment Colonel Ohara came up from behind, and said, "I hope you're not talking about me, when you're talking about a hard-headed Irishman who needs his proverbial Episcopalian ass kicked."

The sergeant major got up and shook the retired chaplain's hand, "No colonel—at least not today."

"That's good, because I was coming out here to tell you that Chloe and I are running into Folsom for a quick meeting about the Christmas Faire. There's plenty of food left in the 'fridge."

"Thanks, colonel. Between me, Sharon, and your son, we'll come up with something worth eating."

Consider our house, yours," the colonel said as he walked over to his fire engine-red 1966 Ford Mustang convertible.

Sean Kennedy nodded his head toward his father and then said, "We have a new Cherokee, a Jaguar, a Bentley and that thirty-year old Ford Mustang! And guess what Pop always drives—that old Mustang!"

"You know why, don't you?"

"I haven't a clue."

"It's easy. The Mustang was his before he met your mom. Everything else comes from her money. Now, I'm not saying that's a bad thing. Hell, the big Victorian we have in Nevada City wasn't paid for with my Army retirement. On the contrary. When the boys went off to college and the Army, Sharon decided there wasn't one good reason for us to own half of

Anaheim, anymore.

"One day, she was sitting out on the front porch when I got home from a round of golf. She had a huge pitcher of lemonade going. Oh, I knew something was up, because every time she got out her mother's lemonade pitcher my life was about to change. And, sure enough after a bit of small talk she announced that a real estate broker was on the way out, and that she wanted to list the property."

"You're kidding, right?" Sean asked.

"Not one bit. Remember, the property belonged to her. And, the way I looked at it, if she wanted to sell it, that was her business. When I asked why she wanted to sell, she just replied, 'I'm done with southern California, and I want to move to up north to an old Victorian.' That was it, plain and simple."

"It didn't bother you, that she made the decision arbitrarily?"

"Listen, Sean. Sharon and I have been married since 1942, and during that time I was traipsing across the world, fighting wars, toppling governments and raising a whole lot of hell. Not once did she complain that I was not there for the boys when they were growing up. Nope, in fact, she pretty much raised them by herself, and did a damn fine job of it, if you ask me. So if she wanted to sell her property without asking, it was alright with me."

"I guess that's one way of looking at it," Sean Ohara replied.

"Let's just say, it works for me. After all, I consider myself damned lucky to have found a woman as wonderful as Sharon."

"I'm beginning to see your point, Sergeant Major."

"Good! Now I can get back to telling you how I won World War Two."

"Okay. You were telling me why you're not the most religious Episcopalian who ever came down the pike."

"First off—you know yourself, that Episcopalians think they are 'God's Chosen Frozen.'"

"As a matter of fact, I've heard my father lament on that very subject more than once."

"Well, when I was young I never prayed, because I was so irritated at God for when I'd gone through with my mom's death and the 'other stuff' that went on in Villisca while I was growing up. As *if* God *had anything to do with it*. I know that, now, but at the time I blamed God for everything. I felt pretty much that way until the latter days of the war."

"So you've said," Sean replied.

"It's true. If it hadn't been for Ian Henry, I don't think I would have gone to church once during the entire time we were rolling across Europe. But when I have this crazy Catholic from New Hampshire ragging my sorry ass about what an ungrateful *schmuck* I was... well, you get my point. I went to church with Henry, because I couldn't stand him being on my case all the time."

A thought flashed inside Sean Ohara's head.

"Sergeant Major, before you continue with your story, you haven't told me if Corporal Henry made it through the war."

CSM Wilkes stopped talking briefly and looked at the teenager, but said nothing.

Noticing the man's lack of response, Sean blurted out, "Oh, hell! You're not gonna tell me that you got within thirty days of the friggin' war's end, and he got killed? Tell me that's not the case!"

A few seconds passed before Wilkes replied. "No. He made it home, all right, but he sure went by a circuitous route. Which I'll get to, but not right now. Okay?"

"Now you've really got me going."

"Why do you say that?" Wilkes asked.

"For the past six days you've been anxiously telling me about your unit during World War Two, and now that you're about to the end, you're getting quiet. What gives?"

"Well... quite honestly, young man, what I have to tell you next makes everything else seem like child's play."

"Phew! You're kidding, right?"

"I wish it were so, but no.... What I'm about to tell you still makes me nauseous. And that's saying a helluva lot, when you consider I spent two years in Korea and three tours in Vietnam before retiring."

"Jesus, am I ready for this?" the teenager asked rhetorically.

"You've gone this far—you might as well hear the rest of it."

SOMEWHERE NEAR HERZBERG, GERMANY
TUESDAY, 10 APRIL 1945, EARLY AFTERNOON

For the past half-hour, the only thing any of the men saw moving in the woods was a few birds. The engineers were just about to stop for the day, when Lieutenant James looked up and spotted a group of German soldiers approaching. Oddly, they had a woman with them.

Soon the rest of the engineers had a bead on them. From where Ian Henry stood, he figured that if any of them tried anything the slightest bit irregular, he'd drop them on the spot.

He also hoped that at least one of them would have a Luger, or something else of value that he could take as a souvenir back to New Hampshire. As the gaggle got closer, he gave up on that idea completely.

CPL Dwight Long was the first soldier to verbalize what they were all thinking about the approaching group. In his distinctly Oklahoma accent, he said, "What a sorry bunch of assholes these characters are."

Lieutenant James spoke up. "Search them, men. Keep an eye out for anything that might pass as intelligence."

The engineers proceeded to search all the German men. In an almost-fatal mistake, none of the engineers searched the woman. It nearly cost them some lives.

After securing their weapons and giving two of the Germans a smoke, the group loaded them into a waiting truck and started to make their way back to their AO. About fifteen minutes later, the woman started making noises that she had to make a nature call.

"Hey, Lieutenant, this Kraut woman has to take a piss," one of the engineers shouted up to Lieutenant James, who was riding in the cab of the two-and-a-half ton truck.

James directed his driver to pull over. Once the truck had stopped, everyone else decided they also might benefit from a trip to the woods.

But when the woman got out of the truck, she pulled out a pistol and let loose, wounding the driver in the head. The other German soldiers made a break for it.

Instantly, CPL Henry raised his Tommy gun and blew away two of the escaping soldiers outright. While Henry was waxing those two soldiers, other men from the unit ran over and tackled the German woman.

SGT Wilkes hollered back to Henry, "Damn good shooting, Henry."

"Yeah, but it shouldn't have ever gone that far. We fucked up. We should've checked that Kraut bitch, too."

"You're right," Wilkes replied. "But it was still damned good shooting."

Henry spat on the ground. "Well, I guess today is as good as any day to kill these bastards! And, trust me—I'll never be so damned stupid again. I don't give a shit if a kid is six years old, I'm gonna search his ass. That was just too damn close!"

"You're right, of course. But I still say it was good shooting," Wilkes added.

"Yeah—I'm such a good shot, two of those Krauts got away."[1]

THE 238TH COMBAT ENGINEERS COMMUNICATIONS CENTER SATURDAY, 12 APRIL 1945, EARLY AFTERNOON

Whenever CPL Ian Henry came into the communications center, he usually would make some sort of comment, tell an anecdote about a recent SNAFU or crack a joke, but not today. He just came in and sat down. At the time, SGT Wilkes was busy working on a message to headquarters, and did not pay any attention to his friend. Once he finished with the message, though, he walked over to where Henry was sitting.

Wilkes waited for Ian to say something, but no words were forthcoming. He was about to say something, when he noticed that his best friend's eyes were red.

Wilkes asked him if everything was all right, but Henry did not respond. He asked him again, "Ian, is everything okay?"

Ian Henry looked up at him, and Wilkes noticed that his comrade from New Hampshire had been crying.

Sonofabitch, I wonder what the hell is going on.

Taking a seat next to him, Wilkes asked, "Hey, what's going on? I've never seen you cry before, and we've been through some shit together. What's up?"

Henry looked up, and said, "FDR is dead."

"What the hell do you mean, 'FDR is dead'?" Wilkes questioned what his ears had just told him.

"I said —'FDR is dead.' I just heard it on Armed Forces Radio, and Lieutenant James verified it. FDR had a stroke this morning, while he was at Warm Springs, Georgia."

"Are you sure about that?" Wilkes said, trying to grasp the enormity of the conversation.

Henry wiped his eyes, looked up and said, "I ain't bullshitting you. Charlie, FDR died of a stroke this morning, in Georgia."

"I'll be a sonofabitch," Wilkes answered, as he reached into his pocket for a smoke.

"He's been president for so long, I was beginning to think he'd always

---

1. With the exception of CPL Henry shooting the escaping Germans, this incident actually occurred on this date.

be around," Henry muttered. Then he looked toward his friend. "I guess the way we ought to look at it, is that God thought he had done enough and it was time for him to come home."

Charlie Wilkes just sat there, stunned. It just did not seem possible that the man who had led the country through the Great Depression, those dark days after Pearl Harbor, and all the way to what looked like the end of *Nazi*sm, could ever be dead.

As Charlie sat, he began to recite the only scripture he knew, the 23rd Psalm. By the time he was on the second line, Ian Henry joined in: "Yea, though I walk through the valley of the shadow of death, I will fear no evil, for thou art with me; thy rod and thy staff they comfort me...."

SATURDAY, 13 APRIL 1945
NEAR OSTERODE (EAST OF GOTTINGEN), GERMANY, 1025 HOURS LOCAL

Even though the men of the 238th Combat Engineers had lost their commander-in-chief the previous day, there was no time for mourning. As such, this Saturday morning they found themselves attached the Seventh Corps in support of the First Division, rolling pell-mell through the northernmost mountain range in Germany, the Harz Mountains, on their way to Berlin.

Yesterday, they had built a Bailey bridge across the Saale River, near Nelben. Today's mission was to continue repairing roads for the infantry troops and armor that were not too far behind. Having driven ten miles in the past two hours, Lieutenant James' convoy was approaching a small country town when they came across a strange sight: a retreat that included numerous stately buildings surrounded by grassy lawns and small wooded areas.

As their convoy slowed, 1LT James was the first to notice a young German *fraülein* pushing a baby carriage. After all the death he had witnessed since Utah Beach, it was a welcome site, indeed. The Army lieutenant thought that, the way things were going, the baby in the carriage would probably never have to hear the sounds of war.

CPL Henry was in the vehicle immediately behind Lieutenant James, and he too noticed the pretty German girl pushing the carriage. Then, from the corner of his eye, he saw another German woman who appeared to be in her mid-twenties. She was pregnant.

Then, he spotted another young woman in the "family way." Then another, and still one more!

What the fuck is going on here?

Damn, Ian! That's damned funny—"What the fuck's going on here?" Obviously, a whole lot of fucking is going on here. Either that or the one sonofabitch that's getting all this stuff is damn potent!

While CPL Henry was amusing himself with his new-found wit, he almost did not stop in time to keep from hitting the lieutenant's vehicle. It had come to a sudden halt.

"Why are we stopping, lieutenant?" someone yelled from a couple of vehicles back.

James didn't respond. Instead, he got out of his jeep and walked over to one of the soon-to-be-mothers. With him was the German-speaking, non-commissioned intelligence officer from headquarters, who was in the process of hitching a ride to another AO.

James nodded toward the NCO, and said, "Ask her why so many women are pregnant here, when there aren't any men around."

"All they need is one, sir."

James smiled. "I know that, sergeant, but something ain't kosher here. Why are so many of these women knocked-up, and there aren't any men?"

The Intel NCO did as directed and waited for a reply. When the response came, it nearly caused his jaw to hit the ground. He whirled around and faced James.

"I'll be a sonofabitch!"

"Sergeant, I didn't come over here to find out if you have two parents. What's the deal with *Fraülein* Titttzenfloppen? What did she say?"

"I'll be go-to-hell, sir. She says that all these women are part of a program intended to breed a new Aryan master race."

"What the hell does that mean?"

The NCO asked more questions, but the answers did not get any better.

"According to what she says, sir, these girls volunteered to come up here and breed with Aryan [SS] soldiers as part of a plan to produce a German master race. Once the babies are born, they become wards of the Third Reich. The boys are raised for an elite fighting force."

"Sergeant, did I hear you right?" James asked with disgust in his voice.

"Yes, sir. In fact, according to her, the little boys are given military training at a nearby military camp from the time they begin to walk."

James looked to the NCO. "Well, I'll bet you a package of pipe tobacco that here's a story you never thought you'd send up channels."

The NCO looked at the lieutenant. "And, how soon, before we shoot that Austrian paper hanger?"

"Not soon enough. Let's get back on the road. I'm getting sick to my stomach."

As James got back into his vehicle, he looked to SGT Wilkes.

"Let's get a move on. I've seen enough of these bastards to last me a lifetime."

"Where to, Lieutenant?"

"Ellrich."

"Where's that?" Wilkes didn't having a map handy.

"It's a small town about thirteen kilometers northeast of Nordhausen. Part of the battalion is there or has plans to bivouac up there. That's where we're headed."

What Lieutenant James was not aware of, was that in the next couple of days he and his men would witness some of the most barbaric behaviors one could ever imagine. For every man present, it would be a life-altering experience. For they were about to plunge into the very abyss of *Nazi* anti-Semitism—the hell-hole referred to in history books as the concentration camps at Nordhausen and Mittelbau-Dora.

> *The least we could have done was to give them a decent burial.*
> *The most we can do is to ensure that they are not forgotten.*
> —Ernest C. James, 1990

THE GRAND ROOM OF COLONEL & MRS. MICHAEL BRANDON OHARA'S RESIDENCE
LOS LAGOS, GRANITE BAY, CALIFORNIA
WEDNESDAY, 4 DECEMBER 1991, 7:30 P.M. LOCAL

A short while after everyone at the table had finished their dinner, Mrs. Ohara announced that Ernie and Faith James were going to stop by for a few minutes. At first, the Oharas' son, Sean, didn't think anything of it. Then he began to wonder what was up. By the time the front doorbell rang, his curiosity was about to drive him up the walls.

Thinking back to the previous Labor Day vacation in Iowa, and the story that Dexter Dannenberg had told, and its surprise ending, he wondered if tonight would be a repeat performance of that dramatic weekend.

But, how could that be? What else is there to tell?

After the greetings, and Colonel Ohara's insistence on mixing MAJ James, (USAR, Ret.) and his wife, Faith, cocktails, Ernie began talking.

"So, where did Charlie leave off?"

CSM Wilkes responded, "We were just about to go into Nordhausen, Ernie."

James took a sip from his drink, and replied, "Before we go there, I'd like to address some comments to you, Sean."

"Sir, being the son of a chaplain, I've pretty much heard it all," the teen responded.

"That may be so. But, suffice it to say, so far we've told you some pretty gruesome stories. And, I must admit that, while Charlie and I were slugging our way across Europe, we saw lot of horrible things. But nothing prepared us for what we were about to see when we entered the Mittlebau-Dora concentration camp.

"The 104th (Timberwolf) Division had moved quickly through the area a day or so before us, in pursuit of the fleeing Germans. We had moved to Ellrich, a small town about thirteen kilometers from Nordhausen.

"The next day we found a condition diametrically opposite to what we'd found in the nursery camp in the Hartz Mountains. Our entry into the city of Nordhausen opened our eyes to the sort of people we were fighting. We quickly understood why Germany's surrender had to be complete, and unconditional. When the leading armored columns drove into the city to ferret out the last *Nazi* defenders, our amazed armored troops and infantrymen discovered two of Germany's infamous concentration camps, Nordhausen and Mittelbau-Dora.[2]

"Our battalion had moved into Nordhausen as part of the VII Corps, and in support of the 1st Division. Our orders were to continue on to Halle with the 104th Infantry Division. As we neared Nordhausen, a strange, peculiar odor permeated the air. I first noticed it when we entered the railroad yards near the camp. The stench became terrible, much worse than we later found in town.

"We noticed that the residents of the city were breaking open the doors

---

2. Nordhausen labor camp and Camp Dora/Mittelbau were satellite camps to Buchenwald, which was approximately fifty miles to the south. Inmates were transferred there to perform labor on the missiles at Peenemunde.

of boxcars containing food and other goods, looting everything they could gather up. One car contained bags of sugar, and it was the scene of fisticuffs as people struggled to get at the stuff.

"But, as we stood there watching the goings-on of the townspeople, I noticed another train standing on a siding, that none of the townspeople went near. Then I noticed fluid dripping from the floor of a car. I got a detail of men together, and they broke open one of the doors.

"My God, we encountered a gruesome sight! Human bodies slithered out like wet eels. The train was full of corpses, at least one hundred people per car. Of course, there were no survivors. The scene was indescribable, for those poor people had been jammed into the boxcar with absolutely no room to spare.

"In retrospect, I assume those people on the train were Jews. We had little knowledge of the Holocaust at that time, and I didn't know to look for yellow stars, or tattoos. They probably were Jews transferred from the other extermination camps that were being overrun by the American and British troops. Those already in the camp were slave laborers of unknown nationality or ethnic origin.

"In the city and elsewhere, we saw the camps and slave barracks, surrounded with barbed wire fences. Slave laborers—men, women and children—and ethnic minorities displaced from Russia, Poland, France, Belgium, the Netherlands, the Balkans and other conquered areas, were kept here to operate the huge V-bomb factory built deep into tunnels drilled into the hillsides a short distance from town. The inhumanity of their living conditions was appalling. By far, the dead outnumbered the living.

"Thousands of bodies, possibly as many as ten thousand, were discovered in the partially-destroyed barracks, lying in the fields or stacked at the crematory waiting to be burned. People were found lying where they had died, or were crammed into rooms set aside for the dead that were so full that their bony remains tumbled out when the doors were opened.

"The dead were horribly emaciated, with protruding eyes, thin arms and legs. Others were stacked indiscriminately in piles, having obviously died of starvation and deprivation. Those still living were practically dead, too, lying in the same rooms, even in the same beds with dead and dying friends and family members, too weak to move.

"Our troops who had to witness this hell-hole needed no urging from me, or any of the other officers in the 238th Combat Engineers, to get back into the fight against those inhuman monsters who cared so little for others' lives.

"A large camp complex, Nordhausen consisted of four or five barracks-type buildings housing thousands of closely-crowded inmates. Later findings revealed that these inmates had been working in the underground factory, located in tunnels outside the camp. The installation included three tunnels where V-1 and V-2 rockets and Messerschmitt airplanes were assembled and built. After this information was reported to higher headquarters, the 238th took on the job of cleaning up, and assisting the survivors.

"On orders of officers from the infantry units in the city, probably the 104th Division, the deputy *Burgermeister* of Nordhausen was routed out and ordered to round up all able-bodied townsmen. These townspeople, mostly older men, claimed no knowledge of the camps. From all of the local civilians came the same answer: 'We didn't know what was happening.' Many of these same civilians presumably supervised the very same people who lay dead and dying in the concentration camp!

"It's inconceivable that they didn't know what was going on. The camp was open to view—one could see through the barbed wire—and the pervasive stench was indescribable. As far as I am concerned, anybody who claimed that was delusional. That, or in total denial!

"The Germans were required to pick up bodies individually, carry them to an assembly area, and bury them in the mass trench grave. We also had the townspeople administer to the survivors. Many objected. But our troops were in no mood to compromise, and they knew it. The smell was overpowering, and it was filthy work picking up all those decaying bodies. So the civilians were forced to continue.

"In retribution for their part in this awful crime, be it the active support of those who directed such horrors or merely of passive acceptance of the regime, the local people were compelled to shape the rough trenches our bulldozers dug on a hillside overlooking the city. Stretchers were fashioned from doors, clothes or other sources. Bodies were placed on these makeshift stretchers and carried by four people to their final resting place, a cemetery that will always bear evidence to *Nazi* sadism and brutality. The locals who carried the dead weren't allowed to cover their faces with masks. We felt they should have to experience the results of what they'd done.

"These people had stripped the Jews and other inmates of their last thread of human dignity. By burying them in an honorable manner, we gave them back a small degree of that dignity.

"Later, while observing the burial of the dead, we went through the crematorium. There I saw the remains of several partially-burned bodies, and watched while they were removed."

Major James stopped talking briefly. He picked up his cocktail and took a sip. Then he continued.

"The capture of the city of Nordhausen gave all of us an eye-opener as to what kind of barbarians we were fighting, and proved to every soldier present that *Nazi* Germany had to be thoroughly beaten. The inhumanity through which they forced prisoners to live was beyond comprehension—absolutely beyond comprehension."

James stopped talking again, this time to wipe his eyes. Sean Kennedy reached over and gave the old soldier a hug.

"Major, I just want to say thank you for your service, and for giving back to those victims of the *Nazi*s their dignity. Although, sadly it came too late for them."

"That's why you absolutely must not let all these anti-Semites get away with denying the Holocaust. We were there! We saw it—it did happen!"

Now Colonel Ohara came into the conversation. "Major, I'd like to offer a prayer for all those poor souls you buried, if you don't mind."

"I think that's a fine idea, colonel," James said, as he bowed his head.

Colonel Ohara began.

"Heavenly Father, we acknowledge our manifold sins and wickedness and it is for that reason we ask forgiveness. Cleanse our hearts, Dear Lord, of impure thoughts of racism, hatred and genocide.

"We beseech you, Heavenly Father, to learn from this story we have heard over the past few days. Help us to stand up to bigotry of all forms, and to remember that the Holocaust began with words.

"We plead for those who died at the hands of the *Nazi*s, and ask that we always remember their sacrifices, acknowledging that it is through your Grace that our salvation depends. This we ask in your Son's name. Amen."

The others repeated their "amens," and the room suddenly went silent. It was an awkward silence, unplanned and painfully long.

Mrs. Kennedy broke it, by suggesting that everyone adjourn to the dining room table and have a piece of pie. All present took her up on her offer.

As the group was finishing their dessert, Sean Kennedy broached the subject that everyone was ignoring.

"CSM Wilkes, after Major James' story of what happened at Nordhausen, I'm wondering what happened next, given the fact that the war in Europe had only about three weeks to go."

CSM Wilkes eagerly jumped into the conversation.

"Within three days we knew that Germany's cause was lost. Hell, you could see it in the prisoners we were capturing. The Germans were turning themselves in. They knew the war was lost and, at that point, I guess they figured they might as well 'call it a day,' and surrender. That way, they might at least get to return to their families. At first, it was one or two, but as the days passed, more and more turned themselves in.

"We liberated many a weapon from them. I know, as I have a footlocker-full of Kraut pistols. By April 18th we were getting thirty POWs a day. And, as the month progressed, it became obvious that all the talk in the newspapers about Germany surrendering probably was true. With each day we became more confident that the war would be over within a matter of days.

"As it turned out, we first got word of the war's end on Saturday, May 5th, 1945. The 238th had been occupying a small town near Eisleben, Germany, functioning as the military government. Eisleben is about thirty kilometers west of Halle, and about seventy kilometers northwest of Leipzig.

"Company A was assigned to a town that doesn't even exist anymore. It was called Wimmelburg, a few kilometers southeast of Eisleben. Their mission was to confiscate all *Nazi* insignia and paraphernalia, armaments and war-type trophies, and turn them in for destruction. I can remember it, as if it were yesterday...."

238TH COMBAT ENGINEERS HEADQUARTERS, NEAR EISLEBEN, GERMANY ATHLETIC FIELD, SATURDAY, 5 MAY 1945, 1430 HOURS LOCAL

"What the hell do you mean, 'he's out'?" SGT Wilkes yelled from inside the dugout, when the officer doubling as an umpire called Ian Henry out as he slid into home base.

The umpire let the insult go. He saw what he saw, and as far as he was concerned CPL Ian Henry was out. That was it, and no debate was going to be tolerated.

The next batter up was the newly-promoted CPL Eric Duncan. As he approached home plate, he took a batting stance, then took a couple of practice swings. Duncan believed he was ready for CPL Edward Baker to unleash a fastball that would fly over the home plate so fast it would make his head spin.

It had been two days since Edward "V-2" Baker had starting pitching for the 238th Yankees, and Duncan firmly believed that today was the day he would actually connect with the Oklahoman's "rocket." Just before Baker began his wind-up, Duncan looked him in the eye and said, "I'm gonna knock it all the way to Berlin!"

"The last I done heard, ain't nothin' in Berlin left standing," PFC Kenny Miller shouted from his third base position.

Baker checked the runner at first base. Nothing going there, but he'd be damned if anyone was going to steal a base from him. Besides, the runner wasn't taking any chances. The last two members of his team who'd tried to steal a base had been thrown out the "Oklahoma Bomber."

The ball came in inside and low, but that didn't stop Duncan from swinging his bat with all his might. S-M-A-C-K!

Duncan was stunned. He hadn't only connected with the baseball—he'd hit it so hard that it went clear out of the makeshift field the engineers had built two weeks ago when the fighting began to die down.

"Way to go, Eric! That's showing 'em!" Wilkes shouted as he started running out toward home plate.

Now we've got two men on, and it's the bottom of the ninth inning. I'll be go to hell if we ain't behind 3-1, and two outs. No time to fuck up here!

Wilkes picked up the bat, and stood in the batter's box. He rearranged himself and then got back in the batter's stance.

"Stop playing with yourself, and hit the ball!" someone from the other team yelled from their bench.

"At least he's got something to play with, dick-head!" One of Charlie's teammates yelled back.

The umpire was getting tired of all the bantering, and was about to say something when he saw 1LT James running toward the field.

Wilkes twisted his head, and he too saw James approaching.

I wonder what the hell this is all about.

Charlie Wilkes didn't have to wait long, because as soon as James got into the field he yelled, "Gentlemen, the war is over! The Krauts have called it quits. The formal surrender ceremonies will take place in a few days!"

From that moment, the baseball game was over. All the men ran to the pitcher's mound and started yelling, jumping up and down, and laughing all the way.

As CPL Henry walked over to where the other soldiers were celebrating, a smile came across his face.

Now, I can go find Genevieve!

As Henry approached the mound, he was met by Charlie Wilkes. "Ian, did you hear, the war is over! We beat the bastards!"

Ian looked his best friend in the eyes, and replied in his inimitable New Hampshire accent, "Yeah, Charlie, I heard. Thank God, this part of the war is over. Praise God!"

CPL Baker joined the celebration. "Charlie, we're almost there. One down, one to go. And, hopefully the Marines will have convinced those damned Japs to surrender before we have to go to the Pacific."

Henry looked at his two old comrades. "Did you ever think, when we were back on those LCTs on Utah Beach, that you'd make it this far?"

CPL Baker wiped his eyes. Under other circumstances he'd have been embarrassed to death for show this much emotion. But after what he had been through with these two men over the past eleven months, he didn't give a damn—let the friggin' tears fall!

He grabbed his two friends, pulled them toward him, and gave them a hug!

The three began to laugh. CPL Baker was so elated he actually pinched himself to see if he was dreaming.

Could it possibly be true, that the nightmare was finally over?

As the trio continued their celebration, SGT Wilkes felt a tug from the back of his jacket. He turned and recognized his fellow Iowan, CPL Daniel Erickson, standing there with a smile wider than the Nodaway River in springtime.

"You heard the news?" Charlie asked.

"A few minutes ago, and I wanted to come right out and say something I should've said eleven months past. Thanks for looking out for me back there on Utah Beach, and for getting me into this unit. I don't think I'd have made it, if I stayed in my old one."

Charlie was touched by his former football foe's thoughtfulness.

"Hey, we Iowans got to stick together!"

"Just the same Charlie, thanks for talking to Lieutenant James about keeping me."

"Shit, you knew?" Wilkes tried not to let his emotions show.

"I didn't know for sure, but I figured you had talked to the L-T," Erickson said.

"Well, we needed another man, and you were available," Charlie said, trying to marginalize his role in getting his friend transferred to the engineers from the infantry.

"I guess," Erickson said, looking at the other three GIs, "all we gotta do now is to kick the crap outta those bastards that bombed Pearl."

Henry looked toward Erickson, and said, "Either that, or pray the Marines do it before we can get a boat lined up for transportation."

Duncan returned to their conversation. "Hell, from what I heard, it's gonna take six months before we can sort out the equipment losses and get the property books right. By then, the Japs will be down for the count. Hell, the Marines have kicked their miserable asses almost back to the home islands. Maybe, by the time they need us, it'll be over."

"One can only hope," Charlie Wilkes replied.

Ian Henry added, "Or pray that the Marines do it for us."

Duncan nodded his head. "God bless the United States Marines!"

SATURDAY, 9 MAY 1945, MARTIN LUTHER SQUARE EISLEBEN, GERMANY, 1000 HOURS LOCAL

For the past half-hour, the men of the 238th Combat Engineer Battalion had been standing around waiting to be put in formation. For SGT Charles Wilkes, the experience was almost surreal. Inwardly, he knew the war in Europe was over. But to him, now, he was having difficulty grasping the concept that the war in Europe was finished.

As he stood smoking a cigarette, he wondered what the final toll in human lives would be. He had heard on the BBC that the Chinese had lost somewhere in the neighborhood of three million soldiers, plus seventeen million civilians.

My God, twenty million people have died in China, alone. If that's the case, how many have our Russian Allies lost? And, to think one sorry sonofabitch from Austria, and his pals from Rome and Tokyo, started it all. Hell, the good news is that Hitler and Mussolini are both dead—hopefully rotting in hell as I stand here!

His thoughts were interrupted when he heard the first sergeant holler, "Battalion, atten-shun!

He quickly scrambled to his place in A Company's formation, the fourth squad's section sergeant.

1SGT Freck then yelled, "Report!"

After hearing the reports from all the sections, SSG Marion P. Davis, from Sheffield, Alabama, reported to Freck, "Company A, all present."

Once Freck was sure that all his men were present, he did an about-face and reported to 1LT James, "A Company, all present."

James returned his salute, then reported into the Battalion commander, who in turn directed the men to make a right face, and march.

As the battalion marched through Martin Luther Square in Eisleben, SGT Wilkes turned his head ever so slightly to talk to CPL Ian Henry.

"Well, Ian, we made it."

"Yes, by the grace of God, we did."

Henry's ever-so-Catholic remark caused Wilkes to snicker, although quietly.

"Ian, I think it was your faith that got us through."

"Maybe so, Charlie, but I have the feeling we also owe a heck of a lot to our officers, and the senior enlisted men in this unit. And, of course, to the men who died over the past eleven months. All twenty-six of them."

Charlie looked over at his buddy.

"We lost twenty-six?"

"Yes, twenty-six—and each one of them was a good man, too."

"Damn—I'd lost count." Wilkes admitted.

"I would have, too, except I that I pray for their souls every night."

From the head of the column, the two soldiers heard another command. "Battalion… halt!"

The battalion commander had them do a left-face, then put them at parade-rest.

Over the next few minutes the commander spoke a few words, none of which Charlie Wilkes heard as he struggled to remember the names and the faces of those brave, young American soldiers who had made the ultimate sacrifice for their country.

As he stood there thinking about his fallen comrades, Charlie suddenly remembered a bit of scripture. It was St. Paul's letter to the Ephesians. His father, the sheriff of Villisca, Iowa, had written it in the bible he'd given him on the day he got on the train to report for active duty, ever so long ago. St. Paul said, "Therefore take the whole armor of God that you may be able to withstand in the evil day, and having done all, to stand."

"…and having done all, to stand."

"What was that, Charlie?" Ian asked.

"Huh?"

"You were saying something about 'standing'," Henry replied with a smile on his face.

"Oh, nothing… just a bit of scripture my father wrote in my bible came to mind. Now, I guess, I know what he meant. That's all."

CPL Henry slapped him lightly on his right shoulder.

"Well, I don't know what's a bigger deal—us winning this friggin' war, or Sergeant Charles Wilkes quoting scripture."

Wilkes started to laugh but controlled himself, because he knew that laughing was not exactly an approved behavior in formation—victors in war, or not.

Suddenly the two GIs were hit with another revelation. The formation had been dismissed. As the pair began walking toward the truck that would take them back to their quarters, Charlie kept thinking about St. Paul's words.

"Therefore take the whole armor of God that you may be able to withstand in the evil day, and having done all, to stand."

IN FRONT OF THE BASE MAIN CHAPEL, FORT DIX, NEW JERSEY SUNDAY, 14 OCTOBER 1945, 1215 HOURS LOCAL

As SGT Charles Wilkes and CPL Ian Henry emerged from the base chapel after mass, both wondered if their paths would ever cross again. They had made promises to keep in touch, but inwardly each wondered if they really would maintain contact. Or would they, for a few months or years and, then, as their memories began to fade, would their friendship do the same?

Charlie Wilkes was especially concerned for Ian, because, in his mind, Henry was obsessed with the idea of sailing back to back to Belgium after he went home for a week or two, with the purpose of finding Miss Genevieve Pelletier, from Verviers. Charlie decided to broach the subject with his friend one last time.

In between putting a piece of gum in this mouth and lighting a cigarette, Charlie said, "So, Ian, tell me something…."

"Just so it doesn't have anything to do with me going back to Belgium…."

"Dammit, Ian, that's no way to treat a buddy. I'm just concerned that Miss Pelletier may have gone back to England by now, and you won't be able to track her down."

"Charlie," Ian said, "How many times do we have to go over this?"

"As many as it takes, to get you to forget about that girl and come back to Anaheim with me. I know damn good and well that Sharon will find you a wife. She's on the altar guild at the cathedral, and says there are at least eight or nine young ladies serving with her who are suitable for marriage. So, why go all the way back to Belgium?"

"Charlie, I'm gonna say this one more time. When we were in Verviers, Genevieve told me that she and her mother were going to stay there until Christmas, figuring that if they hadn't heard from her father by then, that the Germans had killed him."

"But that letter was dated back in June. It's now August, and you haven't heard a word from her," Charlie replied.

Henry answered immediately. "Charlie, first of all, June was only two months ago. Besides, how many different places did we hang our hats during those last days of the war? Hell, we were here one day there, the next—you know, you were there! It was a friggin' circus! Besides, you don't really think the Army delivered all of our mail to us?"

"Yeah, I know. But, listen," Charlie retorted, "you couldn't find her when you did go back, during that three-day leave Lieutenant James got for you. So what makes you think she's still there?"

Henry looked at his friend, and frowned. "Charlie, are you just plain dense, or what? I told you, that two of those three days I was gone were spent trying to get to Verviers and back to the unit. And that the only time I had to look around for Genevieve was on a day that her school was closed."

"Well, yes, you did say that. But one would think that someone in town would've known about her. After all, how many British girls were at that school?"

"According to Genevieve, there were two others. Besides, why do you care if I go chasing all over Europe to find her?"

"What are you saying?" Charlie asked pointedly.

"I'm saying that I'm going back to Belgium to find Genevieve Pelletier. And, if I don't find her there, I'm going to go over to England and hunt her down there. And I'm not going to rest until I do!"

"Okay," Charlie said, pursuing a different approach. "What happens when you do find her, and she turns you down?"

Charlie's question brought a big smile to Ian's face. "Charlie Wilkes, how in the name of God Almighty would any woman in the world turn down a man as good-looking as me?"

"Oh, my God!" Charlie replied, laughing. "You're worse than Lieutenant James."

""What do you mean?" Henry replied.

"You know that, as soon as we're discharged, he's headed for Glens Falls, New York, to marry that woman, Faith."

"Yeah, I do. And, what's more, I think a guy who got two Bronze Stars, and another with a "V" device from General Lawton Collins personally, and who led us from Utah Beach all the way to the friggin' Elbe River, ought to be smart enough to find a woman he wants to marry."

Charlie laughed, and admitted, "Yeah, I think you're right. But what amazes me is that neither one of you has spent any real time with the woman you plan to marry."

"Charlie Wilkes! You, of all people, shouldn't say a damn thing about how long someone knew his wife before they got married. I mean, how long had you known Sharon before you two got married?"

"Ian, for God's sake, I've known Sharon since grade school."

"Charlie, yes, you went to school with Sharon. But you never dated her. In fact, if my memory serves me right, she avoided you like the plague."

"Well, it just tells you she's a good judgment of character," Charlie replied, laughing.

"You're so full of shit, Charlie...." Henry said, then stopped himself from completing his sentence.

"Well, that certainly ain't a state secret. So, what's your point?"

Charlie took a drag from his Camel, exhaled it, but didn't say anything right away. Instead he kept walking, which was a good thing, because CPL Henry was starved. The reason for his hunger was due to his Catholicism, and something his grandmother had pounded into his head since he was a boy: Good Catholics did not eat before mass on Sunday!

"Come on, Wilkes, what's your point?" Ian said as he picked up the pace.

"I'm thinking," Charlie replied.

"Well—while you're mentally jerking off, I am going to hurry my starving Catholic butt over to the mess hall. It closes in thirty minutes, and I haven't eaten anything, yet."

As the two soldiers walked, their conversation changed to the current baseball season and which team would win the World Series.

Initially, Charlie expressed no opinion. But after Ian Henry said he believed the pennant was going to the Dodgers, he got very animated.

"Are you crazy? Detroit is gonna go all the way!"

"What the hell are you talking about—Detroit? They don't stand a chance, the Dodgers are going to kick their asses," Henry replied forcefully.

"Why, I'll bet you a cold can of Old Style beer that the World Series this year will be between the Chicago Cubs and Detroit. And, the Tigers take it all," Charlie came back.

"You're on! I can't wait to collect this bet!"

"Just don't hold your breath, waiting for it," Charlie chimed in.

As the two GIs neared the consolidated mess hall, Ian Henry suddenly stopped walking. It caused Charlie to turn around and ask his friend why he was no longer walking to the place he'd originally insisted they go.

"I just remembered something that Lieutenant James told me to tell you."

"What's that?" Wilkes inquired.

"Lieutenant James has invited us to his wedding."

"I'll be go to hell."

Ian considered his friend's response, then joked, "You seem determined to go to hell, Charlie. If I were you, I'd come up with another way to show your amazement. Otherwise, the devil just might take you up on your insistence about where you're going to be spending the afterlife."

"Dammit, Ian, it's just an expression. Besides, what's this about Lieutenant James inviting us to his wedding?"

"He did it this morning, when I ran into him over at payroll."

"I wonder why he did that?" Wilkes asked.

"What do you mean, 'I wonder why he did that'?"

"Simple—we're not officers," Wilkes replied.

"That's true. But remember, we knew him when he was enlisted, back at Camp Roberts."

"And how many millions of years ago *was that*? Wilkes said, as he thought about how many different places he and Henry had been, these past four years.

Ian Henry thought about what Charlie Wilkes had just said, and replied, "You know, it does seem like a million years ago, doesn't it?"

"A million and one, if you really want to know the truth."

Ian started walking again. "So, are you gonna go?"

"I don't know… if we should."

"Why do you say that? He asked us, Charlie."

When Charlie didn't respond right away, Ian added, "Charlie, let me refresh your memory. Lieutenant James is the guy who got us from Utah Beach, all the way to Martin Luther Platz in Eisleben, Germany. I think we owe it to him, if you ask me."

"It ain't that I don't want to attend his wedding, Ian. I just don't want to be in the way."

"Knowing the lieutenant like we do, I don't think that's going to happen."

Wilkes again did not reply right away, but when he did, he said, "Okay, let him know we'll be there, if we've been discharged by then."

"I am supposed to see him this afternoon," Henry said, as he put out his cigarette and began field stripping it.

Watching Henry fieldstrip his smoke caused Wilkes to wonder aloud, "Do you think you'll be doing that in five years?"

"Absolutely not," Ian replied, emphatically.

"How do you know?" Charlie and Ian now stood in the line in front of the enlisted men's consolidated mess hall.

"Because, if I'm still smoking in five years, you have my permission to kick me in the ass," Henry said.

"Why do you say that?" asked Wilkes.

"Because I have a feeling that smoking probably ain't good for you. And, besides, I only started doing it because I was bored. And now I ain't bored!"

"Well, since you put it that way, I guess there are a whole lot of things neither one of us is gonna be doing in five years."

The line inched forward. The two soldiers moved with it, and within fifteen minutes they were both seated inside the hall next to three other veterans from the European Theater of Operations. After a bit of small talk, Wilkes and Henry continued their conversation.

"Does Lieutenant James have any idea when we'll be getting discharged?"

"Quite honestly, it's a crap-shoot. But, from what Ernie said, we should be getting out tomorrow morning," Ian Henry replied.

Charlie had to think about what his friend had just said. He was sort of zoned-out.

Who the hell's 'Ernie'? Oh, shit—that's Lieutenant James' first name! Fuck, have I been in the Army too long, or what?

After figuring out who Ian meant when he referred to Lieutenant James by his first name instead of his rank, Wilkes wondered aloud, "Who would have thought it? Sergeant Charlie Wilkes, formerly with the United States Army, specifically the 238th Combat Engineer Battalion, is soon to be Mr.

Charlie Wilkes, of Anaheim, California. Private citizen, the proud father of three boys and married to one magnificent woman."

"With any luck at all, Charlie, I'll find Genevieve within a few months, and we'll get married and set up house in Paso Robles. In fact, I think I'm even going to apply for admission to Cal Poly at San Luis Obispo and get a college degree. I'm thinking about becoming a high school teacher, and raising grapes on the side."

While Ian sat there contemplating his soon-to-be future, Charlie's mind wandered back to a conversation he'd had with Randy Roberts on a Friday afternoon in July 1939, after Charlie was thrown out of his house by the man Charlie believed to be his father.

Randy had been the exact opposite of Charlie Wilkes. Randy was a place-kicker on the Villisca High football team, while Charlie was a tailback. Randy could quote both Shakespeare and the Bible, while Charlie never read anything more difficult than dime store novels. Randy could sing Billie Holiday's music and dance like no other teenager in southwestern Iowa, whereas Charlie could barely carry a tune, and all the dancing he'd ever done when a youth was to tiptoe around the law. Last, Randy Roberts was probably the best-looking young man in Villisca, and homosexual. Charlie also was good looking, and he'd managed to mount every girl in Montgomery County who put out, at least once before he graduated from high school.

Yet it was Randy Roberts who married Sharon in the fall of 1939, and had moved to California after Charlie's FBI-agent uncle got him a position on the Cal football team.

Tragically, and through an odd twist of fate, it also had been Randy Roberts who was killed on board the USS *Arizona* on that December morning, those oh-so many years ago.

Ever so softly, Charlie Wilkes could hear the calming voice of the young man who had been his wife's first husband, saying to him, "Someday, Charlie, things will turn out just fine for you."

Charlie sat still for a while, quietly reflecting on the words of his lost friend. A minute or so passed, and then Charlie uttered, "I guess this is someday."

Ian Henry, who'd just finished his lunch, looked toward his friend and asked if he'd said something. Charlie replied, "No, I was just remembering something Sharon's first husband said to me—that's all."

"You want to talk about it?" Ian asked.

Charlie looked at his friend and said, "Honestly, I don't. I just want to savor this moment."

Henry shrugged his shoulders, then picked up his coffee and took a sip.

After mentally reliving the summer of 1939 and the subsequent events at Pearl Harbor, Charlie Wilkes had an epiphany—it was time for him to start living in the "someday" Randy had spoken of in that hot, upper room of the Roberts home in Iowa.

A smile came over his face. He looked at Ian and said, "So tell me about Lieutenant James' wedding plans."

"Okay. He plans to meet Faith in a couple of days in New York City. He's going by rail and, from what Ernie said, he's gonna get off the train, pick up Faith and they'll continue on up to Glens Falls...."

EPILOGUE

Ask the Lord for rain in the springtime;
it is the Lord who makes the storm clouds.
—Zechariah

IN THE LIVING ROOM OF COLONEL AND MRS. SEAN OHARA
LOS LAGOS, GRANITE BAY, CALIFORNIA
WEDNESDAY, 4 DECEMBER 1991, 9:30 P.M. LOCAL

Now CSM Wilkes was finishing his story.

"We did attend Ernie and Faith's wedding and, in a way, I think by going up there to Glens Falls and seeing Lieutenant James and Faith get married in the rectory of that Catholic church renewed my faith in humankind.

"I remember it so clearly. Ernie all dressed up in his uniform, and Faith as beautiful a bride as one could imagine...."

Sean Ohara spoke up. "Yes, I imagine after all the hell the three of you had been through, for you to see two people in love probably made your day."

"It did, indeed. And, to be honest with you, even today when someone or something irritates the hell out of me I think back to Ernie and Faith's wedding on that beautiful October day in 1945. After I do that for a few minutes, things seem to fall into their proper place again."

Sean's mother, Chloe Mountbatten Ohara, wiped her eyes and said, "Sergeant Major, I never knew you were an old softie at heart. Good for you."

The sergeant major's wife, Sharon Wilkes, laughed. "Yeah, all that command sergeant major stuff is 'there,' but inside Charlie's a wonderful man. I thank God for him every night."

CSM Wilkes looked to Sharon and smiled.

You did good, Charlie, when you married her!

There came a pause in the storytelling for a few minutes, while Sharon and Charlie discussed whether to drive back to Nevada City, or stay the night in one of the Oharas' many spare rooms.

Chloe Ohara put an end to the discussion, when she said, "After we finish up tonight, I'm going to break out some cognac and put another log on the fire."

Looking at her husband, then Chloe said, "Colonel, could I entice you into getting enough snifters for all the adults, and a small one for Sean?"

The command sergeant major looked toward his wife, and said, "I think we've been invited to spend the night."

Sharon Wilkes nodded her thanks to Mrs. Ohara.

"Your invitation is gratefully accepted."

With the question of the night's lodging resolved, the guests once again began to make their way to the Ohara's grand room, as that is where the bar was located.

On the way into the room, as Sean Ohara walked alongside the command sergeant major, he asked, "If you don't mind, sir, there is one question you haven't answered."

"What's that? I thought we'd won the war," Wilkes said, taking his seat on the sofa.

The teenager sat down next to the retired senior noncommissioned officer.

"Did Corporal Henry ever marry Genevieve?"

A broad smile came over Charlie Wilkes' face.

"Well? Did he marry her or not?" Sean demanded.

"Oh, he did. Eventually."

"What do you mean by that?"

"What I mean by *that*, is he did marry her. But that's not the story here."

"Why not?" Sean asked.

"What I mean to say, is that never in a million years would you be able to guess where I learned that Corporal Ian Henry, of Hooksett, New Hampshire had married Miss Genevieve Pelletier of Verviers, Belgium."

From across the room, the man's wife shouted, "Charlie Wilkes, if you start telling that story tonight, none of us will get to bed!"

CSM Wilkes looked to the young man and said, "You heard the boss, not tonight. But, I will leave you with this thought: Sergeant Ian Henry told me in a general purpose medium tent in Korea in December, 1951, how he'd found Genevieve Pelletier in London, on New Year's Day, 1946."

"He did what?" Sean questioned.

You see, when I got back to California I enlisted in the California Army National Guard. As it turned out, so did Corporal Ian Henry, after he and

Genevieve Pelletier got married. Well, after the Reds came over the 38th Parallel in 1950, we soon found our butts in of all places, Korea."

"Charlie, not tonight," Sharon begged.

Charlie smiled at his wife, and the young man. "How about you coming up to the house at sometime in the near future and I tell you the story?"

"You're on, command sergeant major."

"Then we all have a date—our house, early next January."

Colonel Ohara smiled, and said, "CSM, I think you're the only person I know of who could out-talk old Ezra at the Watergate."

"I'll take that as a compliment, as long as all of you come up after Christmas to hear how Ian Henry again found the teenaged girl he'd met in Belgium, in 1945—and how we both personally won the war in Korea."

"You're on, sergeant major."

PAUL MICHAEL FRAZEÉ

Raised in the East Bay area of San Francisco, the author enlisted in the United States Army on his eighteenth birthday. After graduation from Hayward High School in June of 1966, he took Basic Training at Fort Ord, California ("A-3-3, Sergeant!").

After the completion of Communications Specialist school at Fort Gordon, Georgia, he spent nearly a year with the 8th Infantry Division at Bad Kreuznach, Germany before volunteering for a tour in Vietnam. Following his military service and graduation from California State University at Hayward, Mr. Frazeé pursued numerous careers, among them banking, retailing and as national sales manager for an import company in the San Francisco Bay Area.

Currently, the author teaches social sciences at the secondary level in the Sacramento schools. In addition to *Cornfield Soldiers—Utah Beach to the Elbe River*, he has published two other works of military fiction, *Waiting For a Rainbow—Coming of Age in Vietnam* and *Summer Storm—Prelude to Pearl Harbor*.

Mr. Frazeé is active in his church, where he serves as a lay reader. Recently retired from the California Army National Guard after a career that spanned forty years, he and his wife reside in the Sacramento area with their two young daughters. His hobbies include reading and traveling–particularly in Mexico and Germany.

Ernest Gaines

CORNFIELD
SOLDIERS

15 January 2015

To David:

Enjoy the read!

Paul M Frazee

USA (Ret)

Duty, Honor, Country!